Sherry A. Burton
The Jerry McNeal Series
Three Books In One
Always Faithful *(Book One)*
Ghostly Guidance *(Book Two)*
Rambling Spirit *(Book Three)*

Dorry Press

Acknowledgements

I will forever be grateful to my mom, who insisted the dog stay in the series.

To my hubby, thanks for helping me stay in the writing chair.

To my editor, Beth, for allowing me to keep my voice.

To Laura, for EVERYTHING you do to keep me current in both my covers and graphics.

To my beta readers for giving the books an early read.

To my proofreader, Latisha Rich, for the extra set of eyes.

To my fans, for the continued support.

Lastly, to my "writing voices," thank you for all the incredible ideas!

Always Faithful

In loving memory of my mother
Mary Juanita Lands, October 1942- May
2019,
who always loved
"the story about the dog."

Prologue

September 8th, 1985

Jerry woke in the wee hours of the morning and rubbed a closed fist against his droopy eyes. It had been months since he'd awoken during the night, not since the time his gums were swollen and irritated, causing him to cry out in a desperate search of relief. He stuck his thumb in his mouth, chomped down, and felt nothing out of the norm. No pain that would have explained his being awake when all was quiet. His diaper was wet; maybe that was what had awoken him. He rolled onto his side, thinking to voice his concerns to his mother and stopped, once again jamming his thumb into his mouth. Something was wrong, but it had nothing to do with his diaper. He focused his attention on the lamp at the far side of the room. A small glow emitted from the lamp, which sat atop a tall brown chest of drawers. He'd seen that same lamp every time he woke, and while it looked the same, in the wee hours of this Sunday morning, a feeling told him there was something different about it. A feeling that the lamp needed watching.

Eyes wide, he did just that. Watched. Lying perfectly still except for his mouth, which worked greedily at his right thumb. Jerry, a thumb sucker since birth, had rejected pacifiers for something more tangible. Of course, he didn't realize the particular advantages of thumb sucking at first, but they'd become clear after several of his playmates were made to give up their own, less permanent devices. Not Jerry. No siree. His was always there at the ready whenever he felt the need for comforting, like at present when something was most assuredly wrong. His mouth tugged at his thumb as he waited, slurping a silent vigil in the darkness for what was about to happen.

He didn't have to wait long.

Within minutes, the wall beside the dresser lit up in a flash of white. Jerry watched in absolute amazement as the bright light traveled from the wall to the lamp. It made a sound like when his mommy was in the kitchen fixing him something to eat. He'd never seen anything so bright. He could feel the warmth coming from the cord. Cords were not supposed to be hot. If they were, his mother would not have let him anywhere near the lamp. He smelled something. It didn't smell like anything his mom had cooked. He wasn't sure what it was, but he didn't like it. He pulled his blanket over his head with his free hand, trying to make the bad smell go away. He wanted his mommy and daddy, but he couldn't see them. The bright light was traveling up the curtains. It was pretty and made the room bright enough to see. The room was empty. It was also very hot. As the heat intensified, he grew more and more afraid. He wasn't sure what that bright light was, but he didn't like it.

Jerry woke from the dream with a strangled cry. He looked out through the bars of his crib, peering out into the darkness. His trusty thumb was stuck securely between his lips, and from the wrinkled texture had been in place for most – if not all – of the night. The lamp that had been drenched in flames only moments before was soft and illuminating. Everything seemed to be as it should be, but he had a feeling it would not be that way for long. It was the first of a long history of what he would come to know as *that feeling*. A knowing that he would embrace, and something that would shape the core of the man he would someday become. For the moment, at eleven days past his second birthday, Jerry was utterly and desperately afraid of that which he could not control.

Where are Mommy and Daddy? I need them.

Chapter One

Holly squinted through the lens, waited for precisely the right second when the bride was between breaths, then, *snap*, captured the photo. She turned the screen to admire her handiwork and sighed, knowing this photo would soon replace the one that was currently showcasing the main page on her website. It was a perfect photo, with the quintessential perfect fairytale couple. The bride's long dark hair was upswept, held in place with a delicate halo of baby's breath flowers and one single red rose. Thin dark wisps of hair hung in tiny ringlets along the sides of her temples, her natural beauty made even more striking by the daring use of bold makeup around her equally dark eyes. The bride's lips had been shaded to match the color of her rose, lending a storybook feel to the photograph, both standing out boldly against the paleness of her skin. Bare milky white shoulders gave way to the intricate lace of her pearly white gown, which hugged her body like a second skin. If the bride had intended to channel Snow White, she had most assuredly obtained her goal. The groom, equally handsome, stood out in an ink-black tuxedo, with waves of dark flowing hair and mischievous brown eyes, which seemed to say *I've found my princess and I cannot wait to have my way with her.* Holly had the couple turn and positioned the groom's hands so they splayed across the small of his new wife's back, fingers placed just so, forming a perfect heart. Several members of the bridal party made comments of approval as they moved to see Holly's placement of the newlyweds. She took a photo, then snapped several more just to be certain, before checking the camera and nodding her satisfaction. People hired her to capture memories; what she gave them was perfection. Images to last a lifetime, or at least until they burned said pictures during a nasty divorce. *Not this couple; this couple will beat the odds.* At least that was what Holly told herself. Of course, she said the same thing about every wedding she photographed. It was her motto at her photography studio, giving every couple enchanting photos that would follow them into their happily ever after.

Barf!

She bit her lower lip to keep from gagging and moved to her left to get a better angle, all the while chastising herself for being so cynical. She pressed the button with her index finger, silently wishing the couple many years of happiness. Something she found difficult to do, since she herself stopped believing in happy endings at the tender age of twelve. The age she'd been when her parents had divorced. Up until that point, she'd thought life perfect, her family perfect. *Nothing's perfect.*

She bent sideways, *except this photo*, she thought and pressed the button to capture the picture. She marveled at how beautiful Morgan, the bride, looked. *I wonder if I would look as beautiful.* Not likely, given the fact she was more comfortable in little to no makeup, jeans, and t-shirts, most likely imprinted with the logo from her website. Hollywood Films, a genius play on her first and last name, Holly Wood. Hey, what could she say, wherever she went, she was assured free advertising. Well, after the cost of the initial printing. Not today, though. Today, she was impeccably dressed to blend in. That was why she'd spent nearly an hour straightening her mane of thick brown hair, only to ruin the whole process by twining the entire mass of hair into a long braid, which rounded her head and draped across her right shoulder. *Maybe I should have added some baby's breath to the braid.* A sudden image of Rapunzel standing next to Snow White floated through her mind. She almost laughed and caught herself. *Get a grip, Holly. It's a long way till midnight, and you still have to film the ball.* This time, she did snicker.

Morgan turned to her, the full-length gown following after her in a trail of shimmering elegance. "Is something wrong?"

Just tell the truth. "No, I just found myself wondering if I'd make as beautiful of a bride as you and, well…" She lifted the braid, then spread her fingers and watched as it fell limp against her shoulder.

"Of course you would, wouldn't she, Grant?" Morgan said, smiling over her shoulder at her new husband.

Grant, who'd obviously been listening, leaned in and spoke in hushed tones, "You are a very lovely lady and, to prove it, I'll have you know my best man has already been making inquiries as to how well I know you." He wiggled his eyebrows at her before nodding towards the opposite side of the room.

Holly casually turned in the direction of where the rest of the wedding party was standing, patiently waiting for her to call them when needed. In the center of the throng was the best man, a tall, lean, and incredibly handsome twenty-something man currently doing handstands while the others cheered him on.

"He's got stamina," Grant said, and the three of them laughed.

"Good to know," Holly said and wondered what else he was good at. Feeling a blush spreading over her, she shook off her curiosity and motioned the duo into another pose.

Just what I need, another child.

Morgan was now holding her bouquet of blood-red roses that matched both her lips' color and the single red rose that Grant wore in his lapel. She was leaning into her new husband in a stance that looked as if they were already comfortable with one another. Like a pair that truly fit together and, now that they were joined, only good things would come their way. As she peered through the camera lens, the newly married Mr. and Mrs. Bilkner looked just like one of those fairytales that she touted on her website, yet she no longer believed in. Holly took the photo and heaved a sigh.

Oh well, let them have their moment and the pictures to prove they were once happy. Lowering the camera, she plastered a smile onto her face. "Okay, let's get the rest of the wedding party over here so we can create some memories."

She snapped a few candid photos as the bridal party took up positions around the happy couple. She liked to sneak these unplanned snapshots to the photograph package at no extra charge. It was what made her sessions special, what got people talking, and what led her to be highly sought after when it came to location shoots. Her reputation was as one of the best, not only in

7

Chambersburg, the Pennsylvania town in which she lived, but the surrounding towns as well. It was what had brought her to Gettysburg today, during one of the worst snowstorms of the season. *Blizzard,* she reminded herself. She took a deep breath, letting it out slowly as she changed the camera lens. The evening had only just begun, and the snow, which had been falling all day, was not projected to stop until well after her current gig was over. It wouldn't be the first time she'd driven in heavy snow. Still, she'd taken precautions, borrowing her father's Jeep – it was older, but had 4-wheel-drive and was much more dependable than her Mustang. *No use worrying about things you can't change*, she thought, raising the camera. She focused on the bride and groom, who seemed to radiate happiness.

Maybe this couple will actually beat the odds.

"Hold still, everyone," Holly called, then pressed the button to freeze the moment forever. The best man, a handsome fellow with pearly white teeth and a devilish smile, closed his eyes just as she'd snapped the photo. He must have realized this, as he made eye contact with her and shrugged an apology.

Flirt! You're too young, and I'm too not interested. At thirty, the last thing she was looking for was a guy whose idea of fun was doing handstands with a rose clenched between his teeth. While the guy might have stamina, he didn't exude much in the maturity department. And that carried a lot of weight. Especially since she had her daughter, Gracie, to consider.

"Do over. Let's all try to keep our eyes open this time," she teased and waited for everyone to return to their previous positions. She continued to pose people and take photos for another twenty minutes before finally releasing the group, most of which whooped with delight as they gathered their belongings and began making their way downstairs to the reception area. Thankfully, the reception was being held in the basement of the church. A lucky break, given the weather conditions – at least she wouldn't have to venture outside until it was time to leave. Holly disconnected the wide-angle lens, then stuffed it into her bag. She'd just turned to follow the group when Morgan came up beside her, her face flushed against her milk-white skin. She seemed hesitant.

"Is something wrong?"

Morgan's blush deepened. "No, I…well… I was just hoping… I know it is probably impractical, but I saw this photo on Pinterest and, well, I was hoping to recreate it."

Pinterest had taken scrapbooking to a whole new level. A person could find virtually anything on there from recipes to hairstyles, to gardening tips and more. The possibilities were endless. Once found, you "pinned" the photo to your board and could come back to it anytime you were ready. No tape, no glue, no mess; all you needed was internet access and a surfing device, such as a cell phone or computer.

"Got to love Pinterest," Holly agreed.

"Totally," Morgan said brightly. "It's where I got most of my ideas for the wedding. Some people are so creative."

"I'm not sure how any of us survived without it," Holly replied. "I use it all the time myself."

"I know! That's where I got the idea from, one of your boards."

"Really?" Holly asked, wondering what photo she'd picked and just how risqué as to make for the proverbial blushing bride. "Does it include nudity?"

"I hope so," Grant said, stepping up behind Morgan and

placing his hands on her bare shoulders.

She laughed and leaned into him. "Not even so much as cleavage."

He started to plant a kiss on top of her head before settling on the nape of her neck instead, careful to avoid the clips that held her hair in place. "Ah well, there's plenty of time for that later."

Morgan's blush deepened. Any redder and Holly would have to do some serious airbrushing to remove the color. "So tell me which picture you're referring to."

"I know it sounds crazy, but I'd like to take a picture in the snow. You know, the one where the bride looks like she's standing in a snow globe?"

So much for not going outside.

Holly knew exactly which photo Morgan was envisioning, and how unattainable it would be in the current weather conditions, since she'd taken the photo herself. The bride, a young woman named Kathy, was standing in the middle of a beautiful snow-covered garden while soft flakes of white flowed around her. The difference was, she'd taken the photo in broad daylight, and the snow had only just started to fall. The sun had filtered perfectly through the snow, and nary even the slightest breeze had lifted the air. All the planets had aligned, giving Holly the perfect setting for the illusion. And it was an illusion, one that could not possibly be duplicated in blinding snow with driving winds. She had also seen the look of determination in Morgan's eyes; she'd be wasting her time trying to reason with the woman. No, some things are better shown. It wouldn't take much, a wintery blast up the delicate gown, or wind tugging at her perfectly fashioned hair. It was little things such as this that guaranteed her future referrals. Not snow, nor sleet, nor wind, nor hail. Holly herself had come from a long line of letter carriers who used to chant that very slogan, all the while wishing they were home with the rest of the world instead of tramping through the elements. Besides, she was reasonably sure this would be her fastest outdoor session ever.

"I'm willing to give it a try if you are," she said, tugging on her coat, motioning towards the door.

Chapter Two

Fingertips pressed together in prayer formation, Trooper Jerry McNeal stared idly at the blank wall of his cubicle. He'd been in the same position for nearly half an hour. It wouldn't be long now before he felt the need to explore. He stood and walked the short distance to the window, at first seeing nothing but the reflection of his shaved head. He leaned closer, peering into the night, watching as snow whirled past the streetlights like an angry swarm of hornets. His breath, warm against the window caused the glass to fog, yet he didn't seem to notice. He was no longer looking at what lay beyond the glass but listening to something no one else could hear. It was a night where he'd rather remain indoors, a night where he wished others would do the same. "If only," he said to the fogged glass. Turning from the window, he started towards his chair, moved to sit, thought better of it, and began pacing the confines of the room instead. He never knew when *the feeling* would show up, but it was here now, and he was listening.

Waiting.

For what, he was not sure. He normally never knew what *it* was until it happened. The feeling was a part of him. A part that told him he was not like everyone else. His grandmother – an Appalachian mountain woman – always told him it was a gift from the gods. His mother referred to it as his super-power. She'd said she first knew he was special when he'd woken in the night screaming the words "HOT! HOT!" A few moments later, his mother was standing beside his crib, still trying to comfort him when she'd smelled smoke and saw a white cloud drifting upwards into the room. A frayed cord on a lamp in Jerry's room had faltered, starting a fire on the upper level. The batteries in the family's smoke detectors were long dead, and no warning had come from the neglected device. All inside would have perished, starting with Jerry himself, if Jerry had not woken them with his cries. That was the first time he could remember having had *that feeling*. He had just turned two years old.

A snowy image flittered through his mind. He sighed. Of course, there would be snow; the whole state and most of the surrounding region was under a blizzard warning. The accumulation had been mounting all day. Roads were already impassable in many areas. Even the state police post was running on a skeleton crew, many of its officers not able to leave the confines of their driveways. He shook off his frustration and continued to pace the small office space. A blinding flash made him stop to gather this second piece of the puzzle. *A transformer, maybe?* He didn't think so. A transformer blowing would not be optimal during current weather conditions, but he didn't think such an event would warrant his increased restlessness. No, this was the type of feeling he normally got when human lives were at stake, the type of feeling that inspired him to become a Pennsylvania State Police Trooper when his enlistment ended with the Marines. He'd thought the Marines would be a good fit, and it was. At first. Then his second deployment changed all that. His feelings were on hyper-alert as every day something bad happened. While Iraq might be a good place for a Marine looking for a bit of excitement, it was not the place for a Marine with a special gift that would warn him when something bad was going to happen. It was Iraq, and there was a war going on. Something bad was always happening. The problem was that knowing something was going to happen and being powerless to stop it was enough to nearly drive him mad. While he'd managed to keep from going insane, the feeling had driven him away from the Marines. Thankfully, he had found a new home, which now allowed him to help when the feeling showed him the way. This evening, that feeling seemed to be on hyperdrive.

It's going to be bad, whatever it is.

Jerry moved down the hall and into the breakroom. Once there, he circled the room like an animal trapped in a cage, his anxiety piquing until he finally decided he had to leave the room or scream. He opted for leaving the room, knowing full well screams would lend way to panic and drawn weapons as his comrades raced to his aid. Instead, he tugged on his heavy black coat and rooted in his pockets for his gloves, pulling them on as well. With a heavy sigh, he headed for the outer office, smiling sheepishly at the bewildered stares of his fellow troopers.

Sergeant Seltzer leaned back in his chair, eyeing Jerry with a cross between wonder and awe. "Jeez, McNeal, you're not actually going out in this crap, are you? Tell me you're just going out for a smoke."

Jerry cast the older man a look he was sure mimicked

the man's puzzled face. "We both know I don't smoke."

"I know, but I was hoping you had suddenly decided to start."

"Beats the alternative, doesn't it?"

"Might."

Jerry was fairly certain Seltzer had been a cop in his previous life, as well as the one before that. The man had a look about him. One that said, "I've seen it all." Suddenly, an image of an old-time sheriff came to mind: same white hair, only longer, smoothly pushed back under a Stetson hat, as well as a double-barrel shotgun lazily draped across his jean-clad lap, matching pearl-handled pistols freshly polished and ready for use. For an instant, Jerry expected the man to turn and spit the juice from what he was chewing into a waiting spittoon. The image cleared as the station commander blew a bubble; the tobacco replaced with chewing gum, jeans with a deep gray regulation uniform, pistol – singular – planted firmly in its holster. Jerry rolled his neck to release the tension. Obviously, fresh air would do him some good.

Sergeant Seltzer leaned forward, his white hair shining brightly in the overhead fluorescents. "I take it you've seen the weather reports. Franklin County just went under a state of emergency. No one on the roads unless it's essential."

Jerry removed his gloves and filled his travel mug with coffee, twisting the plastic lid tightly against the rim. "When did that ever stop people from their stupidity?"

"You know we don't have enough manpower to double up, much less send someone along on a joy ride."

Jerry gave an involuntary shudder. "Let's hope that's all this turns out to be."

Seltzer met his eyes. "Not likely, though, is it, son?"

"No."

"So you got a destination in mind or just going for a drive?" Sergeant Seltzer asked. He sighed and made to reach for his brimmed hat.

Jerry waved a hand in dismissal. "No use both of us freezing our asses off. The feeling's not urgent. Just enough to make me want to take a drive."

It was a lie, as the feeling had been blaring like a siren for hours, but something about this one felt different. More personal.

Seltzer looked relieved. "Well, all the same, take Manning's SUV. He's still on leave, and your cruiser's no match for this storm. Check in with dispatch as soon as you figure out what direction you're headed. I'd rather have a heads up if I have to send anyone out."

When, Jerry thought. *When you have to send others out. Soon, but not yet.*

Jerry nodded in agreement before plucking the keys from the board. He squeezed them gently, sending a silent condolence to Manning, who had been on leave since the loss of his partner seven days earlier. Bracing against the wind, Jerry opened the door stepping out into the swirling chill. He picked his way carefully across the parking lot towards the row of SUVs, using the key fob to find his way. He brushed the snow from the windshield with his gloved hand, thankful it was a dry snow. After buckling his seatbelt, he started the SUV to let the engine warm, closed his eyes, and listened. He likened it to a homing device; only the device was his body. The feeling would pull at him, much like a game of Hot or Cold. If he were moving in the right direction, it would just feel right. If not, the clutter inside his head would grow until he turned around and silenced it. Try explaining that to a medical

16

doctor. "You have a gift," one MD had told him.

"No, I have a feeling," he'd replied.

"Yes, but that feeling is a gift."

"Call it what you want. Just give me something to make it go away."

The doctor had stared at him in disbelief. "Surely you jest."

"Yeah, Doc. I just came from a fatal accident. One that I knew about before it happened, yet was powerless to do anything to stop. I always joke about crap like that." He hadn't meant to take out his frustrations on the poor guy, but it had been an extremely difficult day. A mother and her unborn child had died, and there was nothing Jerry could have done to prevent it. That was the same reason he'd walked away from the Marine Corps when he was nearly halfway through to retirement. People died, and there was nothing he could do about it. Knowing something was going to happen didn't usually stop it from happening. Sure, sometimes the gift would clue him in well in advance, and he could route his men in a different direction, but more often than not, he was kept in the dark until his services were needed. He got out because he was tired of being the freaking cleanup crew.

The doctor had moved to the sink to wash his hands. There was a calmness in the way the man stood there staring at the water coming from the faucet. Methodically, he ran his hands under the rushing water, then reached for the soap dispenser. As the soap bubbled within his palms, he turned his face to Jerry and spoke. "I have a gift."

The words had so shocked Jerry that he had jerked his head up in surprise.

"Oh, not the kind you have. But do you think mine is all that different?" The doctor turned off the faucet, pulled two paper towels from the holder, and began to dry his hands. "I went to medical school. With a simple exam, or not so simple medical test, I can make a diagnosis. The majority of the time, I'm correct and can, as you said, make it all go away. But for the others, I'm left feeling helpless, wondering why I bother. Would you have me give up helping those I can because of those I cannot?" The doctor tossed the towels into the trash and left the room before Jerry could reply.

Wow. The doctor was good.

That was six years ago. Jerry had just celebrated his first year on the job. A few days earlier was when he'd gotten a feeling, been led to the scene, only to find there was nothing he could do. He'd felt once again that he was simply part of the cleanup crew and was considering putting in his resignation yet again. Since that time, no matter the outcome, Jerry had never questioned his gift. He was currently serving his seventh year as a Pennsylvania State Trooper.

Jerry put the SUV into gear, crept to the edge of the parking lot, hesitated, and then took a left towards the interstate. Once at the main intersection, he moved to merge onto Interstate 81. At the last second, he whipped the wheel, nearly spinning in a complete circle and headed left towards US Route 30 instead. Apparently, he was now heading in the right direction, as his hands relaxed against the steering wheel. Sometimes, the feeling would begin before the trouble even existed. He was pretty certain this was one of those times.

Chapter Three

Dennis Young looked into the worried eyes of his wife of nine years. Lifting his hand, he smoothed the crease between her dark eyes. "Get rid of that," he said softly.

Selina managed a smile. "It's always hard to see you leave on nights like this."

"I know, but try to remember I'm driving the safest thing on the road," he said, speaking of the county snowplow truck he drove. He felt her sigh as he wrapped his arms around her, pulling her as tight as both their enormous stomachs would allow. They'd had this same conversation nearly every time he headed out to work. Dennis tried to soothe her the best he could, which was not easy. His Latino wife was extremely superstitious and exceedingly hormonal, both of which had him walking on eggshells of late. Not totally her fault, but not the best combination for the husband of a fiery woman in her last trimester of pregnancy.

"I know. I just have a bad feeling tonight," Selina said softly.

He laughed. "You always have a bad feeling, and yet I

manage to come home every time."

She made a halfhearted attempt to pull away from him. "Stop teasing me. I'm your wife. The mother of your children. Am I not allowed to worry? I'm your wife; it's my job."

"Yes, you are allowed." He kissed her on the temple. "And you're very good at it."

"I'm also very good at this," she said, placing her mouth on his.

Her lips were soft and warm. He'd love more than anything to be able to explore them in more detail, but he was already running late. Reluctantly he pulled away and placed a hand on her protruding belly. "I promise to stay safe, Mamacita."

"You'd better," she said, turning from him.

He followed her into the kitchen and watched as she pulled several bags from the fridge, placing each carefully inside his lunchbox. It was a child's lunchbox with a likeness of Superman on the outside, his Father's Day present from his boys, Cory and Cooper, twin seven-year-olds. They'd picked it out themselves, saying he was their hero. When he'd asked them why, they said *it was because he kept the roads safe for everyone to drive on.* He smiled as he did every time he remembered how excited they were at finding him the perfect gift. They had dashed into his room upon waking, smiling matching missing-tooth grins – they'd both lost the same front tooth only one week before – begging him to open the package. *Please, Papa, don't wait. You must open it now!* He was a lucky man to have such an amazing family. To them, he *was* their Superman. Who needed a cape when you had a sixty-thousand-pound truck at your disposal?

Selina closed the lunchbox and peered at him, her gaze

serious. "You have a turkey sandwich with mustard and lettuce. Celery and carrots and hummus and just because I know you, there is a slice of angel food cake," she said, handing him the case.

"I bet Superman was never on a low-fat diet," Dennis said, frowning at the bag.

This brought a smile to her face.

"That's because Superman didn't have high cholesterol." She reached for his medication. Opening the container, she handed him a small pill.

"I bet Superman didn't get treated like a baby."

"Si, but Superman doesn't have a belly to match his pregnant wife's either. You do. Besides, Superman would likely remember to take his pills."

A low blow, followed by a direct hit. Both painful but also painfully true. Dennis was overweight to begin with, and his weight had steadily increased as Selina's pregnancy progressed. At first, Selina hadn't mentioned it, but then Dennis had developed heart palpitations. A trip to the doctor showed that Dennis was well on his way to a heart attack if he didn't make some serious changes. One of those changes meant lowering his cholesterol. This was to be accomplished by diet and medication. Medication that Dennis didn't remember to take, which was the precise reason why his wife had taken over dispensing the pills. He opened his mouth, waiting for Selina to place the pill on his tongue before washing it down with the remnants of his coffee. His wife blew out a sigh, then placed the pills back on top of the fridge.

"I'm pretty sure the bottle says to take with water," she said, turning to him.

"I took it with water. It just happened to be flavored with coffee grounds," he said gruffly.

Selina leveled a look at him. "Just make sure you eat the lunch I prepared. No stopping at the drive-thru."

"It's a blizzard out there. I doubt anything is open," he reminded her.

Her eyes narrowed in response.

"Yes, Mom," he said, and stuck out his tongue. At least in his head. He would not dare provoke the woman standing in front of him any more than necessary. Being treated like a child was bad enough, but his wife could punish him much more effectively than his mother ever could. Sleeping on the couch was just the beginning. Taking away other more intimate things was something he'd rather avoid. He pressed his lips together in remembrance of her recent kiss. "Turkey, rabbit food, and a slice of angel food cake given to me by my angel," he replied instead.

"No stopping at Rutter's either," she said, referring to one of the local gas stations along his route.

Before he could think of a witty reply, his radio crackled, then announced that the roads were worsening and reminded everyone that they were still under a state of emergency. Seeing the worry lines crease her face, he sat his lunch on the counter and folded his arms around her once more.

"See there; we are under a state of emergency. There won't be anyone on the roads but me." She chuckled in response. They both knew that not everyone heeded weather-related warnings. "That's better, Lina. You know I hate leaving you, but it's my job, and I happen to be pretty darn good at it."

He lifted her chin with a gentle hand and lowered his mouth to hers. What he thought would be a simple peck in farewell turned steamy and left him hungry for more.

Mood swings were only a small portion of things that had increased during her pregnancy. Though Selina had always been eager, she had been rabid with a heightened sex drive since the beginning of her unplanned pregnancy, a tricky thing as both their stomachs expanded. He glanced at the kitchen clock. *Way too late to call in sick.* He wondered, momentarily, if it would help to just tell the truth. As far as he knew, no one on his crew had ever called in horny. It would probably earn him hero status with all the guys as well. Thinking better of it, he picked up his lunchbox and headed for the door.

***

The short drive to work proved Selina's fears to be valid. The snow was already well over a foot deep, and that was on top of several feet that were already on the ground. While the snow on the roads was not as deep as on the fields, it was plenty deep enough to wreak havoc on the roadways, and the white stuff was not showing any signs of letting up anytime soon. It would be all the plows could do just to keep up. He'd used the plow on his Jeep Wrangler to make his way the short distance from his house off Duffield Road to the county garage on Highway 997 to pick up his work truck, an impressive yellow beast he'd named Hercules. It was midnight when Dennis officially began his shift. Normally, he'd do eight hours and be done, but for a storm this size, the shifts had been expanded to twelve on twelve off, with trucks running around the clock. The trucks were well maintained and could handle the added demand. A plus to rotating the trucks, his truck was warm and ready when he arrived. As Hercules idled, he checked all the gauges. Next, he tilted the blade, checking the readings on his monitors for any issues. Finding everything in order, he said a short prayer and moved to the loading area to get his truck filled with a mixture of calcium chloride and salt. He watched in the large side mirror as Pete, the loader driver, maneuvered the Caterpillar into position, lowered the bucket into the pile, and moved forward. Once the bucket was full, he lifted the contents into the air, carefully positioning it over the edge of the dump bed before tilting the scoop. The truck jerked as the contents landed, then settled with a final shiver.

Pete's voice drifted through the radio, speaking over the rumble of the truck. "That will do it for now."

Dennis keyed the mike of his radio. "Thanks, man. I'm off to make the streets safe for all those who dare to venture out."

"Yeah, you and a dozen others. Stay safe out there. I'll catch you on your return."

Dennis pulled to the edge of the parking lot, lowered the blade, and took a left onto Highway 997. The truck burrowed a path along the winding road that led to US Route 30 – also known as Lincoln Highway. He caught a green light at Rutter's and made an easy right onto Lincoln Highway and began clearing his official route – US Route 30 from the borough's edge to the Franklin/Adams county line. He'd turn around just the other side of the county line in the Adams County lot, then make his way back to the edge of the borough before doing it all again, only deviating when time to reload the truck. Monotonous to some, but not to him; he knew this road like the back of his hand. Knew every curve, hill, and hidden driveway. Knew when he needed to slow down and exactly what speed to maintain to make the clearest path, providing people stayed out of his way. With a few exceptions, businesses were closed, even those that normally remained open throughout the night. He preferred it this way; it was much easier and safer than to slam on the brakes when a car pulled out in front of him. Obviously, most people did not realize what was involved in stopping a fully loaded salt truck. As if on cue, a Chevy Tahoe pulled out in front of him. Dennis managed to get the truck stopped just in time to avoid crashing into the rear of the SUV. He wondered at his wife's feeling. *Don't get jumpy, Dennis. She's just on edge right now. Worried about the baby is all.* They'd both been, as it seemed another child was not in the cards for them. They'd tried for years after the boys; two pregnancies followed, and neither made it to term. Then years went by with nothing happening. Dennis and Selina had resigned themselves to being a family of four. Each had gained weight and settled into a comfortable routine. For Dennis, that included work and joining the family at soccer practice when his schedule allowed. For Selina, it involved all the wifely and motherly duties and a newfound love of cooking and baking, which was what had led to some of the family's weight issues. Selina had not even known she was pregnant until the second trimester. By then, the doctors said she had a high chance of making it to full term. They both knew this baby would most likely be their last, so both were anxious for her to be born. Each had been thrilled to learn the child Selina was expecting was a girl. Dennis tried hard to picture a small replica of his wife, with rich brown skin and eyes the color of coffee. Or would she resemble the boys with their olive tones? Maybe she would surprise them all and come out looking like Dennis, pasty white with green eyes. *For her sake, I hope not.* He smiled. *All I know is, she's going to be beautiful.*

Hercules muscled its way east, throwing a rooster tail of snow in its path. Dennis listened to the mindless chatter on his work radio and settled in for the long night ahead. He passed Rutter's with only a side glance. He had a turkey sandwich and willpower. Not really. He'd had a green light. That willpower could very well have been tested if the light had been red. He would pass this way many more times before his shift was through. Chances were pretty decent that said willpower would be tested numerous times over the course of the night.

Chapter Four

The lights of the reception room blinked: one, two, three times. The third wink kept the room dark for several seconds before illuminating the basement once more. Cheers erupted from the wedding guests, whoops and hoorays all joyfully echoing off the painted concrete walls of the church basement. While Holly was pleased the lights had withstood the latest wintery blast, she was pretty sure that would not remain the case much longer. She looked around to see if anyone shared her thoughts. She made eye contact with Sandy, the mother of the bride, and was relieved to see a look of resignation on the woman's face. Sandy shrugged and glanced at the lights as if asking for confirmation.

Holly nodded her agreement and felt guilty after having done so. While she was pretty sure the power would be out shortly, ending the event, she would prefer that end to come sooner than later and was more than ready to be home. She'd had an uneasy feeling ever since she'd followed Morgan and Grant outside a few hours earlier. While she'd known it had been snowing the entire time they'd been inside, she was surprised at just how much snow had fallen since she'd arrived. Driving home would be interesting, to say the least.

"Okay, people, I think that's our warning," Sandy shouted above the cheers. "Let's wrap this up before we lose power completely."

Thank God, Holly thought and then felt better at hearing the mumbles of agreement from others in the room. She took one final picture, then set to work breaking down her camera equipment, carefully removing the lenses and placing them between the dividers of her camera bag. One of the dividers had come loose. Instead of wasting time with it, she pulled her knit hat out of her coat pocket and placed the camera inside. *Just call me Miss MacGyver,* she thought and zipped the bag shut. *Not too bad with a camera either, Miss Mac,* she added, taking a mental inventory of some of the photos she'd taken. She'd been stalking the partygoers for hours, finding them unaware and capturing random photos that would fill albums and, God-willing, delight the bride and groom for years to come. It was well past midnight; the bride and groom had already departed, slipping out unnoticed. Or so they thought. She had noticed and had the picture to prove it. She didn't always stay on the job this long, but the bride's parents had paid for the deluxe package. Normally, the late hour wouldn't be such a big deal, but they were under a blizzard warning, and she still had a twenty-three-mile drive home. Eighteen-plus inches was the expected total, at least the last time she'd had a chance to check the news. They were well on their way. At least ten inches of the white stuff had made it to the ground the last time she'd peeked outside. That was over two hours ago. She'd just finished packing her supplies when Sandy approached her.

"Are you sure you don't want to spend the night?" She was still wearing the taupe dress she'd worn to the wedding but had removed the heels and covered her stockings with thick wool socks that stretched the length of her slender calves. Her dark hair was still pulled up, but strands had fallen, and others strained against the pins that held them in place. She smelled of a mix of perfume and alcohol, and was well past tipsy, but Holly didn't think she would be considered drunk. Relaxed, yes – maybe for the first time in months – tired – most assuredly – but not drunk. Holly had heard the woman extend the same offer to others over the last few moments – some had taken her up on her hospitality, and others declined, saying they had made other arrangements. Sandy looked about ready to drop, not unusual for a haggard mother of the bride, but her smile was warm, the invite genuine. Holly thought about taking her up on her offer but just couldn't bring herself to say yes.

"Thank you for the offer, but I'm going to have to pass. I promised my daughter that I'd be there in the morning when she woke up."

Sandy leaned against the wall for support and tucked a few fallen strands of hair behind her ear. "How old is your daughter?"

"She turns five tomorrow." Holly wanted to add that she wasn't sure how many birthdays they would get to spend together, but let that thought go unsaid. She wasn't going to add to the woman's troubles. Grace was in remission. Holly had to keep thinking positive. Still, regression was always a possibility, thus the reason she refused to stay the night. All the support groups stressed never to take a single moment for granted. They also said you had to take care of yourself too and probably would not consider driving home in a blizzard a smart thing, but Holly had her priorities. Being there for Grace was at the top of that list.

Sandy rested a hand on Holly's shoulder, blinking back tears. "You cherish every moment you have with your little girl. They grow up so quickly, and then they don't need you anymore."

For an instant, Holly thought the woman had read her mind, but one look in Sandy's eyes let her know she was referring to her own daughter. The one she thought lost to her now that she'd found someone else to take care of her. An odd feeling of kinship washed over her. They were both trying to hang on to their little girls. She took Sandy's hand and gave it a gentle squeeze. "She's just distracted at the moment. Take it from me; we always need our mamas."

The overhead lights flickered another warning. Sandy pushed off the wall and rose from her melancholy, like a benched player being pulled back into the game. "If you are not going to stay, then you'd better get going. Did my husband pay you?"

"He did." *And then some,* she thought, referring to the generous tip he'd given her.

"Good. Now get going before someone else decides to call you back for another picture," Sandy said firmly.

Holly didn't have to be told twice. She hurried into her coat and slipped out the same door the love-struck couple had used only twenty minutes before. A blast of arctic air sent snow flying into her face. All of a sudden, she was regretting the MacGyver'd use of her hat. Oh well, at least the camera was warm. She hurried to her car, head lowered against the brutal northern wind. Winter in Pennsylvania could be treacherous at times.

This was one of those times.

She hadn't expected to be leaving so late. After seeing the weather reports, she thought the party would have ended earlier than it did. She could have left sooner; the family would have understood, but she had a reputation to protect. Staying until the end was the package they'd paid for. It was expected of her, and it wasn't like the couple had planned to get married in a blinding snowstorm. The wedding had been on her books for nearly a year. It was one of the hazards of accepting a wedding gig in late January, one she'd agreed on, even knowing she would have a half-hour's drive home. "Yeah, right," she mumbled against the wind. She'd be lucky to get home at all in these conditions. She lost her footing, slipping, but managed to lift the camera case high before she hit the pavement. Fortunately, the blanket of snow helped to cushion her fall. She pushed from the fluff, managing to right herself, all while keeping the camera equipment tucked close to her body. She was not about to sacrifice hours' worth of work, especially since the bride's father had tipped her so generously for showing up in such deplorable conditions. Of course she'd showed up; she was a professional. *Neither rain, nor wind, nor sleet, nor snow. So what if that was the United States Postal Service's motto. If it worked for her father, it worked for her.* Besides, she was driving her father's Jeep, and it had seen its share of snowstorms.

Reaching the Jeep, she tugged the door against the wind, barely making it inside without falling a second time. *Maybe I should have accepted Sandy's offer.* While the smart thing, her heart pulled her in the other direction. She was going home, keeping the promise she'd made to her daughter. She waited for the engine to warm, thankful she'd raised the wiper blades upon arriving. At least they would not be stuck to the windows. As the snow started to slide down the windshield, she took off her heels and pulled on sweatpants, wool socks, and boots. No easy task while she was sitting in the driver's seat, but she managed. She wasn't making much of a fashion statement with her navy blue dress, but she was heading straight home. It wasn't like anyone would see her.

She grimaced, realizing she'd forgotten to lower the wiper blades. The wind caught the door as she opened it, flying out of her hand with enough force she was afraid it would be pulled from its hinges. Grabbing hold of the edge, she pushed it shut, hurried to scrape the remaining snow off the windshield, lowered the blades, and returned to the car, stamping the snow from her feet. She warmed her hands, cursing the fact that she'd left her gloves on the seat instead of placing them on her hands. *Oh well, at least they are still dry*, she thought, slipping them on. She considered calling her dad to let him know she was on her way, then reconsidered. If he were still awake, he would have called. No sense interrupting perfectly good sleep just to say she was okay. She placed the phone in the cup holder and placed the car in gear.

"God, please watch over me and guide me home safely," she repeated as she made her way out of the church parking lot.

Chapter Five

Having made several passes along the stretch of Route 30 to the county line, Officer Jerry McNeal was now idling in the snow-covered parking lot of Greenwood Hills Chapel. He felt certain he was close to where he would be needed and although not ready to radio for reinforcements, he knew the time was getting near. On an ordinary day – if there were such a thing when dealing with that feeling – Jerry would have asked for backup or had stations on standby, but this was no ordinary day. The roads were treacherous, the snow falling so quickly even the snowplows were having trouble keeping up. He watched the computer monitor in his patrol car scroll the latest weather advisory, which now predicted over twenty-four inches of snow by the time the system moved out. He locked his fingers together in a meditative state, extended his two index fingers, and tapped them against his mouth, watching the snow fall against the windshield. The wet flakes would barely settle before being tossed forcefully aside by the wiper blades. Out of the corner of his left eye, he saw the flashing yellow lights of a snowplow hulking its way through the intersection where 997 met Route 30. Heading east on Route 30, the blade skimmed the road, tilted slightly, shooting everything in its path to the right shoulder of the road. A shiver traveled the length of him as the truck disappeared behind a whiteout of snow, then reappeared a short time later. "God in Heaven, please watch over us all," Jerry said as the truck passed in a spray of snow followed by a beacon of yellow lights. Lights that could not be seen only seconds earlier. He felt hot air brush against the back of his neck and instantly pressed his hand to the area in question. He had a sudden feeling that he wasn't alone, yet when he looked in the mirror, he saw nothing but darkness amongst the faint glow of his parking lights reflecting in the snow.

His cell phone rang, startling him. "McNeal," he said, tearing his gaze away from the mirror.

"How's things looking out there, Jerry?" the sergeant asked.

"A little freaky."

"Say again?"

"Whiteouts so bad you can't see. I just watched an entire snowplow disappear right before my very eyes," Jerry said, checking the mirror once more.

"And the civilian traffic?"

"I wish I could say nonexistent," Jerry said, watching a late model pickup truck drive past much faster than was safe, considering the current road conditions. He considered citing the driver, but his feeling told him he was needed elsewhere.

"When they have an accident, you can bet your ass they'll blame the road commission for not having the roads cleared. How about you? That radar of yours picking up anything?"

Jerry knew his sergeant was not referring to his police radar. Not the one in his vehicle anyway. "Yeah, I think it's about that time. I don't know what yet, but pretty close to the county line on 30."

"Need me to send backup?"

"I wish I knew," Jerry said with a sigh. "I just can't see bringing everyone out in these conditions when I don't have a clue what I'm dealing with. I think I'm going to take another pass down that way. I got a really bad feeling when that snowplow went past a few moments ago."

"You do that. I'll have a couple of the boys start heading in your direction," the sergeant said.

"Okay, but tell them to take their time. I'll be back in touch as soon as I know something."

"Roger that."

Jerry switched off his phone and checked the rearview mirror one last time. He wasn't sure which was stronger, the feeling that something was going to happen or the feeling that he was no longer alone in the SUV.

***

Conditions were deteriorating at an alarming rate as Dennis made his fifth pass down Route 30. Thankfully, it seemed most were heeding the warnings, with only a few exceptions. He passed Wal-Mart, which remained open despite the conditions. He pulled into the Lowe's parking lot and let the engine idle while he unzipped his lunchbox. He opened the baggie, pulled out his turkey sandwich, peeling the bread back with the tip of his index finger, and sighed. He was glad his truck was facing west; had he turned the other direction, he would be able to see both the Wendy's and Arby's signs. Not that either was open, but that wasn't the point. He took a bite, felt the crunch of the lettuce followed by the tangy bite of yellow mustard, and chewed halfheartedly. *Boring.* That was the only way to describe it. He ate another bite, wishing he had some chips to go with it. He thought about returning to Wal-Mart. No, he couldn't do that, as technically, he was still on lunch. And he'd promised to eat only what Selina had fixed him for lunch. But if he were to stop at Rutter's during his next pass, he would be able to get something he could sink his teeth into and eat it with a clear conscience. If Selina asked if he had only eaten what she'd packed him for lunch, he could, with a clear conscience, say yes. He would just refrain from telling her about anything he'd eaten afterward. He finished eating his sandwich, which seemed to taste a bit better now that he'd worked out a plan. Next, he dove into the veggies, dipping each stick into the hummus before popping them into his mouth and crunching them into oblivion. When he finished, he ran his index finger around the container, licking the remnants from the digit before covering the container and returning it to the lunchbox. He smiled as he picked up the container that held the angel food cake. Only then did he see the note. Sitting the container in his lap, he unfolded the note.

My darling Dennis, I'm so proud of you for sticking to your diet. I know how hard it is for you, but I thank you for making this commitment to your health. The boys and I need you and would be so lost without you. You can do this. You are stronger than any craving. Please remember this anytime you get weak.

I'll reward you later,
Selina.

Dennis sighed. Lina knew him too well. Of course she'd known what he was planning. A plan he could no longer follow through with. He opened the container, removed the slice of cake, and took a small bite, chewing it slowly in an effort to make it last. He finished the cake, plucked a couple of crumbs from his shirt, and ate those as well. Halfheartedly, he closed the lid to his lunchbox. While he was no longer hungry, his tummy still wasn't quite satisfied. It was going to be a long night. He made a right turn out of the parking lot, lowering his blade as he rounded the corner, leaving a trail of dirty white in his path. Just as he passed Norlo Park, he went through a whiteout that lasted several moments. He'd driven through several more by the time he'd reached Highway 997. He caught the red light at Rutter's and shook his head. Fate was tempting him. He eased his grip on the steering wheel, only then realizing how hard he'd been gripping the wheel. He didn't mind driving in the snow. Driving blind in the midst of whiteouts was another thing altogether. If he could not see the road, chances were others on the road could not see him. At least he had the added security of the flashing lights. His security blanket vanished when a wall of white suddenly blocked his view of the red traffic light he'd seen just seconds before. The veil of snow lifted just seconds before the light switched to green.

Gripping the steering wheel, he continued on his way. He passed by Rutter's and averted his eyes to avoid further temptation. He noticed a State Trooper idling in the parking lot of Greenwood Hills Chapel and chuckled. If anyone was speeding on these roads, they deserved to be pulled over. Probably didn't even have his radar on. Taking a nap or watching a movie on his phone. *Porn*. That thought evoked another chuckle. Dark parking lot, not many people on the roads. *Yes, most definitely porn. Must be nice, being a cop. I could be a cop. I could watch porn in a snow-covered parking lot. It would beat the heck out of driving in blinding snowstorms. But hey, not everyone can be Superman.*

***

The roads were worse than Holly had imagined. A part of her wished she'd taken Sandy up on her offer to stay. A moot point now that she'd already driven far enough that turning around would defeat the point. The snow would be the same in both directions, so she might as well keep going. She saw a billboard touting Mr. Ed's Elephant Museum, one of the local touristy places. The museum housed glass cases full of elephant figurines and memorabilia and nearly as much selection when it came to candy, nuts, and fudge, which could be purchased by the piece or pound. Her mouth watered at the thought of cinnamon-flavored almonds, which were her personal favorite. She smiled, remembering the childish excitement on Grace's steroid-bloated face when she'd run through the store filling her little tin bucket with candy. How she'd stood outside bald as a billiard ball answering Miss Ellie, the talking elephant statue that was on guard near the road at the museum's entrance.

That was two years ago, when Grace first started undergoing chemo. Two long years. Grace's hair still hadn't returned, but the child always insisted Holly blow the horn every time they drove past so Miss Ellie would know they were thinking of her. Her mind drifted to her daughter, who'd been in remission for half a year. The doctors called this a positive sign, but others who'd been through the same ordeal warned her to be diligent of any signs and symptoms. Always one to think positive, Holly had not allowed such thoughts to dictate her life, still working and accepting jobs. She had bills to pay after all – but she refused to miss any important events in her daughter's life, including Grace's fifth birthday tomorrow – today, actually, as it was well past midnight.

She passed the store with the concrete monuments, gasping when the building disappeared in a haze of white before her eyes. She focused her attention back on driving, sat taller in the seat, and strained to see the road. While the roads had been plowed, the snow was still plenty deep and conditions slippery. She nearly lost control of the Jeep as she passed Cashtown Road. Such a drastic change from when she'd shot a wedding at the historic Round Barn in August. That had been a hot summer afternoon, so hot she could almost feel the warmth of the afternoon sun just thinking about it. Almost but not quite. As it was, the heater in the Jeep struggled to keep up against the wind outside, making her grateful she'd had the forethought to pull on her sweats and boots before heading out.

As she drove down the hill, she passed a snow-covered elephant on the right that announced the beginning of the elephant museum property. Just past the trees would be the museum and the famous Miss Ellie. Holly smiled, wondering if anyone would notice if she parked alongside Miss Ellie and spent the night, then, realizing she'd run out of gas before daybreak, opted to toot the horn instead. "Hi, Miss Ellie," she shouted as she drove past, then made a mental note to take Grace back to the museum once the weather cleared. It would be worth the sugar high just to have new memories of the place.

As she continued west on Route 30, the snow

intensified. Whiteouts were becoming commonplace. Thankfully, she had only met three vehicles in the last ten minutes, and none appeared to be traveling in the same direction as she. The road began to level out; she could just make out the yellow flashing lights alerting her of the traffic light.

She was almost home.

Just a few more miles, and she'd be able to tiptoe into Grace's room to check on her before jumping into a warm shower to thaw out. She gripped the wheel tighter as another whiteout blocked her vision. As the snow shower cleared, she could see the yellow flashing lights looming closer. *Weren't they supposed to be higher? When had they added more lights? Why hadn't she noticed the second set of lights on her way out of town?* She squinted through the snow, trying to figure out what she was seeing before her mind registered she was heading straight into the path of a snowplow. Screaming, she whipped the steering wheel to the left, sending the Jeep fishtailing out of control. Barely missing the guardrail, she careened down the embankment and headlong into a stand of trees.

Chapter Six

Jerry crept his way along the snow-covered road, the feeling of urgency escalating with every turn of the wheel. He knew it was nearing the time when he would be needed. He traveled at what seemed a snail's pace, reminding himself he would be of no help if he ended up in a ditch. An image of the snowplow entered his mind, but something else nagged at the recesses. Something he'd yet to put his finger on. Even though the plow had passed by only moments before, the roads were so thick with freshly fallen snow that the large truck's tire tracks were already covered with snow. It didn't help that the wind was blowing so fiercely that he was driving blind most of the time, whiteouts sending veils of snow to obscure his view. A seasoned driver, he knew the truck could be right in front of him, and he wouldn't see it until it was too late. The windy road proved tricky, but he was able to stay in his lane. The snow blind lifted, the yellow caution lights dancing into view, warning of the traffic light at Route 233. Just past that would be Caledonia State Park, then the Franklin/Adams county line. A county snowplow would have to turn around soon. Jerry guessed the best spot for this was just across the county line at the Adams County fill site. The truck would have to cross traffic but could make a right turn when exiting the parking lot. The light turned red as he was approaching. Jerry looked to make certain the path was clear before proceeding through the intersection without stopping.

Just as he cleared the light, he saw what he was looking for; the large snowplow had careened into the hill on the opposite side of the road. It looked as if the blade of the plow had dug into the hillside so hard that it had slung the truck to the side, lifting the whole right side of the truck completely off the road. The truck was left teetering on the left wheels, held precariously in that position by the blade, which was embedded in the snow-covered hill. *How in the heck did he manage that?* Jerry wondered. The yellow lights on the truck were still flashing, which would hopefully keep the truck visible to oncoming traffic. Just in case, Jerry parked his SUV in the center of the road and hit the switches to every light available to him. The snow lit up in a brilliant array of blues, reds, and whites. He turned on the siren, hoping that what could not be seen could at least be heard. The wail of the siren bounced off the snow, wound down, then increased once again, echoing off the hillside. Annoying but effective, especially when conditions were at their worst.

He used his spotlight to survey the area. Not seeing anything else out of the norm, he keyed the radio, alerting dispatch. "Dispatch, this is unit 7. I've got a single vehicle accident located on Route 997 just east of the Adams County line, approximately a quarter mile past Route 233. Clear." For the sake of the driver's privacy, Jerry used the SUV's in-unit computer, quickly typing a message to dispatch, letting them know the vehicle involved was a county snowplow, asking for a large tow truck and other equipment needed to handle the scene.

"Clear, unit 7; other units are being dispatched. Please be advised due to weather conditions, response time will be hindered. Clear?"

"Clear." Jerry zipped his coat to his chin, pulling on his gloves before climbing out of his vehicle. He started towards the truck, then returned to the SUV for a first aid kit, feeling sure he'd need it. He checked under the seat, then opened the back door. The wind caught the door, whisking it from his grasp. He could have sworn he felt a rush of warm air sail past him. Not possible on a night like this, but eerie all the same. He looked around, half expecting to see someone standing behind him. No one was there. *Get a grip, Jerry.* He shrugged off the feeling of unease, found the first aid kit, and hurried to the truck. His boots sank into the depths of snow as he cautiously approached the left side of the cab. Studying the wreckage to make sure there was no chance of the truck rolling further, he squeezed his way between the truck and the hill. He tried the door, but it was locked. Not that he'd be able to open it, as there was barely enough room for him to squeeze between the truck and the hill. The windows were covered with snow; there didn't appear to be any movement within the cab. He reached for his flashlight, brushed the snow away from the side window, and illuminated the inside.

The driver was still fastened in his seat-belt, the only thing keeping the large man in his seat. Jerry was impressed the belt had held, considering the man's weight. The driver's head was hanging limp, double chin resting high on the man's chest. Jerry shouted to be heard above the siren. This did not evoke a response. He could see blood coming from the left side of the man's head. *He must have hit his head on the side window.* Jerry tapped at the window with his flashlight. Still, the man did not move. *Come on, fella, don't be dead.* Jerry pulled his cell phone out of his pocket, opting for discretion, knowing there was a good possibility the man's wife owned a police scanner. He found the number he was looking for and pressed send. "Sergeant, I need a name for the county snowplow driver running 997. Also, please verify there is an ambulance en route to this location."

"I'll get dispatch working on the name. The ambulance has been dispatched, but road conditions are keeping them from responding at present."

Jerry could hear the helplessness in the sergeant's voice, which matched the panic he was starting to feel. Something nudging at him was telling him to hurry. *Give me a break already. Can't you see I'm trying?*

"I don't care if they have to use a dog sled, get them en route," Jerry said heatedly.

"Roger. And, McNeal, we are doing the best we can. Clear?"

"Clear," Jerry said, keeping his anger in check. He was angrier at himself than at the sergeant. *If he'd only gone with his instincts and asked for backup earlier.* He tapped on the window once more and was relieved when he saw the man's eyes flicker in response. *Unconscious, not dead. Thank you, Jesus.* He tugged at the driver's side door again to no avail. Swallowing, he knew the only way in would be the passenger's side door, which meant he'd have to climb his way inside. First, he trudged his way around to the front of the truck. He aimed the beam of light at the blade, which still appeared to be firmly embedded in the hillside. He climbed onto the blade, then, using the snow-covered hillside as leverage, tried to dislodge the blade. He slipped but managed to leap clear of the blade. He was somewhat satisfied that the truck wasn't going anywhere. At least, he hoped so. *Wouldn't be much help if I were under a truck.* The siren was still wailing. He considered turning it off, but decided he'd rather put up with a bit of noise than to have someone plow into the underside of the truck. As the siren lessened, he heard a howl in the distance. He froze, listening. It too seemed to be echoing off the hillside. There were a few homes in the area, but this stretch was mostly forest. *Could be a wolf or coyote, most likely something less sinister. Probably just a family dog from one of the neighboring houses. Poor devil is probably half frozen and upset by the sirens. Can't say as I blame you, pal. If I had time, I'd find your owners and have a talk with them about leaving you outside on a night like this.* He turned his attention back to the situation at hand. He went back to the driver's side window, pounding on the glass. "Driver, can you hear me?"

No response.

His instincts shouted to break the window so that he could get to the man, but given the man's size, there was no way Jerry would be able to pull him through the narrow opening. No, all it would do would be to further expose the man to the elements. That the man was not wearing his coat would not help his situation. Given no other choice, Jerry gripped the doorframe and began his slippery ascent up the side of the truck.

Chapter Seven

The blinking lights, the snow clearing to reveal the enormous snowplow headed straight for her; it all happened so quickly that all Holly could do was scream. She applied the brakes, but it didn't seem to help as the Jeep careened out of control. Just missing the guardrail, she felt the Jeep take flight, leaving the road, and sailing over the bed of snow. *Oh God, please don't let me die!* Limbs crashed against the Jeep as it floated down the ravine. She heard something hit the door as the Jeep passed a stand of young saplings. The Jeep headed straight towards a thicket of large, established trees. *No! No! Please no*! She made a fruitless attempt at turning the wheel, then braced for impact. She hit hard, a spray of snow billowing out in all directions. Something crashed through the windshield, plummeting to the seat beside her. She felt the Jeep buckle as it hit a sturdy tree. At the same instant, a searing pain shot through her right leg, traveling all the way up her thigh. She screamed as the airbag deployed, crashing into her so hard it stifled her scream, knocking the air out of her lungs and forcing her backward into the seat.

And then it was over.

The airbag deflated, releasing the pressure on her chest. *Am I dead?* she wondered. *Probably not, considering how bad my leg hurts.* She was trembling but had not lost consciousness. Holly took inventory. Her face hurt, but she was pretty sure the blood she tasted was from a busted lip. Her leg hurt something fierce and felt as if it was jammed into the floorboard. She tried to move it. *Holy crap!* It felt as if her leg was on fire, a searing pain that traveled all the way to her hip. Tears streamed down her face, threatening to freeze where they fell. She held her breath, clenching her teeth through the pain, and tried to pull her leg free. *Oh God!* Her breath was coming in tiny gasps as she pulled yet again, the pain racing through her like hot embers traveling the length of her torso. Still, the leg wouldn't budge. She reached for her phone, but it was not where she'd left it. She leaned forward in an attempt at finding it; her leg screamed its displeasure. She sat back in her seat, her teeth biting her lower lip as she waited for the pain to ease. She was not getting out of the car, at least not without assistance. *Is the other driver okay? Maybe he's already called for help. But what if he didn't? I'll freeze to death.*

Heavy wet snow streamed in through the broken windshield, pushed forward by the brutal force of the wind blowing into the Jeep. It was too dark to tell just how bad her situation really was. She would need to get help soon or would likely die out here. An image of Gracie came to mind. *I will not leave you, Gracie. At least not without a fight.* Holly pushed at the airbag until she could get a firm grip on the steering wheel. She held fast to the wheel as she made another attempt to pull her leg free, screaming as the Jeep played tug-o-war with her trapped limb. It was no use; the vehicle was not letting go. *Now what?* The truck driver would call for help and tell them her location. *If he were okay, he would have been down to check on me by now.* The thought chilled her further.

"Hello…HELP!" she called louder. The only sound was the wind and the occasional tree branch cracking under the weight of the snow. She brushed at the icy snow that pelted her face. *Think, Holly.* She reached into the side pocket of the door and felt something hard. Stretching her fingers further, she gripped what felt to be a flashlight. Pulling it free, she clicked the button, breathing a sigh of relief when it illuminated the inside of the cab. The relief was short-lived when she saw the condition of the Jeep. She took a breath and took stock of her situation. The window had shattered into a spider web but was intact except for a hole the size of a large beach ball where snow now streamed through. She turned the beam on the seat. A branch, which looked more like a large boulder, rested in the passenger seat. *That would have killed me if it had hit on my side.* She felt her body tremble and knew it was from more than the cold. The front end was caved around a rather large tree, her leg pinned within the wreckage. She wasn't going anywhere anytime soon. *Then I need to make sure I'm still alive when someone finally comes for me.* She shined the light in the compartment where she'd found the flashlight and saw an umbrella. Leaning to the left as carefully as she could, without moving the bottom half of her body, she reached for it, pulling it free with the tips of her fingers. She placed the flashlight into the cup holder, removed the shield from the umbrella, and held it to the side, flinching as it sprang to life. Maneuvering the umbrella, she pushed it towards the shattered windshield, the pain clawing up her leg like burning rods with each movement. After several attempts, she was able to position the umbrella in front of the windshield to offer some protection.

She sat back, brushed newly fallen tears from her face, and admired her handiwork. *Good job, MacGyver! What else you got?* she thought as she looked around the dimly lit compartment. Her gaze stopped at the camera bag. *Little good that will do me.* The bag was still in the passenger seat where she'd left it. Unfortunately, the limb that had broken the window was resting on top of it. Extending her right arm, she pulled at the log. When that didn't work, she grabbed hold of the camera bag and began to tug, straining against her injured leg. Releasing the bag, her hands flew to her leg, rubbing against the pain. Gathering her courage, she gripped the bag, tugging with all her might until, at last, she pulled the bag free. Her fingers trembled from cold and pain as she unzipped the bag. Opening the flap, Holly smiled. She'd completely forgot that she put her scarf inside when entering the church earlier that evening. She pulled out the red silk scarf, which was more for style than function. Still, it was better than nothing. She unrolled it and wrapped it around her head several times, covering her cheeks, mouth, and neck. It helped, at least a little. *How long does it take for hypothermia to kick in?* she wondered.

She removed the camera, checking for damage, and found none. Removing the lens cover, she turned on the flash and snapped a few photos of the dashboard resting on her leg, the umbrella, and the log. She lifted the umbrella, holding tight as the wind tried to blow it out of her hand, and blindly snapped several shots of the mangled car nestled against the snow-covered tree. Surely photos from the victim's point of view would be worth something. *If... she lived to share them. If not, at least Gracie would know*

she had been lucid enough to take photos before she died.
The thought of her daughter brought forth a new round of
tears. *What would she think when her momma failed to
come home?* Would she think she'd broken her promise?
Or would she grow up feeling guilty, thinking it her fault
that her mom had been killed? That if she hadn't made the
promise to return, she wouldn't have been in the snow. *It's
not your fault, baby.* Holly's feeling of helplessness was
replaced with a renewed sense of determination. She
returned the camera to the bag and began rubbing her
gloved hands along her arms to keep the circulation
flowing.

Her cell phone rang, causing her to jump, the
movement leaving her gasping in pain. The floorboard on
the passenger side lit up, showcasing the phone's
whereabouts. The ringtone – ACDC's "Hells Bells" – let
her know her dad had woken and was worried about her.
"I'm not okay, send help," she called as the melody kept
playing. The music stopped. Several seconds of silence
passed before she heard the chime letting her know she had
a new voicemail. Regret engulfed her as she recalled her
decision not to text to let him know she was on her way.
He would probably think she was still working. Or worse,
that she'd decided to spend the night. *Note to self, if you
get out of this, come up with a better plan of action for
future situations such as this.* "Yeah, like not driving in
blizzards," she said through chattering teeth. *God, I'm
cold.*

An image of Dory – the blue and yellow fish from the
Disney movie *Finding Nemo* – came to mind. "Just keep
swimming, just keep swimming," the fish had repeated.
"Just keep moving. Just keep moving," she said, rubbing
her arms. She was still chattering the words when she

heard it. A siren wailing from the top of the ridge. The sound echoing off the surrounding mountains. Rising and falling like treacherous ocean waves. Ominous on any other occasion. Tonight, the most wonderful sound she'd ever heard. *Help was coming! The snowplow driver must have called for help. He would tell them she was in the ravine and someone would come for her.*

"I'm down here!" she said, pulling the fabric away from her mouth.

She waited for a reply. And waited. "Hello, it's pretty dang cold down here." All she could hear was the sound of the siren echoing off the rise of the hill. *Good thing they know I'm here. They would never hear me above the sound of the siren.* She pulled the mirror from where it had landed on the dashboard, held it up to look out of the rear window. The window was covered with snow, so she tossed the mirror on the seat beside the branch.

She was trembling from her head to her toes. Well, at least the toes on her left foot. Her right leg seemed to be growing numb. At least it wasn't throbbing any longer. While a relief, it probably wasn't the best of signs. *Maybe I should move it to wake it up.* A thought she discounted when just the simple act of trying to wiggle her toes sent tears streaming down her face. *Knock off the crying before the tears freeze the scarf to your face.* She wiped her eyes with a gloved hand, stopping when she had a sudden overwhelming feeling she was no longer alone.

As the siren waned, she heard a branch snap just outside the driver's side door, confirming her suspicions. "Hello? Is anyone out there?" she asked, wishing she could power down the window. She aimed the flashlight at the window, seeing nothing but her reflection in the snow-coated glass. She turned the light towards the passenger window, which once again showed nothing but her reflection.

She tried to open the door, but it wouldn't give. *Sorry, I broke your truck, Dad.* "Hello? Is anyone out there? Please, if you are there, can you get me out?" *Why wasn't anyone answering?*

She heard a thump on the hood, felt the Jeep move. Fear washed over her. *Bigfoot?* Her hands trembled as she pulled the umbrella away from the window, screaming as she saw the hulking form of a very large wolf staring in through the large hole. The animal turned its head, deep brown eyes surveying her intensely. *Not a wolf, thank God. A dog. A huge German Shepherd. A police dog?* "Good Boy." God, please let him be a good boy. *Surely I didn't survive the accident just to be eaten by a dog.* She thought about asking him if he was hungry, but since she didn't have anything to offer him, decided against it. *No use giving him any ideas.*

Snow was blowing around the dog and drifting in through the broken windshield. Holly wanted to replace the umbrella but was afraid to make any sudden movements. She thought about using the umbrella to shoo the dog away, but he didn't look like the kind of animal who would be easily shooed. He looked more like the type that would get extremely pissed off if she even tried.

"Help?" The word came out in a whisper.

In response, the dog tilted its enormous head, opened its mouth, and began to howl. The animal's cry came from deep within, as if desperate to be heard over the continuing wail of the siren.

Chapter Eight

Jerry climbed his way up the slippery truck to the passenger side door. Once there, he pushed the snow away from the window and peered inside. Just as he'd expected, the door was locked. He tapped his flashlight against the window. "Driver? Can you hear me?" *I'd be surprised if you can hear anything over that darn siren,* he thought, regretting his decision to leave it on.

He palmed his hand against the window once more. "DRIVER!" *Dammit, what's this guy's name?*

Jerry's phone rang. "Talk to me," he said, forgoing the formalities.

"The driver's name is Dennis Young," the sergeant said into the phone. "Is he alive?"

"I think so. He's unconscious; I'm trying to get to him now. How about some help with that?" he added a bit more tersely.

"Take it easy, McNeal. Don't let this get personal. We both know he'd be much worse off if you'd not been called into action by that gift of yours. You know the weather conditions. Just hold on until we get there."

Holding on was precisely what he was doing, squatting on the side of a truck held in place by the blade bolted to the front. The wind and weight of the snow that was quickly piling up on the side of the truck didn't help. Jerry was afraid it wouldn't take much for the blade to become dislodged and knew the situation could go from bad to worse at any moment. "Roger that," he said, ending the call. It was his fault. He'd known the proximity even before finding the wreckage. *Yes, but he hadn't actually known how serious the situation was going to be. Let's just hope my caution doesn't cost the man his life.*

Jerry tapped the window once more. He hesitated until the siren eased, then called to the driver, "Dennis? DENNIS! WAKE UP!" he shouted and nearly slipped off the truck when Dennis opened his eyes, lifted his head, and looked at him, blinking as if trying to focus. He watched in horror as the man's left hand went in search of the seatbelt release.

"NO!" Jerry shouted, knocking the flashlight against the glass. "Don't release that buckle!" The seatbelt was the only thing holding the man in place. Jerry was afraid that by releasing the belt, the man's weight could be the catalyst that dislodged the plow blade, the only thing keeping the truck from landing on its side.

Dennis turned his head in Jerry's direction. His brows knit together, questioning.

Jerry aimed the light into the driver's compartment. "The truck is not stable. Listen to me; I'm a Pennsylvania State Police Officer. My name is Trooper McNeal. Whatever you do, don't release that seatbelt," Jerry shouted through the glass.

The man nodded, a movement that must have caused considerable pain as his hand flew to the side of his head.

His eyes closed, then opened just as suddenly. A look of concern replaced the confusion as he brought the blood-covered hand to his face for further inspection. The man looked like a frightened rabbit.

A very large rabbit with dilated eyes.

Jerry was going to have to break the window. He took out his nightstick. "Dennis, listen to me. I'm going to help you. But to do that, I will need to break the window. Your coat is near your lap. Put your hands down, and you'll be able to feel it."

Jerry watched as Dennis' right hand found the heavy coat. "Okay, put it over your head to protect you from the glass. It's going to shatter, but it shouldn't cut you. Understand?"

Wordlessly, Dennis did as Jerry had told him.

It took two tries to break the glass. When it finally let go, it shattered into thousands of tiny, non-threatening pellets. When the spray finished, Dennis slowly lowered the coat. "I don't think the boss is going to be very happy about this." And with that, he turned his head to the left, vomiting all over the driver's side window.

Buddy, that window is the least of your worries, Jerry thought, recognizing the symptoms of a traumatic brain injury. The fact that Dennis had never once mentioned being cold also raised concerns. Jerry himself felt as though his teeth were going to shatter from chattering together.

"Dennis, I'm going to lower down into the truck with you. Okay?" Without waiting for an answer, Jerry slid the flashlight into his pocket, keeping it on so that it helped to illuminate his way. Grabbing hold of the windowsill, he lowered himself in feet first until he was somewhat sitting in the seat beside Dennis. He removed the flashlight from his pocket and positioned it so that it would light the cab but leave his hands free to attend to the driver. The stench of vomit inside the truck was overwhelming. Jerry felt his own stomach flip as the smell permeated his nostrils. *Breathe through your mouth, or you're going to lose it.* He opened his mouth slightly, then unwrapped the emergency blanket. Using the sun visor and door frame, he managed to drape the blanket enough to create a makeshift tent to protect them both from the wind and snow. Not perfect by any means, but it should hold until help arrived.

Opening the first aid kit, he fumbled for the gauze, opened the package, and placed it alongside Dennis' head. As soon as he applied pressure to the wound, Dennis jumped as if just realizing someone was with him. "Easy, big guy, it's just me, Trooper McNeal," Jerry said softly.

"The cop from outside," Dennis said, sounding groggy.

"That's right, the cop from outside," Jerry repeated. *Keep him talking, Jerry.* "You had an accident. Do you remember what happened?"

"What happened?"

Jerry continued to apply pressure to the wound with one hand and shook the glass from Dennis' coat with the other. "That's what I'm asking you, Dennis. Do you remember what happened?" he said, tucking the coat around the man.

"A bright light," Dennis said.

Jerry caught his breath. *Had he missed something?* Another vehicle perhaps. "What kind of light, Dennis?"

"There's a cop with a bright light banging on the window."

Jerry relaxed. "That was me, Dennis; I was the one knocking on the window."

"Can you tell the cop to turn off the siren? It's hurting

my head."

"I can't turn off the siren. I'm here with you. How long have you been driving the truck, Dennis?"

"I'm not driving it."

Where the heck was everyone? "Are you married, Dennis?"

"Yes."

A glimmer of hope. "What's your wife's name, Dennis?"

"Selina." The edges of his mouth turned up. "She's my angel." Even dazed, there was no doubt the man loved his wife.

"Selina, that's a beautiful name," Jerry said, still holding pressure to Dennis' head.

"She's my angel," Dennis repeated, closing his eyes.

Don't go to sleep on me. "Tell me about Selina," Jerry said, raising his voice.

"She's my beautiful firecracker with smoldering brown eyes. She's a good wife. She takes care of me." A tear trickled down his cheek. "She's the center of my world, and I don't know what my life would have been like without her."

Okay, time to change the subject. Crying was not going to solve anything. "Got any kids, Dennis?"

"I got…" Dennis stopped in midsentence. "Do you hear that?"

Actually, for the first time in nearly thirty minutes, he could hear. *Someone had turned off the siren.* He rather hoped that someone was the help they'd been waiting on.

"McNeal!?"

Thank God! "In here, Sergeant."

Jerry nearly jumped out of his skin several seconds later when a face appeared in the driver's side window.

"How are you doing in there, McNeal?" he asked, shining a light through the glass.

Freezing my nuts off.

"We're doing good. We'd be a bit better if you'd turn off your light." The light was a heavy-duty mag light and bright even to him. "Dennis here has a bit of a bump on his head. He's grateful you turned off the siren."

"Him and half the county. We've had over a dozen complaints. Between the siren and the dog howling."

As if on cue, a howl pierced the air.

"Maybe people shouldn't leave their dogs out in this weather in the first place," Jerry answered heatedly. Jerry had a soft spot for animals, as they seemed to share the same gift as he. A knack for knowing when something was going to happen. A feeling that strangely had not lessened since he'd arrived on the scene, which was precisely why he'd left the siren on in the first place. He had a strong feeling that the worst was yet to come.

"Yes, while I'm sure most of the callers would agree with you, the rest would still like to get their beauty sleep."

"As much as I'd like to continue the conversation, I'd much rather do it from inside a warm building. Any chance of getting us out of here anytime soon?"

"I wanna go home," Dennis said in agreement.

The only place you're going is to the hospital. "We're going to get you out of here, pal," Jerry said reassuringly.

"We have help on the scene. Since there was minimal traffic on the roads, I had them come in silent. We've had enough calls. Make any more noise than necessary, and we'd be in a heck of a pickle. All we need is rubberneckers and ambulance chasers coming to see what's going on and ending up in ditches, or worse. So what do you think the chances are that your friend here can get out the same way you got in?" Sergeant Seltzer said, looking at Jerry.

Not a chance. Even without the head injury, the man's size alone would keep him from it. Jerry simply shook his head in reply.

"Didn't hurt to ask. You two hold tight. I'm going to have a chat with the rescue team to see if they've formed a plan yet."

"You go right ahead, sir. Dennis and I will be right here when you figure it out. You still with me, Dennis? Hang in there. They will have us out of here in no time," Jerry said once the sergeant had left.

In the distance, he heard a dog howl. He could hear the hum of engines just beyond the cab of the truck but didn't think that was what was causing the dog's sorrowful call. It was brutally cold out. He used his free hand to tuck the heavy coat closer to Dennis. *Please God, let this man survive, and, if you're not too busy, could you please send someone to see what's bothering that dog?*

Chapter Nine

Several moments had passed and yet no one had come to check on her. No one except the dog, which now crouched on her hood staring in at her. The dog was large-boned, brown with areas of black. His ears rose up into the night, pointed and alert. The brown on his face gave way to black markings that led to a full black mask on his face. Intense, deep-set brown eyes appeared to be sizing her up as if wondering how she would taste.

"You don't want to eat me, do you, boy? How about being a good doggy and run up the hill and drag whoever is up there down here? What do you say?"

The dog licked its lips in response.

"If you're going to eat me, could you please wait until after I'm dead? It probably won't be long now, at least I don't think so. I can't feel my leg anymore; that has to mean I'm getting close to dying right?"

The dog cocked its head as if trying to decipher her words.

"Maybe you could start with my hurt leg. Just chew it off so that I can hobble out of here before I freeze to death.

I don't even care if you eat the rest of that leg. I have pretty good calves; I'm sure there is enough meat on them to fill your belly. What do you say, fellow? Want to help a desperate lady out? You get to eat, and I get to live? Sound like a workable plan to you? Huh, big boy?" *What is this? Let's Make a Deal? You're losing it, Holly.*

The dog snorted its response, pushing away the umbrella and inching its massive body in through the hole and onto the dashboard.

"Oh God! HELP! Please no, please don't eat me!" she cried, using the umbrella as a shield. The large dog wasn't deterred. It brushed its way past and continued to crawl through the window, slowly making its way into the cab of the truck.

Once inside, the animal stood with its front legs on the center console, its hind legs still awkwardly resting on the dashboard. The flashlight, resting in the cupholder between the dog's legs, shot a beam upwards, showcasing the animal's rather fierce looking fangs. She closed her eyes, bracing for the impact of the teeth. She waited for several seconds before cautiously opening one eye. The beast was hulking merely inches from her face. As she opened her eye, the dog's tongue snaked from its mouth, licking her cheek. No doubt sampling before digging in.

He licked her face once more. This time, the action included a slight wag of the tail.

"Tall, dark, and friendly huh? I'd ask you to sit, but I'm afraid that seat is taken," Holly said, looking at the limb that was still resting on the passenger's seat. "I'd gladly give you my chair, but I seem to be stuck." She tried once again to pull her leg free. Either it had gone numb or her entire body was frozen.

Undeterred, the canine finished its descent into the cab

before gingerly easing between Holly and the steering wheel, stretching across her lap, and covering her with its body. She removed a glove and touched a trembling hand to his fur, surprised at how warm the animal felt despite the fact that he – at least she thought it was a he – had been outside. Now that she had a chance to look more closely, she found it funny he was not covered in snow. Stranger still, he didn't appear to have any snow on him at all. *I must be hallucinating.* This thought comforted her. If she were, in fact, hallucinating, the dog probably wasn't going to eat her. *Did she imagine the siren as well? Can someone imagine something that loud? Maybe this whole thing is a dream, and I'm really home in my bed. Yes, this is all a dream. All I have to do is close my eyes and go back to sleep,* she thought, lowering her eyelids.

An instant later, her eyes flew open as the dog once again began to howl. Not a dream at all. Cold, terrified, slightly deafened by being in such close proximity to a howling dog, and trapped beneath the weight of the animal, she had been fairly certain she was in the depths of a nightmare. At least her leg didn't hurt anymore. Surprisingly, nothing hurt. But, she was cold, so terribly cold. Snow and wind drifted in through the windshield, swirling around the umbrella, which she hadn't thought to push back into its previous position. *I should fix it.* The thought passed without her acting on it. She was so very tired. She just needed to sleep.

A warm sensation aroused her once more, blinking into awareness as the dog's tongue licked the snowy flakes from her face. *I'll need a hot shower when I get home. If I live. And if I don't, what will happen to Gracie? She'll be all alone.* Holly had been hopelessly in love with Gracie's father and thought he'd felt the same way about her. At least that was the way he acted until the day Holly had shared her wonderful news with him. News he didn't think was as wonderful as she did. He made that perfectly clear when he accused Holly of trying to trap him into marriage. Her mother had told her she was a disgrace and that the child would ruin her life as she – Holly – had ruined hers, by trapping her in her own loveless marriage. Holly felt differently and considered the child her saving grace, going so far as to name her Amy Grace. A part of her wanted to name her Amazing Grace just to spite all who said the child was not welcomed, but thankfully, Holly had come to her senses before filling out the birth certificate. Even though Gracie – as she preferred to call her – was amazing, the name was too over-the-top. Holly had told her dad of the name, and he adopted it for the pet name he often used for Gracie. Her dad, while still alive, was not in the best health. What would become of Gracie if he too were not around?

Who will take care of my little Gracie!? Just the thought of her daughter all alone in the world brought a new onslaught of tears. As if sharing in her grief, the shepherd tilted its head in a cry of solidarity. As Holly sobbed into the animal's fur, she was not aware of idling motors coming from the rise above, nor did she realize the siren had been silenced.

Chapter Ten

Jerry sat in the SUV, sipping a welcomed cup of black coffee. He normally added a bit of cream, but tonight, just the warmth of the slightly bitter brew was enough. Every bone in his body ached. He'd spent nearly three hours in the truck with Dennis, comforting him, stanching his wound, and all the while balancing so as not to fall on the man. It had taken longer than usual to round up the equipment needed at the scene, including a tow truck large enough to handle a truck that size, and a driver that was brave enough to venture out on a night such as this. After much deliberation, it was decided that the safest way to free the driver was to move the truck while Dennis and Jerry were still inside. Risky, but less so than adding the weight of a crew large enough to handle hoisting a man Dennis' size out the passenger side door. The added weight would have most likely dislodged the blade, thus sending the truck catapulting to its side. Trying to right the truck on a good day would be a fairly lengthy and complicated task; doing so in a blizzard was unthinkable. As it was, they placed blankets and pillows between Dennis' head and the window, while Jerry braced for possible impact if anything went wrong. The tow truck was able to come in from the west side and ease the truck onto all four wheels with barely any effort, leaving everyone with a sense of relief and conviction that they'd formed the best plan. The paramedics were stabilizing Dennis for the trip to the hospital. Even though he had an obvious head injury, they were fairly certain the long-term outlook was a positive one. Even with this bit of good news, Jerry still felt as if something was off. The snow had halted at some point during the rescue. Even the wind had eased its relentless assault, yet the feeling that he'd had since long before the accident had never diminished. If anything, it had increased dramatically.

What am I missing?

He'd just started to mentally retrace his steps when a light tap startled him into the present. He lowered the window, exposing the weary face of Sergeant Seltzer. The man looked every bit as exhausted as Jerry felt and just as cold.

"You doing all right, McNeal?" he asked, the words coming out in steamed breaths.

"Doing fine," Jerry lied.

"You've had one heck of a night. Why don't you go home and take a hot shower?"

God, that sounds tempting. "Not just yet, Sergeant."

Sergeant Seltzer blew into his gloved hands. "No?"

"I'm not entirely sure, but I don't think this night is over." *Not by a long shot*, he thought but neglected to add.

Seltzer sighed. "Any idea where or when?"

Now. Here. Everywhere. Focus, Jerry, he willed silently. "I wish I knew."

"Is this the same as before? I mean, the accident scene

is not even fully cleared. Maybe it's just some residual ESP or something," Seltzer offered with a nod towards the ambulance.

Jerry followed his gaze, taking in the surroundings. The road was blocked in both directions. A handful of cars idled, waiting until the path cleared. Normal procedure would be to set up a detour, but the back roads were impassable. Several firetrucks, the tow truck, two ambulances – a second rig had been requested just in case the truck had toppled with Jerry still inside. Since the second ambulance was not yet needed elsewhere, the crew remained on-site and were currently chatting with other emergency personnel. People were milling about, offering comments about what they supposed had happened, most deciding the driver had swerved to miss hitting a deer or bear – unanimously adding he should have hit the animal instead of driving into the mountain. In every way a normal post-accident scene, which projected a sense of relief that help had arrived in time. Not one to justify the hairs on the back of Jerry's neck prickling as if infested with lice. But that was exactly what it felt like, as if he were going to crawl right out of his skin.

"I hope you're right." *Not a chance.* He'd never had a feeling this strong before, and he'd had some pretty big hunches to contend with. *No, this felt as if his life depended on it. Whatever "it" was.*

What am I missing? The thought hammered at him like a jackhammer surging through concrete.

"Looks like the ambulance crew is getting ready to roll. Want to go check on the patient?"

"Nah, you go on ahead. I want to stay in front of the heater a bit longer," Jerry said, powering up the window. He needed to concentrate, and he could not do that with all the pats on the back, telling him he'd done it again. Or using the "H" word. Jerry was a guy who sometimes knew things; in his mind, that did not make him a hero. He put his hands together in prayer form, resting his chin on his thumbs and pressing both index fingers against his mouth; he closed his eyes. He was not sure why this seemed to work, but often, it did.

What am I missing?

Instantly, he was back parked at the chapel, watching as the snowplow drove past. The driver had looked in his direction and smiled. *Did he see him smile or did he imagine it? It didn't really matter. Or did it? Had the driver planned the accident? Had he intentionally driven towards the side of the mountain, gotten cold feet at the very last second, veering so that the side of the plow was the only thing that hit? Maybe, but doubtful.* By the time Jerry had arrived, his tracks had been covered by blowing snow, so, unless the driver remembered what happened, they likely might never know.

What am I missing?

What about the theory the crew had? That he had swerved to miss hitting an animal. Unlikely. According to dispatch, the driver was seasoned; he would have known an animal wouldn't have damaged the truck. Doubtful he would chance wrecking the truck just to avoid Bambi. Unless he was an animal lover. Plausible, but Jerry didn't think so. Jerry, an animal lover himself, would have put his own safety first.

What am I missing?

Could have been another vehicle. Except for the fact that the guardrail is intact. It was; that was the first thing Jerry had observed when he'd arrived at the scene and did his initial assessment.

Once again, Jerry was lured back to the present as the ambulance door slammed, signaling they were ready to head out. *God be with you all.* He watched as they slowly drove away, lights dancing off the freshly fallen snow. Sergeant Seltzer was heading his way. Sighing, Jerry drank the last of his coffee and got out to meet the man, who looked as if he were about to drop. It had been a long night for everyone.

"How's that feeling of yours, McNeal?" he asked as he approached.

"Still there," Jerry said reluctantly. *No use sugarcoating it.*

"So what do you want to do about it? Everyone is freezing their balls off and ready to head back in."

Before Jerry could answer, a sorrowful howl echoed off the mountainside. Anger fueled his answer. "Tell them to do jumping jacks for all I care! I'm going to find that dog, and get him inside where it's warm."

Jerry knew he was out of line, but he was on edge. The feeling that he was missing something nagged at him like buzzards circling fresh roadkill on a busy highway. Relentless, but just out of grasp.

"You sure that's such a good idea? He's down in the ravine from the sound of it. That snow has got to be at least three feet deep."

"I think it's a splendid idea," Jerry said heatedly. "I'm going to find that dog, see if he's got a collar, and if he does, I'm going to shove it up his owner's ass. Maybe then he'll think twice about leaving the poor thing out on a night like this."

"Easy, Trooper," Seltzer said evenly. "I know you are off your feed but try to keep it together."

Jerry stormed past, nearly slipping as he did.

"McNeal...Jerry!" Seltzer called after him when he didn't answer.

It wasn't really about the dog. Sure he felt sorry for the beast, but he was a dog after all. It was more the act of actually doing something that Jerry needed. Something, anything that would distract him enough so that he could figure out what he was missing. As he neared the guardrail, the feeling of urgency intensified. *Was it the dog he was meant to save after all?* He pulled out his flashlight, aiming it towards the ravine. The beam shone brightly against the snow. The trees were covered in layers of brilliant white. At first, he didn't see anything. Nothing out of the ordinary anyway. Then all the pieces of the puzzle came slamming into place, like a floodgate blocking rushing water. The beam of his flashlight had reflected off the smallest glint of metal, miraculously left uncovered from the blowing winds and out of place in a forest laced with trees. Jerry knew what it was the instant he saw it. The feeling that he was missing something lifted the second his mind embraced what he was seeing.

Another vehicle!

Chapter Eleven

"We have a second vehicle!" Jerry shouted over his shoulder. The instant the feeling of imminent doom lifted, he felt rejuvenated. He rushed down the ravine, oblivious of anything except reaching the wreckage and seeing if whoever was inside was okay. *Of course they are not okay. If they were, they would have made their way up the hill by now. At least let them be alive.* Now that the feeling had lifted, another took its place, one of regret. He should have looked closer. The beam from his flashlight wavered, then brightened once more. As it dimmed yet again, he tripped over a log and nearly plummeted into the deep snow. He'd nearly taxed the batteries while waiting with the other driver. *Slow down, Jerry. Not going to be of any help if you faceplant into a tree.* He slowed his pace, picking his way carefully down the slippery slope. His thoughts traveled to the dog. *It must have been calling for help. That dog is the real hero. If not for that animal, we would have all driven away.* He glanced over his shoulder and was relieved to see lights. Help was on its way. *Please don't let it be too late.* He took comfort in the fact that the dog had survived.

Maybe there is still hope for whoever else was in the vehicle. Still, with the length of time that had passed, hypothermia was a given.

Jerry reached the vehicle, a smaller Jeep. *Four people at the most.* The Jeep had skimmed a tree, which appeared to be blocking the driver's door. *At least it didn't hit it head-on.* The relief was short-lived when the faded beam from his flashlight showed a much larger tree had indeed stopped the Jeep's descent, and it had hit hard enough to cave in the front of the truck. A second later, he saw the broken window on the front right side. *Had someone been ejected upon impact?* He aimed the beam to the front of the Jeep, knowing that if anyone were indeed ejected, there would not be any need to hurry. He took a breath as he rounded the Jeep, stepping as carefully as possible just in case a body lay beneath the snow. Once on the passenger side, he peered into the side window, letting out the breath only when he found the seat empty, except for a large limb that rested in the passenger seat. *Not a body, a limb. Thank you, Jesus!* He made a quick sweep of the vehicle, checking for other occupants before turning his attention to the driver. He couldn't see her face, but from the clothing – long black coat and the bright red scarf wrapped around her mouth and neck – he was fairly certain the victim was a female. "Ma'am. I'm Trooper Jerry McNeal of the Pennsylvania State Police Department. Can you hear me?"

"What took you so long?" The voice was weak but surprisingly lucid.

I'm sorry…I was stupid. I should have checked. I knew something was wrong. I didn't see any tracks and the guardrail was intact. I should have looked closer. I trusted my eyes instead of my feeling.

"Hello? Please tell me you're not a dream."

"No, I'm not a dream. It took me longer than it should have, but I'm here now," he said, shivering against the chill. While the actual snow had stopped, the wind continued to blow, causing the snow to whirl in icy blasts. A huge branch fell, just missing him, disappearing into the snow in a puff of white. He pulled the passenger door, which was locked. "Ma'am, can you unlock the door?"

"Where did your dog go?"

My dog? She must be confused.

Jerry looked in the back seat once more. The second sweep of the interior confirmed what he'd already determined. Except for the driver, the Jeep was empty. *He must have gotten scared and ran away when he heard me coming.* "Don't worry, ma'am, we'll find *your* dog," he said, putting emphasis on the word "your." "But first, we need to get you out. Can you unlock the door?"

The woman leaned to the side, fumbled with the lock, then stopped. She closed her eyes briefly before trying again, pressing it with the bare fingers of her right hand. It was then he noticed the gloves, which rested on the center console, well within reach. *Why on earth would she have taken her gloves off? Or not put them on in the first place?* Obviously, the woman was not thinking clearly. *Yet she has enough presence of mind to do as I ask,* he thought as the latch sprang up, unlocking the door to allow him access. Opening the door, he wrapped his arms around the log and wrestled it from the seat. *She was darn lucky.* He moved the bag and slid into the seat beside her. He removed her flashlight from the cup dispenser, pushed the button, and nothing happened. *Darn! How long has this thing been dead?* He tossed the light aside, placing his dwindling light in the holder. Removing his gloves, he reached for her hands, his only thought to keep them warm until the others arrived. Her grip was amazingly warm. *How could her hands be so warm after being trapped for so long?* At first glance, there were no obvious signs of hypothermia. A miracle, considering how long she'd been exposed to the elements. He marveled at the umbrella, which was shoved into the open windshield, and admired her ingenuity. *Could that simple wind block be the reason she had not succumbed to hypothermia? Not likely. It would have helped, but it wouldn't explain how warm her hands felt.*

"Can you move?"

She shook her head in response. "My leg is trapped. It hurt at first, but I can't feel it anymore. Probably not a good sign."

Probably not. "We'll get you out of here in no time. The firemen will be here any moment." He tried to sound positive. "Ma'am, can you tell me your name?"

"Holly."

Pretty name. It reminds me of Christmas. "A Christmas baby?" he asked, following his hunch.

"How'd… you …guess?" Her teeth were chattering. Funny, she hadn't seemed that cold when he'd arrived.

"I'm a cop, remember. It's what we do."

"You must be pretty good at your job."

If I'd been better, I'd have found you sooner. "I do my best."

"You found me, didn't you? I… thin…k that mmmakes you pretty good. I'm sooo cold."

It seemed as if she were deteriorating before his very eyes. As if she was just now feeling the cold, even though she'd been exposed to the elements for several hours. *Why now?*

Jerry rubbed her fingers between his bare hands. "You weren't cold before?"

"No, your dog kept me warm."

My dog?

He was just about to voice the question aloud when the interior of the cab lit up, announcing the rescue workers' arrival. Multiple voices could be heard just outside the window. The lights became brighter as gloved hands began clearing the snow away from the Jeep.

She turned towards him, pulled the scarf away from her mouth, and gave him a trembling smile. "Nice to finally meet you, Trooper McNeal."

"It's you!" If he hadn't already been sitting, the jolt would have sent him hurtling back. While he didn't personally know her, he'd seen this lady multiple times over the last couple of weeks. In the halls of the hospital mostly, when he'd been there visiting his elderly neighbor, who was declining in health. Once he'd almost gotten up the nerve to speak to her, almost. How could he not have recognized her? Maybe it was because of all the dark mascara that trailed down her cheeks, showing the path of her tears. *Tears because she'd been left alone in the dark for so long. I'm sorry, Holly.* He longed to wrap his arms around her, tell her she was safe, and apologize for not finding her sooner. Instead, he continued to rub her hands with his. It was enough. *For now.*

"How is the other driver?"

"He's pretty banged up, but he should make it."

"There was a horrible whiteout. I thought the light I was seeing was the caution light, but then the snow cleared, and I realized there were two sets of lights. The caution light and those from the snowplow and I was heading straight for the center of the blade. I turned the wheel and pressed on the gas, hoping to get out of the way. I think I may have been airborne when I left the road. I guess I overreacted. Oh well, at least I also missed the guardrail. Lucky me," she said through chattering teeth.

But if you'd hit the guardrail, I would have found you sooner. How many hours had the blood supply been cut off from her injured leg? "Lucky you," Jerry repeated with a gentle squeeze to her hand.

"Why, hello, young lady. It appears you might have made a wrong turn," Sergeant Seltzer said as his face appeared in front of the broken window.

Jerry watched as a calculating look crossed Holly's face. "Someone told me the snow might be good for sledding. I thought I'd check it out myself before bringing my daughter out and disappointing her."

Jerry felt an irrational twinge of jealousy at the mention of a daughter; the emotion left as quickly as it had arisen. Could it have been because, at that exact moment, his fingers were tracing the spot where a ring should have been if she'd been married? *Feeling protective over someone who needs your assistance is part of the job.*

"Is there anyone you want us to call to let know you are okay?" Seltzer asked as he handed Jerry several pouches through the open windshield.

"My dad. He's all I got. Besides my daughter, that is."

She's not married. The admission pleased him more than he could have imagined as he fumbled to open one of the pouches. "Blankets," he said as he finally ripped open the small pouch.

"What are we supposed to do with it? Piece it together ourselves?"

Pretty and quick-witted. "Don't worry; they are plenty big," he said, unraveling the silver emergency blanket.

"They don't look like much, but they were designed by astronauts and do a pretty good job at holding in the heat."

He began to cover her with the blanket, tucking it in and around her to help get her warm. *If you had any to hold in*, he thought, looking at her blue-tinged lips. "Sergeant, can you see if you can get us some hot packs?"

"And coffee?" Holly asked hopefully.

"Not worried it will keep you awake?"

"It's way past my bedtime. What's a few more hours?"

"Coffee it is, then. Oh, waiter," he said the next time Seltzer stuck his head in the window, "we'd like two piping hot coffees to go."

"How about a couple of hot packs instead?" Seltzer said, handing in several more small packages.

"What is he? The small package king?" Holly quipped, then blushed when she realized what she'd said.

"I've heard rumors to that effect," Jerry said as he pushed into the plastic to activate the hot pack.

"Very funny, McNeal. Ask your wife about my package the next time you see her," Seltzer said and turned away in a huff.

"I'm sorry, I didn't mean to bring your wife into it," Holly said quietly.

Jerry laughed. "The joke's on him. I'm not married."

He watched as a smile touched her eyes. *Had she been worried that he was?*

"Well, then, nice to meet you, Trooper McNeal," Holly said and reached her hand out of the blanket.

Easy, Jerry, don't let a simple rescue turn into a date, he reminded himself. Instead of taking her exposed hand, he pushed a warm pack into her palm.

"Ooohhh, this feels so good."

"Yes, maybe you shouldn't have offended the guy. You

never know what kind of goodies he might bring," Jerry said, trying to keep her mind off her situation.

"Like doughnuts?"

Jerry rolled his eyes. *If he had a nickel for every doughnut quip he'd heard since becoming a cop...*

"Sorry, I tend to make jokes when I'm nervous."

"So do I and I've not made one single joke. That should let you know everything will be just fine."

"Promise?" She looked towards her leg, which while trapped and resting at a slightly odd angle, didn't seem to be causing her any undue discomfort.

God, please don't let her lose her leg.

As if she'd heard his thoughts, she turned her head towards him, blinking at him as pools of liquid rimmed her soft doe eyes. Hopeful, yet not fully trusting as they waited for him to respond.

Don't say it, Jerry. "I promise."

Crap...

Chapter Twelve

In his line of work, he'd often said things like: *You're going to be okay. It's not as bad as it looks. It's just a flesh wound* – just to ease the situation. Until this moment, saying those things had just been part of the job. Now, as he sat next to her, he needed the words he'd said to be true. Why was it so important to him? That was the part that was unclear. Maybe it was the way she'd been looking at him when he assured her she was going to be okay. *Yeah, that had to be it.* It wasn't as if he had any actual feelings for the woman. He'd just met her after all. Sure, he'd noticed her in passing once or twice. Maybe that was why the feeling had grown so intense in the first place because he knew the person involved. Near the end, he'd felt like he was going to explode. *And why was that?* The feeling had totally engulfed him. Almost as if his life had depended on it. And then just merely finding the wreckage, the sense of dread had lifted. As if he knew at that exact point everything was going to be okay. Only it wasn't, not totally anyway. She was still trapped, and even though he wasn't a doctor, he was pretty sure the blood flow had been cut off from her leg for way too long. They sat huddled under a tarp, which had been spread inside the car, while the rescue team figured the best route to freeing Holly from the wreckage.

They had the silver blanket wrapped around them, and a fistful of charcoal-activated warming packets. All in all, they were fairly comfortable. A new flashlight lit the confines of the tarp, making it seem more like a tent and reminding him of his days as a Boy Scout camping under the stars. She'd asked him to stay with her, refusing to allow a paramedic to take his place. He would have left if asked but was grateful she had insisted he stay and would have considered this a romantic setting – if not for the dire circumstances and the questionable outcome. What if she lost her leg? *Don't go there, Jerry.*

"You are awful quiet over there," she said, pulling him away from his thoughts. "I'm not stupid."

"Excuse me?"

"I'm going to lose my right leg. You know it too; that's why you turned away as soon as you made the promise."

"I know no such thing." *Only he did, at least on some level.*

"It's okay; I figured as much when the pain went away." Her voice sounded resigned to the fact.

"We have some of the best people there are working to help you. You have to think positive." Wow, that sounded as rehearsed as when he read the Miranda rights.

She laughed.

"What's so funny?" As if he didn't know.

"I gave the same speech to my daughter when she was going through her chemo."

Cancer? That would explain why she spent so much time in the hospital. And he'd thought she worked there.

"Leukemia. She's in remission," she said before he could ask.

He could hear the team outside. They were getting ready to begin using the Jaws of Life. With luck, they'd have her out soon. "What's your daughter's name?" he asked, hoping to keep her distracted.

"Grace. I call her Gracie. It's her birthday. She's five. There were times when I wasn't sure if she would make it to her birthday, and then she started getting better." Her voice cracked. "I promised her I'd be home for it. I should have stayed the night in Gettysburg, but I promised."

Tears slipped from her eyes and began dripping onto the silver blanket. He started to wipe them from her face, then reconsidered. Better to let her worry about her daughter. Love could be a mighty big motivator. "How long has she been in remission?"

"Six months. Six wonderful, amazing months."

The tarp lifted and Seltzer poked his head in through the windshield. "How are you holding up, ma'am?"

"I'd be better if I could get out of here," Holly said, wiping at the tears.

"We are going to have you out soon. You are going to hear a lot of popping and cracking as we cut the car away from you. Understand?"

Jerry watched as she appeared to swallow her fear. "I guess my dad's not going to be getting his Jeep back?"

"He's getting his daughter back, and I'm sure that is all that will matter to him. You let us know if you need anything." He gave Jerry a pointed look – which Jerry knew meant to keep her calm – before lowering the flap to keep the heat from escaping.

A sharp pop followed by the sound of something pelting against the tarp caused Holly to jump. He watched as her eyes flew open. She moved a hand towards the tarp.

"Leave it," he said briskly. "Sorry, it was glass from the side window. Next, they are going to be removing the door and roof." Instantly, he could hear popping and creaking as the Jaws of Life began eating away at the steel.

"Why were you in Gettysburg?" Jerry asked.

"What?" she asked absently.

"You said you should have spent the night in Gettysburg. Never mind what's going on outside. It's just you and me. Talk to me." *Please.*

"I...I was taking pictures. At a wedding. I'm a photographer."

Crap! He reached into the floor between his legs and brought up the bag he'd carelessly pushed to the side when entering. He frowned, noting the bag was slightly wet where the snow had melted from his boots. Unzipping the bag, he withdrew the camera and inspected it for any visible damage, breathing a sigh of relief when he saw it seemed to be unscathed. He was just about to return it to its case when Holly reached for it. Turning it on, she snapped a photo of him.

"You would probably do better with this," he said and handed her the flash attachment.

Holly slipped the flash into the horseshoe-shaped crease and took several more photos, the flash looking like a strobe within the confines of the tarp.

He closed his eyes, trying to get rid of the light that momentarily burned into his retinas.

She aimed the camera for yet another shot when someone on the other side of the tarp yelled for others to lift the roof from the car. "I guess things are about to get interesting," she said as she lowered the camera. "Maybe I could get them to remove the tarp so I can get some decent shots."

"You're kidding, right?"

"I took some earlier. Ya know, to document what had happened in case…" Her voice trailed off.

"In case we didn't find you in time," he said, finishing her sentence.

"It had crossed my mind at first," she admitted.

"I'm sorry I didn't find you earlier." Guilt clawed at him. He'd known something was wrong. Why the heck hadn't he listened to his feeling?

Her brows knitted together. "But you knew I was here. That's why you sent your dog."

It was the second time she'd assumed the dog to be his. *What had happened to the thing?* "My dog?"

"Yes, the police dog. He scared me at first, but then I knew you'd sent him to keep me warm. How do you train them to do that?"

Now he was even more confused. "Trained him to what?"

"To keep people warm."

"Holly, I'm afraid I don't have any idea what you are talking about. I don't have a dog."

"Well, someone sent him. One of the other officers, maybe?"

There was no one else with me. "So what makes you so sure this dog was a police dog?"

"The tag on his collar, PSPD090."

PSPD090, Pennsylvania State Police Department. A chill raced across his arms. He knew that number. Everyone in his department knew that number. They also knew the number was officially retired. K-9 090, AKA Gunter, had received a medal of commendation last week. Only he was not here to accept the award; he'd died in the line of duty days earlier when he'd leapt in front of a bullet. A bullet intended for his partner, handler Sergeant Brad Manning. Manning was still on mandatory leave. In fact, it was Manning's SUV Jerry had driven this evening. A sudden recollection of having felt he'd not been alone in the patrol unit had Jerry's heart racing. *Don't lose your head, Jerry; there has to be a logical explanation for this.* "What do you mean the dog kept you warm?" He hoped his voice sounded calmer than he felt.

"He crawled into my lap and kept licking my face. My hands were freezing, even with my gloves on, so I got the idea to take them off and place them under the dog's fur. It worked."

That explained why she seemed to have suffered no ill effects from prolonged exposure. The dog's body heat had kept her warm. Except for the fact that a ghost dog wouldn't be warm. Would it? *Hold it together, McNeal.* "Are you sure of the tag?" *Of course she's sure. Probably read an article about the dog's heroism in the paper and had hallucinated the whole thing. Then why was she so warm?*

"Yes, I mean, I think so… There was a tag. I guess I could be wrong about the number, though."

Of course, you are. But then where did the dog come from? And more importantly, where did it go? Yeah, just the facts, ma'am. You need to take your own advice, Jerry. Like the fact that if a police dog had gotten loose from another district, then the police department would have sent out a BOLO. So why hadn't the police department sent one out? Easy, Jerry, because you can't Be On the Look Out for a dead dog.

Holly gasped, pulling him abruptly from his musings. In his peripheral vision, he saw the camera gliding to the floor, seemingly in slow motion. He reacted in time to keep the camera from hitting the floor, grasping it triumphantly between his first finger and thumb. He was just about to proclaim his heroics when Holly's screams filled the early morning air.

Chapter Thirteen

Jerry paced the halls of the emergency room at the Chambersburg Hospital, where they'd taken Holly. Normally, they would have flown her to a trauma center, but weather conditions did not allow for the helicopter to take flight. Instead, paramedics routed to the nearest hospital for stabilization. He'd followed the ambulance, just to be sure she arrived safe, then found he couldn't leave. Not without knowing she'd be okay. Her screams still haunted him. He'd been sure they'd cut her leg off when extricating her from the car, but thankfully, that had not been the case. The sudden intense pain was caused by the release of pressure. Once her leg was cut free, the nerve endings reawakened, sending pain signals to the brain. A good sign, according to the paramedics on scene.

As he started down the corridor for the umpteenth time, the lobby entrance doors at the end of the hallway slid open. An elderly man trudged into the corridor, carrying a bleary-eyed little girl. While the child was well past the age of needing carrying, he seemed in no hurry to put her down. The old man's face looked haggard under his gray bed-tossed hair. Bootlaces trailed behind, as if he'd dressed too hastily to have bothered with them. Jerry's eyes shifted to the child, who had fared better than the man carrying her. She was wearing a bright pink coat with a matching knitted hat that covered her head. What looked to be pajama pants were tucked securely into boots, which were laced and tied at the top. Unnecessary, since by the looks of it, the child's feet had never actually touched the snow. The girl blinked against the brightness, yawned, and rubbed a tight fist against her eye. As she lowered her hand, he could see the red-rimmed lids of her eyes – eyes that looked exceedingly bright despite her puffy white face. *Is she hurt or sick?* Even as his mind registered the question, Jerry realized he had instinctively moved towards the duo. Jerry took a step closer, but before he could fully reach them, the man grabbed on to the sleeve of a passing hospital worker. *A lab tech*, Jerry noted upon seeing the plastic basket that held slender glass tubes in the worker's right hand.

"My daughter was in an accident. They told me she was in Bed Three. Can you show me where it is?" the man asked frantically.

The lab tech shifted the basket to his left hand before placing his now free hand reassuringly under the man's arm. The technician was good. Jerry held back as the tech led them over to the nurses' station. Jerry was pleased to see the worker stay with the man and child until he'd gotten the information needed. Within moments, the tech brushed past Jerry with the man and child following. The older man made eye contact with Jerry as he passed. Jerry offered a nod of encouragement and was surprised at the twinge of envy he experienced as the trio disappeared behind the curtain where they were keeping Holly. *That must have been Holly's dad and her daughter. Not sick then, not anymore.* He smiled, remembering Holly said the child was in remission. For some reason, that thought lifted his spirits. The child is a fighter. *Gracie,* he thought, remembering her name. She had to get her fighting spirit from someone. *I hope that someone is her mother.*

Jerry moved closer to the curtain, wishing he too had been allowed inside. *You're going above and beyond, Jer. Just go home and get some sleep. It's been a difficult day; you can call and check on her status in the morning.* He was tired. A hot shower and firm bed sounded exceedingly inviting. Still, he made no move to leave. He patted the pocket of his heavy winter coat, which was draped across his left arm, and started as the curtain leading to Holly's cubicle parted. The lab tech stepped out into the hall, scanned the hallway, and set off in his earlier direction. Jerry took off his hat and rubbed his free hand across his smooth head. As his hand trailed down the back of his skull, the curtain slid open. The old man walked out, followed by the little girl. She peered up at him, and for the first time, he could see her resemblance to her mother. As the man stepped around him, Jerry saw unshed tears brimming in his eyes. *Are they tears of remorse or relief?* He moved to ask the man when he felt something tug at the coat he was holding. He looked down into the worried face of Holly's daughter.

"The doctors will fix you," Gracie said in a solemn voice.

Puzzled, he knelt down to her level. "Excuse me?"

Gracie pointed to his head, then pulled off her cap to display her own hairless scalp. "I was sick too, but the doctors fixed me. They are fixing my mommy too. Mommy said they are angels; they will fix you too."

Jerry felt his eyes moisten. *She thinks I'm sick. Worried about strangers at a time like this.* "Oh, honey, I'm not sick. My hair will grow back."

"Mine too!" Gracie said before trailing her grandfather down the hall.

Jerry thought about going after her and explaining he'd shaved his head by choice but didn't want to leave Holly. He was not leaving until he knew she was going to be all right. He leaned against the wall, waiting. Suddenly, the nurse stuck her head out of the enclosure. The tall, thin woman with her hair pulled back in a no-nonsense bun, looked at him with an expression that said *I'm in charge and you'd best remember that.* "Trooper McNeal?" the woman asked upon seeing him.

He pushed off the wall. "Yes?"

She appraised him briefly, then smiled. It was a slight smile, one that he may have missed if he hadn't seen the transition. "Miss Wood is asking to see you. She said you are the one who saved her life."

"Among others."

"Yes, well, she wants to see you." She leveled a look at him, and for a second, he thought she was going to renege on her invitation. "Don't stay long; she's been through a lot this evening."

That's putting it mildly. "Yes, ma'am," Jerry said and stepped around the woman. As he passed through the opening in the curtain, he was once more surprised to find his heart rate elevated. *Get a grip, Jer. You're acting like a schoolboy.* A schoolboy who nearly leaped for joy when he saw Holly smiling up at him from her hospital bed. Her face was bruised, her nose swollen but didn't appear to be broken. Her lip was split and coated with a glistening salve. She would no doubt have double black eyes by the day's end, but all in all, Jerry thought she looked beautiful. As beautiful as someone who looked as if she'd just spent a round in a boxing ring with Mike Tyson could.

"Miss Wood, how are you feeling?" he asked in his best cop voice.

"Seriously? With everything we've been through, you can't call me by my first name?"

"How are you feeling, Holly?" he said more gently.

She lifted her arm to show him the IV. "Pretty darn good. I'm not sure what's in here, but I could have used some of this stuff earlier."

He remembered her scream. Something told him he would always remember that scream. "I thought…"

"Truth be told, so did I."

"How is it? Your leg?" he asked, nodding toward the covers. *I don't care as long as the rest of you is okay.*

"They're not sure yet, but they think I may be able to keep it. I'm not sure how it will look in a pair of shorts, but I guess we can't have everything."

"Oh thank God," he said, voicing his relief out loud.

"He had help," she said, beaming up at him. "He sent me an angel."

You may be more right than you know. An image of Gunter floated through his mind.

"You have a hard time with this whole hero thing, don't you?" she asked.

He held two fingers together near his face. "A wee bit. Besides, I think most of the credit belongs to the dog. Wouldn't you say?"

A frown replaced her smile. "Did you ever find him?"

"We did not." If he was even ever there. *You heard him yourself, Jerry.*

"But you are positive you didn't send him?"

He wanted to humor her, to tell her he'd been mistaken, that he'd watched him flee the scene, but he couldn't lie to her. "I did not."

"And no one else did?"

He shook his head.

"You don't believe me, do you?"

God help me, but I do. "I heard the dog myself. But it would have been nice to have actually seen the thing." *Just so I could be sure...*

"Oh, that's easy." The smile returned to her face.

"It is?"

"Sure! I took a picture of him!" The smile left her face. "Please tell me my camera survived."

A picture?! He slid into the chair beside her bed, fished in his coat pocket, and withdrew the camera. "I'm afraid the bag itself didn't make it." He tugged on the coat, found the inside pocket, and withdrew the flash, which he'd dismantled. Thankfully, his service coat had deep utility pockets.

"You didn't look through the photos?" she asked, taking the camera from him.

"Of course not; that would have been an invasion of privacy, and the law frowns upon that sort of thing." What he didn't tell her was that his fingers had caressed that camera repeatedly while he'd struggled with his mind, which was trying to coax him into having just one little peek. A glimpse into a world seen through her eyes. How close he'd come to invading her privacy. How sure he'd been that if she hadn't made it, her family would never have known he'd taken the camera. It would be his link to her. To this woman who'd first captured his heart weeks ago, when he had seen her roaming the halls of this very hospital. *Oh, Jerry, they would take away your gun if they knew how bonkers you…*

"Here he is," Holly said, thrusting the camera in his direction. "See? Told you I wasn't hallucinating!"

***

He'd only gotten a brief look at the photo before the orderly had pulled back the curtain, bursting through like Jack Nicholson in the movie *The Shining* – here's Johnny! Actually, he'd said something more along the lines of *Miss Wood, my name is Donny, and I'm here to take you down to x-ray,* but it had had the same surreal feel. Especially when Jerry had just seen a photo of a dog who was supposed to be dead. He was dead, darn it; Jerry was sure of that. Jerry thought it would have been a coincidence: two shepherds with the same markings, the same torn ear – a crackhead had bitten the dog in retaliation from the dog biting him – but no sort of coincidence would account for the tag. Holly was good at her job, yes sir; not many in her situation would have thought to focus on that tag. The numbers were clear. No mistake about it, the dog in the picture was the same dog. The question now was, did he tell her? *Um, I hate to tell you this, but the dog in the photo is a ghost. Maybe you should not tell anyone because they will think you are crazy.* He would need to figure it out by the time they next spoke. And they would speak. A smile crossed his lips, remembering her last words. *You still owe me a coffee; we'll consider it our second date.* Maybe it had been the contents of the IV speaking, but he thought she sounded sincere.

"You did a fine job, McNeal," Seltzer said, clapping him on the shoulder with a firm hand.

"Yeah, I'd have done a better one if I'd found her

sooner. If only…"

The sergeant dug his fingers into Jerry's shoulder. "If only what?!"

Jerry shook his head. "I knew something wasn't right. I should have looked harder when I first arrived at the scene."

Seltzer released his grip. "Darn it, Jerry. Quit beating yourself up. If only. I have your 'if only.' If only you didn't have that wonderful gift of yours, that little lady would still be at the bottom of that ravine. Sure, someone would probably have happened along the snowplow at some point, but do you think they would have found the girl? By the time someone would have filed a missing person's report, the buzzards would have been circling overhead. The only reason she is still alive is because of you. And only you. *Comprende?*"

"I understand." *I also understand I had help out there tonight.* "Sergeant? Did anyone ever find that dog?"

With that, the man burst out laughing. "Jeez, Jerry, give it a rest. I'm sure that mutt has found its way home by now. Although come to think of it, you may owe the dog a nice juicy bone. If you hadn't been all fired up about it being left in the cold, you might not have stumbled onto the girl. I guess it's safe to say you had help with this one."

Jerry felt the tension leave his shoulders. "I'd put money on it."

Chapter Fourteen

Pennsylvania State Police Trooper Jerry McNeal slipped two fingers into the elastic waistband of his briefs, sliding them across his hips, watching as they fell without protest to the cold tiled floor. He pulled open the shower door, turned on the faucet, and stepped inside without waiting for the water to warm. He needed the shock value, which was exactly what he got. It was bitterly cold outside and the water coming in through the pipes jolted his senses in a way even a steamy cup of coffee couldn't equal. He screamed obscenities the second the icy fingers touched his skin. He pressed his hands against the wall, leaning into the spray and swearing once more as the water trailed lower down his exposed flesh. He tilted his head, closing his eyes as the stream bounced off his freshly shaved skull. He shivered as he waited for the water to warm. "Suck it up, McNeal. It's too early on a Sunday morning for you to be talking crap," he scolded. It was early, four a.m. – not that he'd gotten much sleep to begin with. As the chill lessened, his body slowly began to relax. He opened his eyes and saw two more staring at him from the other side of the shower door. "Pervert."

As if in response, the orange cat lifted its hind leg and began licking where his testicles had once been.

"Showoff," Jerry said and proceeded to wash his own in a more acceptable way.

The cat lifted its head and looked at him as if to say, *you know you're jealous,* then meowed.

Not for the first time since remodeling the bathroom the previous summer, Jerry regretted having installed a see-through shower door. He'd felt the same way ever since opening the back door to the deck and watching in disbelief as the half-starved cat scooted between his legs and into the safe confines of the house. Jerry had told the cat at the time it was only temporary. Apparently, the cat didn't believe him. Six months later the cat, who Jerry still referred to as Cat, was still here, amazing since Jerry had never considered himself a cat person. Jerry finished his shower and opened the door to relieved meows. As soon as Jerry stepped out of the shower, Cat leaped from the counter and rubbed against Jerry's still wet legs, singing a mix of soft mews and purrs. Jerry snapped the towel at the cat, who turned and snagged the edge of the towel in one of its nails. *You're on borrowed time, Cat.* As Jerry untangled the paw, the cat pulled back, cutting a single scrape across the back of Jerry's hand. *It was so much easier when he lived alone.*

Jerry dressed in sweats, then made his way down the hallway and into the kitchen. The smell of freshly brewed coffee greeted him as he entered the room. *What did people do before timers?* He poured a cup, then moved to the table. The cat jumped onto the table. Jerry scooped him up and placed him on the floor. "Stay off the table, Cat."

The cat meowed his discontent.

"Remember, Cat: my house, my rules. And my rules state that I do not have to feed you until after I have had my morning coffee."

He took a sip of coffee, grateful for its warmth. It had been two days since the blizzard incident, and he still had trouble getting warm. Not that the icy shower had helped, but at least he was now fully awake. Both parties involved in the accident were going to recover fully, and Holly was going to keep her leg. He smiled just thinking of her. He reached for his cell phone, thinking to call and ask her how she was feeling this morning, remembered the time, and returned the phone to the table. *Easy, Jerry; you keep this up, and people might get the wrong impression.* "Can't have that now, can we?" he said, picking up the neglected stack of unopened mail.

He sifted through the stack, tossing the obvious junk to the side. He came to a business envelope and paused. The envelope was addressed to Trooper Jerry McNeal, with no return address. He looked closer at the postmark, which showed Michigan. To some, this would appear to be spam, but the hairs on the back of Jerry's neck told him otherwise. He took another sip of coffee before tearing into the envelope and pulling out its contents.

Dear Mr. McNeal,

A friend of mine was visiting Gettysburg last month and happened to stumble upon an article about you in one of the local papers. Forgive me for not knowing which paper, as my friend did not think to save the whole paper, instead just clipping the article in which your story appeared. Carrie, that is my friend's name, was fascinated when she read about what you described as your feelings. Carrie knew I would be interested, so she saved the article for me.

I've had the article for several weeks, not meaning to do anything about it, until now.

My daughter, Max —at least that's what she calls herself; it's short for Maxine, although why she'd prefer to go by a boy's name instead of the beautiful name of her great-grandmother, I'll never know. Please forgive me for rambling. I just am not sure what I need to say to you. Oh, the heck with it, I will just tell you what is on my mind. Max also has "those feelings." Sometimes, they come to her in a dream. Other times, she just seems to know things. There have also been times when she doesn't know what is wrong, but she is uneasy for days until "it" happens. So far, they've been small things, well, most of the time. Anyway, over the past week, my daughter has been having a recurring dream that involves someone being killed. I cannot very well walk into our local police station and tell them this as they would surely have me committed, and where would my daughter be then? Please, Mr. McNeal, I need to ask you, knowing what you know (that the feelings are indeed real) what would you do in my place?

My daughter is twelve years old.
Mrs. April Buchanan
810-555-5555

Jerry reread the letter twice before placing it back in the envelope. He knew the article of which the woman spoke. He'd not been happy when his sergeant insisted he give the interview. Since the story's release, Jerry had gotten multiple letters, all telling him about their feelings, some even telling what they thought of his so-called feelings, but this one just felt different. Yes, okay, he had a feeling about it. He picked up the phone, debated about the early hour, and dialed the number. As his call was answered, and a young voice drifted through the receiver, that feeling intensified...

Ghostly Guidance

To all the working dogs and those K-9s who have lost their lives while protecting others.

Chapter One

Jerry poured himself a cup of coffee, resisting an urge to football-kick the cat who was currently purring incessantly against his leg. He palmed his coffee cup, dodging the feline as he walked to the table to read his mail. Tired of being ignored, the cat jumped onto the table, voicing his need to be fed.

"Stay off the table, Cat," Jerry said, calling him by name and scooping him onto the floor.

Not one to be dismissed, Cat jumped up once more as Jerry tapped the phone number into his cell phone. When he'd finished dialing, Jerry used his free hand to place the cat back on the floor. Incensed, the cat sat staring at Jerry, its tail whipping from side to side as if contemplating his next move.

"This had better be worth waking up for," came a groggy voice on the other end of the phone.

Jerry instantly regretted calling at such an early hour. He debated hanging up but knew the person on the other end already had his number. Hoping to avoid confrontation, he opted for a formal introduction. "This is

Trooper First Class Jerry McNeal in Chambersburg, Pennsylvania; I'm calling in regard to a letter I received."

"Mr. McNeal, I sent that letter weeks ago." The woman sighed heavily into the phone. "I didn't think you were going to call."

Jerry picked up the letter and scanned the signature – April Buchanan. He could make up an excuse or just tell her the truth – that he got so many letters from people claiming to either be like him or wanting him to use his gift to help them out of their financial bind, that he hated opening his mail. He opted instead for a simple apology. "I'm sorry it's taken me so long to get in touch."

"I'm sorry. I know you must be busy. I'm just grateful that you took the time to call. Hang on, and I'll wake Maxine."

"I apologize for the early morning call. I can call back this evening if you'd prefer."

"No!... Please don't hang up. It will just take me a moment to get up the stairs. Max will be happy to hear from you. Lord knows she needs to talk to someone who understands."

Jerry smiled a triumphant smile as Cat once again decided to weave in and around his legs, purring and covering his pants with orange fur. Never being around a cat before, he'd quickly grown wise to the cat's wicked ways of shedding hair all over the legs of his neatly pressed uniform. After the first few times of playing dodge-the-cat, he decided it was much easier to dress in sweatpants until time to change into his work uniform. "So, this doesn't run in the family?"

"Heavens, no. Is that how it normally works?"

Darned if I know. "Just making conversation, ma'am." Actually, if he could establish a family connection, it would give Max's intuitions credibility.

"Have any of her premonitions come true?"

"Oh yes, all the time. Why, just last night, she blessed me before I even sneezed."

"I wouldn't exactly call that a premonition." Jerry resisted rolling his eyes.

"I sneezed a second later. What would you call it?"

"Maybe I should wait to speak to Max." *Or hang up and let you go back to bed.* Jerry could hear muffled talking on the other end of the phone.

"Hello?" The voice sounded much like that of her mother. "Trooper McNeal, is it really you?"

"Yeah, Max, it's me. Sorry it took so long to call. Your mom tells me you've had some disturbing dreams."

"Yes, sir."

"How about you tell me about them." While he'd hoped they were just nightmares, his own radar currently told him there was more to it.

"There's not much to tell. Everything is still blurry in my dream. I see a lady and know she's going to die."

"Do you know this lady?"

"I don't think so."

"Are you sure?"

"She feels familiar, but I don't think it's anyone I know."

"I think you need to give it some time."

"How much time?"

"I don't know."

"What do you mean you don't know? Mom said you could help."

Jerry could feel her anxiety rising and took in a calming breath. "Max, I'm not trying to brush you off. I'll do everything in my power to help. What I'm saying is you need to be sure."

"How?"

"Keep a notebook beside your bed. Revisit your dream. Write everything down the moment it comes to you. Think back to see if you might have watched something on TV or read anything in the paper that could be influencing your dreams."

"Can't I just call the police?"

"You can. The problem is getting them to believe you."

"Then you can call them for me. Tell them what I told you."

Please don't ask me to do that.

"Do you believe me?" she asked when he didn't answer. He could hear the tremble in her voice.

"I want to," he answered as honestly as he could.

"But you don't."

He could tell she was crying. "Max, I know you believe it, and it feels very real to you. But you're not the first person to have reached out to me. People call, send letters, stop me on the street. At first, I was happy to have found kindred spirits and so I believed them all. A few were legitimate, some a complete farce, and others were just simply people having recurring dreams, much like when people get songs stuck in their heads."

"If I do nothing, someone is going to die." This time, her voice held conviction.

"It would be easier for you and the police if you knew who that someone was. That's why I need you to start keeping a journal."

"I can almost see her."

"That's good. Give it some time, Max. Maybe it'll come to you. Even then, you may have trouble getting people to listen to you."

"Because I'm a kid?"

Partly. "Because people have a difficult time believing things they can't understand."

"Do people believe you?"

"A few. But that didn't happen overnight." His grandmother had the gift, but it had skipped over his mother and younger brother. His father had always shied away from discussing it. Some of the guys he worked with seemed to accept it; others held him at arm's length, making the odd joke about him knowing things about their personal business. Sergeant Seltzer was a believer, which helped when Jerry needed to go off to follow a feeling.

"Jerry?"

"Yeah, Max?"

"I hope I can figure out what I'm supposed to know before it's too late."

"Me too, kid."

"Jerry?"

"Yeah, Max?"

"I'm sorry about your dog."

Jerry stiffened in his chair. He'd not told a soul about what happened during the blizzard. "My dog?"

"I'm sorry." She sniffed.

He decided to rephrase the question. "What about my dog?"

"I thought you knew."

"Knew what?"

"Your dog is dead."

"Max. What does my dog look like?"

She laughed a nervous giggle. "Is this some kind of exercise?"

"I just want to see how accurate you can perceive things." He spoke softly, trying to put her at ease.

"A German shepherd. He's beautiful, by the way. Or was."

"Go on," Jerry encouraged.

"Brown with black markings on his face. His ears go straight up, and he's missing part of one. A gun. He got shot, but there's more. Gun – is that his name, or is it Gunner...his ear...a fight...Jerry, did someone bite off your dog's ear?" Her voice was incredulous.

Jerry stared into the phone. *The girl's good. She's going to need help. How are you going to help her when you can't even help yourself?*

"Are you there, Jerry?"

"I'm here, Max. The dog's name is Gunter, and he's not my dog. He's a police dog. Or he was."

"It's weird."

"What's weird?"

"I know he's dead. But I feel like he's alive."

"What if I told you you're right?"

"Which one?"

"Both."

"I don't understand."

"Gunter is dead, but I saw him."

"You saw him get killed?"

"I saw him after he was dead and buried." *Great, she's going to go to school and blab it to all her friends.*

"Cool!"

"Max, I haven't told anyone except you about that."

"Why not?"

"When you're a kid, and you walk into a police station and tell someone you're having dreams of someone getting murdered, they're going to treat you like a kid. I'm a police officer. If I go telling people I see ghosts, they're going to have me committed."

"Even though they know what you can do?"

"Remember what I told you about people being scared of what they can't explain."

"Will it ever get easier for us?"

I've asked myself that a million times. Not wanting to dash her hopes, he said the only thing that came to mind. "Kids can be cruel – be careful who you tell. Some will think it's cool, but others will expect things from you that you might not be able to deliver."

"I've already found that out." Her voice cracked. "It kind of sucks sometimes."

"It sure does." Jerry watched as Cat, having given up on getting his food from Jerry, decided to go straight to the source – jumping onto the counter and pawing open the cabinet that contained the cat food. "Listen, I've got to be going. Keep my number and let me know if I can answer any more questions. And Max?"

"Yeah, Jerry."

"If you want me to call your police station for you, I will. Just let me know when you're ready."

"Does that mean you believe me?"

"You're the only one that knows about the dog."

"It must be pretty cool having a ghost dog."

"I don't have him. He just showed up at the accident scene and helped me find a lady that probably wouldn't have been found if he wasn't there."

"Cool!"

"Yeah, it was pretty cool." He smiled.

"Like Christmas."

"What?"

"The lady's name – Holly, it sounds like Christmas."

Wow, she's good. "Max?"

"Yeah, Jerry."

"Remind me never to play poker with you."

"That's what my dad says."

"Have a good day, Max."

"You too, Jerry. And don't worry about the dog. He'll be back."

That's exactly what I'm worried about, Jerry thought, clicking off the phone. The second he placed the phone on the table, Cat jumped up, sniffing the phone.

"You're not going to win," Jerry said, placing him onto the floor once more. "I have many things in my life that I can't control, but keeping you off my table isn't one of them. I will win this battle."

Cat meowed his answer, which to Jerry meant "challenge accepted."

Chapter Two

Jerry scanned the parking lot of the state police post, saw Manning's lime-green pickup, and turned the opposite direction. That Manning was here didn't come as a surprise – Sergeant Seltzer had told Jerry of his impending return the previous day. What did come as a surprise was that Manning was early. While he didn't dislike the man, Jerry had hoped to be on the road well before he arrived. He parked his truck, started toward the building, and hesitated when his inner radar told him he wasn't alone. Though he couldn't see the dog, the hairs on his arms told him he was near.

Maybe Manning being here wasn't a bad thing after all. Perhaps the dog was confused. After all, Gunter had showed up when Jerry was forced to drive Manning's SUV during the snowstorm. It all made sense now; the dog wasn't attached to him – it was attached to the SUV. That was why he hadn't seen the K-9 in the days since the accident. *What a relief.* "Okay, dog, let's take a walk. It's time for you to attach yourself to someone who actually cares about you."

"Yo, McNeal, what are you doing here?" Manning asked the second Jerry entered the building. Manning's cubicle was nowhere near the front door, making it obvious the man had been waiting for him.

"Last I saw, I still work here." Jerry resisted the temptation to look to see if the dog was visible. The lack of emotion on Manning's chiseled face told him what he needed to know. He started toward the back, pausing when Manning blocked his way. Jerry caught a glimpse of white hair, saw Sergeant Seltzer looking in their direction, and gave a subtle nod, letting his boss know he had things under control.

"I see the psychic convention's in town. I guess I figured you'd be there with the others."

"Some of us have to have real jobs," Jerry quipped.

"Wait. Say it isn't true. You're going to stand there and tell me you don't believe in that crap." Manning snorted.

I don't know what I believe. "Let it go, Manning."

Anger flashed in Manning's eyes. "No, I'm not going to let it go. You go around like a cowboy on a white horse saving the day, and you think you're the only one? So I'm to believe you've cornered the market on the psychic crap. It's just you, and all other psychics are frauds."

Not all of them. Jerry could tell by the set of Manning's shoulders he was looking for an argument and had a pretty good idea why he had singled him out – he needed someone to blame for what had happened to his partner and had decided that someone should be Jerry. No shock; Jerry was used to being the scapegoat. He'd been nowhere near the scene when the dog got shot. And therein lay the problem. "Step aside, Manning."

"Look at you hiding behind that uniform. I see you for what you really are. You know you ain't nothing but a darn coward." Manning grabbed him by the arm as he tried to pass. "Always running away. Couldn't cut it as a Marine, so you joined the State Police. The reason you aren't at the convention is you know you can't cut it as a psychic either."

Instinct took over. Jerry jerked his arm out of Manning's grip, pushed him against the wall, and leaned in close. "What's your beef, Manning?"

"My beef is you. You use your ...whatever it is...to help everyone but those close to you. Maybe if you quit running when things get a bit tough, you could focus your energy on what matters."

Jerry narrowed his eyes, hoping Manning hadn't seen he'd touched a nerve. "Yeah, and what's that?"

"Family. Me, your fellow officers, my freaking dog. Maybe if you would have let us in, you would've felt something the night Gunter got shot." Manning's voice cracked as he said the dog's name.

So it was true. Manning did blame him. It made perfect sense; why would he want to blame the whack-job that had fired the gun that actually killed the dog. *Crap. Is that why the dog's haunting me? Because he blames me for getting him killed? Easy, Jerry, you're losing it.* "I'm sorry your dog's dead." Jerry released the man.

"He was more than just a dog." Manning was calmer now. "He saved my life."

"I know," Jerry replied, wishing he could tell him of the dog's latest heroics.

"I heard about the crash on Route 30 the other day," Manning said as Jerry stepped around him. "That was a good save."

Manning was talking about the accident involving a very intriguing photographer named Holly and a snowplow. What he didn't know was that the dog he was mourning had been instrumental in finding the woman whose car had veered off the side of the road during the blizzard and was buried at the bottom of the ravine. While Jerry's gift had led him to the accident, it had not led him to Holly, who would have died if not for the dog. Over the last couple of days, he'd contemplated telling the man, but any hope of convincing him now would be construed as a way for Jerry to ease his conscience. Besides, what would he say? *Sorry you miss your dog, but if it's any consolation, the dog's now a ghost and seems to like me more than you.* Jerry decided to take the easy way out. "Thanks."

"We good?" Manning asked, moving aside.

"Good as we always were." While Jerry didn't see the dog, he held his arm to his side, spreading his fingers, giving the sign for stay, hoping Gunter would see it and know to stay with his old partner.

"Problem?" Seltzer asked when Jerry went into the sergeant's office.

Jerry shrugged. "He blames me for not saving his dog."

"Want me to talk to him?"

"You talk to him, you're going to have to talk to Jackson as well. He stopped me the other day."

"Jackson's not sore about the dog too, is he?"

"He wanted the winning lottery numbers."

"What'd he say when you told him you don't know?" Seltzer leaned forward in his chair. "You don't know, do you?"

"If I did, I wouldn't be here."

"It would solve a lot of problems," Seltzer said, running a hand through his white hair.

"Me not being here?"

"You knowing the lottery numbers. I wonder why that is?"

"I'm not sure I'm following you," Jerry replied.

"Why people like you can know some things and not know others. So, what are you going to do about Manning?" Seltzer asked, not waiting for an answer to the previous question.

Jerry waited for Seltzer to take a drink of coffee. "I was thinking about telling him his dog's a ghost."

Seltzer spit coffee from his nose. " Jeez, McNeal, you can't go around joking like that."

Jerry stared at the dog who'd materialized and now lay just in front of Seltzer's desk.

His boss's eyes grew wide as he stood and peeked over the desk. Blowing out a breath of air, the man sat back down. "You had me there for a moment."

Jerry looked to the now empty spot where the dog had been lying just a second before. *No need to bring him in on your little delusion, Jerry.* He smiled. "Just trying to keep you on your toes, sir."

"More like trying to send me to an early grave. Can you imagine the press if something like that were to get out? Might help with the budget, though."

"How's that?"

"Because now we have to fund another K-9. Do you think they really exist?"

"K-9s?"

"No, ghosts. You're wired into that stuff. Have you ever seen one?"

Jerry slid a glance to Gunter, who'd not only materialized but now looked at him with his head tilted to the side as if waiting to hear his answer. He focused his gaze on Seltzer. "I guess if I can know when something's going to happen before it does, then I'd have to say ghosts are plausible."

"But you've never seen one yourself?"

Easy, Jerry, time to tread lightly. "Sir, I have so much crap floating around in my head, it's hard at times to know what's real and what isn't."

"Yeah, I guess it would be at that," Seltzer agreed.

"Hey, about that K-9. I have a friend in North Carolina who trains dogs and donates them to police. I believe he only does search and rescue, but I can reach out to him if you'd like." Jerry hoped Seltzer would say yes, as it would give him an opportunity to ask some questions of his own.

"Donate, you say? And they're already trained?"

"Highly trained. Mike knows his stuff and has plenty of references."

"See what you can find out and get back to me. Anything else?" Seltzer asked when Jerry made no move to leave.

"I may need you to make a call for me."

"Go on." Seltzer leaned back in his chair.

"There's this girl." Seltzer cocked an eyebrow, and Jerry shook his head. "Max is a kid. Her mother sent me a letter asking me to speak to the girl."

"This one for real?"

"I'm afraid so."

"You say that like it's a bad thing."

"She needs a mentor."

"So mentor her."

"You make it sound easy."

"I won't pretend to know what it's like, but I know you and know you're not going to lead anyone astray."

"Not on purpose."

"So, who do you need me to call?"

"No one yet. Max doesn't have enough information." Jerry blew out a frustrated sigh. "She has dreams about someone being murdered, only that's pretty much all she knows. And that she thinks it's a woman."

"Pretty thin."

"That's what I told her."

"What makes you so sure she's legit?"

Because she knew about the dog. "Because when I was talking to her, she picked up on Holly."

"Who?"

"Ms. Wood, the woman from the blizzard."

"Why would she pick up on her?"

Because I was thinking about her at the time. Don't go there, Jerry. He shrugged. "I talked to the girl right after the accident."

"Let me know if you need me to help." Seltzer pulled out a pack of gum, removed a stick, and returned the pack to the drawer. "You want to go further out in the state today? I was thinking to send you over to Hershey. Might give you a chance to check in on Ms. Wood."

That was the thing about Seltzer; he believed in Jerry – so much so, he allowed him to choose where he wanted to patrol. Probably because Jerry never took advantage of the man's generosity. Jerry started to shake his head; ever since Manning had mentioned the psychic convention, the hairs on the back of Jerry's neck were tingling. But whatever he was feeling wasn't demanding his immediate attention.

Jerry looked at the dog, who was lying with his head resting on his front paws. "I think that'll be okay."

"Let me know if anything changes. And, McNeal, if that girl's as good as you think she is, you tell her to come see me when she's ready to go to work."

"I'll be sure to pass it along." Jerry stood, and the dog instantly joined him at his side. Jerry made it a point to walk past Manning's cubicle in hopes of getting the dog to stay with his old partner. Jerry stopped at the door and motioned him to stay. Gunter hesitated, and Jerry made a beeline to the door. When he opened it, Gunter was there, wagging his tail.

Chapter Three

Gunter stayed by Jerry's side the whole way to his cruiser, jumping inside and sitting in the passenger's seat when he opened the door.

Jerry looked at the dog and motioned to the rear of the car. "Backseat."

The dog tilted his head, pointing his long ears toward the dashboard.

"Come on. It's freaking cold out here. Get in the backseat."

Gunter answered with a single bark. Jerry sighed and slid behind the wheel. "Just so you know, I'm not a dog person. For the record, I'm not a cat person either." Jerry clicked on his seatbelt and headed out of the parking lot, leaving out the fact that he currently shared his house with an orange tabby that didn't listen any better.

Jerry thought about his promise to help find a replacement dog for Manning. He was pretty sure his friend Mike could help. The guy was prior Navy. Not that Jerry held it against the man – not everyone was cut out to be a Marine. Mike was one of the good guys. He worked with the K-9s while in the Navy and then spent years training dogs for the police department. After retiring, he began running a nonprofit that trained dogs to their highest level before donating the K-9s to police departments. He also worked to partner therapy dogs with military veterans to help them manage their PTSD. Jerry checked the time and debated calling Mike to inquire about a dog. Deciding to chance it, he made the call.

"Hello?"

"I was afraid I'd catch you in bed," Jerry replied.

"Been at it for hours. The dogs get restless if they don't get their breakfast on time. What can I do for you, Jerry?"

"I told my sergeant I'd see if you had any K-9s available." Jerry glanced over at Gunter and lowered his voice. "One of our dogs was killed in the line of duty."

"That's a darn shame. What kind of dog was he?"

"German shepherd."

"No, I mean a patrol K-9 or SAR?"

"Darned if I know. A patrol dog, I guess. The dog was trained to go on runs with the officer." Jerry covered the phone. "What kind of dog are you?"

Gunter barked his reply.

"Is that a dog I hear?"

Crap. "Yeah."

"Good. It's about time you listened to me and got yourself a PTSD companion."

"I don't think he qualifies as a PTSD companion." Jerry slid a glance to Gunter, who'd had him on edge since the moment he'd shown up. "He doesn't listen very well."

"Has he had any training?"

Not in this lifetime. "I'm sure he's had some."

"Well, if you can get him to do the basics – sit, stay, lie down – that's a start."

"I tried to get him to get in the back seat. I think he may have laughed at me."

"That's not good, Jerry."

"Tell me about it."

"No, I mean you have to let the dog know who's in charge."

Jerry looked at the dog once more. "I'm pretty sure he knows who's in charge."

"No, that's not right. You're in charge, Jerry. You're the one who feeds him and takes him out on a leash."

"Crap."

"Crap, what? You haven't fed him or taken him out?"

Jerry realized he'd backed himself into a corner. "I guess I don't know much about dogs."

"Dogs have to eat, Jerry. How long have you had him?"

Too long. "He first showed up a couple days ago."

"A couple of days, and you haven't fed him?"

"He disappeared for a while."

"Well, he's back now, so you've got to feed him."

"I'll stop at the store on the way home."

"Not just any store; go to the pet store and get a quality dog food. Make sure the first couple of ingredients are meat. Understand? And get a good collar and a leash. What kind of dog is he?"

Jerry swallowed. "A German shepherd."

"Okay, make that a harness. And get a leash. Make sure to get a real leash, not one of those retractable ones – I don't trust those things. They snap and you're in trouble. Good choice on the dog, by the way. GSDs are good dogs, smart and very dependable. Treat him right, and he'll stay with you a long time."

"That's what I'm worried about," Jerry groaned.

"What?"

"I said I'll take care of him. You've nothing to worry about."

"So, some pointers. Don't let him on the furniture. Not until he knows you are the boss. And if he shows any sign of food aggression, feed him by hand. You need to let him know you are the provider. What's his name?"

Jerry started to say the dog's real name then stopped. The last thing he wanted was for the man to mention it to anyone. "I've just been calling him Dog."

Mike laughed. "Most dogs name themselves. Give it some time; he'll do something that'll set him apart from all the rest."

Jerry thought to ask if being dead counted. *Maybe I should call him Casper.* "Thanks for the advice. I have to get going."

"Okay, you give your sergeant my cell number and have him give me a call. He tells me what he's looking for, and we'll find him a dog. And, Jerry?"

"Yeah, Mike?"

"You need help training that dog of yours, let me know. I've been doing this a long time. There's not a dog on this earth I can't handle."

"Okay, Mike, I'll be in touch." Jerry set the phone in the console and glanced at Gunter. "Mike said I'm supposed to show you who's boss."

Gunter curled his lip and growled a soft growl.

"Yeah, that's what I thought."

***

Never having been in a pet supply store before, Jerry wandered down the aisle marveling at all the choices. The toy aisle alone almost made him glad to have a dog. Gunter, who'd plastered himself by Jerry's side the moment they entered, stopped in front of the ball section.

120

"You like balls?"

Gunter gave a puppy-like yip and wagged his tail.

"Okay, a ball it is."

Jerry reached for a lime-green tennis ball, and Gunter growled. Jerry moved his hand to the right, hovering it over a smaller orange ball that reminded him of a mini basketball. Gunter yipped his approval. Jerry put the ball in the basket and continued down the aisle, stopping in front of a section of squeaky toys. He saw one that looked like an opossum, tossed it into the cart without asking the dog's approval, then continued on to the next aisle. The moment he rounded the corner, Jerry knew he was in over his head. The entire row was filled on both sides with collars, leashes, and harnesses in every color imaginable. He stopped the cart and gave a nod toward Gunter. "See anything that strikes your fancy?"

Gunter yawned his reply.

Undeterred, Jerry walked to where the harnesses were hanging, picked a red one that looked as if it would fit, then searched for a matching leash, placing them in the cart with the toys. That wasn't so bad. Now to get a bag of food and be done. The second Jerry rounded the corner to the dog food aisle, he saw a middle-aged woman with grey-streaked hair stuff a can of dog food into her coat. She had another can in her left hand, and from the bulk of the fabric, the single can of dog food wasn't the only thing hiding under the coat. She looked up as he rounded the corner and reminded him of a deer caught in the headlights. She took in his uniform, tossed the second can to the floor, then sprinted off in the opposite direction.

Before Jerry could respond, Gunter raced after the woman. Tackling her from behind, he sent her sliding along the floor a good three feet, then stood breathing down her neck, tail wagging as if it was all a glorious game.

Crap! "Dog! Get over here." Gunter did one better and disappeared.

Jerry walked to the end of the aisle and offered the woman a hand.

She slapped his hand away. "Help! Help! Police brutality!"

Several people came running, including several store employees and a man with a pit bull – both man and dog looked as if they'd never missed a meal. The dog strained against his spiked collar, and the man kept reeling in the retractable leash. Jerry thought of what Mike had said and sent out a silent prayer that the leash would hold. The man holding the leash was breathing heavy, and it was hard to tell which one was slobbering more, the man or the dog.

The man narrowed his eyes at Jerry. "You push her down?"

Jerry ignored the question, watching as the employees helped the woman to her feet.

Tears rolled from the woman's eyes. Jerry wondered if she were truly injured or afraid of getting arrested for shoplifting.

She put a hand above her heart. "I was standing there minding my own business when that cop pushed me to the floor. I could even feel the heat of his breath on the back of my neck!"

The manager showed up before Jerry could respond. "What happened?"

"He pushed my wife!" The man with the dog let out a length of leash. "Easy, Tiny, ain't no one going to hurt your momma no more."

Jerry gave the man a closer look, wondering if the girth

beneath his coat were real or if he too had been padding his beltline.

"He did. I'm going to sue. You'll hear from my attorney. All of you! I'll own this store!" She shrugged out of the employee's grip, gave her husband a nod, and they both started to walk away.

Jerry, who'd been silent up until this point, keyed his radio and requested another unit sent to his location – also specifying a female officer. Releasing the mike, he turned to the woman. "Ma'am, you need to stay where you are."

"You don't get to manhandle me and then order me around," she said over her shoulder.

"Ma'am, I'd advise you to listen. You don't want a simple case of shoplifting to turn into resisting arrest."

The woman stopped but motioned for her husband to continue.

The manager blinked his surprise. "You tackled her for shoplifting?"

"I didn't touch the woman." Jerry maneuvered himself in front of the couple, all the while hoping the dog's leash would hold. "Sir, I suggest you stay put as well."

The man started forward once more. Jerry felt for his taser, wondering if he should use it on the man or the dog, which didn't appear happy to have Jerry so close to his human mom. Tiny growled at Jerry, barking and straining even more than before. Jerry thought back to his conversation with Mike and wondered what the man would do in his current situation. Suddenly, Jerry felt the hair on the back of his neck bristle. He held up a hand to the dog. "Easy, boy. No one's going to hurt you."

The dog's demeanor instantly changed. Cowering, he tucked his tail between his legs and began whining.

"What did you do to him?"

Jerry held up his palms. "I didn't do anything."

One of the salesmen – a young boy with the name Tim on his name tag – elbowed the other. "Check it out; the man's a real dog whisperer."

"Cesar don't have nothing on him," the other clerk agreed.

Jerry put the name of the dog and the clerk together and resisted the urge to laugh. And he wasn't a dog whisperer; he hadn't done anything except raise his hand, pretending to quiet the dog the second he felt Gunter appear. The fact that no one had mentioned the shepherd let him know they couldn't see him. While he wasn't sure if the pit bull could see Gunter, it was obvious Tiny could feel the K-9's ghostly presence. Jerry breathed a sigh of relief when he heard a local Derry Township police unit radio they'd arrived on the scene.

Jerry saw two officers enter through the sliding door. Having patrolled in the area multiple times, he recognized both Cahill and Martinez and stepped into the main aisle, positioning himself where they could see him. The door slid open a second time and admitted a third officer Jerry didn't recognize.

As the first two officers reached him, the woman pushed her way past and pointed a meaty finger at Jerry. "Thank god you're here, officers. I want you to arrest this man. I'm making a citizen's arrest, but I want you to do the arresting."

The third officer came up and quickly took charge, telling the female officer to get the woman's statement.

Jerry gave a nod to the officer, whose nametag read Barnes. "Better get one from the husband as well."

Cahill took the man and dog in the opposite direction. Though the man seemed reluctant, the dog was more than eager to leave the area.

As soon as Jerry had the man to himself, he motioned the store manager forward. "Your video cameras work?"

The manager bobbed his head. "Of course."

"Wind them back to when the couple came in. Follow them to see what the videos show. Let us know when you have it, and one of us will come take a look."

"Yes, sir, officer."

"Shoplifting," Jerry said by explanation. He looked at Gunter, who was sitting at his side looking mighty pleased with himself.

Barnes followed his gaze, appearing nonplussed. "I figured as much."

"The woman tried to run and lost her balance. She was embarrassed and blamed me for her clumsiness." Okay, it was a lie, but the video would back it up. Besides, it was better than trying to explain what really transpired.

Barnes gave a nod to the basket Jerry had left at the end of the aisle. "Is that their cart?"

"No, it's mine. I was doing a bit of shopping when I happened upon the woman feeding dog food to her coat."

Barnes looked in the cart. "Finish your shopping. I'll go have a look at the video."

While the other employee followed Barnes, Tim wavered, as if wondering if he should follow. After a few seconds of indecision, he turned his attention to Jerry. "Can I help you find something, officer?"

"Dog food."

The kid waved his hand to encompass the row of food. "What kind?"

Darned if I know. "Something with meat."

The boy laughed. "They all have meat. Some just have more than others."

Jerry looked at Gunter and shrugged. "I think the dog would like one with a lot of meat."

The boy sighed. "How big is your dog?"

Jerry held out a hand to show the height. "German shepherd."

"Okay, that helps. You're probably going to want a large breed dog food." He pointed to a bag. "This is what I feed my dog."

"You got a shepherd?"

"No, a pit. They're a wonderful breed with the right owner." He cast a glance toward the man and dog. "It was pretty cool how you got him to calm down. Your dog must be pretty well trained."

Jerry slid a glance toward Gunter, who had turned and was now staring at the boy and wagging his tail. "Son, my dog's so good, he could be right in front of you right now, and you wouldn't even know he's here."

Chapter Four

Jerry sat in the parking garage at Penn State Health Complex in Hershey, PA questioning why he was even there. To add to his distress, he'd spent the last ten minutes chiding himself for purchasing the leash and harness for the dog that seemed determined to go into the hospital with him.

I've officially lost what's left of my mind – the dog's not even real. Jerry looked at the dog, who was currently panting and dribbling droplets of saliva onto the leather seat. *Real enough to ruin the leather and to cause trouble if anyone saw him.* Though no one at the pet store could see Gunter, Holly had. Jerry wasn't sure if it was because she'd been in trouble at the time or if it was because the dog had wanted her to see him. And therein lay the problem. If some could see the dog and others could not, how would he handle the situation if confronted while walking through the hospital with an unleashed dog. And if he were actually able to put the harness and leash on the dog – without said dog biting him – what would it look like to those unable to see him?

Jerry recalled those stiff fake collared leashes of his childhood bent to look as if one were actually walking a dog. So much so, the toy companies had marketed them as invisible dogs. *I served two tours with the Marines. I'm a Pennsylvania State Trooper, and this is what my life has become. Am I really supposed to walk around pretending to walk an invisible dog? Maybe I could pretend it's a joke. No one will believe you, Jerry.*

It was all getting to be too much. Jerry looked at the dog, who sat staring at him, apparently just as confused by Jerry's indecision as Jerry himself. Jerry turned his frustration on the dog.

"Why me? You had the whole populace of earth, and you pick the one person who's not thrilled to have you here. Wouldn't you be happier with a boy who would run and play with you or, better yet, with your old partner? Sure, Manning can be a jerk, but at least he likes you."

Gunter growled, and Jerry put out his hands. "Oh no, you don't get to be angry. You're a ghost. You're not supposed to have feelings. This is all about me – I'm the one who gets to be mad."

Gunter barked a deep, throaty bark. Jerry was just about to open the door and make a run for it when he saw an older woman wearing a beige coat standing to the left of his patrol car. Leaning heavily on a cane, she had her right hand on her chest and kept turning from side to side.

Jerry set the leash and harness aside and got out of the car. "Can I help you, ma'am?"

"Oh, I don't want to be a bother. It's just that I can't seem to find my car. I thought for sure I'd parked on this level. I was almost certain of it. But it's not here."

Jerry looked at Gunter, who'd followed him out of the car. "We'll help you find it."

The woman looked from Jerry to the car and back to Jerry again. "We?"

Crap. "You and me together. Do you have your car keys?"

"My keys aren't going to do me any good if I can't find my car."

"Ah, but they will." At least he hoped so. "Dig them out, and I'll show you a trick."

She unzipped her purse and dug around inside before finally retrieving a set of keys and handing them over with trembling hands. "I still don't know what good they'll do without the car."

Jerry held them up then pressed the lock button. Though he couldn't hear anything, Gunter barked then took off running. Jerry thought about following then changed his mind. "I think you are on a different level."

She looked uncertain. "How can you be so sure. I thought for sure I'd parked on this level. Perhaps someone stole it. Maybe you should call it in on that there radio of yours."

"How about we check the garage first? If we don't find your car, I promise to call it in." He took her by the elbow. "Come on, and I'll give you a ride."

Her blue eyes twinkled. "I've never ridden in a police car before."

Jerry led her to the passenger side and started to open the front door, when she stopped him.

"Could I maybe ride in the back seat?"

Jerry suppressed a chuckle. "Sure."

She retrieved her cell phone from her right coat pocket and held it out to him. "And could you maybe take a picture of me to prove it?"

Jerry thought to ask if she wanted him to handcuff her

but decided against it. She grinned a wide grin while he took several photos. He started to hand the phone back, then hesitated. "You know, most criminals are not smiling when they are sitting back there."

"Oh…Oh." She rifled her hand through her hair and scrunched her face into a frown. "How's this?"

Jerry snapped a couple more photos and handed her the phone so she could see for herself.

The woman snickered her approval and placed the phone back in her pocket. "Just wait until I post these on the Facebook. My friends at the bingo hall are going to be so jealous."

Crap. Way to go, Jerry. Why don't you cruise around with lights and sirens blaring for good measure? He shut the door, walked to the driver's side of the cruiser, and got in. He pulled out of the space and watched in his rearview mirror as someone claimed the spot that had taken three full turns around the parking garage to find. He circled to the next floor and onto the next before seeing Gunter standing in front of a blue PT Cruiser. He pulled up next to the car and looked in the mirror once more. "Would that be yours?"

She looked out the window and gasped her surprise. "Why, yes, it is. How did you know?"

"It matches your eyes." *Jeez, Jerry.*

"That's exactly what my husband said when he bought it for me."

Jerry placed the cruiser in park and walked around, opening the door for her. As he helped her from his car, he pointed to the concrete pillar. "Next time you come, use your cell phone to take a photo of the sign. When you're finished with your appointment, you can check the picture to see where you parked your car."

"What a smart young man you are."

"And don't put your keys in your purse. Keep them in your pocket, so you don't have to dig for them in case anyone is following you."

"That's a good idea. People are always following me when I'm in here."

Jerry raised an eyebrow. "They are?"

"Oh yes, it's the only way to get a parking place. Speaking of which, you'd better take mine when I leave. You're not likely to get your old spot back."

Jerry helped her to her car, declined the tip she offered, then backed up and waited for her to pull out so he could snag her parking spot. He turned to Gunter, who'd returned to the passenger seat. "You should go home with her. She seems nice enough."

Gunter growled his answer.

"What? At least if she forgets you in the car, you'll be able to get out on your own." Jerry held up the harness, moved to place it over Gunter's head, then made a mental note to return it to the store when the dog bared his teeth. "Okay, but I'll deny knowing you if anyone sees you."

Jerry's cell rang, the ringtone letting him know it was Sergeant Seltzer. "Hey, Sarge, what's up?"

"Just letting you know I got a call from Derry Township."

"They reviewed the video while I was still in the store. I never touched the woman."

"Never said you did."

"So why'd they call?"

"When the woman threatened to sue, the watch captain decided to review the videos a second time. Though he agreed you were nowhere near the woman, he questioned your overall behavior. He seems to think you were acting a bit odd in the store."

"How so?"

"He claims you were talking to yourself. I told him there must be a reasonable explanation for your actions."

"In other words, you lied." Or *covered my ass, again.*

"I give all my officers the benefit of the doubt until I see the evidence."

Jerry closed his eyes and let out a sigh. Even before the dog came into the picture, he knew his days at the post to be numbered. Still, he'd thought he had a bit more time to figure things out. "What do you think?"

"I try not to when it comes to you."

Jerry cast a glance toward the dog. "When are you going to review the clip?"

"The store manager's waiting for approval from his boss. Then he'll e-mail it over."

"So why tell me. Why not just hit me with it when I come in?"

"What, and deprive you of a chance to come up with a plausible explanation?"

"Maybe I should just tell the truth."

"Would it get you kicked off the force?"

Jerry looked at the dog once more. "Probably."

Seltzer sighed into the phone. "Work on your story, McNeal. We'll talk tomorrow."

Jerry clicked off the phone and stuck it into his pocket. *Tomorrow it is.*

***

Gunter stayed with Jerry the entire way to the visitor information station. Several hospital volunteers sat behind the desk. One looked up when he approached. Gunter jumped up, placing his paws on the counter directly in front of the woman. Jerry smiled a disarming smile and asked for Holly's room number. The woman looked him over and frowned.

Crap, she sees the dog. Jerry decided to face the dilemma head-on. "Is there a problem?"

"What? No, I was about to ask you the same thing, officer."

The uniform. Jerry felt his tension ease. "Not at all. Just here visiting a friend."

"Oh, good." She wrote Holly's room number on a map of the complex and handed it to him. As she slid the paper over, Gunter licked the back of the woman's age-spotted hand. Though she didn't acknowledge the dog's gesture, she covered the spot with her other hand when she pulled it away. She smiled a confused smile. "You have a good day, officer."

Why is it everyone else gets tail wags and licks, and all I get are growls? For the first time, Jerry realized the dog's rejection actually bothered him. Why had Gunter attached himself to him when it was apparent from his actions that the dog didn't even like him? Jerry pondered that question the whole way through the maze of hallways and onto the elevator. He was still questioning things when he approached Holly's room. The door to the room was open, but the curtain was pulled so that Jerry could not see inside. He started to knock then hesitated when Gunter moved between him and the door. Frustrated, Jerry began to reach over the dog.

Gunter growled his objection.

This is getting ridiculous. Jerry was about to say something about calling an exorcist, when he heard Holly's voice.

"I can't do this anymore, Dad. It's not fair to Gracie."

"You're overreacting. Gracie is doing much better."

"I know she's better, and that's precisely the point. If I'm going to make the move, I need to do it now. Get her settled into a new life and established with doctors now while she is healthy."

"But why move at all?"

"Because she needs to be around family. If this had been worse…"

"It wasn't."

"But it almost was, Dad. Then what would have happened to her?"

"I would have taken care of her."

"Dad, you know I love you, but you can barely take care of yourself."

"Who will take care of me if you're not here?"

There was a moment of silence. "I was hoping you would come with us."

"I don't know."

"They are your family too. It just makes sense. Gracie needs to know her extended family. That way, if anything happens to us, she won't be thrust into a sea of strangers. She has aunts and uncles that she's only seen a handful of times. Please, Dad. Aunt Edna said we can stay with her until we find a place of our own."

"What about that nice young man you were telling me about? I thought you said there was a connection."

"You mean the one I haven't heard from since the accident? He's a cop, Dad. He was only doing his job."

No, I'm here. Jerry tried to step around the dog, hoping to let Holly know she was wrong. Gunter bared his teeth, once again refusing to allow him to enter the room.

"I don't need any distractions, Dad. I need stability."

"You both need someone dependable in your life."

"We do, which is why I'm hoping you'll move with us.

I can't imagine not having you close, but in the end, I need to do what is best for my daughter."

"Okay, Holly. I'll go with you."

Jerry turned away from the room and retraced his steps to the elevator. As he stood waiting for the doors to open, he looked at Gunter, who was now staring up at him with soft brown eyes. If not for the K-9, he would've gone into the room and possibly changed the direction of Holly's life. The woman needed dependable, and that wasn't him. It had never been him. At the moment, it was unclear if he'd even have a job much longer.

"Is this it? Is this why you're here? To keep me from ruining her life?" As if in answer to Jerry's question, Gunter wagged his tail. A second later, the dog disappeared.

Chapter Five

Jerry woke with the feeling of being watched. He opened his eyes, expecting to see the cat staring at him, but Cat was nowhere in sight. Odd, as it was well past his normal feeding time.

Jerry sat on the edge of the bed, doing his best to shake his unease. He showered, then dressed and made his way to the kitchen. The feeling intensified as he poured himself a cup of coffee and took a sip, lingering as he placed the cup on the table. *What's going on, Jerry?*

Jerry made a show of getting out the can of cat food, opening the container, and putting it on the floor with a clang. Cat was not one for missing a meal, and Jerry was surprised he wasn't already rubbing against his leg, purring in excited anticipation.

"Yo, Cat, breakfast is ready." *Where the heck are you?* Jerry retrieved his cup and walked through the house, searching his usual hangouts. By the time he'd walked through the whole place, Jerry had to admit feeling concerned, wondering if he had accidentally left him outside. Just as he was about to give up, he caught sight of the cat out of the corner of his eye. Ears plastered back and eyes wide, Cat sat on top of the refrigerator watching his every move.

"How the heck did you get up there?" Jerry walked over to help him down, surprised when Cat hissed at him. Another attempt had the cat emitting a low warning growl. What the heck was it with animals growling at him?

Jerry withdrew his hand. "What the heck has gotten into you, Cat? It was your idea to stay. You don't like it here, you're welcome to leave. If I'd wanted a cat, I would've given you a name other than Cat. I remember distinctly warning you that I don't even like cats."

Jerry's comment evoked another low growl.

"Geesh, Cat, you got rabies or something?" Jerry asked, only half-joking. His brain told him the stray had been here so long that rabies would have presented itself by now, but something sure had the animal on edge. It reminded him of a person dealing with PTSD – that was one ailment Jerry was well-versed in.

He walked across the room, picked up the can of cat food, and brought it back to the cat. Cat sniffed the contents and took a bite. As he ate, he continued to grumble his discontent.

"Cat, I don't mind if you eat up there, but you'd better not use the area as a litterbox. That crap will get your ass booted out for sure."

Jerry moved to the window and stood drinking his coffee. Even though his head and neck were freshly shaven, he felt tingling on the back of his neck where the hair should be, crawling like a zillion bugs up and down his neck and across his arms as he stared off into the distance.

As he took another sip from his cup, he saw something

move. Looking closer, Jerry realized what he saw was not outside the window but a reflection of something moving behind him. The practical part of his brain told him Cat had finally evacuated his hiding place, but the part of his brain that looked elsewhere warned him this was not the case. Palming the cup in case he needed to use it as a weapon, he turned from the window. His breath caught, and his grip tightened around the cup, even though he knew it would prove ineffective against the current threat.

In the center of the floor, crouched but alert, Gunter stared back at him – eyes so intense that Jerry could barely breathe. So much for his theory that the dog had come to keep him from ruining Holly's life. Also now debunked was Jerry's original theory that the K-9's appearance was limited to police activities. His presence in the apartment seemed to have Gunter confused as well – the ghostly apparition stared at him as if it were Jerry who was out of place.

Cat hissed, drawing Jerry's attention.

"Yeah, I see him too. The bad news, he's a ghost. The good news, I don't think he can actually eat either one of us."

The dog barked, making Jerry question his earlier deduction. Cat crouched down, pressing himself further against the back wall above the fridge. For a brief second, Jerry considered joining him.

Take it easy, Jerry. If the dog were going to eat you, he would have done so already. He was fine – well, mostly fine – in the car yesterday. Something must be upsetting him. Or maybe it's just because he doesn't like unfamiliar settings. Then again, he's a police dog. He's been trained to handle the unknown. Does training transfer over to the other realm? Think of Cujo. Cujo wasn't dead; he had rabies. Okay, what about the cat from Pet Cemetery? What was his name? Before he could recall the cat's name, the dog growled a throaty growl. *Do something, Jerry. What was it Manning used to say to him?*

"At ease, Dog," Jerry commanded.

The dog barked his answer.

"At ease, Gunter!" Jerry firmed the command and called the dog by name. It was a long shot, but he'd heard Manning give the dog the same command on multiple occasions to call the dog off.

Instantly, the dog's demeanor changed. No longer on alert, the dog crouched, wagging his tail. Jerry rolled his shoulders. *Okay, that's more like it.*

"You want some grub, dog?" Jerry walked to the fridge, pulled out a slice of ham, and tossed it in front of the dog.

The dog sniffed it but made no move to eat.

"Go on, dog, take it."

Nothing.

"Eat, Gunter." Still nothing. Jerry shook his head and took another sip of coffee. "Why me, Lord? First, I have a cat I didn't ask for, and now I'm being haunted by Cujo."

The dog growled. A second later, there was a knock on the front door. Jerry glanced at the door. When he looked back, the dog was gone. Also missing was the feeling that had been hanging in the air before he appeared.

Jerry crossed the living space of the small upstairs apartment he rented and opened the door to find his landlord, Todd Wells, standing on the landing, shivering and blowing into his ungloved hands. Wells appeared agitated, and Jerry braced himself for another tirade from the man who'd been onto Jerry for the last couple of weeks, asking if he was going to renew his lease. Jerry had signed the original lease, three years with an option for three more, to coincide with his patrol rotation. While he'd initially intended to stay, recently, something was telling Jerry to hold off. Though he didn't know the reason, Jerry knew better than to question his feelings – especially one so strong.

The thing was, Jerry had spent the better part of the previous year making improvements to the place. The agreement was that Jerry would do the renovations, and Wells would deduct the materials from the price of rent. Jerry had thought it a good deal at the time, as the man had given him the go-ahead to pick the finishes, meaning Jerry was able to get the look he wanted without shelling out the dough for a high-end apartment. Wells hadn't objected, as the deal assured him free labor. Both had been happy with the agreement until the renovations were completed – Wells took one look at the newly updated garage apartment and saw dollar signs. From that moment, he'd tried every underhanded trick available to convince Jerry not to renew his lease.

Jerry was not stupid. If Wells could force him out, he could ask three times the price Jerry currently paid for the formerly outdated unit. While Jerry liked the place, he wasn't sure if he liked it enough to deal with Wells' crap for the next three years. But that didn't mean he intended to give his landlord the satisfaction of leaving early. The contract was not due to expire for two months, and he was only required to provide a thirty-day notice.

Jerry stared at the man, wondering what new thing he'd invented to needle him about today.

"Mr. McNeal, do you think carrying a badge gives you the right to break the law?" Jerry blinked his confusion as Wells stood on his tippy toes and tried to look around him.

It wasn't the first time the man had tried this tactic.

"What law would I be breaking this time?"

"I heard a dog." Wells held up what looked to be his copy of the contract. "Our agreement specifically states no pets, and I heard a dog. Erma heard it too."

Crap! "Mr. Wells, I assure you I don't own a dog." Technically, it was the truth.

Wells was not convinced. "McNeal, it's bad enough you're standing there lying to me, but Erma heard it too. Shame on you, and you being a police officer and all."

Erma was Well's hundred-plus-pound Old English bulldog who did nothing but eat, bark, and crap all over the yard. It was disgusting enough dodging the piles in the summertime, but he despised looking at them in the winter. Dark cigar-length blemishes marring all the fresh white snow. While dogs had never liked Jerry, his disdain for dogs took on a whole new level after meeting Erma – not that it was the dog's fault. Jerry didn't want a dog. Any dog. The last thing he wanted was to run after some mutt and pick up crap all day.

Jerry pulled himself to attention and raised his voice just in case the dog had any plans to make itself visible to the man at the door. "I'm a Pennsylvania State Trooper. I do not own nor do I wish to have a dog!"

"Well, you don't have to yell," Wells admonished. "Just let me come in and have a look around, and that will be the end of it."

Wells attempted to enter, and Jerry blocked his way. "Do you have a search warrant?"

"I don't need a blasted search warrant to enter my own property."

"No, but you do need to give me twenty-four hours' notice according to that lease in your hand."

"What about probable cause?"

"That only works for the police," Jerry reminded him.

"What if I call the police? They would have to come, right?"

Jerry chuckled. "The police would come, eventually. Then they would take your statement. Next, they would come up here and ask me if I have a dog."

"And you would lie to them, just like you're lying to me right now."

"I would tell them the truth. The same as I already told you."

"And they would believe you because you have a badge."

Jerry sighed. "Because I'm telling the truth."

Wells cupped his hands and blew air into them.

"You're cold, Mr. Wells. Go home and come back tomorrow."

Wells cocked his head.

"You've asked to see inside. Come back tomorrow at this time, and I'll let you in."

"You trying to be cute?"

"No, sir, just trying to uphold the law. You asked to see inside. I'll let you in when the required twenty-four-hour notice is up."

"I see what you're doing. It will give you time to tamper with the evidence."

Jerry resisted the urge to push the man down the stairs. "Go home, Wells."

"And if I refuse?"

"Then I'll help you down the stairs. I'm sure they are mighty slippery with all this new snow. It'd be too bad if you were to happen to fall down a couple on the way down."

Wells narrowed his eyes. "That would be police brutality."

"I'm not in uniform. Besides, I have a darn good lawyer. I'm pretty sure we can get you on faulty upkeep of the premises. Might even be able to call in the sewer commissioner to give you a fine for not picking up after your dog. I'm fairly certain there is an ordinance about feces going into the storm drains. While I'm at it, I will insist they call PETA because I'm pretty sure that hound of yours is grossly overweight." Jerry was reaching for stuff, but from the look on Wells' face, the man was buying into it.

"I'll be back in the morning. And you can believe I will be watching you. You try to sneak a dog out of here, and I'll know it."

Not if the dog is invisible. Jerry closed the door. The second he did, the dog reappeared.

Chapter Six

Weary from the long drive from Louisville, Savannah pulled into her sister's driveway in Chambersburg, Pennsylvania, happy to have finally reached her destination. She grabbed her phone to text her sister of her arrival, when the speakers in the car's dashboard alerted her of her sister's call. Savannah pressed the button on the display. "Reading my mind again?"

"I'd love to say yes, but I got an alert on my phone telling me someone was in the driveway."

"You're not home?"

"No, I just got off work. My car is still in the shop. It was supposed to be finished this morning, but now they're saying Monday. Anyway, I rode in with a friend last night. Want to pick me up? He doesn't get off for another hour."

Savannah stared at the dashboard. "He?"

"Just a co-worker. You going to pick me up or not?"

"Sure, but I'm going to need a nap when we get back here."

"No time for that. We've got to set things up before everyone arrives."

Savannah sighed. "Ugh, I tossed and turned until two and finally said the heck with it and got on the road. The weather in the mountains was awful, and I'm beat."

"Yeah, well, I worked a double, so we get to be miserable together."

"I'm going to need a huge amount of caffeine to make it through the day."

"You and me both. Straight up Lincoln Highway and follow the signs to the hospital, remember?"

"I remember."

"Just come to the Emergency entrance. I'll keep an eye out for you."

Savannah put her car in reverse and drove the short distance, stifling a yawn as she made the right onto Lincoln Highway. She cruised through several traffic lights before finally getting caught by a red. There was a combination gas station convenience store on the right, so she clicked on her turn signal, thinking to pick up a coffee. The light changed just as she began to turn the wheel, and she reconsidered, deciding she was too tired to get out of the car. A few short blocks later, she saw the sign to the hospital, turned right onto North 7th Street, then made a right and navigated into the Emergency bay. Still dressed in scrubs, Cassidy stood just inside the door. She hurried to the car and immediately started fiddling with the heater.

Savannah batted her hand away. "If you're cold, zip your coat. It took me two hundred miles, but I finally had it adjusted to where I wanted it."

Cassidy looked her over. "You look like crap."

Savannah let off of the brake and eased out from underneath the overhang. "You don't look so hot yourself. Are those bags under your eyes?"

Her sister shrugged. "Nothing a bit of makeup won't

hide. Take a right."

"Aren't we going back to Lincoln Highway?"

"Yes, but you can't make a left from this street. Go right, take your first left, then it will take you around where you can turn left at the light."

Savannah turned the wheel and followed her sister's instructions. "Why'd you work a double if you knew you'd be hosting the convention tonight?"

"A friend's kid got sick, and she didn't have anyone to watch her." She pointed, motioning for Savannah to make a turn. "It's all good. She covered for me a few weeks ago."

"That's sweet of you, Cass."

"I know. And it's Raven."

"What is?"

"My name."

"When did that happen?"

"Today. It goes better with my outfit. I've got one for you too."

"I like my name."

"That's because you like the history that surrounds it."

It was true. Their mother used to regale the girls with stories of why she'd chosen their names. Savannah was named after the city where their parents had spent their honeymoon. Cassidy, on the other hand, was named after the band their mother was listening to the first time her parents had done the deed. Why their mother couldn't have simply told Cassidy she'd been named after Mama Cass and been done with it remained a mystery.

"Because Mom took pleasure in torturing me."

"Stop reading my mind."

Cassidy laughed. "I didn't have to; your mind always goes there when we talk about how we got our names."

"It's hard not to go there. Mom shared the story enough

over the years."

"Which is why she's going to stay with you when she gets old and senile. It's bad enough listening to the story while she has all her faculties. I refuse to do so when I can't tell her to knock it off."

"I don't think we have to worry about her losing her mind anytime soon. Her memory is better than mine."

"That's good. Hey, I got you an outfit to show off the ladies."

Savannah slid a glance in her sister's direction, knowing the comment to be a thinly veiled dig at their mother, who, in Cassidy's mind, had purposely saved the breast gene for Savannah. She'd heard it many times over the years, *Mom likes you best; she gave you a better name and better breasts.* It wasn't that Savannah minded showing off her breasts, but not having much to show for herself, she felt that Cassidy sometimes pushed things to the extreme. "Still trying to dress me like a slut?"

"We've been through this before. You'll probably be the youngest reader in the room. That's not a bad thing, but people might see your youth as a sign of inexperience. I've seen it before; people gravitate to the older psychics because they think they're wiser."

Savannah held up her left hand to show her newly acquired wedding ring. "I'm old enough to be married."

Cassidy ignored both the ring and comment. "You're still young. If you want to stand out, you have to let the ladies breathe."

"So I can draw in the creeps." Savannah pulled into the convenience store she'd almost stopped at on her way to pick up her sister. "I need caffeine."

Cassidy unbuckled her seatbelt and turned to face her. "It's not like you're leaving with any of them. I'll put you in the front row so I can keep an eye on you. We'll work out a signal, then if you need me to save you, I will. Listen, it won't always be like this. You have the gift; I've seen it firsthand. Being at the convention will help you gain confidence."

Cassidy had a point. While she had no trouble picking up on things, she lacked the experience to give a proper reading, especially if the message she received was one the person sitting across from her wouldn't enjoy hearing. As much as she enjoyed her ability, she despised being the bearer of bad news. Her sister, on the other hand, was extremely adept at handling every situation thrown at her. "Okay, I'll listen to your advice."

Cassidy opened the door. "You coming in?"

"No, I'm saving my energy for tonight. Forget the coffee, get me a monster drink – the more caffeine the better. Don't look now, but the cops are here." Savannah nodded to the state cruiser, which had pulled in and was currently backing into a parking space near the road.

Cassidy shrugged off the comment. "They're always here. The state police post is not too far away."

The moment her sister shut the door, Savannah readjusted the heat. She looked through the store window, wishing she'd told Cassidy to bring her a donut. Smiling, she closed her eyes, pictured her sister's face, and conjured up the image of a chocolate donut with multicolored sprinkles. As she concentrated, she felt someone watching her. She opened her eyes, half expecting to see Cassidy staring out the window sticking out her tongue. She wasn't there, but the feeling of being watched intensified. She scanned the parking lot, a chill racing down her spine when her gaze came to rest on the police cruiser. Though the officer had gone inside, the car was idling – white smoke drifting out from the tailpipe.

She wiped the fog from her window, surprised to see a large German shepherd staring back at her from the patrol car's passenger seat. Strange that he was watching her and not the door that his owner had used. It also struck her odd that the dog was sitting in the front seat, as she'd always thought them confined to the back. The intensity of the dog's stare pulled at her, that and the fact that she'd always been fascinated with German shepherds.

Hoping to get a better look, she put her car in reverse and drove past the cop car. The dog locked eyes on her, watching her as she passed. Brown with black markings, the dog's ears pointed straight to the roof of the car. Well, one of them did. The other seemed to have a piece missing. Even with the defect, it was a stunning dog. A car came up behind her, and she moved forward, then turned around, driving slowly to get another look. She lowered the side window and whistled – smiling when the dog tilted its head in response.

A horn blared. Savannah looked in her rearview mirror and saw a red truck pressed close to the back of her car. When she looked back at the police car, the dog was gone. She circled around the pumps and reached the door just as her sister exited the store.

Cassidy opened the passenger door, got in, and immediately adjusted the thermostat. "Now this is what I call service. I got you your donut; sorry, they were all out of sprinkles."

"I can't believe it still works."

Cassidy pulled a chocolate donut from the bag and handed it to her. "Always has."

Savannah drove past the police car on the way out of the back parking lot. "I wanted to get a better look at the police dog. He must have lay down."

"I should have known. You've always been drawn to animals." Cassidy pulled the top on the can and handed it to her. "Maybe that's the direction you should go."

"A K-9 officer?"

"God, no. You'd shoot someone. But there's big money in pet psychics."

"Seriously?" She loved working with animals and wouldn't mind getting paid for it.

"Sure. The pet business is a billion-dollar industry. It's something to think about."

"Does that mean I don't have to wear the dress?"

Cassidy laughed. "Oh, you're going to wear the dress. You might even meet yourself a nice guy."

So her sister hadn't missed the comment about being married. It wouldn't surprise her if she'd been dwelling on it the whole time. It was no secret that Cassidy disapproved of her relationship with Alex – enough so that she had even made excuses for not being able to take time off from work to drive to Kentucky to attend the private ceremony. "Somehow, I doubt Alex would like that."

"Ah yes, Alex. How is married life treating you?"

"I couldn't be happier." Hoping to avoid another fight over the fact that Cassidy hadn't so much as sent a card, Savannah changed the subject. "There was something about the dog. No, I think there's more to it than that. The moment I saw the car – even before I saw the dog – I got chills."

"I felt it too."

"With the cop car?"

"No, the cop. I saw him inside. He felt it too. I could tell."

"Really? Did he say anything?"

"No, but it was there. Something in the way he looked at me."

The light turned green, and Savannah moved forward with the traffic. "Maybe he has a thing for nurses."

"Perhaps. Though he'd have to be desperate to find me attractive today."

"That's true."

"Hey!"

"You're wearing scrubs and a pink puff coat. Your hair is in a bun, and you look as if you haven't slept in a week."

"I hate to break it to you, but you don't look much better."

Savannah checked the mirror and sighed. "We're going to need a lot of makeup!"

Cassidy held up a bag with several cans of caffeinated beverages. "And a lot more caffeine."

Chapter Seven

Jerry knew something was wrong when he stepped inside the station, and everyone turned in his direction. Instead of the usual *hey, Jerry, what's happening*, his fellow officers now stared at him much the way one stared at a criminal that had perpetrated a particularly heinous crime. Manning stepped out from behind his cubicle, made eye contact, then looked past Jerry as if looking for someone – or something.

It occurred to Jerry that Gunter might have taken this moment to reveal himself to the unit and resisted looking over his shoulder. What if he had? Should he feign shock? Would it matter? They already thought him to be a bit off – not that he cared what any of them thought. Only he did. They were a great bunch of guys. Outstanding officers that had treated him like just one of the guys – until he proved them wrong. It had been that way throughout his life – which was why he was more comfortable on his own.

Perhaps it wasn't the dog at all; maybe in his bid to reclaim some semblance of order between Cat and the dog, he'd somehow forgotten to put on pants. No, he specifically remembered changing into his uniform pants after Wells left. *Don't try to kid yourself, Jerry; you know good and well what Manning's looking for – he darn sure isn't trying to figure out if you're wearing boxers or briefs. The dog.* He wasn't sure how they'd found out, but it was pretty obvious they had. It was the only explanation for his fellow officers standing there looking at him as if he had the plague.

Ignoring their stares, Jerry walked to his cubicle, placed his hat in the chair, and continued to the coffee station, taking his time to fill his cup. *Just act normal, Jerry. What a joke; there's nothing normal about you. Never has been and never will be.*

Most of the time, he didn't give a rat's ass what anyone else thought, but ever since the dog had shown up, even he had questioned his sanity. *Come on, Jerry, stop being so dramatic – it's not like you haven't seen ghosts before.*

Jerry wondered what Seltzer thought of the situation. It wasn't like he hadn't tried to warn the man. *Yeah, and then you passed it off as a joke the second he acted as if he didn't believe you. You should have tried harder.* The fact that his sergeant hadn't already made an appearance spoke for itself. It was clear the man had finally reached his limit. Unable to delay any longer, Jerry went to Seltzer's office.

The door was open. Seltzer looked up and motioned him in. "Kick the door around, McNeal."

Jerry shut the door and stood rigid in front of his desk.

Seltzer waved him off. "At ease, McNeal. You're not on report."

Jerry relaxed but continued to stand.

Seltzer got up and looked around the room before walking to the window and looking out. "The video came in from Hershey. I'm not the only one who saw it. Peters saw it as well. He's worked a few cases with them, so I'm guessing they already had his e-mail plugged in. Still, he didn't have to show it to the others."

"I didn't push the woman."

"That part was obvious."

"I get the feeling there's a but in there."

"What the heck were you doing in the store?"

"Shopping."

"For a dog you don't own and talking to a person that wasn't there," Seltzer blurted.

So that was it. The guys didn't know about his ghostly visitor. They just thought he was crazy. Jerry pondered his new dilemma. Was one level of crazy better than the other? Would either option allow him to remain on the job? Did he even want to stay? Too many questions and not enough answers. He needed some time to work out his response. "Can I see the evidence?"

Seltzer hesitated briefly, then shrugged. "You're going to see it eventually. Might as well have a look."

Jerry waited for Seltzer to pull up the video, watching the set of the man's mouth as he turned the screen around. It must be bad if the sergeant couldn't find a reason to make a quip. The video clip began with Jerry walking into the store. Uniform pressed and brimmed hat sitting high upon his sleek head, Jerry walked through the sliding door like a man on a mission. Though Jerry knew Gunter to have been at his side, the dog wasn't present in the video. *Then why had he shown up in the photo Holly took?* Just thinking of Holly pulled at his heart.

Focus, Jerry.

Jerry blinked and refocused his attention on the video, which showed him starting up the aisle that held the dog toys. He stopped pushing the cart and appeared to be speaking to someone. He was getting ready to tell his boss that he'd been singing along with the music when the video showed him reaching for a ball. He questioned the invisible entity then chose another. The evidence showed him doing something similar twice more before leaving the aisle. By the time he'd watched the entire clip, even Jerry further questioned his mental stability.

Seltzer canceled the file then pulled up another one that started with Jerry coming face to face with his accuser. The woman bolted the second she saw him – running away on her own accord. A second before she fell, Jerry lifted a hand and splayed his fingers – mouthing something that sent her sliding across the floor. *Crap.*

"There's another clip if you want to see it. It zooms in on your mouth and clearly shows you telling the woman to stop."

"Would you have preferred me to shoot her for shoplifting?"

Seltzer eyeballed him before replaying the last scene. He stopped at the point where Jerry lifted his hand. "I watched this a dozen times. The more I view it, the more I feel like I'm watching a movie where the sorcerer casts a spell on someone. A few special effects and you've got yourself a viral Tik-Tok video. Seriously, McNeal, I don't know what to tell Derry, much less the guys in the department."

Jerry wasn't worried about Derry. After telling the woman they had video of her and her husband shoplifting, both had admitted to their crimes. "Hershey isn't a problem."

"And the men in the other room?"

No guts, no glory, Jerry. "Tell them the truth."

Seltzer raised an eyebrow. "How about you start by

telling me?"

"I did. Or at least I tried to. Right here in this room yesterday."

Seltzer stared at Jerry, mouth agape. "The dog?"

"Yep."

Seltzer pulled a stick of gum from a pack, unwrapped it, and stuck it in his mouth, then offered one to Jerry, who declined. "You mean to tell me that Gunter has returned from the dead?"

"Yep."

"And it was the dog that pushed the woman down?"

"It's the truth. Listen, I know that I can feel things before they happen and see things that aren't there, but that's where my abilities stop." Jerry held out his hands, turning them to show they were simply hands. "If you want to call those things magic, so be it. But I assure you that is where my 'gift' ends. I'm not a sorcerer, warlock, or any of the other things your mind might conjure up."

Seltzer blew out a whistle. "So you're telling me the dog did it?"

Jerry nodded.

"I always thought of ghosts as a mist of some sort. I didn't know they could be firm enough to send a person flying like that."

Jerry was genuinely surprised his sergeant admitted to having given ghosts any thought at all. "Not every accident is as innocent as it seems. Have you ever tripped over your own two feet, stumbled up the stairs, or caught your finger in a car door?"

Seltzer's eyes grew wide. "Jeez, McNeal, we have a hard enough time trying to prosecute the living. You can't go around telling people stuff like that."

"I don't intend to."

Seltzer stopped chewing his gum. "You want me to tell them?"

Jerry shook his head. "Those guys aren't going to believe either of us."

"I'm not following you, McNeal."

"We just need to convince one."

Seltzer leaned back in his chair. "If we convince Manning, he does the rest."

Jerry nodded.

"Any idea how you intend on getting the man to believe you?"

"Not a clue."

Seltzer smiled. "Glad to hear you have things under control. When do you want to do this?"

"I guess now's as good a time as any."

"You mean the dog's here?"

"Appeared a few minutes after I came into the room."

Seltzer stood, peered over the desk, and sighed his disappointment. "McNeal, if I didn't know better, I would swear you're pulling my leg."

"I wouldn't do that, sir."

"I know, which is the only reason I haven't requested your gun and badge. What now?"

"Call Manning in and pray something comes to me."

Seltzer lifted his phone, punched in the numbers to Manning's desk, telling him to come to his office, then lowered the receiver. "I hope this works."

"You and me both."

Gunter jumped up, placing his paws on Seltzer's desk, and barked at the monitor. Not only did Jerry know what the dog was trying to convey, but he thought it was a splendid idea. "Did Derry send you the whole video?"

"They did, but I haven't looked at it all." He smiled a

sheepish grin. "I kind of lost my stomach for it after I saw you cast the spell."

"Understood. While I'm talking to Manning, pull it up. Pause it when you see me first get to the toy aisle." Jerry felt Manning's presence even before the man cleared his throat to announce his appearance.

"You wanted to see me, sir?"

Seltzer motioned him in and pointed at the chair next to Jerry. Manning pulled the chair to the side and sat leaning far away from Jerry.

Jerry gripped the sidearms of his chair, thinking to slide his chair closer. Seltzer shot him a look that said *you wanted this meeting*, and Jerry thought better of it. Staying where he was, he turned his body toward Manning. "There's no easy way to say this, so I'll just say it and be done. Gunter's ghost is here, and he seems to have taken an interest in me."

Manning fist-pumped the air, grinning like a boy who'd just gotten his first kiss. "I knew it!"

No way it could be that easy. Jerry looked at Seltzer, who also blinked his disbelief, then turned back to Manning. "You're not surprised?"

"No offense, McNeal, but when it comes to you, nothing surprises me."

"None taken. So you're saying you've seen him?"

"No, just a feeling. Not like your feelings," Manning added a little too quickly. "But ever since our little run-in yesterday, I've gotten the feeling I wasn't alone. Not all the time, but enough to know something was up."

"Do you feel him now?"

Manning nodded his head and looked beside his chair. The problem was that the dog was nowhere near where the man was looking.

Jerry did a head tilt to let Seltzer know the situation. Great, either the man was trying to humor him or was still grieving so much he wanted to feel the dog's presence. Jerry decided to go with the latter. "I think he thinks he's still alive. He's still on the job and has helped me twice."

Manning bristled. "Why's he helping you? I'm his partner."

"Maybe it's because I can see him."

Manning's face turned red, and he pulled back the hand that had been pretending to pet the dog. "You can?"

"When he wants me to. He was just at your side."

Manning looked at the spot beside the chair, and Jerry looked at Seltzer, who'd obviously caught the lie. "You got that video, Sergeant?"

"I do." Seltzer turned the screen around.

Jerry pointed to the monitor. "You've seen the video, right?"

Manning nodded. "I have."

"Go ahead and push play."

Seltzer did, and Jerry pointed to the screen once more. "Gunter was with me in the store. Walking on my left side."

"He always walked on my left." Manning sighed a heavy sigh. "I wish I could see him."

"You will. In just a minute." Seltzer started to object, and Jerry raised a hand to silence him. The video showed Jerry reaching for a ball. "Stop the video. I started to pick out a ball, and Gunter stopped me because he didn't like the ball. Start the video."

Manning gasped when Jerry moved his hand to a different ball. "That kind was always his favorite. He never liked tennis balls, only the rubber ones."

The video showed Jerry coming face to face with the

woman and showed her dropping the can. She took off running, then crashed to the floor. Manning jumped up and bit at the back of his knuckle while pointing at the screen with his other hand. "Oh man, I could see him running and slamming into her. Not on the video, but I've seen Gunter do it enough that I could tell what happened."

Sergeant Seltzer started to stop the video, and Jerry shook his head. "Let it run."

Seltzer moved to see the screen better, and they all watched as the manager and several employees came into view. A man joined them, struggling to maintain control of an obese pit bull that seemed to have taken exception to Jerry.

"His name's Tiny." Jerry motioned to the screen. "Gunter is about to take control of the scene. He'd disappeared after the manager showed up but came back just as I thought the leash would break. The instant I felt him appear, I raised my right hand. Of course, they thought I'd done something amazing, but the only thing I was guilty of was trying to decide if I was going to climb up the shelves or try to make it to the door if Tiny got loose. Keep watching. Here it comes."

Seltzer and Manning leaned toward the screen, watching as the big dog went from full Cujo to absolute wimp in a matter of seconds.

Manning looked at Jerry. "What'd Gunter do?"

"He didn't do anything. He just appeared. I'm not sure if Tiny actually saw him or just felt his presence, but he was having no part of it."

Seltzer shook his head. "Well, I'll be..."

Jerry smiled at Manning, who was beaming like a proud papa. "The thing is, we can't let him keep doing things like this."

Both Seltzer and Manning stared at him. It was Seltzer who finally spoke. "We can't?"

"No, it's not fair to the dog. He's lived his life and needs to cross over to the other side."

Manning brushed his hand through his hair. "How do you get him to do that?"

"Not me, you."

"Me? I thought you said he's attached to you."

"Only because I can see him. He needed to come and make sure you were okay. Now that he knows you are – you are, aren't you?"

"I guess. I mean, yes, I am."

"Okay, so now you need to tell him it's time to go."

Manning looked around the room. "Is he here?"

"He is." Jerry pointed to where Gunter sat, intently watching the three of them. "Right over there."

Manning walked to the spot where Jerry indicated. "It's time to cross over now. I'm going to be just fine."

Jerry sighed when the dog looked at him and yawned. "Try it again. A little firmer this time."

"Maybe he doesn't want to go."

I want him to go. "Try it again."

"Okay, Gunter, enough of the heroics. You're off duty. Now go." Manning looked at Jerry, and Jerry smiled. "You mean he's gone?"

Jerry walked over and clamped the man on the shoulder. "You'll not have to worry about him anymore."

"He's gone. I knew it. I felt it the moment he left. He's in a good place now. Happier. I'm glad you let me know he's okay."

"Now I just have to convince the rest of the guys that I'm not crazy."

Manning brightened. "Don't you worry about that. I'll

tell them."

"You're a good man, Manning."

"You're not so bad yourself, McNeal."

Seltzer waited for Manning to leave the room before speaking. "The dog's still here, isn't he?"

"Yep."

"Shouldn't it have worked?"

"It did on *The Ghost Whisperer.*"

"Do you know how crazy this all sounds?"

"Yep."

"Now what?"

Jerry looked at the dog, which had once again plastered himself by his side. "I haven't got a clue."

Chapter Eight

Jerry made a beeline for Manning's SUV parked on the far side of the parking lot. Once there, he opened the back door and waited for Gunter to jump inside before slamming the door behind him. With the dog placed in his rightful ride, Jerry hurried to his cruiser, started it, and took off without even giving the car a chance to warm up. As he made a left out of the lot, he glanced in the rearview mirror and saw Gunter's golden-brown eyes staring back at him.

"You know I'm used to working alone, right?" Gunter tilted his head in response. "Listen, Boy, it's not that I have anything against dogs, but the thing is, I've never actually owned one. Given you don't seem to like me, I think it's best if we part ways."

His words prompted a head-tilt in the opposite direction. Not sure what else to say, Jerry concentrated on the road, avoiding the constant impulse to look in the mirror to see if the dog was still there. Not that he had to, as he could feel the dog's presence.

Over the next few hours, Jerry covered the interstate

between Carlisle and Greencastle. Each time he neared Chambersburg, the feeling that something was going to happen intensified. While he didn't know what his senses were picking up, experience told him he still had time to figure it out. He drove around all the area schools and felt certain those were not the intended target.

Just for the heck of it, he drove past Wilson College, happy when his feeling of dread didn't peak. He turned around, then cut through Norland Avenue, making a pass around each of the medical complexes before heading over to Lincoln Highway and stopping at Sheetz for a cup of coffee and hotdog.

The parking lot was full, so he backed into a space near the road and left the car idling, surprised when Gunter seemed content to wait in the cruiser. Jerry headed straight to the coffee station and smiled at an elderly man, who looked up when he neared. The man returned his smile and backed out the way long enough for Jerry to pour himself a cup of black coffee. Jerry recognized the man, who liked his coffee sweet and took his time doctoring it to his satisfaction. Jerry thanked him and went to the kiosk, tapping the screen to order his lunch. He started to complete his transaction, then reconsidered. Though he'd set out some dog food this morning, the dog had refused to eat. Using the back key, he added a second hotdog to his order.

As Jerry stood waiting for them to call his number, the hair on the back of his neck began to tingle. Instantly on alert, he scanned the store. Several men in business suits stood chatting about a stock they were following. A young man in military fatigues now stood near the coffee station waiting his turn at the counter, while the same older gentleman continued to fumble with his creamers. There were seven open pods on the counter in front of him and three more at the ready. Jerry made eye contact with the younger man and took a sip of his black coffee. The young man smiled and shook his head. While the man fidgeted with impatience, he didn't set off any alarm bells.

Looking in the opposite direction, Jerry saw a young woman wearing a pink puff coat with maroon medical scrubs underneath, pulling several caffeine-laden drinks from behind the glass door of the refrigerator section. The woman looked tired, as if just ending a long shift.

She should be going to bed, so why the need for so much caffeine?

She turned, saw him looking, brushed the hair from her face, and headed for the donut case.

Though Jerry could empathize with the woman, she nor any of the others set off further alarm bells. And yet, the skin on his neck continued to crawl.

Come on, Jerry, you're missing something. Focus.

"Number 51," a voice called from behind the counter.

Jerry started to walk toward the counter, and the man who'd been fumbling with the creamers cut him off. He waited for the man to hobble out of the way and then moved in to claim his order.

"Have a good day, officer," the brown-eyed girl said, handing him the bag.

As Jerry took it, the feeling of dread dissolved. He turned, making another visual sweep of the area. The two men in suits were gone, as was the woman wearing scrubs. He hurried to the counter in long, determined strides while pulling several singles from his wallet. He handed the woman the ticket along with enough to cover the total with a few pennies left over, then made a beeline for the door.

"Stay safe out there," the woman behind the counter

called after him.

Jerry heard the pennies clink in the extra penny tray that sat on the counter and waved a hand over his shoulder in response. The two men he'd seen inside now continued their conversation just outside the door. Jerry made a point of walking near where they were standing, resisting a sigh when his intuition didn't key on either of them. That left the young woman in scrubs, who was nowhere in sight. What he could see was the German shepherd, who'd moved to the front passenger seat in his absence.

"I don't suppose you saw where the woman went," he asked as he slid behind the wheel. Gunter cocked his head to the side in response. Jerry pulled a hotdog from the bag, unwrapped the foil, and set it on the console. He pulled out the second one, unwrapped it, and took a bite. Gunter licked his lips but made no move to retrieve the hotdog Jerry had placed for him. Jerry nodded toward the hotdog. "Go on, eat."

Gunter bent, sniffed the offering, and promptly disappeared.

Jerry finished his hotdog then, deciding the dog wasn't coming back, ate the other one as well. As he sat drinking his coffee, he thought of the woman who'd set off his inner alarm. While Jerry knew her to be involved, the feeling hadn't been strong enough to consider her the main threat, target, or victim, or whatever his radar was picking up on. Still, he wished he'd been alert enough not to let her slip through his fingers. Following her could have led to the person or persons who would need his help.

He recalled his conversation with Manning and sighed. The man had been right; Jerry was able to pick up on everyone but still not able to save friends. Okay, so technically, the dog wasn't a friend. He looked over his shoulder, half expecting the dog to be there, surprised to feel somewhat disappointed that he wasn't. Manning thought the dog was gone; would it be so bad to let him hang around? *Give it a rest, Jerry. You don't even like dogs.*

Jerry crumpled the foil and tossed it into the sack. He started to set the bag on the floorboard then changed his mind. Exiting the car, he walked to the front of the building, stepped around the two men who continued to chat despite the frigid air, and tossed the bag in the trash.

"Have a good day," he said, stepping around them for the third time.

"You too," both men replied, confirming what he already knew. Neither of the men had triggered his early warning system. Returning to his police cruiser, he hesitated at seeing a shadow in the backseat. Not only had the dog returned, he was currently lying across the length of the backseat chewing on a meaty bone.

The dog paused from his gnawing, tilting his head as if asking if Jerry were going to stand out in the cold all day.

Jerry looked in the mirror, making eye contact with the dog as he slid behind the wheel. "I don't want to know where you got that. And no blood on the seat; we're already on thin ice with the sergeant."

Gunter licked his lips and went back to chewing on the bone.

Jerry pulled out of his parking spot and drove to the exit debating his next move. The woman had been wearing scrubs. She'd looked tired, but the drink she'd purchased had enough caffeine to keep her awake most of the day. *Maybe she plans to work a double shift. Logical. Okay, hospital or medical office?* Though he'd already made passes around both Chambersburg Hospital and the largest medical complex in town, he decided to give the area another sweep to see if doing so would tweak his inner radar. He turned right and drove the short distance to the hospital. He didn't have to go inside; if the threat had been there, he would have known. He saw the sign that read emergency entrance and thought of Holly.

Focus, Jerry.

Leaving the hospital parking lot, he made his way back to Norland Road; knowing the duration of the drive, he was following the wrong lead. He decided to make another sweep of 81 and started toward Carlisle. Once again, his intuition told him he was going the wrong way, so he pulled into the center median, intending to turn back in the direction he'd just come. Instead of pulling out, he shifted the cruiser into park and sat with his hands pressed together watching the traffic pass. Sitting there served two purposes – it gave him time to clear his mind and slowed traffic – at least until the drivers thought they were out of radar range.

He smiled, knowing the only radar they were on was the one hardwired into his brain. He wondered how the conversation would go if he actually got a hit.

"Sir or madam, step out of your vehicle."

"Is there a problem, officer?"

"Yes, my spider senses told me you're about to do something awful." He didn't like the term spider – or spidey senses – the names Sergeant Seltzer had given his ability – but he'd never been able to come up with anything better. As it was, none of the cars triggered any feelings, so he decided to take his search elsewhere. He waited for an opening then eased into traffic. The moment he turned back to Chambersburg, he knew he'd made the right decision. He took the Lincoln Highway exit, and Gunter whined.

Jerry looked in the mirror, watching as the dog paced from one side of the car to the other. "Either you need to go to the bathroom or you approve of my choice."

The dog answered with a single bark.

"You let yourself in. I suppose you can let yourself out." Jerry changed lanes then took the Lincoln Highway exit. Having chosen the same exit multiple times, he knew whatever was to take place would occur on or near that highway. He'd no sooner given in to that thought when he saw the banners announcing the psychic convention. Had he missed them before, or had someone just set them out? He decided it was the latter, as surely he would have seen them blowing against the wind. He turned on his turn signal and eased into the parking lot, and instantly knew he'd found what he was searching for.

"Do you feel it too?" Jerry asked when the hairs on the back of his neck began to prickle. Since he normally worked on his own, it came as a surprise how excited he was to share the feeling with someone – even if the someone in question was a ninety-pound German shepherd no longer of this world. "It's a bit early yet, don't you think? Probably another day, maybe two?"

Gunter paced the backseat, barking his disappointment as Jerry cruised through the parking lot and pulled back onto Lincoln Highway without stopping.

"Nothing's stopping you from getting out," Jerry said when the shepherd turned and looked out the back window, sealing his discontent with a low growl. The dog stayed put, stretching across the backseat to chew on the bone as Jerry turned toward the Borough to make another pass. He drove to the far side of town before circling back and veering his police cruiser into the parking lot across the street from where the psychic convention was to be held. He parked in the rear of the lot, angling so that he could see the main entrance to the building across the street without drawing unwanted attention. The second he put the shifter into park, Gunter materialized onto the passenger side seat, panting so hard, the front windshield began to fog.

"You're a ghost. How can your breath be so warm?"

Gunter curled his lip and growled a soft growl.

Jerry chuckled. "You're offended at being called a ghost?"

Another growl.

"You do know you're dead, right? I mean, that would explain your walking through walls and disappearing and reappearing in the front seat."

This statement provoked a full snarl.

"Hey, don't be sore at me. I'm not the one that killed you. Okay, full disclosure," Jerry said when the dog tilted his head. "You got shot protecting your partner. You had a grand funeral, and for some reason neither of us has figured out, you came back. Only instead of haunting your former partner, I seem to be stuck with you."

Gunter barked a ferocious bark.

"Okay, okay. For some reason, you've decided I deserve your company. Better?"

Gunter looked at Jerry and licked his lips.

Recalling the bloody bone, Jerry rolled his neck from side to side. "I'm not sure I like that answer."

It wasn't that Jerry didn't like dogs, not really anyway. Saying he didn't like them was a defense mechanism – they were the ones that had built that barrier – running from him – barking whenever he was near and growling when he happened to look in their direction. It had been that way since he was a child. As he sat there staring at the dog, he realized he'd never even gotten close enough to one to feel the softness of their fur. He reached his hand, wondering if it would feel as warm as the breath steaming up the windows. As he neared the dog's head, Gunter whipped around, capturing his hand between his teeth. He gave a warning growl before letting go.

Jerry retracted his hand, nervously inspecting it for tooth marks. "If you don't like me, why are you here?"

The dog cocked his head to the side as if saying, *I've been wondering the same thing myself.*

Chapter Nine

Manning was sitting in his SUV when Jerry arrived at the station at the end of their shift. Seeing Jerry, he climbed out and hurried to greet him. "Is he still gone?"

"Close your eyes."

Manning did as told.

"Do you feel him?"

Manning's brow furrowed then relaxed as he opened his eyes. "No, I think I did it. I helped him find his peace. I think helping him helped me. I've felt so calm today."

"Good deal." Jerry cast a glance at Gunter, who was standing at his side wagging his tail. *At least someone is getting some peace.*

"Maybe that's my new calling. Helping people cross over."

Oh, boy. "I don't think it works like that. I think it worked this time because you had a personal connection to the spirit."

"But it couldn't hurt to try, right? I mean, I don't see them like you do, but if I feel one near, maybe I should tell him it's okay to cross over. That would be alright, don't you think?"

"Sure, Manning."

"Cool. Oh, and I talked to the guys. They were skeptical at first, but then I showed them the tape, and they all saw it too. They think it's pretty cool that Gunter was still on the job. Too bad he had to cross over; we'd make national news. Boy, what a great dog he was." Gunter jumped up on Manning, licking the side of his cheek, and Jerry felt a tinge of jealousy. Manning looked to the sky and brushed away the moisture. "Hey, we'd better get inside; I think it's starting to rain. Glad it held off until the end of our shift."

They walked into the building together, and everyone greeted them with casual indifference. Jerry tossed his hat onto his chair, changed out of his uniform, and headed to Seltzer's office.

"Is he with you?" Sergeant Seltzer asked the moment Jerry entered.

"Joined at the hip."

Seltzer's eyes twinkled. "That must be amazing."

"More like a pain in the ass. I don't know what's worse, him or the cat." *At least the cat seems to like me.*

Seltzer raised an eyebrow. "I never pictured you as a cat guy."

"I'm full of surprises."

"To say the least. Any trouble with the guys?"

"No, apparently, seeing ghosts trumps crazy."

Seltzer chuckled. "Seeing ghosts trumps everything."

"You might want to keep an eye on Manning."

"Is there a problem?"

"I think helping the dog cross was akin to a religious experience. He thinks he has a gift."

"Well, crap."

"Yep."

"You got any preference for patrols tomorrow?"

"I'm going to stay local."

"Your spidey senses tingling?"

Jerry rolled his neck. "Something's brewing."

"Big?"

"I picked up something today. Might be something minor, but whatever it is will need a delicate touch."

Seltzer popped a stick of gum into his mouth and leaned back in his chair. "And you think that's you?"

"Just call me Mr. Finesse."

Seltzer frowned. "Should I bring in more guys?"

"No. I don't think that's necessary."

"You're the boss," Seltzer said, then laughed at the irony.

Jerry knew the risk his boss took each time he allowed him to take the lead on his hunches. Jerry smiled a weak smile. "I'll let you know if anything changes."

Seltzer studied him for a moment. "It's not like you to change before going home."

The man was good. Still, Jerry decided not to share his decision to investigate the psychic convention a bit further. "Thought I'd stop off for a beer."

"You need anything, call my cell." Seltzer hadn't bought the ruse, not that Jerry expected him to.

"Roger that, sir."

"You sure you don't want to tell me where you're going just in case?"

Jerry raised an eyebrow. "So you can have some units in the area? I don't think it's necessary tonight."

"I could order you to tell me."

"I'd lie. Besides, not knowing gives you plausible deniability." Jerry looked at the dog, whose pointed ears had been following the conversation like a beacon. "I'm not going alone."

"Who?"

Jerry jerked his thumb toward Gunter. "He might not like me much, but he seems to be good in a pinch. I have your number on speed dial."

Seltzer looked in the direction of Jerry's hip. "Watch over him, Gunter."

Jerry smiled. He didn't have the heart to tell the man that the dog he was addressing had already moved to the door.

***

Jerry opened the door to his beat-down old Chevy truck, and the dog cut him off, entering with a single leap and moving to the passenger side. Jerry followed him in, sliding behind the wheel and sticking the key into the ignition. He stepped his left foot on the brake, pumping the gas with his right as he turned the key, listening as the engine rolled over a couple of times before sputtering to life. Jerry breathed a sigh of relief then fiddled with the heater, blowing into his hands as he waited for the engine to warm up. He glanced at Gunter, who yawned his disapproval. "You don't approve, find another ride."

Unwavering, the dog licked his lips.

"It's ugly, but it's paid for and dependable, at least most of the time." Jerry pushed on the brake and moved the gearshift into reverse. He crept from the parking lot, then shifted several times as the truck got up to speed. At the end of the road, he geared down, made another left onto Lincoln Highway, shifting and downshifting as traffic warranted. As he drove, Gunter grew restless, whining his aggravation with each delay. Jerry fully understood the dog's frustration and continued down the road as if being led by an invisible guide wire that pulled him toward the building he'd staked out earlier in the day. While the energy pull had escalated, Jerry knew they still had time until the main event.

He backed into a parking space at the far corner of the lot, then headed toward the building with the dog at his side. He reached for the door then hesitated. "You're not wearing a collar or leash. Maybe you should stay outside."

The dog barked then looked toward the door.

"Okay, but if anyone sees you, I'll deny knowing you." With that, Jerry pulled open the door and walked inside, hesitating momentarily as the energy within the building nearly overloaded his senses.

After several seconds of angst, a sudden calmness washed over him. He looked to see a woman with unnaturally black hair making her way toward him. Despite the weather, she wore open sandals and a multicolored kimono that swept the floor as she walked. Her gaze settled on Gunter and her brows knitted. Her lids lifted with sudden realization, and she visibly swallowed her fear. Jerry instantly knew she was the real deal. Recovering her composure, she smiled broadly, greeting him as one would an old friend. "Welcome. Did you come for a reading?"

I'm not sure why I'm here. Jerry shrugged. "Just thought I'd see what all the fuss is about."

"You've come for answers. I would tell you which tables to avoid," she looked at Gunter once more, "but something tells me you don't need my help with that."

He wasn't sure what to say, so he said nothing.

Unfazed, she licked her painted lips. "Take a walk around. You'll know when you find what you're looking for – and, officer, thank you for not coming in uniform."

Jerry cocked his head and looked at the woman more closely. It took him a second, but he recognized her as the woman he'd seen wearing scrubs earlier in the day. Sporting heavy make-up, she no longer looked as haggard as she'd appeared when he'd first seen her. The feeling that he'd gotten earlier was no longer linked solely to the woman but more to the building they were standing in. There was more to it, but he knew she was not directly involved with whatever "it" was.

Jerry stood near the opening to the main room, which was alive with excited energy and calming music. Healing drums beat in the distance, luring some in the crowd to the far corner of the room. People of all ages and ethnicity walked about with casual curiosity, inspecting tables covered with crystals, candles, and healing stones. Others sat, desperately holding on to what the medium across the table was telling them. A few held the tepid energy of skeptics – walking around bemused – as if wondering what had led them there. Jerry felt a kinship to those individuals – though he'd been pulled to the space by the "feeling" – he mostly identified with the tepid skeptics, the ones who wanted all the answers but were too cynical to believe anyone capable of delivering them.

He didn't have to enter to find what he was looking for, as the feeling pulled at him like a homing device until, at last, he found himself staring at a young woman who looked to be in her early twenties. She sat at a table close to the door. A stand-up display behind her chair showed a pendulum hovering over a spread-out deck of tarot cards and bold gold lettering introducing her as Mistress Savannah. The write-up underneath her name promised to guide you to what you're looking for, primarily focusing on LOVE, HAPPINESS, and SUCCESS.

Savannah. Jerry wondered if that was the girl's given name or one she'd selected to go with her profession. *It works either way.* The girl emitted an aura of mystery. Round face with even rounder eyes, both deeply shadowed to give her a sultry look, she licked her richly painted lips, pulled another card from the deck, and placed it on the table with the rest.

The man sitting at her table stared straight ahead, making Jerry wonder if he was listening to anything she said. From his puppy-dog infatuated expression, she could just as well be reading from the sports page. It was apparent why he'd chosen her table – the girl was "gifted" in other ways. That she'd chosen to embrace her attributes was evident, as her purple dress showed enough cleavage to allow her to stand out from those not so well-endowed.

Savannah looked up, saw Jerry staring at her, and smiled a brilliant smile. She slid the tip of her tongue over her lips, batted her long lashes, and motioned him over with a crook of the finger. "I'll be with you shortly," she said, reaching around the man at her table to hand Jerry a business card.

Jerry glanced at the card. *Why go on not knowing about your life? Let Mistress Savannah, healer of the heart, lead you out of the dark.* There was a phone number listed on the back of the card. One look at the number told him it wasn't a local number. Not a surprise, as it was not unusual for conventions to bring in people from out of state. Jerry winked and made a show of tucking the card into his pocket. While he wasn't interested in the girl's thoughts on Love, Happiness, or Success, he was highly interested in why his radar told him she was in trouble – furthermore, the cynical part of him wanted to ask why she didn't already know it.

Deciding to stay inconspicuous, Jerry started walking, thinking to circle the room, intending to slip into the chair once the gentleman that currently occupied it left. He realized Gunter was no longer with him and turned to see the dog sitting beside the table, staring at Savannah with his golden-brown puppy-dog eyes.

Wow, she's good.

Jerry clapped the side of his leg. Gunter's ears twitched, but the dog made no move to join him. He thought to go get him but decided against it. *Not my dog, not my problem.* Besides, the woman hadn't even acknowledged Gunter's presence. *Maybe she can't see him. Perhaps you're the only one that can, Jerry. Not true. Holly not only saw him, she has proof of his existence on her camera. The woman at the door saw him too!* "I'm not the only one."

"Excuse me?"

Jerry turned to see an older woman staring at him. He made a show of removing something from his ear and stuffing it into his pocket. "Sorry, I was on the phone. Bluetooth."

"Oh." The woman smiled, then continued on her way.

Keep it up, Jerry, and they'll have you committed. Just as the thought came to him, a short, stocky man wearing a helmet made entirely of aluminum foil strolled past, muttering to himself. *Great, Jerry McNeal, prior Marine and current Pennsylvania State Trooper, finds himself right at home in a room full of...full of what, Jerry? What makes these people any different than you? You're the one that keeps running away. The guy with the foil might be a complete nutjob, but at least he owns his crazy, not walking through the crowd hiding who he really is. You're the imposter, Jerry. Heck, even the dog is sitting out in the open.*

As the realization hit him, Jerry turned and headed toward the exit. With each step, a voice pulled at him, telling him he hadn't accomplished what he'd come here to do. No, but he was doing something he was good at – running away. He'd run away from home – not in the physical sense – but he'd left as soon as he was old enough to go without being made to return.

He'd run from the Marines – when time and time again, he'd not been able to save his brothers from dying, even though he knew tragedy was about to occur. Manning had been right – he'd even failed to protect the dog. He could have. He'd felt something that morning – a strong pull when he'd seen Manning heading to his SUV with the dog at his side. But it was Manning – something about the guy rubbed him the wrong way, and the dog had paid the price. The thing that haunted Jerry – aside from the dog – was that it could have been Manning that Chambersburg had to bury. In ignoring his so-called gift, had he in some way played God? Was that why the dog decided to haunt him? As penance for not helping his partner?

Just as Jerry reached the door, Gunter barked. Jerry turned and saw the chair in front of Savannah was vacant. She noticed him looking and smiled. In that instant, Jerry knew if he left, he'd be making another fatal mistake. *She's going to die if I don't figure out what is going to happen.*

Jerry turned, retracing his steps. Just before he reached her table, a man cut him off, sinking into the empty chair. As soon as Jerry saw the two together, his feeling of doom escalated to a whole new level.

The dog tilted his head to the side, looking at Jerry as if to say, *You had your chance and blew it. Again.*

Crap.

Chapter Ten

With the two key players identified, Jerry's training took over. While instincts told him to scoop the man up and drag him from the room, the cop in him knew the man hadn't done anything to warrant intervention. Even though Jerry had earned a reputation for knowing when something might happen, the legal system still needed a crime. Telling a judge he had a feeling the man was going to commit a crime would get him nowhere. Besides, while the feeling was strong, it wasn't call-the-cavalry strong. Savannah was safe – at least for the time being.

A man walked past, bumped into Jerry, and mumbled something about him blocking the aisle.

Go easy, Jerry. Stop drawing attention to yourself. You still have plenty of time.

Taking his own advice, Jerry walked to the closest wall, positioning himself so he could see both Savannah and her new client. The man was cleanshaven, appropriately dressed in jeans and jacket, and appeared calm enough. Unlike the previous man, this guy actually seemed to be staring at the girl's face and not her breasts.

Savannah slid a credit card reader across the table, waited for her client to insert his card, then pulled the reader out of his reach, simultaneously pushing the button on a small timer and turning it for him to see. So far, everything seemed above board.

Savannah chatted with the man for a moment, then shuffled the tarot cards, placing them onto the table in groups of three. Still chatting with the man, she lifted a card, frowned, then instantly covered with the same brilliant smile she'd used on Jerry earlier. If the man had noticed the fleeting frown, he didn't let on. Instead, he tapped a second card. Savannah lifted the card, sucked in a breath of air, then returned it to the table without comment. Still talking to the man, she snuck a peek at the last card. Her expression remained nonplussed as she gathered the cards and placed them to the side without explanation. The man looked at the table, a frown creasing his forehead. The frown lessened the instant Savannah took his hand in hers.

She flipped the hand so she could see his palm, studied it briefly, then pointed something out with the index finger of her right hand. Whatever she told him must have resonated, as his shoulders relaxed. He said something to her, and she pointed to his palm once more. Savannah seemed slightly more at ease now, though her smile still seemed a bit forced. She chatted with the man for several more moments before lifting her hands, as if telling him that was all. As if to firm her point, she pressed the button on the timer and pulled his card from the reader, handing it over to him. He stood, returned the card to his wallet, and left. Unlike others who continued to walk through the room, the man headed straight for the door. As he neared, Jerry went into cop mode, making a mental note of the man's description – brown hair, hazel eyes, and a faded scar just over the guy's left eyebrow. He also noted red clay on the edge of the guy's work boot and used the doorframe to gauge his height as he exited the room. Though the guy was smiling when he left, the feeling of unease hovered over him like a dark raincloud as he left.

Jerry thought about following him, but experience told him there was no need. Whatever was going to happen was going to take place on these premises. Soon, but not tonight. While he still didn't know what it was, he knew it would involve the mysterious Savannah.

Jerry pushed off the wall, walked to Savannah's table, and claimed the empty chair.

"I'm sorry about before," she said, glancing toward the door. "I thought about telling the guy you were next, but I wasn't sure if you were actually interested in a reading or just hanging around for the view."

Jerry smiled, keeping his eyes above her neckline. "You're a lovely young lady."

She cocked her head to the side. "I detect a 'but' in there."

"But...you're not my type."

She smiled. "And yet here you are."

"Here I am," Jerry agreed.

Savannah slid the card reader across the table, waited for Jerry to insert his card, then pressed the timer as she'd done with her previous client. Pulling the card reader out of reach, she turned her palms up, sweeping them across the table. "So, what will it be, cards or palm?"

"How about I let you decide?"

"Cards it is." She picked up the tarot deck and began shuffling. "Ask the cards your question as I'm shuffling. What will it be: Love, Happiness, or Success?"

Jerry shrugged. "Why don't we let the cards decide what they want me to know?"

"Suit yourself." After a moment, she stopped shuffling and dealt them onto the table in three separate piles. After placing the final card onto the center pile, she lifted her gaze to him. "Pick three in any order."

Jerry studied the deck for a moment, then tapped the center pile, the one to the left, and lastly, tapped a finger on the card to the right.

Savannah hesitated for a moment before turning over the middle card. Once she did, she let out an audible sigh then turned the other two over in order. "If that isn't a clear message, I don't know what is."

Jerry looked at the cards. "All I see is a shepherd in a flowing white robe, a man driving a chariot, and a man holding a wand."

Savannah laughed a carefree laugh. "That's why you're paying me to interpret for you."

Also known as throwing money out the window. Jerry resisted voicing that aloud as she pointed to the first card.

"The Hermit signifies a journey." She motioned to the card with the chariot. "This also signifies a journey. Care to guess what this one means?"

Jerry looked at the card with the man holding the wand. "That you're going to wave your magic wand and send me away?"

"Not me, but it's the King of Wands, which shows the journey could begin at any moment. Are you planning on taking a trip?"

Jerry thought to tell her he'd been moments from fleeing when his conscience made him come back, but decided against it. "Nope."

She frowned and mumbled something under her breath.

"Excuse me?"

"What? Oh, nothing." She scooped the cards into a pile, set them aside, and reached for his hand. "I'm much better at reading palms."

Jerry raised a brow. "I couldn't help notice you had trouble with the last gentleman who occupied this chair."

Savannah's mouth fell open, and she narrowed her eyes. "You were watching?"

"Waiting my turn," Jerry corrected.

"Invading a man's privacy's more like it," she said sharply.

Too sharply – leading Jerry to believe she was more embarrassed she'd been caught than worried about privacy in a place where anyone walking past a table couldn't help but overhear what was said. Intuition told him the conversation they'd had was pivotal, so he decided to press the issue. "I couldn't help notice his cards seemed to upset you."

She remained quiet for a good moment as if debating her answer, then lowered her voice. "The man gave me the creeps the moment he sat down. Then when I turned the cards over…"

"Bad?"

She closed her eyes for a moment rubbing her arms with her hands. "To say the least. The Devil, the Tower, and Death."

They're just cards. Jerry fought to keep the cynicism from his voice. "Sounds bad."

"The worst."

"Couldn't have been too bad. The man was smiling when he left."

She looked around once more. "That's because I lied."

The hairs on Jerry's neck prickled. "That doesn't sound

very ethical."

She laughed. "I'm not a doctor."

"No, but people come to you for advice." This time, he let his anger show.

She shrugged. "I gave him advice."

"Just not the advice he needed to hear."

"You know I charge by the minute, right? I mean, I don't mind idle chit-chat, but this isn't a date. While you're sitting in that chair, it's your dime."

"Hooker wages." She blushed, and he instantly regretted his words.

Instead of shrinking away from his words, she pulled herself taller in the chair. "I can think of worse ways to make a living. And I might show a bit of cleavage, but I like to think of it as window dressing. How many times have you browsed through a catalog knowing good and well you couldn't afford what was inside the cover?" She raised a hand and motioned around the room. "There are many tables to choose from, and I'm the youngest reader in the room. I know why men sit in my chair – that's why I dress the way I do. But it stops at this table. Oh, sure, I've had men offer me more if I were to leave with them, but I've never taken any of them up on their offer. I'm not that kind of a girl."

Are you trying to convince yourself or me? Jerry smiled a disarming smile. "So, what did you tell the man?"

She sighed. "What are you, a cop or something?"

He thought about telling her about his feeling, but something told him she wouldn't believe him any more than he believed her. "Just trying to figure out why a man who'd pulled such a bad hand left the building walking like he'd won the lottery."

"Aside from the view?" She winked, then leaned in and

lowered her voice once more. "Listen, I did the guy a favor. He told me he was tired of living in a dump and wanted to see if he'd be moving anytime soon."

"Too bad he didn't draw my hand."

"Too bad. Listen, if I had told him what his cards really said, he would have freaked out. I've seen it happen. The guy would've probably stayed all night, and it would've cost him a fortune." She glanced at the credit card reader and winked. "I hope you have a good job."

The state will pay for this one. "So you did him a favor. What happens when he finds out you lied?"

She leaned back in her chair. "The convention's over tomorrow. I'll be long gone by the time his luck changes."

Doubtful. "And if you're not?"

"Then I'll tell him I made a mistake."

It was Jerry's turn to sigh. "I hope you didn't make a bigger mistake than you bargained for."

Her face turned serious. "Do you think he's dangerous?"

The last thing Jerry wanted to do was escalate the situation. "I think he's a guy. Sometimes guys do things without thinking them through."

She held her hand out, and he offered her his palm. She shook her head. "No, I'd like something personal."

"My hands are attached to my person."

"Your watch. I'm not going to steal it," she said when he hesitated.

Jerry slipped the watch off and handed it to her, shifting in his seat as she wrapped her fingers around it and closed her eyes. A frown tugged at her lips, and he resisted the urge to demand she return it.

When at last she opened her eyes, they were brimming with tears. "You hold on to a lot of pain."

187

You have no idea. Jerry forced a smile. "I'm in the prime of my life."

"I'm not talking physical pain, and you know it."

Lucky guess. Even still, he thought about snatching the watch and making a beeline for the door.

"I didn't read the cards right."

For a moment, he wondered if she meant his or the man before him. He got his answer when next she spoke.

"You're not going on a trip. You're running away."

He reached for his watch, and she pulled it back, keeping it just out of his reach. "You've done it before. You're always seeking answers for things you don't understand, and when you don't get the answers you want, you run away."

This was more than just a lucky guess. Jerry struggled to keep his voice even. "I'll take my watch back now."

"You'll never get the answers you seek if you keep running." She looked him in the eye. "Your friends' deaths are not your fault."

Jerry pushed from his chair, all pretense of remaining calm forgotten. "Give me my watch."

She stood keeping her fingers closed. "I understand why you were afraid to get your own reading. What I don't understand is why you came here in the first place."

Because I was stupid enough to think this was all a bunch of smoke and mirrors. "Do me a favor. You see that man come through those doors, get up and go to the bathroom. Hide behind a table or go out the back door."

Her eyebrows knitted together. "You know something you're not telling me."

Jerry laughed at the irony. "You're the medium. Figure it out."

She opened her hand, letting the watch fall into his

open palm. "Mr. McNeal?" she called as he turned to leave.

Jerry hesitated. He hadn't given her his name. *Max picked up on Holly's name sounding like Christmas.* He turned, thinking to ask her how she'd zeroed in on his precise name.

"Forgot your credit card," she said, holding it for him to see.

Jerry took the card, feeling instantly relieved. Savannah hadn't read him; she'd guessed. *Good job, Jerry; you fed her the information she needed.* Shaking his head at the misstep, he pocketed the credit card with a Marine corps emblem on it. *Then how'd she known about the running away? Another lucky guess.*

She called his name again, and he turned for a second time. Before he could ask what she wanted, she nodded to the side of the table where Gunter was lying with his muzzle resting on his front paws. "Don't forget to take your dog."

"I don't have a dog," Jerry said, bolting for the door.

Chapter Eleven

Jerry rushed from the building, the only thing on his mind getting as far away as possible. Not just from the building but away from things he couldn't control. Women that knew too much about his thoughts and dogs who could appear and disappear at will. He didn't stop to consider the logic of running from a dog who could move between realms, not that it mattered, since he was in no state of mind to listen to logic – not that there was anything logical about ghosts.

The truck started on the first turn, and Jerry sped out of the parking lot with no destination in mind. His decisions were made on a clear path – if the traffic light was green, he continued in that direction. If red, he turned. He stopped at a stop sign, saw a car to his right, and turned left, following the path of least resistance. He drove, staring straight ahead with both hands on the wheel, only removing his right to shift gears. Sweat beaded on his forehead and his heart raced so fast, he wondered if he was having more than a panic attack. Though he knew what set him off, all he kept thinking was what if. What if – this time it was real? What if – they found him in a field after having run off the road because this time he was actually having the heart attack he'd imagined so many times before? That was all his life seemed to be anymore: a perpetual game of what-ifs.

It wasn't until he was nearly to the Mason-Dixon line that the panic ebbed, and he became rational enough to pull to the side of the road. He sat there for several moments, flexing his fingers, which ached from gripping the steering wheel, rolled his neck from side to side to relieve the tension, and took in his surroundings as he waited for his heart rate to return to normal.

Jerry saw movement to his left, looked out the window, and saw a long line of black cows standing near the fence, each stretching their neck over the wire as if to see what was going on. Jerry wondered if they were welcoming him or hoping he'd come bearing food. Either way, having them standing nearby was a tad comforting. If he were still on the brink of panic, they would have picked up on it and stayed clear.

It had been some time since he'd experienced an anxiety attack of this magnitude, and he was glad he wasn't on duty. They'd take away his gun. The last thing he wanted was to be stuck at a desk job for the rest of his career. *Get your crap together, Jerry!*

Jerry dug his cell phone from his pocket, found the number he was looking for, and hit dial.

The call was answered on the third ring. "McNeal, talk to me, buddy."

Jerry struggled to keep his voice casual. "Hey, Doc, how's it going?"

Laughter drifted from the phone. "Working hard, drinking harder."

That Doc was drinking didn't come as a surprise; that he'd mentioned it made the hair on the back of Jerry's neck tingle. "Anything I need to be worried about?"

"Not until I start mixing the two. I start drinking on the job, then I've got trouble." Doc was the Navy Corpsman who'd been assigned to Jerry's Marine unit and, as such, had made two trips into Bagdad with Jerry and the others. While most of the unit had gotten out when their enlistment was over, Doc was still serving. Instead of being in the field, he'd advanced to the rank of Chief and was currently stationed in Maryland at the Bethesda Navy Hospital just outside of DC.

"Heard from any of the others?"

"Boz, Turner, and Delong."

"Everything cool?"

"Nothing a few moments on the phone with me couldn't cure."

Though the man on the other end couldn't see him, Jerry nodded his understanding. In turn, Doc had approached each man in the unit, making them promise that if they ever needed to talk, they would give him a call. He was so dedicated to that quest, he'd purchased a separate satellite phone so that he'd never miss any of their calls. Turner had told Jerry that Doc once answered his call, even though he'd been in a closed meeting with his commanding officer at the time. When Jerry had asked Doc if it was true, he'd confirmed, saying he'd gotten himself out of being court-martialed by giving the CO his private number to give to the man's son, also a Marine, serving in a different unit.

"How are things in PA?" Doc asked after a moment.

"Good." It was a lie, and both men knew it. Still, even though Doc knew the reason for the call, he never asked for details unless Jerry brought it up. It wasn't the first time Jerry had phoned his lifeline. Just hearing the man's voice was enough. It wasn't about what was said or not said, it was about knowing someone was there. After hearing the Chief's voice, Jerry was feeling calm enough to be embarrassed to have needed him in the first place. "Listen, I've got to be going."

"Doing some of that cop crap?"

"Something like that."

"You cool, Jerry?"

"Better than," Jerry said, ending the call. He gripped the phone, picturing the man's face. *Thank you.* Why he couldn't say the words directly to the man, he didn't know. Maybe because doing so would show Doc how vulnerable he really was. Calling on the pretense of a casual phone call was one thing. Letting on that he'd had another panic attack was another. Putting the truck into gear, Jerry turned the wheel and headed back toward Chambersburg.

***

While he was feeling better, Jerry had no desire to go home. Craving breakfast, he headed for the Waffle House, pleased when he pulled up to the building, looked through the windows, and saw an empty booth. As he entered, he made eye contact with his regular waitress. Tall and thin, Roxy had worked there for as long as Jerry had lived in the area. Though she knew Jerry was a state trooper, she never gave away his secret when he was out of uniform.

"The usual?" she asked, setting silverware and black coffee on the table in front of him.

Jerry nodded and wrapped his hands around the cup. Now that he was out of the truck, he allowed his mind to wander, trying to pinpoint what exactly had set off this latest panic attack. Savannah told him he'd be running away. Yes, but there was more to it. She'd touched on the fact that he hadn't been able to save his friends. She'd said he wasn't responsible, as if saying it would make it true. But he was there, had felt something about to happen, and yet he wasn't able to prevent it. *Not his fault – tell it to the men who died.*

"Need a top-off?"

Jerry looked to see Roxy standing next to him, holding a coffee pot. He started to hand her his cup then realized he'd yet to take a drink. "I'm good at the moment."

"Your food will be out shortly," she said, walking away.

Jerry felt a blast of cold air, looked toward the door, and sighed. Savannah and the woman he'd seen wearing scrubs were standing in the doorway searching for a place to sit.

Jerry scanned the room, hoping to see an empty table. There were none.

The ladies looked in his direction, their gaze settling on him.

Crap!

The unnamed woman smiled, stepped in his direction, and Savannah grabbed hold of her arm, pulling her back. Jerry was about to sigh his relief, when his arm went up, seemingly on its own, waving them over. *Double crap. Why, Jerry?* Before he could answer his own question, the woman pulled her arm free and walked the short distance to his booth.

"Mind if we join you?"

Yes. Jerry swiped his hand to the opposite side. "Be my guest."

"Thanks," she said, sliding across the bench.

Though her body language told him she'd prefer not to,

Savannah joined them, sitting beside her friend.

"Thank you for sharing your table. I've been craving breakfast all day. I'm Raven, by the way, and this is Savannah, but I believe you two have already met. She said she scared you off. Ow!" she said when Savannah jabbed her with her elbow. "What? That's what you said."

"And yet, you wish to humiliate me more by making me sit with him?"

"Jerry McNeal." He looked at Savannah. "Why, pray tell, would you be humiliated for giving me a reading?"

Cassidy waved a hand to summon the waitress then looked at Jerry. "She's new, so she didn't know how to react when you ran off. You went out the door, and she ran to the bathroom. I wasn't sure what had happened until I went in and found her sobbing her head off."

"That's enough, Cassidy," Savannah said through gritted teeth.

"Okay, now I've really done it. She's using her mom voice, calling me by my real name. We're sisters, in case you can't tell."

"Which is why she was able to con me into coming up for the convention," Savannah explained. "Cassidy told me she was lonely and wanted some company. The next thing I know, she's sticking me in a dress a size too small and telling me to read the cards."

Roxy came to drop off Jerry's plate and gave the girls a once over. By the set of her jaw, Jerry could see she disapproved of how they were dressed. "Can I get you two… ladies something to eat?"

"I'll have what he's having," Cassidy said, studying Jerry's plate of smothered and covered hashbrowns with scrambled eggs.

Savannah wrinkled her nose. "I'll have scrambled eggs,

bacon, crispy hashbrowns, and white toast."

"And to drink?"

"Large orange juice," both girls said at once.

"That looks so good. I'm starving," Cassidy said when Jerry picked up his fork.

Jerry set his fork aside and pushed his plate across the table. "Go ahead. I can wait."

Cassidy pulled the plate closer and started in on the food without apology. She took a bite and moaned her approval.

Savannah rolled her eyes. "Really, Cass?"

"What? I worked all night and most of the day covering another shift and worked as hostess at the convention. I'm starving."

"That explains the monster drink."

Cassidy stopped chewing and looked at him. "God, was that this morning? It's been a long day."

"I don't know why you didn't let me play hostess. You're better at the cards than I am."

"You know what you're doing. That's why you agreed to come in the first place. You've just got to build up your confidence with the cards."

"Maybe I could be more confident if you quit dressing me like a whore."

For a moment, Jerry wondered if they'd forgotten he was there. Roxy came to the table to drop off the orange juices, saw Cassidy eating Jerry's meal, and shook her head.

Jerry looked at Roxy and shrugged. "She was hungry."

"She's something," Roxy grumbled.

Cassidy grabbed Roxy's arm, studied her palm, and winked. "You're no saint yourself."

Roxy pulled her hand away and left without a word.

Jerry looked at her over his coffee cup. "You know you shouldn't piss off the people who handle your food."

Cassidy fired off another wink. "I've already got my food."

"Touché." Jerry turned his attention to Savannah. "So, what made you want to be a psychic?"

"It was her idea."

"She's got the gift. We both do, even though she doesn't always believe it. Our mom and grandmother have it. Or had – our grandmother's dead."

"I've heard it can sometimes skip a generation. Or come on without any family ties." Jerry tried to make his questions sound random. While he had the gift, his mother did not. His grandmother did some of what she'd referred to as conjuring, but his brother hadn't had the gift.

"I guess it can be either way. Are you the only one in your family who has the gift?"

Savannah's mouth dropped open. "You have the gift?"

"Of course he does. Don't tell me you didn't pick up on it."

Savannah blushed. "No, the guy before him threw me off. By the time Jerry sat down, all I could get from him was he was a nonbeliever."

"Is it true that you don't believe?" Cassidy sat her fork on her plate and laughed when Jerry shrugged.

Roxy brought the remaining plates. "Anything else?" Everyone shook their head, and she placed the food on the table and left.

Cassidy smiled at Jerry. "I see my little sister isn't the only one who needs to learn to embrace their gift."

"That ship sailed a long time ago."

"Okay, so you believe. So what? Do you think you're the only one with intuition?"

"I think there are a lot of frauds out there." He nodded toward Savannah. "I also think if you go around giving people bad advice, it could come back to haunt you."

Cassidy smiled. "Speaking of which, where's your dog?"

"I have no clue. The last time I saw him, he was with your sister."

Savannah's eyes flew open. "I don't have him. I turned my head, and when I looked back, he was gone. I thought he went looking for you. I hope he didn't go out on his own; he's liable to get killed. You don't think someone stole him, do you?"

Cassidy looked at Jerry and smiled a sly smile. "Do you want to tell her, or should I?"

Jerry lifted his coffee cup and gave her a nod. "You better do it. She's not going to believe me."

Chapter Twelve

Garrett Lutz, a man of many titles – husband, father, liar – was sitting on a house of cards, so flimsy one misstep, and he would lose everything. A few short months ago, he was on top of the world, with a beautiful wife, a new baby daughter, and a job offer that allowed him to be home every night to help with the baby. It also held the promise of moving his precious family out of the dump in which they currently lived.

The dream job had lasted precisely one week – that was how long it took his new employer to discover Garrett had lied about having a college degree. Why they'd waited until after hiring him to do an in-depth background check was beyond him. A simple computer check could have saved them all a lot of heartache, and he'd still have his job at the warehouse. While it wasn't his dream job, it had kept the roof over his family's head and allowed him to stick money into savings each month – savings that were nearly gone, as he'd been using it to pay the bills since his termination.

Termination – he could think of a few people he'd like

to terminate.

Garrett opened the briefcase his wife Rene had surprised him with on the first day of his new job and pulled out a notebook. Maybe if he made a list of everyone who'd done him wrong, it would help calm his nerves. He clicked the pen and wrote the name, Patrick Menendez. The man who'd taken great pleasure in telling him he was fired and pointing toward the door like a parent sending a child to the corner. Boy, had that pissed him off – especially since everyone was watching. Menendez further humiliated him when he crossed his arms like a bodyguard and wouldn't let Garrett explain to the boss why he'd falsified his resume. If only Menendez would've allowed him into the man's office to show him the photo he'd taken on his camera phone the night before, this could have all been sorted out. The photo, showing the tears of joy in his wife's eyes when she'd pulled up some new home listings, would melt anyone's heart. It certainly had warmed his. They'd spent the next few hours making a wish list of all the things they wanted for their new home. He couldn't remember the last time he'd seen her that happy. She'd had such a rough go of it as of late. Postpartum. The doctors promised it would be temporary. He couldn't bear to add to her sadness, which was why he refused to tell her the truth, at least not until he had a replacement job under his belt.

Garrett searched his mind for another name. Pam. He didn't know her last name, but that was okay – he knew where she worked. He looked about the room, surprised to see her looking directly at him. He hated her. Loathed the way she'd told him he wasn't allowed to take up a table unless he was a paying customer. Hated that she'd cost him a small fortune in fancy coffee drinks over the past three months. You don't treat a person like that, especially not one that's in your place of business eight hours a day. He lifted his cup, took a drink, and smiled as she turned away.

Garrett used the pen to write another name: Shockley. Now there was a man he'd like to terminate. How dare Shockley refuse to give him his old job back. The man knew how desperate he was, especially since Garrett had explained everything. Yeah, he'd sure like to terminate Shockley.

Using the pen, he wrote another name: Garrett Lutz. Garrett stared at the name – his name – as if thinking of someone else. *Now there's a man that needs terminating. For a smart man, he sure is dumb.* Taking a bad situation and making it worse by not being honest with his wife. How stupid of him to have dipped into what little savings they had to pay the bills while sitting in the coffee shop all day using his laptop to look for work. He could've easily found a job – heck, even the coffee shop he used as his office had a sign in the window. But he refused to lower his standards. *Yeah, that guy sure needs terminating.*

Garrett shook his head to clear it and lined out his name. He was being too hard on himself. Any man in his situation would've done the same thing if they'd seen the look of hope on Rene's face when she'd learned of the promised paid vacations, health insurance, and a whole host of other things. Rene immediately pulled out her phone to call her mother to tell her the news. She'd then asked if it would be alright to purchase a few things. Unable to tell her no, he'd laughed and told her to spend away, as their income had more than doubled.

Garrett couldn't bear to tell her he'd screwed up again. So he didn't. He continued to set his alarm, pretended to go to work, then came home each day and listened to her tell him how proud she was of him. And each day, their savings dwindled a little more. He'd cringe when she told him she'd used her credit card to purchase a little something new for the house or the baby. It wasn't her fault; she'd never been frivolous with money before, and since he paid the bills, she had no idea how precarious their situation was. If only he'd told her the truth, then he might not be in this mess, but he hadn't, and no amount of wishing he had was going to change that. Everything was going to be okay. He just needed a bit of time.

His hand shook as he prepared to press send on yet another resume, a job he was qualified for in every way except for the lack of the same degree that had gotten him fired before. Still, he'd faked it before; he might get away with it again. He had the experience – he'd been working warehouse jobs for years. He'd even filled in for his boss a time or two.

Garrett pounded his fist on the table, startling a couple sitting next to him. He was glad Shockley hadn't taken him back. The last thing he wanted was to start at the bottom again. The bottom meant third shift, and he'd promised Rene he would be there to help with Lydia when she woke during the night. He needed days, and he needed enough money to buy his wife that beautiful new house she dreamed of. She deserved it. They deserved it. It had worked before and would work again – it had to.

***

Garrett pulled into the driveway, his heart clenching when he saw Rene standing in the front window holding the baby. The little woman waiting for her provider to come home, only he wasn't a provider; he was a deadbeat. A knot formed in the pit of his stomach, and he struggled to contain the self-loathing as he gathered his briefcase and headed to the house, continuing the charade he'd started weeks ago.

Rene failed to smile when he entered. He set his briefcase on the table and turned to her, saw her trembling, and for a moment, thought there was something wrong with the baby. He was just about to ask, when his wife spoke.

"Where have you been?"

"What do you mean? You know I've been at work."

She narrowed her beautiful eyes. "Liar."

She knew. He didn't know how she knew, but she did. Still, she could be upset at something else. "Excuse me?"

"You don't have a job. You've been lying to me all this time."

"How'd you find out?"

Tears brimmed her eyes. "We got the results from the radium test today. It was positive. I called to see how much it was to have the basement sealed. I wanted to surprise you by taking care of it since you've been working so hard. I gave them my credit card number, and it was declined. I thought there'd been a mistake, so I signed in to the account to check. Garrett, we are nearly broke!"

"I can explain."

"You don't have to. I tried to call you, and your phone went to voice mail, so I called the number you gave me for your office. The man who answered said you got fired months ago."

Garrett reached into his pocket, pulled out his cell phone, pushed a couple of buttons, and got nothing. "It's dead. I must have forgotten to charge it."

She hugged the baby tighter. "That's all you have to say to me?"

"For now. You're upset. It wouldn't do any good to try

and explain myself right now."

"You're darn right I'm upset. Where do you go every day, and what have you been spending our money on?"

Garrett sighed. This was the ugly side of his wife – the one he preferred not to see. He walked to the table, plugged in his phone, and waited until there was enough power to turn it back on before answering. "There was a little problem with my job, and I didn't want to stress you out. You were already on edge with the baby and all. Not to worry; I've been looking for a new job. I'm not going back to my old one either. We both know I'm much too smart to take a pay cut."

She stared at him for a moment before speaking. "You're unemployed. I'm pretty sure anything would be better than that."

"I'm not going to accept anything less than a management position. Something will come along soon; just you wait and see." Actually, he was glad she found out. Now he could stop pretending. Plus, it would save money not paying for all that coffee. He thought of the list and wondered if he should remove Pam's name.

The baby started to fuss, and Rene bounced her in her arms. "What are we going to do about the radium? I'll not have Lydia exposed to that."

He started to ask her how much it would cost to fix and decided against it. Obviously, there wasn't enough left in the account, or they wouldn't be having this discussion. "I'll fix it myself."

"You?"

He didn't like the way she'd spat the word – as if she didn't think him capable of keeping her and Lydia safe. "Yes, me. See, there's an upside to my not working. If I was, we'd have to pay someone to take care of it. As it is,

I have plenty of time to do it myself."

Lydia started to cry, and Garrett decided to let Rene tend to her while he went to change out of his suit. By the time he returned, Rene was sitting in the rocker nursing Lydia. He'd never truly appreciated the task before but was suddenly thankful they didn't have the added burden of purchasing formula. That was the thing about his wife; she could be frugal when she needed to, and with his secret out, they'd have to find creative ways to stretch what money they had left until he landed another job.

Garrett pulled on his old coat, picked up the flashlight, and went to take a look around the house. Truth be told, he hadn't a clue what he was doing, but Rene didn't know that. All he had to do was poke around some and pretend to take care of the issue. It would take weeks to order another test and wait for the results. By then, he'd be working and would have enough money to pay to have it fixed – at least until it was time to move to a better house.

Garrett trudged through the snow, aiming the flashlight at the foundation until he came to a spot where the snow had drifted away. He kicked at the dirt with the toe of his work boot, grimacing when he hit the red clay. He wasn't going to convince Rene it was fixed if he couldn't show her where he'd dug.

He made his way back to the front door, opened it, and stuck in his head. "I'm going to town to get a shovel. Do you need anything?"

She shook her head without answering. The baby must have fallen asleep. He started to leave, then went back to the door, stepping inside, mindless of the mess he was leaving, and collected her car keys from the table.

Garrett was on his way to the hardware store when he saw the signs announcing the psychic convention. He'd never had his fortune read and felt a bit silly spending money so frivolously, but he needed some assurance that everything was going to be okay. A chair opened up at a table close to the door, and he decided it was a sign. To his surprise, the moment he sat down, the girl slid a credit card reader in front of him. He didn't want to look like a cheapskate, so he inserted his card, hoping it wouldn't get rejected. When it went through, he considered it another sign that the beautiful girl in front of him would show him the way.

Chapter Thirteen

Jerry arrived at work early, anxious to speak with Seltzer, only to find his sergeant in a closed-door meeting with the captain. Unable to relax, Jerry walked a path between the coffeepot and his cubicle – walking the route so much, even Gunter grew tired of following and lay on the floor beside Jerry's chair with his head resting on his front paws. Though the dog didn't follow, he continued to watch Jerry's every move.

Several of the guys came in, Manning among them. Seeing Jerry, he said something to the others and joined him at the coffee station. "McNeal, you're in early."

Jerry forced a smile. "Yep."

"Who's the sergeant in with?"

"The captain."

A sly smile appeared on Manning's face, and he quickly covered it by lifting an eyebrow. "Awful early for him to come by."

Tell me about it. "Yep."

"You're a man of few words, huh, McNeal."

Only when I don't like you. Instead of answering, Jerry

just stared at the guy.

Manning shrugged. "Where are you patrolling today?"

"I'm staying local."

"I thought you were local yesterday."

"I was." Jerry knew some of the guys took exception to his special liberties. But Seltzer always managed to smooth them over – at least until now. The second Manning mentioned it, Jerry's intuition told him that was precisely what they were discussing in the other room. *Please don't let it be an issue. Not today.*

Manning leaned in and lowered his voice. "I might have overheard some of the guys talking. I think someone might have gone over the sergeant's head."

Jerry tightened his grip on his coffee cup. "Geez, I wonder who that could be?"

Manning threw up his hands. "Not me, bro; you and I are pals. We've got a connection now since we can both do the same thing. As a matter of fact, I planned on talking to the sergeant about that very thing. I've got a hunch that something big is going to happen around here soon. No, today. Definitely today."

Jerry looked toward the dog and willed him to hear his words. *Bite him.* He sighed when the dog failed to respond. He turned his attention back to Manning, who looked past him to where Gunter lay on the floor.

"Whatcha looking at, Jerry?"

Trying to see where you'd land if I clubbed you with this cup. "Just thinking about grabbing my cover and getting on the road."

Manning didn't buy his answer, and it showed. Before Jerry could say anything, Seltzer's door opened, and the sergeant stuck his head out and waved him over.

Crap.

"Kick the door around." He waited for Jerry to close the door before continuing. "The captain has had a complaint. It seems someone thinks I've been giving you special privileges."

Jerry looked at the captain. "Someone?"

The captain nodded. "Anonymous."

"Anyway, the captain here feels you need to do some farther patrols and let some of the other guys stay local for a bit."

"Okay, but not today."

The captain's head jerked up. "Excuse me? Who's in charge here?"

"You two are, but today, I need to stay local." He wanted to add that his spidey senses were sending shockwaves throughout his body but didn't think sharing that would help his case. At least not with the captain.

Seltzer knew Jerry well enough to know why Jerry had bucked at the change and nodded his agreement. "Very well; local it is."

The captain looked between the two. "That is not what we discussed."

Seltzer held firm. "What we discussed was for future scheduling. I already have Jerry patrolling Chambersburg today."

"Then switch him."

Jerry looked at Seltzer and shook his head.

Seltzer held firm. "The schedule stays the way it is today. Any changes will be on next week's schedule. That will be all, Trooper McNeal."

Jerry hesitated. He'd hoped to talk to Seltzer alone and fill him in with what little details he knew.

"I said you may leave, McNeal."

"Yes, sir." *Crap. I can't let him take the heat for this.*

Jerry faced the captain. "Sir, I'm not sure what the sergeant here has told you, but I have a gift. The sergeant calls it my spidey sense, but whatever it is, I can sometimes see things before they happen."

"So I've heard." The captain didn't sound convinced.

"Something is going to happen here today, and I need to be here to make sure innocent people don't die."

"So why not just tell your sergeant what's going to take place and let him send some troopers?"

"It doesn't work that way. I'm led to where I'm needed." Okay, so that was only a minor lie. He did know where it was going to happen. But he also knew he was the one that needed to defuse the situation so others didn't get hurt.

Indecision pulled at the captain's face. "Why you, McNeal?"

Jerry sighed. "Sir, I ask myself that same thing each and every day."

The captain stood. "You have it your way today, trooper, but things in this department will change, and we will run this post by the book. And for what it's worth, I wish you luck with whatever you think is going to happen."

Still hoping to have a word with the sergeant, Jerry stepped to the side.

The captain looked over his shoulder. "I think I'll stay in town for a while today just in case you need anything."

The moment he left, Sergeant Seltzer reached into his drawer and pulled out a pack of gum. "Well, that was fun."

Jerry chuckled. "I can think of other words for it."

"Ah, no worries. I needed to lose a few pounds. I haven't had an ass-chewing like that in a long time. Any idea who anonymous is?"

Jerry gave a nod to Manning, who was in the outer room talking to the captain. "A pretty good one."

Seltzer stood and looked out his inner office window. "Manning? I thought the two of you found some common ground."

"Too common."

"How so?"

"I'd make a wager he's telling the captain he has a feeling something big is going down today."

Seltzer raised an eyebrow. "How'd he come by that information?"

"Guessed it when I told him I was planning on staying local."

"The captain is going to think I'm running a loony bin. No offense."

Jerry laughed once more. "None taken. Hey, about today. I know the where and also have an idea who the key players are."

"Give me the names, and I'll have them brought in."

"You know it doesn't work that way. You saw the captain. The only reason he agreed to it today is my track record. No crime, no arrest. Something's going to happen at the psychic convention. I'm going to drive my pickup. I can't get close enough in the cruiser. I'm not sure when – probably a few hours yet. They don't let people in until nine."

"Okay, you know how it works – you need us – we'll be there."

Jerry smiled. "That's what I'm counting on."

***

Jerry parked in the same space he'd had the previous day. Backed in and hunkered in the seat, he had a clear view of the front door. Not that it mattered, as Gunter was sitting in the seat beside him, pointed ears turning like radar antennas. Jerry nodded toward the door. "Can you feel it? Not much longer."

Gunter woofed his agreement.

Several moments later, Gunter growled. Jerry looked and heaved a heavy sigh as a State Police SUV pulled into the parking lot and backed in beside him.

Manning lowered his window, and Jerry resisted the sudden urge to shoot the man. "What the heck are you doing here?"

"I followed my instincts, and they led me here."

Jerry was tired of playing nice. Things were going to go down soon, and he didn't need to be babysitting. "That's a load of crap, and you know it. You saw my truck. Now get out of here before it's too late."

Instead of leaving, Manning closed his window.

"Jeez, how did you ever…." Realizing the dog was no longer in the truck, he stopped without finishing his sentence. *Okay, dog, why'd you leave?* His spidey senses were on full alert as he searched the parking lot. *Come on, Jerry, concentrate.* Jerry's cell rang, causing Jerry to jump.

"McNeal? Why the heck haven't you called?"

"Excuse me?"

"The sheriff's department just got a call about a nut job with a knife at the psychic convention."

Crap! "Manning!"

"Manning's got a knife?"

"No, he distracted me. I've got to go." Jerry saw Manning getting out of his cruiser and ended the call. "Manning, where do you think you're going?"

"Inside. Didn't you get the call? Every cop in the county is on the way."

"You're not going in."

"Last time I checked, you weren't the boss."

Think, Jerry. A chill ran the length of him, and Jerry saw Manning lying on the floor in a pool of blood. "You can't go in. If you do, you'll be killed."

"Killed?"

I'm sure of it. "That's right, remember when you accused me of not knowing when something was going to happen to my friends? You were right. But this time, I know, and that's why I can't let you go in."

"We're friends?"

Not really. "Yes, and that's why you need to stay out here and control the situation. Don't let anyone inside unless I request them. Can you do that, buddy? I'm counting on you."

"Go on, McNeal. I've got your back."

Jerry drew his pistol and quietly made his way inside the building. A crowd of onlookers stood close to the man as he wielded a knife and screamed obscenities. *They're too close. He could stab any one of them before I get to him.* Jerry closed the distance while keeping an eye on the blade. *Knife?* It didn't make sense; the vision showed Manning with a bullet wound. Jerry hoped he wouldn't have to drop the man but knew he might not have a choice.

As Jerry approached, Cassidy saw him and caught her breath. He wanted to ask where her sister was, but there was no time as the suspect raised the knife in Jerry's direction. Training told Jerry to fire, but instinct told him to wait. While the man was clearly in distress, Jerry knew he was not the person the guy wished to harm.

Keeping his pistol trained on the guy, Jerry raised his left hand. "Put the knife down."

"I can't." The man's voice cracked as he spoke.

"Sure you can. Just lower your arm."

"Where's the girl?"

Jerry kept his eyes on the knife, the blade glistening against the bright overhead lights with every move. *Play along, Jerry.* "What girl?"

"The freaking psychic!" the man screamed.

Keep the focus, Jerry. He'd allowed himself to get distracted once. He'd not let it happen again. "Is there someone in particular you're hoping to find?"

"She was here last night, but I can't find her now."

"Maybe she has the day off." Not likely, but it would explain Savannah's absence from the table.

"It's a two-day convention. They don't take days off. She's here, I know it. She knows what she did and is hiding from me."

As if to prove his point, the tablecloth moved, and Jerry knew Savannah was hiding under the table. *Don't do anything stupid, kid; he doesn't know you're there.*

Jerry took a step closer, keeping his pistol trained on the man's chest. "What's your name?"

"My name is back the freak off!" the man yelled in response.

Easy, Jerry. Taking his own advice, Jerry planted in place, squaring his knees. "I'm not going to be able to do that, sir. Just tell me your name, and I'll help you figure out where she is."

The man hesitated a moment before answering, "Garrett."

"Garrett, you got a last name?"

"No way, man. I'm not stupid – I give you my last name, and you can do that cop crap. You ain't got no reason to know my full name."

"Just trying to get to know you, sir."

Garrett grabbed his crotch. "Yeah, get to know this."

Jerry could hear sirens in the distance. *Come on, Manning, I'm counting on you.* He'd no sooner keyed on the man than he again saw him lying in a pool of blood— *not going to happen.* Jerry reached up, carefully opening his mike for others to hear. "Come on, man. Right now, it's just you and me – there's no reason to get anyone else involved. In a few moments, the whole district will be here. That happens, and things can get messy. You don't want that. You just want to find your girl."

"She ain't my girl. She's nothing to me."

Easy, Jerry. "Why didn't you say so? You don't need a knife to talk to one of these pretty ladies. I'm sure any of them will be more than happy to give you a free reading."

"I don't want a freaking reading! What do you think started all of this to begin with?"

Jerry kept his voice calm. "That's what I am trying to figure out. I'm trying to help you, Garrett. We get this misunderstanding cleared up, and we can all go home tonight."

Garrett lowered the knife. It was only a slight dip, but they were heading in the right direction. "I can't go home. My old lady took the baby and left me this morning. It don't make any sense, dude. I was in here yesterday and told the woman I was tired of living in a dump. I told her I'd applied for a new job, and the woman – this Savannah – was like, I know, I can see it. You're going places. She said not to worry, that I would be moving to new digs real soon."

Jerry had to give it to Savannah – she was right on that aspect. Garrett would be moving to the county jail as soon as it was safe to handcuff him. Jerry spoke clearly, hoping to let the other units know he was making progress. "What do you say you lower that knife some more, and we go find this girl together. We'll have her give you a new reading and ask her what the mix-up was. I'm pretty sure when she finds out how much she missed the mark, she'll give you a refund from yesterday. You can use the money, right?"

Garrett lowered his arm another notch. "Yeah...yes, I can. That crap ain't right. She didn't say anything about my wife leaving me or this here today. You know what I think?"

That she lied to you? "No, dude, tell me what you think."

"I think she saw me losing my wife, and she wanted me to come back here for another reading so she could tell me what I am supposed to do now."

If the situation weren't so dire, Jerry would have laughed. "I'll tell you what, you lower the knife, and I'll pay for today's reading myself."

"For real, dude?"

Geez, the poor son of a gun actually believes me. "For real. You drop the knife, and I'll see to it personally."

Just as Garrett started to lower the knife, Jerry heard a noise behind him. Someone said something about them sending in another cop, and Jerry felt more than knew that Manning was on his way inside. Garrett reached for his waistband, and Jerry saw the handle of a pistol.

Crap!

Jerry's finger was on the trigger when he caught sight of brown and black fur sailing past in a single leap. Garrett screamed and fired. Gunter disappeared just as Garrett slammed into Savannah's table. "Suspect down! I repeat, the suspect is down!"

Jerry jammed his pistol into its holster, kicked the knife and gun away, and pulled out his cuffs. He clamped them onto Garrett's wrists as he reached up and turned off his mike.

"Where is he?" Garrett's voice was a panic.

You killed him. Don't be ridiculous, Jerry. The dog's already dead. "Where's who?"

"The dog, man. I didn't see him until he was flying through the air."

Savannah peeked out from under the table, and Jerry saw tears rolling down her cheeks.

Speaking low, Jerry whispered in Garrett's ear, "You want to know your future, here it is. There was no dog. It was a ghost. How else would you explain the way he disappeared? Ask anyone here, and they'll deny seeing it. Don't believe me, have your lawyer request the video from the cameras. The other officers are coming in now. Tell them you were trying to give me the gun, and it accidentally went off. Get yourself a good lawyer who can get you help for the demons inside your mind. But heed my words, you bother that girl or anyone else ever again, and that dog will find you and rip out your heart. Trust me on this."

Jerry pulled Garrett to his feet and handed him off to a local officer. As the cop led him away, Jerry reached a hand to help Savannah from under the table.

Her hands shook as she batted tears from her face. She kept her words to a whisper. "I heard what you said to him, but he's right. Your dog grabbed hold of my arm and pulled me from the chair a second before the guy came in. I was getting ready to call for help when I saw him. I remembered what you said and hid under the table."

Before Jerry could answer, Manning joined them, his face pale. "It didn't sound like the guy was listening, and I wanted to help. I saw him pull the gun and dove for cover as he took the shot. Seriously, Jerry, he was aiming right for me. I don't know how he missed. I guess I must have a guardian angel watching over me."

Jerry looked about the room, disappointed when he didn't see Gunter. He made eye contact with Savannah and Manning in turn. "I'd say you both had an angel looking out for you today."

Chapter Fourteen

Jerry woke from a nightmare, looked at the clock, and groaned. Two forty in the morning on a day he wasn't scheduled to work. He closed his eyes, replaying the dream in his head for several moments before finally deciding he wasn't going back to sleep. Opening his eyes once more, he realized Cat was staring at him from the pillow next to his head. "What are you doing here, Cat?"

He got his answer an instant later when he felt the dog's presence and turned to find Gunter standing next to him, the dog's head even with Jerry's face. It was Gunter's first appearance since the incident at the convention, and Jerry found himself glad to see him. He reached his hand toward the dog and Gunter growled.

Jerry recoiled, Cat hissed and took off running, and Gunter gave chase. Jerry pulled himself up, sitting on the side of the bed and trying to pinpoint the precise moment when his life had become a cartoon.

Deciding to let the animals sort things out for themselves, he dressed for his morning run. The moment he opened the door, Gunter bolted down the stairs in front of him, bouncing around in the snow like an eager puppy.

"You'd better not let Wells see you." As the words left his mouth, he realized that though the dog was racing through the yard, he wasn't leaving any pawprints behind. Nor were there any new yellow marks in the freshly fallen snow. Maybe Gunter wasn't so bad after all.

Jerry rolled his neck and took off in a slow jog. After allowing his leg muscles to warm, he increased his pace, running along the snowy street, oblivious of the biting air.

As he ran, the shepherd raced along at his side. Jerry couldn't help but wonder if the dog were chasing some unseen demon – or running away like he was. He usually loved running on mornings like this, enjoying the peacefulness of the freshly fallen snow, as if the white blanket somehow created a barrier from the ugliness in the world. But not today – this morning, he ran from dreams he could not shake and decisions that needed to be made. Should he renew his lease? Doing so would mean another three-year commitment, and as such, would be the longest he'd remained in one place since reaching adulthood. He liked his job well enough, but wasn't sure he could deal with the new restrictions. It was the same thing that had helped make his decision to leave the Marine Corps; his instincts would tell him to go one way, and his commanding officers would send him another.

The captain had made it clear that he would not receive any special treatment. If the sergeant didn't follow those orders, it would likely mean the end of the man's career. Not a problem if Jerry could agree to the new rules, but he couldn't, not when lives were at stake. If he hadn't been there yesterday, people would have gotten killed.

Are you sure, Jerry? It's not like it was you who stopped the guy from shooting Manning. Is that why

Gunter returned? To save his old partner? There had to be more to it than that. Jerry slowed his pace and finally stopped walking altogether. Gunter circled back around and stood watching him. "Manning's safe. Why are you still here?"

Gunter barked his answer.

"I don't understand."

Gunter barked once more, and Jerry's frustration grew. It was just like in the dream he'd had with Joseph standing in the fog trying to show him something he couldn't see. In his dream, the fog had lifted, and their grandmother was standing there mouthing words he couldn't understand. Jerry told her so, and she'd looked at him with sad brown eyes similar to the ones staring at him right now. Gunter took a step forward and then another until he was standing close enough for Jerry to touch. Jerry crouched, staring the dog directly in the eye. *What do you want from me, dog?* Jerry reached a hand toward Gunter. As he did, the cell phone in his pocket rang. Jerry jumped and Gunter disappeared. Jerry sighed his frustration as he answered the phone. "You're calling early."

"That's because I got called early. One of those ladies from the psychic convention called and tried to convince me to give her your phone number – said she has something for you."

"What'd you tell her?"

"I told her it was against policy and that I'd pass along the message, so consider it passed. Oh, she told me to tell you it was kind of urgent."

"Did she leave a number?"

"Nope. She said something about being hungry and that you'd know where to find her."

Jerry smiled and started for his apartment. "Anything

else?"

"Not from her, but I got a call from Chambersburg PD. Seems our guy lawyered up, and his attorney wants the video from the cameras. It's pretty soon for the request; anything on there I need to be concerned about?"

"Nothing that's going to help him."

"That's what I wanted to hear. PD still hasn't found the bullet – they plan to give it another go today."

"They won't find it." Jerry replayed the scene in his head, his stomach clenching when the bullet entered the dog. If not for Gunter, Manning would have been shot and Holly would have died. His intuition led him to both places, and yet it was the dog who'd saved the day both times. *Then why was I there?*

"Are you still there, McNeal?"

"I'm here."

"You did good in there yesterday. Turns out the guy's a real nutjob. PD found a hit list in his briefcase. The girl must have really upset him, as he moved her name to the top of the list. I don't know how that radar of yours works, but it was really on point with this one. I wish I could tell you I was able to smooth things over with the captain, but he's determined to run this post by the books. You'd think he'd see things differently after yesterday."

That was the thing – nothing happened that should have changed anyone's mind. Jerry had allowed himself to get distracted. If not for that, he would have seen Garrett enter and had reasonable cause to search and disarm him. As it was, he was just a Pennsylvania State Trooper doing his job. "The captain's just doing his job, Sergeant. At the end of the day, that's all any of us can do."

"That's a load of manure, and you know it. Manning told me you warned him not to go inside, said that was the only reason he ducked when he saw the gun. You might not want to admit it, but you saved the man's life."

Jerry started into his driveway and saw Wells standing on the stairwell to his apartment. "Crap. I got to go."

"Something wrong?"

"Nothing I can't handle." Jerry clicked off the phone, intending to have it out with Wells. Instead, he found himself getting into his truck and driving away just as Wells made it to the bottom of the steps. He was still trying to figure out why he felt the need to avoid speaking to the guy when he stopped a block down the road to clean the snow from his windshield.

***

Jerry stepped inside the Waffle House and saw Savannah sitting in the same booth they'd shared with her sister two days earlier. Dressed much more conservatively in a purple sweater and simple makeup, she lowered her cell phone and motioned him over the moment she saw him. "I see you got my message."

"It appears so." He raised an eyebrow when the waitress approached the table with his usual order along with a cup of black coffee.

"I took the liberty of ordering for you. Day off?"

Jerry looked at his sweats. "Does it show?"

"A little."

He took a sip of the coffee, grateful for its warmth. "My sergeant said you have something for me."

Savannah lowered her fork and blew out a long breath. "More like a message."

Instantly on alert, Jerry mirrored her actions.

"He spoke to me yesterday when you took my hand, but I didn't have a chance to tell you."

"This should be good."

"I know you're not a believer, but your brother says he's been trying to reach you."

Joseph? The dream. Jerry struggled to keep all emotion from his face. "Say I was to believe you. Just what is it my brother wants me to know?"

Another sigh. "I'm not sure what it means, but he wants me to tell you to stop being cheap."

Jerry laughed. "That sounds like him."

"Do you understand the message?"

"You mean that's it? Is this your way of getting me to pay for breakfast?"

"No, of course not. I owe you more than breakfast for saving my life."

"But we both know I wasn't the one who saved it."

She stared at him, unblinking. "What do you mean? If not for you, I'd be sitting at my table when the guy came back. I wouldn't have known anything was wrong, and he would've probably stabbed me, shot me, or both."

No doubt. "But it was the dog who did the saving."

"He wants to know why you don't like him."

"You're going to sit there and tell me you're talking to my brother right now?"

She pointed her thumb toward the floor. "Not unless your brother has four legs and a tail."

Jerry looked to where she was pointing and saw Gunter staring up at him. He rolled his neck to relieve the tension. "Nice try."

"What?"

"We both know you can see him. That doesn't mean you can talk to him, much less understand him."

She ignored his comment. "It's one of my gifts. He was sent here to help you, and you keep trying to send him away."

"Sent here by who?"

"Your brother."

"Doubtful. He knows I don't like dogs."

"He says you told him the only reason you don't like them is because they don't like you."

Jerry's mouth went dry. If his brother was here, why couldn't he see or feel him? "Joseph's here?"

"He just showed up."

It was getting a bit too crowded in the small diner. Jerry looked to the door.

"She doesn't want you to go."

The woman was all over the place. "You can't even keep your own story straight. He, she, the dog."

"Was your grandmother very religious?"

Granny's here too? He snickered into his coffee cup. "Only on Sunday."

"She said to watch your manners."

Now that sounds like Granny.

"She's mad at you."

Missed the mark again, lady. "I was her favorite."

"Wait – I can't understand when you're both speaking."

"I think I'll be going." Jerry started to leave and found himself unable to move. "What the heck?"

"I think your brother is playing tricks on you. Are you sure your grandmother wasn't religious?"

He didn't want to believe, but something – or someone – was keeping him from leaving. "Why do you think she's religious?"

"Just a phrase she keeps repeating. Jesus, Mary, and Joseph."

Jerry laughed a hearty laugh. "That's not what she's saying. My brother's name was Joseph. Anytime the two of us started carrying on, she would always scold us by saying, 'Jesus, Jerry and Joseph, behave yourselves.'"

Savannah bit at her bottom lip. "So you believe me now?"

Kind of hard not to. Jerry nodded, then frowned. "I've seen spirits before. Why can't I see or feel them?"

"I don't know. Maybe they didn't think you'd listen to them."

"You said she's mad at me?"

"She's upset you're driving her truck."

"She left it to me."

"Only because she didn't know what else to do with it. Your brother's saying you're driving it because you're cheap. He said to spend some of the money he left you to get a new one, and your grandmother is echoing his words."

"Tell him he didn't leave me any money; it was his life insurance policy."

"Same thing." She held out a hand as if to silence someone. "They both say you are not living up to your potential. They don't like the way you keep beating yourself up when you don't get the results you want. They think you need help and said that's why they sent you the dog."

Jerry blinked his surprise. "They sent him?"

"Yes, to help you. They said you shouldn't have to do this on your own."

"Do what?"

"Fight crime."

"I'm not sure I can do this anymore."

"This what? Talking to your family?"

He shook his head. "Being a cop."

"You're not happy with the state police?"

"I'm not happy period."

"You're not thinking?"

"Of killing myself? No. It wouldn't do any good anyway, since I'd probably be like the dog and come back as a ghost. At least now I get to eat real food."

"When I did your reading, I picked up that you'd be running away. It seemed to be cut and dry. I felt you'd done the same thing before."

"I have."

"What if I read you wrong?"

"Doubtful; that's my MO. I run when things get bad."

"Are things bad now?"

"Not bad, just confusing. I feel like a fraud."

"Oh, you're the real deal, alright."

"Not with this. With the police department. I feel like I don't belong. I ride around following my feelings. It's rare that I do any real police work, and it's not only me. I put my sergeant at risk every time I go out." *Shut up, Jerry.*

"You're conflicted."

"You think?"

"So why fight it? Maybe you should go." She smiled. "They're agreeing with me."

"I thought you weren't supposed to tell people what they wanted to hear?"

"I'm not. I'm totally serious. It's only a matter of time before something happens to make you leave anyway. So why not leave on your own terms? You regret your decision to leave the Marines because you ran away. Running away as you did and leaving things unfinished makes you feel like a coward. We both know it isn't true, but it doesn't keep it from nagging at you, especially when things aren't going well on the outside. If you leave the State Police on a whim, it will be another nail in your already fragile inner infrastructure. Wouldn't it be best for all involved – especially you – to leave while you're on an upward curve? You leave on good terms; they would be more apt to take you back or put in a good word at another department should you ever decide you're ready to return."

"Is this you talking, or them?"

Another smile. "A little of all of us, I think."

They had a point. Jerry rolled his neck once more. "I'm not sure if I just had a reading or a counseling session."

"Does it matter?"

"Only because I think I need to fire my counselor." He smiled. "Do you do phone readings?"

"I've never tried, but I think it's worth a try if you ever need me. So, does that mean you're going to take my...our advice?"

"It means you've given me a lot to think about. Although I'm not sure what I'm supposed to do about Cat."

"The dog said the cat must go." She shrugged. "I like cats. I'll take him."

"You've never even met him."

"It doesn't matter. He's a cat. Cats are cool."

He liked her. A lot. He looked at her wedding ring. "Your husband is a lucky man."

"Wife."

"Excuse me?"

"My wife is a lucky lady."

He shook his head. "I didn't see that coming."

She winked. "That's why I get paid the big bucks."

"Because you married a woman?"

She laughed an easy laugh. "Because I can see things most can't. Mr. McNeal?"

"What happened to Jerry?"

"Okay, Jerry. I think you're overthinking things."

"What things."

"With the dog."

"How so?"

"You're trying to treat him like a dog."

"Okay."

"No, I mean, it's obvious he's a dog. But he's a spirit first and foremost."

"So that's why they sent him to me?"

"They may have sent him, but he had to play some part in it. I think it's more like he chose you."

"Why would he do that when he could have picked Manning or anyone else on the planet?"

"Manning would have treated him like a dog. I think he chose you because you're more like him. You feel things." She held up her hand before he could object. "I think he knows what your purpose is on earth, and he's here to help guide you."

"How can he know my purpose when I don't know?"

"He will help you."

"You mean like Lassie?"

She looked at Gunter and shook her head. "I'd say more like Rin Tin Tin."

***

Wells was sitting at Jerry's table when he entered. He had a copy of Jerry's lease in front of him and drummed it with his index finger. "Before you go touting laws on trespassing, I'll have you remember I gave you notice."

Jerry walked to the table, pulled the lease from under the man's finger, scribbled on the paper, and handed it back to him. "No, Mr. Wells, it is I who's giving you notice. I will be out of here by the end of the month."

Wells studied the paper as if expecting the ink to disappear. "Leaving. What a shame. I'll hate to see you

229

go."

Jerry resisted the urge to toss the man out by the seat of his pants. "If we've nothing more to discuss…"

Wells took the hint and hurried out the door, which Jerry locked behind the man. As he wrenched the deadbolt, it felt like a weight had suddenly lifted from his shoulders. When he turned, he saw Gunter staring at him.

"She said you were sent here to show me the way. I'm cool with you hanging around if you are."

Gunter answered with a single bark.

Jerry laughed a carefree laugh. "If we are going to be partners, we're going to have to work on our communication skills."

Taking a chance, Jerry kneeled.

Gunter took a tentative step and then another until he reached Jerry, pushing his forehead into Jerry's chest. Jerry moved slowly, raking his fingers through the dog's black and tan coat, enjoying the softness of the K-9's surprisingly warm fur. In that moment, Jerry felt a peace he'd never felt before.

Rambling Spirit

*To our daughter, Brandy, for overcoming the odds
and giving us a reason to smile.*

Chapter One

Jerry stood at the top of the stairs watching as two men loaded his pickup truck onto the back of a flatbed truck. Gunter sat next to him, leaning against his leg as if offering moral support for finally agreeing to let go of the truck his grandmother left him.

It wasn't that he was overly fond of the truck, which took its time starting on occasion, but in the years since he'd owned it, it had never let him down.

Jerry glanced at the new silver Durango Hellcat he'd chosen to take its place, chuckling as he recalled the look on the salesman's face when he'd driven the '73 Ford onto the lot and asked what he could get for a trade. A look significantly trumped when the salesman asked him how long he'd like to finance the loan for, and Jerry told him he intended to pay cash. It wasn't that he was trying to show off – between his inheritance and living a minimalistic lifestyle, he had the money to pay in full. Doing so enabled him to negotiate a significantly reduced sticker price and keep the Ford – opting to donate it to a charity that helped veterans instead.

Gunter gave a low growl. Jerry looked to see the driver headed in his direction. He motioned for Gunter to stay and hurried down the stairs to meet him.

"She's all strapped down. Here's your receipt for the tax write-off." The driver started to leave, then hesitated. "You know you could have gotten a lot more for her if you'd decided to sell her outright."

At least he knew the salesman had been telling the truth. "I know, but it was my granny's truck, and I didn't feel right selling it."

The man wrinkled his brow. "But it felt okay to give it away?"

Jerry shrugged. "I needed something that wouldn't stand out as much."

This comment drew a full-fledged brow raise. "That's your Hellcat, right? You consider it to be less noticeable?"

"I was in a hurry, and it was between that and a minivan. At least with the Durango, I don't have to worry about getting caught." *There's no one chasing you, Jerry. You're the one doing the running.*

The man rocked back on his heels. "Buddy, I don't know what line of work you're in, but if you're hiring, I'm your guy."

There's no correct answer to that, Jerry, so don't even try. "We good here?"

The man sighed his disappointment. "All set."

Jerry waited for him to return to the flatbed before starting up the stairs. As he neared the top of the stairs, Gunter barked, and Jerry looked to see what had gotten the dog's attention. A box truck was at the end of the driveway, waiting to pull in.

Gunter alerted him once more, and Jerry saw his landlord, Todd Wells, standing in the side yard watching the comings and goings while Erma, his Old English Bulldog, balanced precariously on legs much too short to keep her girth from touching the ground.

"What do you think this is, Grand Central Station?" Wells called to him.

Jerry started to give the man the finger, then buried them all into the palm of his hand instead. "You wanted me out. I'm getting out."

The sour expression on Wells' face lifted. "You're leaving today?"

Wells had already pushed him into moving out earlier than the lease called for, though Jerry had every intention of spending the next couple of days in a motel, he decided not to give the man the satisfaction of driving him out even sooner. "You'll get the keys at the end of the month."

The smile disappeared. "If those trucks make ruts in the yard, I'm sending you the bill to have them fixed."

"Don't look now, Wells, but Erma's eating her crap." It was a lie, but Wells jerked the leash so hard, he couldn't have possibly known that the dog was too far away from the pile. Besides, it was rather obvious by looking at the dark mounds around the yard that neither dog nor owner cared enough to clean up the waste.

Jerry looked down and saw Gunter staring back at him with a particularly judgmental expression. "What?"

Gunter yawned and disappeared.

Not for the first time, Jerry envied the dog's ability to disappear at will. "Chicken."

"Excuse me?"

Jerry looked up and saw two men standing just steps away. Both matched him in height. The man who'd spoken held a clipboard and appeared to be at least twenty years his senior. The second man was much younger and seemed on edge as his eyes darted from side to side. If they'd been up to no good, they would've had him at a disadvantage – *Way to go, Marine. Not only did you allow them to get close to you without your knowing it, but here you are talking to yourself.* "I was trying to decide what I wanted for lunch. Come on in."

The man scribbled something on the clipboard he was holding. "What do you have for us?"

Jerry waved a hand around the room, encompassing the couch, a recliner, computer desk, and multiple boxes stacked against the wall. "Take it all. There's a bed and dresser in the bedroom through that door as well. Don't open that door. There's a cat in there that's mad enough by now to scratch your eyes out."

The second man snaked his head around Jerry. "What about the dog?"

Jerry appraised the man for a moment. Unless the dog wanted to be seen, it was rare anyone could see his ghostly K-9 companion. Since the other man hadn't mentioned seeing him, he doubted that to be the case. "My dog's in the bathroom with the cat."

The man tilted his head. "But…"

Jerry cut him off. "It's a large bathroom."

The man with the clipboard walked over to the sofa. "Come on, Jose, we still have two more stops to get in before we can call it a day."

Jose glanced at the bathroom door. "Si, Carlos."

It took eleven trips up and down the stairs to move everything out. Each time Jose returned to the apartment, he looked as if he wanted to question Jerry further about the dog's disappearance. When Carlos came up to have Jerry sign the receipt, he shook his head.

"Jose is new to the job, but I don't think he's going to

last long."

"Why is that?"

"He thinks your dog is a *fantasma.*"

"Fantasma?"

"Si. He thinks your dog is a ghost."

He is. Jerry forced a smile. "What gave him that idea?"

"He said you didn't have time to put him in the bathroom, and that if there was a dog, why didn't he bark?"

"That's a good question. One would think if I had a dog in here, he should bark." *Come on, Gunter, take the hint.*

"I told him he was probably a good dog and didn't need to bark."

"Did he believe you?"

"No, and I'm too close to retirement for this. I don't want to work with someone who's loco."

"How about I show him the dog? Would that let him keep his job?"

"He's coming up now. Si, I think that would do it."

Jerry walked to the bathroom door and placed his hand on the handle. "Okay, but if the cat gets out, I can't be held responsible."

Jose entered the room, and Carlos pointed to Jerry. "He wants to show you the dog is real."

Jose's eyes grew wide.

Carlos held up a hand to stop Jerry from opening the door. "Can't you just get him to bark or something?"

Jeez, Jerry, how is this your life? Jerry knocked on the door. "Gunter, I need you to bark." Nothing happened.

Jose whispered something to Carlos.

"Come on, Gunter. There is a lot at stake here." *Like proving I shouldn't be committed and letting this nice man keep his job.* Jerry knocked once more. Relief washed over him when Gunter's bark sounded on the other side of the

237

door. The relief was short-lived when hissing and thuds followed. "Crap! He's trying to kill the cat!"

Jerry reached for the doorknob, intending to defuse the chaos he'd created, and heard another thud – this one coming from the door behind him. When he turned, the two men were gone. Gunter materialized, and they both hurried to the door in time to see both Jose and Carlos running to their collection truck. Jerry looked at Gunter and sighed. "It's a good thing I'm leaving town. My reputation in this one is shot."

Gunter wagged his tail in response.

"You look awfully guilty. Tell me you didn't actually kill the cat."

Gunter licked his lips.

Jerry walked to the bathroom, holding his breath as he opened the door. While the plastic carrier he'd left open was now on its side beside the toilet, Cat was still in one piece and currently sitting on the seabag he'd placed in the shower to keep the collection guys from taking the last of his possessions. Cat growled when Jerry entered, his tail swishing from side to side as his eyes blazed with fear. At that moment, all reservations Jerry had about his decision to rehome the feline were gone. The dog had made it abundantly clear he was not going anywhere, and as long as Gunter was near, the cat would continue to live in fear.

***

Sergeant Seltzer was at the coffee station when Jerry arrived. The two men locked eyes. His boss finished filling his cup, and Jerry followed him to his office. A lump formed in Jerry's throat as he shut the door and faced the man.

"Why do I have the feeling I'm not going to like what you're getting ready to tell me?"

For a man who claimed to lack intuition, Seltzer always seemed wired into Jerry's feelings. "Because you're probably not."

Seltzer leaned back in his chair and took a sip from his mug.

Just give it to him straight, Jer. "I'm leaving the force."

Seltzer put the cup on his desk and pulled out a pack of gum. He took his time unwrapping two sticks. Jerry knew the man well enough to know he was gathering his thoughts. "I guess I kind of figured this day was coming. We had a good run, you and me."

Seltzer was speaking of the fact that he never treated Jerry like a cop, instead allowing Jerry to act more like a free agent, giving him the freedom to follow his intuition to fight crime. Unlike some, Sergeant Seltzer believed in him and trusted Jerry to act for the greater good of all around him. Jerry smiled. "That we did, sir."

"You good with your decision?"

Not in the least. "Good as I can get."

"You got a plan?"

"Not even an inkling."

"Have a seat, McNeal."

As Jerry sank into the chair, a melancholy crept over him. How many times had he sat across from the man, telling him about a feeling – the two of them bouncing ideas back and forth. Stepping away from the force was one thing, but walking away from a man who'd never once questioned Jerry's authenticity was another. Jerry laced his fingers together to keep them from giving away his anxiety.

Seltzer leaned forward in his chair. "I have faith in you,

son. I always have."

Crap. Jerry rolled his neck to ease the tension. "That makes one of us, sir."

Seltzer looked over the desk. "Is your dog going with you?"

"Gunter's not my dog."

Seltzer met his gaze. "The heck he isn't."

"He's here, and so I guess he plans on going."

"Good. I'll sleep better at night knowing someone's got your six."

Jerry ran a hand across the top of his scalp.

"What's troubling you, McNeal?"

Jerry rolled his neck. "What the heck am I doing? For the second time in my life, I'm throwing away a perfectly good career."

"Depends on your definition of 'perfectly good'."

"I'm afraid I'm not following you."

"What's perfectly good for me or, say, Manning in there might not be the same as what's perfectly good for you. Take me, for instance. I'm perfectly fine sitting behind this desk and telling everyone else what to do. Manning is a bit obnoxious, but he's a good police officer. You, on the other hand, have..."

Jerry waited as Sergeant Seltzer searched his mind. *Please don't say spidey senses.*

"You have this gift of knowledge that allows you to know things. That knowledge burdens you with a sense of responsibility to be there when the time comes. Near as I can tell, something like that doesn't fit well in a society with rules and obligations that come with having a real job.

"So how do I make it fit?"

"Darned if I know. You're the one with the spidey senses." Seltzer winked. "Listen, I know you don't like when I call it that, but whether you refer to it as spidey senses, a gift, or a feeling, you were put on this earth with something special. It would be a God-awful shame if you don't get to use it because some of the men in the other room got butthurt because they have to drive a bit further than you on any given day. Take what the man upstairs gave you and do with it what you will. Do it on your own terms and piss on everyone else."

Once Seltzer stepped on his soapbox, he sounded like a Sunday morning preacher. Jerry waited for him to finish his sermon before speaking. "Sir, I sure am going to miss you."

"Miss me? Jeez, boy, I'm not going anywhere. I've been saving your sorry ass for six years, and I don't intend to stop now. You find yourself in trouble or just need an ear, I expect you to ring me up on that phone of yours. Understand?"

"Yes, sir, Sergeant!"

Sergeant Seltzer beamed like a proud papa. "Good, now get out there and save the world."

Chapter Two

Jerry glanced in the mirror at the oversized red pickup truck that had been tailgating him for the last eleven miles. Not for the first time, he wished he were driving the old truck his grandmother had left him. If not for the fact his new Durango had less than four hundred miles on it, he would be tempted to slam on the brakes and let the man eat his bumper.

Jerry clamped his hand around the back of his neck, rolling his head from side to side to relieve the tension. In his old life, he would pull the man over. Then again, he doubted the guy would be riding his ass if he knew he was a Pennsylvania State Trooper. Only as of three days ago, he was neither a cop nor a resident of Pennsylvania. *Homeless.*

Jerry laughed. "Don't be so melodramatic, Jerry. You're homeless by choice."

At the sound of his voice, Cat resumed singing the song of a prisoner who'd been tossed into the clink without any hope of parole. Jerry glanced toward Gunter, who sat in the passenger seat beside him. "You were sent here to help, so help. Either beam yourself into that truck behind me and tell that jerk to quit tailgating me or get the cat to be quiet."

Gunter licked his lips in response.

"I don't have a problem with you biting the guy in the truck, but I can't allow you to eat the cat." Why he felt the need to negotiate with the ghost of a K9 police dog, he didn't know.

Gunter yawned.

"Don't give me any of that. If you're bored, go haunt someone else." Jerry checked the mirror once more. "Preferably the man in the truck. Just a quick in and out appearance in the front seat should scare him into backing off."

Jerry turned on his blinker and slid into the passing lane. As happened each time before, the truck followed him into the lane then back into the right lane once more. Jerry wasn't sure if the man was screwing with him on purpose or had simply chosen to follow, hoping to use him as a block against the cops. "I am the cops, dummy!" *At least I used to be.*

Gunter turned his head toward the front windshield and barked a single bark.

Jerry looked to see what had gotten the dog's attention. "Not a bad idea." Jerry waited until the last second and took the exit ramp, smiling as the truck continued down the interstate. Jerry slowed to a stop, looked both ways, and took the ramp back to the interstate. Instead of feeling better for ditching the truck, warning bells told him he needed to stop the man. An image of a minivan stopped at the rear of a long line of vehicles waiting to get through construction flashed into his mind. In a rare moment of clarity, Jerry saw the pickup cruise into the back of the same minivan without once tapping the brakes.

Crap.

Jerry's right foot pressed against the gas pedal, a broad smile spreading across his face as the Hemi engine kicked in and he sailed down the onramp, merging back onto Interstate 68. Gliding around a long, winding curve, he pushed the pedal further when the truck came into view, and an image of the carnage soon to occur flashed into his mind.

Gunter barked. Jerry shook off the vision, looked in the side mirror, and saw a state trooper gaining on him. Unless the man was a kindred spirit who'd also picked up on the accident soon to occur, the blue lights were intended for him. The cat wailed its discontent, and Jerry realized it wasn't Cat but the siren from the police car. He knew better than to keep going, but while stopping would keep him out of trouble, doing so would be fatal to the family of five the man in the pickup was going to encounter in the next couple of miles.

Seltzer. Jerry pushed the button on the steering wheel to bring the Uconnect to life. "Call Seltzer."

"McNeal? Tell me this means you've reconsidered your resignation."

Jerry didn't have time for pleasantries. "I need that life ring you offered."

Seltzer laughed a nervous laugh. "Jeez, McNeal, what's it been? Seventy-two hours? Are those sirens I hear?"

"Long story. Listen, I'm in West Virginia, Interstate 68, just before Morgantown. I've got a trooper on my ass and can't stop."

"West Virginia? What do you mean you can't stop? Are your brakes out?"

"Come on, Seltzer, I don't have time to play Twenty

Questions. Just make the call. I doubt they have more than one police chase going on around here. Tell them I'll stop as soon as I get the truck pulled over." Jerry switched off the phone and crossed into the left lane. Pulling alongside the truck, he honked the horn to get the driver's attention. It took nearly a full minute for the man to look in his direction. When he did, Jerry jerked a thumb behind him and motioned the man to pull over.

The guy looked in his mirror and immediately slowed, moving to the emergency lane. In that instant, the feeling of doom that surrounded the man lessened, leaving a small mountain of worry in its path. Knowing the trooper would not put himself in harm's way by pulling in front of him, Jerry maneuvered his SUV in front of the pickup truck so he wouldn't be able to pull out without backing up. Jerry breathed easier when the trooper followed protocol and pulled in behind the truck. *Calm down, Jerry; you did what you needed to do.*

Jerry pulled out his wallet and temporary registration, placing them in his lap, then rolled down his windows before placing both hands on the wheel.

While Gunter made himself scarce, Cat revved up the volume, meowing his discontent.

The trooper made no move to get out of his cruiser, and Jerry knew he was waiting for backup. All for the best. It would give Seltzer more time to contact them and smooth things over. An image of Seltzer leaning back in his chair, chewing on a stick of gum and trying to explain why he'd known to call came to mind. *Crap, Jerry, you're causing more problems for the man now than you ever did when you worked for him. How's it going to sound when he tells them you get feelings and they should just let you go?* "Quiet, Cat."

Two additional units – one carrying two officers – pulled up. Jerry watched as the team cleared the pickup truck – one taking the man back to a waiting cruiser. Once they had the truck secured, the three remaining officers proceeded toward Jerry, approaching on each side of his vehicle. One positioned himself at the right rear of the Durango; the original trooper kept his hand on the handle of his pistol as he and the other officer stopped just behind the left passenger door.

"Don't look now, boys, but I think I'm about to be arrested." The words had no sooner left his mouth than Gunter disappeared. *So much for having my back.*

The officer to the right moved forward, checking the cargo space before signaling for the original trooper to proceed.

The trooper searched the inside of the front cabin with his eyes. "License and registration."

"I need to lower my hands."

"Any weapons in the vehicle?"

Jerry kept his hands in place, knowing his personal arsenal lay tucked beneath the seats. "Yes, sir." *Please don't ask how many.*

"How about I just have you step out of the vehicle."

Crap! Don't let them put you in handcuffs. Handcuffs mean jail. Keep them talking; give Seltzer time to work his magic. "I'm going to take my hands off the wheel to open my door."

The officer nodded then stepped back to give him room. "Move around to the front of the vehicle."

Jerry did as told.

"Care to tell me why you took so long to stop?"

Jerry pointed to his SUV where the cat's angry cries filled the air and shrugged. "Didn't hear you."

"I guess you didn't see my lights either."

"The sun was in my eyes." *How many times had he heard that one?*

The officer glanced at the Durango. "Do you give us permission to search the vehicle?"

Jerry took in a deep breath, wondering how many guns his weapons permit covered. *He has probable cause. Admit it, Jerry; you've used it with less evidence.* He shook his head. "No."

"We can get a warrant."

You can, but it will take some time. Come on, Seltzer, make the call. Jerry sighed and leaned against the front of his Durango. "Listen, you've got me on speeding, but that's it. I admitted to having a weapon, which I have a permit to carry. That doesn't give you the right to search my vehicle."

"You were speeding down the onramp, took your time stopping, and when you did, you involved another vehicle. It's enough."

"The guy was tailgating me. I decided to give him some room, so I took the off-ramp. I looked at him as he passed, intending to give him the bird, and thought I saw him nodding off behind the wheel. Instead of letting him kill someone, I thought I'd try to stop him." Okay, it was mostly true – he'd only left off the most crucial part. *Better to have them think you're a nut job than to have them sifting through the burned remains of a minivan with a family inside.*

"And you want to make a citizen's arrest?"

Something like that. Before Jerry could drum up an answer, a second officer joined them.

"Here's your license and registration, Trooper McNeal."

Trooper?

"You mean you're on the job?"

Not anymore.

The officer handed Jerry his license and registration then looked at the West Virginia State Trooper. "McNeal here is one of you, out of Pennsylvania."

The trooper didn't seem amused. "You didn't feel the need to share that with me when I asked if you have any weapons?"

The officer laughed. "He was probably too embarrassed. According to the database, McNeal lost his ID and badge and is waiting for a replacement."

He had to give it to Seltzer; the man was creative.

The fourth officer joined them. "Everything under control?"

"Yeah. What's the deal with your guy? Our friend here thought he was nodding off at the wheel."

"Could have been. He said he hasn't slept much in the last couple of days – broke up with his girlfriend and is pretty upset. It's probably a good thing he got stopped, as it gave him a chance to get his head together. He's on his way to her place now to pick up his belongings. It's in county, so I'm going to follow him to make sure there aren't any problems."

The trooper gave a nod to Jerry. "You're free to go, but a word of advice: next time, suck up the embarrassment and save everyone a lot of trouble. Miller, hold up, I'll follow you, and we'll grab some grub afterward."

The other two officers smiled then followed at a slower pace. Jerry instantly felt the remaining anxiety lift. Most of it anyway, as he still had another four hundred miles to go with the cat, who continued to wail the blues from inside the Durango. *Five and a half hours. Maybe I should have let them arrest me. At least then I'd have gotten a few hours of peace.*

Jerry rolled up the windows and dialed Seltzer's number, pulling back onto the freeway as he waited for the man to pick up.

"It's too early for your one phone call, so I take it my little ruse worked?"

"If you mean did they think me an oaf for losing my badge and ID and let me go out of pity, then yes."

"Is that sirens?"

"No, it's my darn cat."

Seltzer chuckled. "Remind me never to ride with you."

"So why not tell them a story and get me off on a professional courtesy?"

"I got to thinking about it after you left the other day. I thought this might be a better solution in case I am not reachable when you need me. This way, they run your record, and it will show up in the database."

"How long do you think we'll be able to get away with this charade?"

"Beats me. I'll keep an eye on things on my end until you figure out your next move."

"And if I don't?"

"You will. But as long as you're not drawing a paycheck, there shouldn't be any reason for anyone in this department to pull your record."

"You're going out on a big limb, Sergeant."

"Did you save the day, McNeal?"

A feeling of absolute certainty washed over him. "Just up the road, there is a family – mother, father, and three children, one of them only a few weeks old – who will now make it to their destination."

"And if you hadn't intervened?"

Jerry shivered. "Not good, sir, not good at all."

"That's all I need to hear. You be careful out there, McNeal. There's a lot of good people depending on you."

"But no pressure."

"Only the pressure you put on yourself."

Chapter Three

Jerry pulled into the driveway, admiring not only the old farmhouse but the land it was sitting on. A line of trees hedged the northwest side of the property; a large barn sat just to the east of the house. Several horses grazed in the field. One looked up and tossed its head, questioning the new arrival. An image of a winged horse flashed in his mind. Jerry did a double-take, needing to ensure they were, in fact, just horses.

A large, fluffy white dog stood just outside his driver's side door, alerting the residents to his arrival. The dog's tail was wagging, and Jerry wished Gunter would return to ensure his safety. Jerry honked the horn, expecting Savannah to call the dog off. When she didn't, he opened the door and stuck out his left foot. When the dog sniffed his boot but didn't attack, the rest of him followed, pulling the cat carrier from his SUV as Cat grumbled his displeasure. Holding the carrier well out of reach of the dog, Jerry shut the door and made his way to the house, pressing his index finger against the doorbell. While he waited, he brought the carrier up so he could see the angry feline. Cat hissed and clawed at the metal grate. Jerry looked at the dog and thought about opening the plastic box. *Sorry, dog. My money's on the cat this time.*

"Not to worry, Cat, you're going to like it so much better here. Lots of land to explore and not a ghost dog in sight." The last part bothered him, as he hadn't seen any sign of Gunter since his run-in with the law in West Virginia.

The door opened. Savannah took one look at Jerry and shook her head. "Don't you look like the sorry soul!"

Wearing grey sweats with her dark hair pulled into a ponytail, she looked like the girl next door. Not the sultry, bosom-flaunting psychic medium she portrayed when giving readings. Jerry handed her the container. "Here's your beast. You're both lucky he's not in a shelter in Maryland right now."

Savannah looked in the carrier and made kissy sounds at the cat. "Long trip?"

"Made even longer by a cat that wouldn't shut up and tried to claw me to death every time I got near the carrier."

"I offered to bring him with me when I left, but you told me no."

"A decision I may regret for the rest of my life."

Savannah peeked in the carrier once more. "It's okay, big guy. I'll save you from that bad man."

"Bad enough to give him a home and feed him so he didn't have to stay outside and freeze to death."

She lowered the carrier. "I guess you're not such a bad guy after all. Care to come in?"

Jerry looked past her. "Your wife won't mind?"

Savannah raised an eyebrow. "I asked you to come into my house, not share my bed."

"Too bad. I could use a nap about now."

Savannah moved away from the door. "Kick your boots off and come into the kitchen. Let me show him where the litterbox is, and I'll make you a cup of coffee. Don't let the dog in – he's a working dog. It's his job to protect the livestock."

Jerry placed his boots on the rug and stood, arching his back for a moment before making his way into the kitchen. "Don't go putting yourself out. You don't have to make a pot on my account."

Savannah laughed an easy laugh and pointed to the pod machine on the counter. "I can bake anything you want, but that there's the extent of my coffee knowledge."

"The shifts I work call for a great deal of caffeine." Jerry sighed a heavy sigh. "Used to work, that is."

"I have to admit I was surprised when you called and said you'd actually done it."

"Not any more surprised than my sergeant when I told him I was resigning."

"Was he mad?"

"Seltzer, nah. I'd like to think I surprised him, but a bigger part of him expected it."

Savannah grew quiet for a moment, and he knew she was reading him. She tilted her head. "Why do I get the feeling you still work for him?"

"I think 'work' is too much of a stretch."

"Maybe. But the two of you are still connected?"

"He knows all my dark secrets."

"Lucky him." She winked. "Why does he come across as a father figure?"

Jerry raised an eyebrow. "Seltzer is the kind of person that's easy to talk to. He listens without judging and I guess you could say he believes in me. Unlike my real father, who has never understood me. Seltzer offered to help out

253

if I find myself in a jam."

"Like the one earlier today? Were you really in a police chase?"

He was glad she was married; a relationship with her wouldn't stand a chance. "Do I need to tell you about it, or can you just beam the information from my mind?"

This elicited a giggle. "I'm not that good."

"If I'm going to tell it, I'm going to need that coffee."

A blush crept over her face, and she pulled a cup from the cabinet and set it under the machine. As she fiddled with the pod, Jerry began to speak. "I had a truck tailgating me. The dog suggested I give him some space, so I took the off-ramp."

She turned toward him, her eyes wide. "The dog's talking to you now?"

Jerry smiled and shook his head. "Not in the sense you're thinking, but he barked, and I knew what he wanted me to do."

"Jerry, that is amazing."

"It is?"

"Sure it is. When I talk to the animals, I don't talk to them like you and I are talking right now. I can just... I don't know, hear them in my mind."

Jerry scratched his head. "I might need some bourbon in that coffee."

"I'm sorry, go on with your story."

"The moment the truck passed, I knew it was a mistake – that I was the only thing between him and something horrific. I tried to catch him and had the whole West Virginia police force on my ass." He'd purposely left out some things and exaggerated others to see how she responded.

She looked him up and down. "Something's changed."

"You mean besides the fact that the cat isn't meowing?"

She handed him the steaming cup of coffee and joined him at the table. "You like it black, right?"

"Yes."

"He's happy to be out of the carrier. That's not what I was talking about. I meant this vision was different."

He nodded.

"Tell me about it."

Though he'd spent the last four hundred miles dissecting it, he still wasn't sure where to start. "As long as I can remember, the feeling always begins with a tingling. A neck crawl or the simple knowledge that something is going to happen."

"And today?"

"It was instantaneous. I knew who, what, and when." He took a sip of the coffee. "I saw it."

"Like a picture or a movie?"

"Both, I guess. First, it came across like a snapshot, and then it was as if a movie was playing in my head. Only I didn't have to concentrate. It was just there."

"Your eyes were open?"

"I sure hope so. I was blasting down the interstate at the time."

"And it's never happened before?"

"Not like that...nothing like that, ever."

"Where was the dog?"

"In the seat beside me."

"And now?"

"Don't know. He disappeared when the police showed up, and I haven't seen him since. I figured he got tired of listening to the cat's bellowing. God knows I did. You don't think he's gone gone, do you?"

She shook her head. "Doubtful. I just wonder if your powers are growing because of the dog."

He looked over the cup at her. "My powers? Now you sound like Sergeant Seltzer. I'm not a superhero and I don't have any powers."

"Would you prefer me to call them your gifts?"

"I've always called them my feelings."

She raised an eyebrow. "Jerry, you and I both know they are more than that."

"Well, I feel things...or at least I used to. Now I see things, unless it was just a one-time thing. Do you think it will happen again? Maybe it was just because I didn't have time to let things play out."

"Why not?"

"For one thing, the police were chasing me, and for another, if I would have let things play out, people would have gotten killed. A whole family. One of them not even old enough to have had a bad dream."

"The timing could've had something to do with it for sure. But I think there's more to it. I think it is because you've finally found your path."

He set down his empty cup and stared at her. "What path? I'm thirty-two years old, unemployed, and currently living out of my vehicle. You may think this is freedom, but frankly, it scares the heck out of me."

If she could tell he was on the verge of a panic attack, it didn't show. She simply licked her lips and continued as if everything was right with the world. Her world maybe, but not his – his was hanging on by a kite string. The cat jumped into her lap, and for a moment, he felt a twinge of jealousy. She lifted her eyes and gave him an incredulous look. "You can't have it both ways."

"I don't know what you're talking about."

"That's a crock. You don't like the cat. How do you expect him to like you?"

"I like him a little."

She rubbed at the side of the cat's face, and Cat purred, pressing into her hand. "You're welcome to take him with you."

Not a chance. "He seems content to stay with you."

"Okay, have it your way, but once you walk out that door, the offer's off the table."

"Promise?"

"You seem calmer now."

He thought she was talking to Cat for a moment, then realized she'd aimed her comment at him. "Maybe. I guess I'm just trying to figure out the age-old question."

"Which is?"

"What am I going to be when I grow up?"

"Who says you have to grow up?"

He laughed. "My father."

"He doesn't have the gift, does he?"

"No. Neither does my mother."

"And yet she understands it."

"Her mother – my grandmother – had it. I guess it's easier to understand when you're raised around it."

"Something tells me that's where you need to start. Yes, yes, I'm sure of it, something to do with family. Something from the past that you need to revisit will help you get closure so you can move forward. Does that make sense?"

More than you know. "I don't think that would be a good idea."

"You haven't told your family that you quit the force?"

"No, and I don't intend to either."

"You don't do well with lies, Jerry."

"That's why I'm not going home."

"Where is home?"

"Parked in your driveway. Everything I own is stuffed inside a seabag in the back seat. Everything else I either donated or gave away. I told you it's a sorry life."

She ignored his attempt to bring her into his pity party. "Where do your parents live?"

"Florida."

"No, that's not right."

He raised an eyebrow. "That's where I send their Christmas card."

"Then why am I seeing mountains?"

Crap. Because someone decided the annual family reunion should be held at Uncle Marvin's house this year. He had had excuses as to why he couldn't attend in the past. As of three days ago, he was a free agent. If anyone in the family found out he was unemployed, he would have no choice but to go – *and tell them what? That he'd quit his job again.* Jerry felt his jaw tense. "I'm not going."

Savannah raised an eyebrow. "I hate to say it, but your grandmother just showed up. She said you're supposed to be nice to the guy."

Jerry knew she was near; he could feel her presence. "If she's here, why is the cat not reacting?"

Savannah shrugged. "My guess is because it's not a malicious spirit."

"That's kind of what I've gotten before. That doesn't explain why I can't hear or see her."

"I don't know. But she's saying you have to go to the family reunion. Something about looking out for Marvin."

"Marvin can go to … I could give a care less what happens to my uncle."

"She's repeating herself. Saying you need to go and

that she knows you feel it."

Jerry fought the anger that threatened to sour his previously good mood. He did feel the pull – that was the problem.

"She told me to remind you that Marvin didn't have anything to do with Joseph's death. And that you holding it against him isn't helping anyone. Tell me about Joseph's death."

Jerry pushed from his chair. "Listen, I appreciate your taking Cat off my hands. And I know that you're only trying to help, but I came here to drop off a cat, not have a therapy session."

Savannah stood and moved to the counter. "I'm sorry, I sometimes forget myself – especially when things come through this strong. Your grandmother – no, she's telling me to call her Granny. Granny wants me to tell you she's sorry too but says it's important that you go."

"Why am I here?"

"You dropped off a cat, remember?"

Jerry laughed. "My ears are still ringing from listening to his constant meowing. But that's the point – he wasn't even my cat. Not really; he just showed up at my door one day."

"Did you try to find his owner?"

"Of course. I called the vets in the area and put up signs. Gosh, I even paid for an ad in the paper."

"I hate to be the bearer of bad news, but if you did all that and didn't take him to the SPCA, he's your cat."

"Let's say for the sake of argument he was my cat. I could have simply opened the door and let him outside. Or, I could have found him a home in Pennsylvania. Why Louisville, Kentucky? Why you?"

"Because I was convenient?"

"Spending eternity locked up inside a vehicle with that cat is not what I'd call convenient." He ran a hand over his head, momentarily surprised to feel stubble, then remembered he'd stopped shaving his scalp two days prior. *Three days off the job, and I've already turned into a wild man.* Jerry shook off the thought.

"Why West Virginia?"

"Excuse me?"

"You could have come through Ohio. Why did you decide to go through West Virginia?"

Jerry looked at the cat, who was investigating every inch of the kitchen. "Glutton for punishment?"

"Or maybe you were guided there. If not for you, that family would have died."

A chill ran down Jerry's spine. "So, what? I'm just to drive around the country and wait for something to happen that I'm supposed to try to fix?"

"It worked for Michael Landon on *Highway to Heaven*."

Jerry closed his eyes then opened them once more. "I'm not an angel."

"Neither was Michael's friend, but you both travel with one."

This evoked a laugh from Jerry. "You've met the dog, right? He's no angel."

"The two of you just have to work on your trust issues."

Jerry lifted his cup from the table and placed it into the sink. "You're in the wrong line of work. You really need to become a therapist."

"Then allow me to give you this bit of advice. You're looking for answers, Jerry. Maybe you should listen to your grandmother's advice and go to the reunion. It seems pretty important to her."

Jerry looked at the orange cat who'd made himself at home and was currently lounging on the counter, purring his contentment as Savannah ran a hand down the length of him. *I think I'll come back as a cat in my next life.* "Cat knows he's not allowed on the counter."

"My house, my rules. Isn't that right, Gus?"

Jerry lifted an eyebrow. "Gus?"

She winked. "It's a lot better than Cat."

"We'll agree to disagree on that." Jerry paced the length of the kitchen then walked to the refrigerator staring at the photos. He keyed on one of Savannah standing next to a woman in a police uniform. The instant he saw the picture, the hair on the back of his neck prickled.

Savannah moved up beside him. "My wife."

"You didn't tell me she's on the job."

"You didn't ask."

Chapter Four

Jerry scanned the photos and selected the one that spoke the clearest. Both Savannah and her wife, Alex, wore simple, long, light purple dresses, and each had their hair pulled away from their face. Each had an arm draped around the other's back, and their facial expressions exuded happiness. He turned, holding the photo for her to see. "Your wedding photo?"

"Yes. Some of our family didn't approve, so it was just a simple ceremony with a few friends and what family chose to attend."

"Your family doesn't like Alex?"

"The problem isn't Alex. She's great. Just ask anyone." Savannah blew out a sigh. "It's that I chose to marry her they have an issue with. You'd think Cassidy would be more open, but my sister is the worst of the bunch."

"Give them time, they'll come around." Jerry wanted to laugh. He was the last one qualified to give family advice.

Savannah shrugged off his comment. "Don't make no

difference to me."

It was a lie, and he knew it. "You two didn't happen to honeymoon in Hawaii, did you?"

"I wish. No, we spent a few days in Myrtle Beach."

Crap. He really wished she would have said yes. "And Alex doesn't have any family there?" He knew the answer but had to ask.

"No." Savannah took the picture from him and studied it. "There is nothing in the picture that even looks like Hawaii. Why all the questions?"

Jerry scratched the back of his scalp. "Just a feeling."

Savannah raised an eyebrow. "That we are going to Hawaii?"

"No."

Savannah held the picture with both hands. "You think Alex is going to Hawaii without me?"

"No. I think Hawaii is coming here."

"Tell me that's a good thing." He hesitated, and she narrowed her eyes. "Dammit, Jerry, Answer me."

He walked to the table, hoping Savannah would follow. When he turned to look at her, she was shaking. *Easy, Jerry.* "It's too early to tell."

"What do you mean too early? You said you got the information instantly today! What are you not telling me, and why the heck can't I feel it?"

He understood her frustration. He'd been feeling the same thing for years. Getting a feeling and not having enough information to stop it in advance or knowing something was going to happen and staying patient enough not to alter the course. "I don't know. Maybe for the same reason I can't see Granny. Maybe you are too close."

"That's not good enough. You have to know! This is Alex." She closed her eyes, blinking away tears. "This is

MY life!"

Jerry waited for her tears to subside before speaking. "I can't give you answers I don't have. All I know... well, I don't know it, but it makes sense. Maybe that's why I'm here – to try to stop whatever it is."

"Try?"

Be honest, Jerry. "I can't always stop it."

"Is she going to die?" Her words came out as a sob.

"Not if I can help it." He raised a hand to silence her. "Whatever it is could be serious. Why else bring me here? With that said, you didn't tell me Alex is a cop, so maybe I just needed to come here so that I could see the picture."

She joined him at the table. "Do you think that's the case?"

"I think it's too early to tell. Maybe that's why it came to me in a movie earlier because it was going to happen soon. Right now, I'm only getting snippets. Snapshots, if you will."

Cat climbed onto Savannah's lap, and she sat absently stroking him. *How many times did he try that with you, Jerry, and you pushed him away? Where's the dog? What's the matter, Jerry? Feeling left out? This is not a popularity contest. Stay on point.* Jerry rolled his neck to get out of his head. "Listen, just because I know something's going to happen doesn't mean things aren't going to work out. Look at what happened with you in Pennsylvania. That turned out alright."

"I just don't understand why I didn't pick up on it." She closed her eyes briefly then opened them once again. "I still don't feel anything."

"I'm not lying."

"I wish you were."

"Me too."

She brushed away a tear. "Now what?"

"We wait."

Savannah pushed off from her chair and placed the cat on the floor. She went to the drawer and pulled out a writing tablet and some pencils, placing them on the table in front of him.

"What are these for?"

"I need to see what you see."

"You expect me to draw what's in my head?"

"Yes, unless your brain is hooked into a printer."

"Not the last time I checked."

"Then draw what you see."

Jerry resisted rolling his eyes. "You know I usually work alone, right?"

"Yep, but that is all behind you. You have me and the dog now."

"I've not seen the dog since I left West Virginia, and when did you get added into the equation?"

"When you set your sights on my wife." She winked and handed him a pencil.

Jerry placed the lead on the paper and drew a circle and several lines. When he finished drawing the stick figure, he turned the paper for her to see.

Savannah sighed. "Really, Jerry?"

"It's Alex. Don't you see the resemblance?"

"I think she needs to eat a sandwich. Seriously, is this the best you can do?"

"When I say it's early, I'm serious. I can see Alex, and I can feel Hawaii."

"Because it feels warm?"

Jerry rubbed at his temples. "This is why I work alone. I should probably go give the image time to grow."

"Go? You're leaving town?" Savannah's eyes were

round, reminding him of a deer caught in the headlights. "What about Alex?"

"I never said I was leaving town. I'm going to find a hotel and take a shower."

"You can stay here. We have three guest rooms."

"I appreciate the offer, but I need to clear my mind. I promise to call if I get anything else."

"What do I tell Alex?"

He turned to face her, keeping his emotions in check. "Nothing."

"I can't do that. Alex will be able to read my face."

"Alex is psychic?"

"No. But she knows me well enough to know when something's wrong."

"Tell her you took a nap and had a dream about what went on in Pennsylvania. She knows how upset you were, so that should pass the sniff test."

"Why not tell her the truth?"

"We don't know what the truth is. Right now, all we know is I see Alex in some kind of trouble."

"Exactly. So we should tell her."

"Telling her could put her in even more danger. Alex is a cop and, as such, has to make split-second decisions every day of her life. What if she starts second-guessing herself or hesitates at the wrong time? It's best for her if we keep this to ourselves for now. We alter her routine, and we could alter whatever I'm feeling. That happens, and I might not be able to do anything. Let me do what I do. I might not be good at much, but this I can do. This works whether I want it to or not. It is already pinging on Alex – let's let it do what it does."

Savannah nodded her head. "Okay, Jerry. We'll do it your way. I promise not to tell Alex."

Jerry started for the door. "I'm going to drive around for a bit and see if I can pick up anything."

"Haven't you had enough driving for one day?"

"It will be nice to have some peace and quiet. Tuck your lip back in; I was talking about the cat."

"He didn't mean that, Gus."

Jerry looked at the orange cat, who didn't seem the least bit upset over his leaving. "Oh, I assure you, I did."

"Jerry, hang on a second." Savannah ran down the hall and returned a moment later, handing him a small picture frame along with a bracelet. "It's a picture of Alex and her favorite bracelet."

"I know what she looks like."

"I know, but I find I can get a better reading if I hold something personal. Louisville is a lot bigger than Chambersburg and has a lot more people, especially with all the Derby festivities. People will be coming in from all over. I wouldn't want you to start following any false leads."

Best to humor her, or you'll never get out of here. "It's probably not a bad idea. Derby festivities?"

"Yes, the Kentucky Derby. It's a horse race. Surely you've heard of it?"

"Yes, I've heard of the Kentucky Derby. But you said Derby festivities."

"Used to only be the race, but now they have all kinds of activities leading up to the race."

"Like what?"

"Thunder over Louisville, Chow Wagons, steamboat races, a parade, Barnstable Brown party. They have the balloon glow and the great balloon race. Oh, and the Oaks race is Friday, but there is another race Thursday night. It started as something for the locals who didn't want to fight the crowds on Derby Day, but it has gotten so big, they named it. Thurby – Thursday and Derby. People dress up, and really it's just a mini-version of the Derby."

Everything pinged, and yet nothing told him that was what he was looking for. "This might sound crazy."

She laughed. "In my line of work, nothing sounds crazy."

"Does a winged horse mean anything?"

Savannah blinked. "You're kidding, right?"

"Not usually."

"Jerry, everything this week has to do with winged horses. Tours, parties. They use the Pegasus pins as admission to some of the big events. Heck, even the parade is called the Pegasus Parade. Jerry, please tell me that's not all you have to go on."

Crap. "It's not, but when I saw your horses, I saw a horse with wings. I figured I'd been on the road too long."

"But we both know there's more to it than that, don't we?"

Jerry placed a hand on her shoulder. "It's early. Don't go getting yourself all worked up. I will call you in the morning, and remember, not a word to Alex."

She nodded, and he knew there would be tears the moment he was gone. He could say something now and open the waterfall, but he didn't do well with tears, so he turned and walked out the door without another word.

***

Once inside the Durango, Jerry placed the photo and bracelet in the center console, leaned his head against the headrest, and closed his eyes. Savannah said there were a lot of festivities, which meant lots of crowds and parties.

Way to go, Jerry. Why'd you even let on there was a problem? Not only did you tell her of imminent doom, but you also led her to believe you're Nicholas Cage here to save the freaking day. And why not bring Alex in on things? She's a patrol cop in a vast city. How do you expect to find her without help?

Jerry put his palms together in prayer form. *Think, Jerry.* The feeling around Alex definitely came across as Hawaii – *maybe a luau? So, what do you search the internet for Louisville or luau? Or, you just let the feeling guide you. Come on, Jerry, this is what you do, so why all of the sudden are you second-guessing your abilities? Because I've let myself get too involved.* Jerry remembered Manning's accusation – you help everyone but those you care about.

Jerry opened his eyes and plucked the bracelet from the console, gripping it in his hand as he'd seen Savannah do with his watch when she'd given him his reading. An image of a rainbow came to mind. *No real surprise there; Alex is gay.* Jerry set the bracelet aside and picked up the photo of Alex in a standard-issue police uniform, staring back at him as if to say *Well, are you going to help me or not?* Jerry started to feel a stab of panic setting in. *Easy, Jerry. You don't have time for this.*

He placed the photo in the console, took his cell phone out of his pocket, scrolled through his preprogrammed numbers, and dialed.

"Talk to me, Jerry?" At the sound of Doc's voice, the panic ebbed.

"I quit the force."

"How's that working out for you?" That was what Jerry liked about his conversations with Doc. The man had heard it all and withheld judgment, at least while on the phone.

"Still trying to figure things out."

"You will."

"Do you really think so?"

"McNeal, if there is one person I don't worry about, it's you. That gift of yours is like a built-in radar. Follow the beacon, and it will lead you to where you're supposed to go."

Good ole Doc, always saying the right thing.

Jerry instantly felt as if a weight lifted from his shoulders. "Got to go, Doc."

"You good, Jerry?"

Jerry nodded his reply. "Thanks, Doc."

Laughter floated through the phone. "Was that gratitude I just heard?"

"There's a first for everything."

"I'll drink to that."

The hairs on the back of Jerry's neck prickled. "You good, Doc?"

"Golden."

"You need anything, you have my number."

Another laugh. "Go save the world, McNeal."

Another prickle. It was the same phrase Seltzer had used. Jerry ended the call and pocketed his phone. *I'll settle for saving a five-foot-nine police officer with hazel eyes.*

Chapter Five

Jerry leaned his head against the headrest and closed his eyes. If not for the tug from his intuition, he would have no trouble putting his seat back and taking a nap. He felt himself falling and jerked his head to prevent it. Opening his eyes, he saw Gunter staring at him. Jerry smiled.

"Welcome back."

Gunter woofed his reply.

"I thought maybe you'd decided to stay with one of the officers in West Virginia."

Gunter growled a low growl.

"It looks like we're staying in the area for a bit. I got a hit on something. I'm not sure how big just yet, but I think it's the reason I'm here."

Gunter growled once more, this one deeper than the first.

"Oh, my bad, the reason we're here."

Gunter gave a yipped response.

"The thing is, I'm a bit nervous about this one."

Gunter tilted his head.

"Yeah, I think I'm too close. I like Savannah."

Gunter's lip curled and he emitted a slight growl.

Jerry suddenly felt as if the dog were scolding him for trying to steal someone's girl. "I know she's married. She's a friend, and therein the problem. I don't want to screw this up. What if I can't figure it out? What if I can't save the day?"

Gunter surprised Jerry by placing his paw on top of Jerry's hand. It was a small gesture, but Jerry felt it just as much as if the dog would have verbally told him to quit worrying. *We will figure this out together*. And at that moment, Jerry knew it to be true.

Jerry spent the next couple of hours driving. He took Interstate 65 through downtown Louisville and continued across the bridge to Indiana, taking the first exit then retracing his path. Traffic was thick – at times, Jerry found himself creeping along at a crawl. Even with Gunter's help, navigating the crush of traffic worried him. Without a siren, he would have no option but to move along at a snail's pace. That scenario did not bode well if his feelings intensified. Jerry looked at Gunter. "Any ideas on how in the heck we're going to make this work?"

Gunter lowered his head and came up holding the end of the photograph in his teeth. Jerry took it from him. *Come on, Jerry, you're not going to get any answers like this.*

Jerry saw a sign for a motel and took the exit. As he pulled up to the front of the building, Gunter groaned.

"You don't approve?" When the dog didn't respond, Jerry went inside.

The lobby was packed full of people waiting to check in. Jerry bided his time until, at last, he was standing at the counter across from a woman whose name tag read "Bev."

Bev had bags under her eyes and looked as if she could use a room of her own. She looked up from the computer screen. Nearly double his age, a pink blush crept over her cheeks as she eyed him up and down. "Checking in?"

"Yes, I'd like a room for the week."

The color faded as she raised an eyebrow. "You don't have reservations?"

"No."

"Honey, I'm sorry. We're full."

Jerry ran a hand over his scalp. "Can you recommend another hotel?"

Bev shook her head. "Derby is our biggest tourist event. The city gets over seven hundred thousand visitors this month. Why, I doubt you're going to find a hotel, bed and breakfast, or air B&B within a hundred-mile radius of the city."

"That explains all the traffic."

"Honey, this is Louisville; there's always traffic." The lobby doors opened. Jerry followed the woman's gaze and saw a middle-aged man wheeling a suitcase. The second Jerry saw him, the hairs on the back of his neck started to prickle. Bev sighed and handed Jerry a brochure that listed the Derby festivities. Their hands touched – instantly, Jerry saw her fighting for her life in the parking lot outside the hotel. As the image progressed, he realized she was lying in a pool of blood, and he knew she had been stabbed. *Crap!*

Jerry pretended to yawn. "I've been on the road all day. Would you have a problem with me taking a nap in my vehicle to take the edge off?"

Bev smiled a sympathetic smile. "No, Sugar, you go right ahead. My car – a white Ford Focus – is parked on the west side of the building. No one likes to park over there because the light is out. I've called, but they're taking their time coming to fix it. Park over there. It'll be darker and quieter for you. There's a bathroom in the lobby if you need it."

Jerry turned and purposely brushed against the arm of the man behind him. Instantly, an image of him changing a tire on the side of the interstate flashed before his eyes. Jerry looked the man in the eye and saw another flash. This time, the guy was clipped by a passing vehicle as he attempted to get back into his car. A third flash saw him being dragged by the vehicle that had sideswiped him. Jerry mumbled his apologies and hurried toward the door. Once outside, he stood processing everything he'd just seen. On the surface, both images appeared to be connected, but as he rolled the images over in his head, he knew he'd just come face-to-face with two unlucky individuals. In a city this large, it was doubtful he would be able to get through the day without pinging on people. So how was he going to be able to keep his spidey senses in check?

Jeez, Jerry, what have you gotten yourself into? Jerry rolled his neck. *Okay, first things first. I need to know what car the man is driving.* His was the only vehicle under the loading zone. Jerry recalled the suitcase the man had wheeled inside. *He might not be coming back to his car tonight. How am I supposed to know which one's his?*

Jerry closed his eyes, replaying the image. The car was a sedan, dark blue...no, black. Jerry opened his eyes and surveyed the parking lot. *Great, only a half a dozen in the lot that come close to matching.* Jerry moved so he could see the counter. The man was still at the desk chatting up Bev. *Okay, so he's still there. What are you going to do? Excuse me, but I need to know which car is yours so I can make sure you don't get killed.* While some might believe him, most would not.

Jerry moved his Durango to the west side of the parking lot, parking where he could clearly see the front of the building along with Bev's Ford. Lowering the windows, he shut off the engine and brought his palms up, tapping the tips of his fingers together. *Come on, Jerry. Think. How are you going to prevent the man's accident? Easy – fix the situation before it happens. Find out which car the man drives and figure out a way to get the tire fixed before he gets on the interstate. Get that done and you can concentrate on the clerk.* At times like this, Jerry wished he had a tracking device. *Or a dog that was trained to track... Gunter!*

The second he willed the dog to come, Gunter showed up sitting in the seat beside him, wagging his tail. Jerry ruffed the dog's fur and pointed toward the building. "See that man inside?"

Gunter gave an eager whine.

"I need to know which car he's driving." Jerry nearly told the dog the color but stopped – best to be sure.

Gunter disappeared and reappeared just outside the driver's side door.

Jerry got out, and Gunter glued himself to his side as he moved to where he could see inside the building. Once in place, Jerry crouched – whispering so that Gunter could hear. "Don't let them see you!"

Gunter took off toward the building, the doors opened, and he walked inside. As the dog entered, both Bev and the man looked to see who'd triggered the doors. Jerry relaxed when they went back to talking as if nothing was wrong. Gunter circled the man, sniffing. Jerry bit his lip as the man shifted from side to side, readjusting himself as the unseen entity got up close and personal with his crotch.

Gunter moved away, the doors opened, and the ghostly

spirit trotted out – his K-9 grin showing him to be vastly enjoying himself. Jerry knew Gunter was triggering the door on purpose, as he'd personally seen the dog walk through walls.

Nose to the ground, Gunter made a beeline across the lot and into the third row sitting next to a late model Buick. Jerry smiled his approval. Not only was the car black, but the hood was also warm to the touch.

"Good job, Trooper." To Jerry's surprise, Gunter jumped up, placing his paws on his chest – further amazed when he ruffled the dog's hair, and Gunter rewarded him with eager whines, sneaking in a lick along his jawline. Jerry wiped his face and looked to see if anyone was watching. *Don't get distracted by all the warm fuzzies, Jer.*

Ordering the dog aside, Jerry took a cursory walk around the car, trying to see if he could locate the faulty tire. Not detecting an issue, Jerry returned to his Durango and drummed his fingers on the steering wheel. "Now what, dog?"

Gunter yawned.

Jerry laughed. "Don't go starting that. We've got work to do."

Gunter tilted his head.

"That's right, work. See that man in there?"

Gunter looked toward the building.

"If we can't figure out a way to stop him, he will get in that car over there tomorrow. Somewhere along his route, he's going to have a flat tire and when he goes to change it, he's going to be killed. And see that woman?"

Once again, Gunter looked to where Jerry pointed.

"She will come outside sometime in the next few hours and be attacked by a man with a knife." Jerry banged the back of his head against the headrest several times. "This is crazy. How am I supposed to help everyone in this city that needs my help and protect Alex?"

Gunter growled a low growl.

"Sorry...we. How are we going to help everyone?"

Gunter yipped a small bark of approval.

"Dog, with that ego, you would've made a great Marine." Jerry leaned his head against the seat. Exhaustion didn't even begin to describe how tired he felt. *Suck it up, McNeal. All you've done is sit on your ass all day. It's not even ten p.m. You had it much worse in the desert.*

Jerry closed his eyes, pulling the images into his mind. The vision showed the man changing a flat tire. *I have to figure out which tire's bad and make it so he needs to get it fixed before getting back on the road.* Jerry opened his eyes, rooted through the glove compartment, and fished out the tire gauge – patting himself on the back for having kept it when cleaning out the old pickup. If he could figure out which tire had the problem, he might be in luck. "Gunter, I need you to watch my back."

The dog barked and disappeared. Jerry heard a second bark and looked to see Gunter standing outside the Durango. Unlike the moment prior, Gunter was wearing his police collar and the K-9 service vest he wore when he was alive and on patrol with the Pennsylvania State Police. In addition, Gunter was missing the portion of his ear that had been chewed off by a crackhead in the line of duty several years before the dog lost his life jumping in front of a bullet intended for the dog's partner, Trooper Brad Manning.

Jerry blinked his surprise. Gunter normally appeared to him in whole form without a collar or vest. He thought back to when Gunter had materialized to save Savannah during the psychic convention – *Was the dog wearing the vest? Yes, I believe he was. Could it be he knew the difference between working and not working? Would a dog even know the difference? Maybe… if the dog was a ghost.*

Jerry opened the door and got out. "Glad to see you're taking the job seriously."

Gunter growled and wagged his tail.

"Okay, here's the plan. I'm going to check out the tires on that car, and you make sure no one sneaks up on me. There is a guy out here somewhere with a knife. I'd prefer to remain in one piece." Jerry remembered Gunter's missing ear. "No offense."

Gunter wagged his tail, and Jerry took that as a sign the dog didn't harbor any ill feelings.

Jerry made his way across the parking lot, keeping out of sight of the lobby door. He returned to the Durango and pulled on a ballcap, hoping it would help shield his face from any hotel cameras – at least the guy hadn't parked in the front row. With any luck, he would be able to find the faulty tire and help it along, better for the man to delay his trip than to let things play out the way they did in Jerry's vision.

Jerry circled around the back of the car and was about to unscrew the cap on the valve stem when Gunter growled, alerting him to a man and woman exiting the hotel. Jerry scrambled behind the car, waiting as the couple got into an SUV in the front row and left. Jerry approached the car for a second time, stopping once more when a vehicle pulled into the parking lot. Jerry stooped as if to tie his shoe, hoping they didn't look close enough to realize he was wearing boots under his jeans. Suddenly pissed off at the absurdity of the situation, Jerry pulled his knife from his pocket and thrust it into the left rear tire. Pocketing the knife, he returned to the truck, surprised to find Gunter sitting in the passenger seat.

The dog's mangled ear was intact; he no longer wore a collar or vest. Gunter stared at him when he slid behind the wheel, and Jerry had the distinct feeling the dog didn't approve of his actions.

"Don't look at me like that. It was either shank the man's tire or play cat and mouse all night."

Gunter yawned.

"I know we don't know if it was the correct tire. But my spidey senses stopped pinging on the guy, so it worked; just hanging around long enough to get it fixed will give the driver of the other vehicle time to get down the road. He does that, the guy should be safe." *Jeez, Jerry, been off the job for only three days and here you are committing crimes and reasoning with ghosts. Your parents would be so proud.*

Chapter Six

The air lay dormant as a heavy blanket of humidity hugged his skin. Jerry wished for the umpteenth time to be able to turn on the air conditioning, if only for a few moments. Gunter growled. Jerry looked to see Bev step outside. It was the second time she'd ventured outside in the last hour. At first, Jerry thought she was taking a smoke break, but she never lit a cigarette – just stood under the overhang rubbing her hands along the length of her arms.

"It was cool inside the lobby. She's probably coming outside to warm up. Unless she feels something more than humidity in the air."

Gunter gave a slight whine.

Jerry roughed the dog's fur. "Easy, boy, we still have some time yet. Remember, a Marine never gives away his position."

Gunter tilted his head and gave him a look as if asking who Jerry was calling a Marine.

Jerry's cell phone chirped. He looked at the screen, surprised to see a text from Manning asking if he was busy. *10:53 p.m. What the heck, Manning.* Jerry returned the phone to the console as Bev went back inside. "Any clue why your old partner thinks we're buds?"

Gunter lifted his lip and gave a snarl.

"Fine, I'll be nice. Maybe chatting with the guy will help me stay awake." Jerry picked up the phone and typed his reply. *What's up?* Within seconds, the phone rang. Jerry swiped to receive the call. "What can I do you for, Manning?"

"Hey, McNeal, just wanted to call and check on you. I know we didn't always see eye to eye, but I at least thought you'd make an effort to say goodbye."

Jerry rolled his neck. "I'm not good with goodbyes."

"So I see. Listen, I can't sleep. You want to get a drink?"

Jerry stared into the phone. Six years on the force, and Manning had never asked him to do anything. "Geez, Manning, I'd love to, but I'm in the wind. Matter of fact, I'm in Louisville."

"Louisville, Kentucky? What are you doing there?"

None of your darn business. "Visiting a friend. Came down for the Derby festivities."

Manning laughed. "Never figured you as a horse man."

I'm not. "There's lots to do besides horse racing."

"Cool. Hey, listen, I wanted to tell you this in person, but thanks for the dog."

Jerry looked over at Gunter. "Dog?"

"Yes, that guy you put Seltzer in contact with came through. I'm getting a replacement for Gunter."

Gunter gave a low growl, and Jerry covered the phone. "Mike's a good guy."

"Good to know. I'll be spending a few weeks in North Carolina working with the dog and learning his routine."

Gunter gave another growl and Jerry pointed a finger

to silence him. "You really like having a dog around, don't you, Manning?"

"Yes. But that's not the whole of it. You might not know it, but I'm not the easiest guy to get along with."

Jerry shook his head but refrained from agreeing with the man.

"I guess I tend to rub people the wrong way."

You got that right.

"I wouldn't do good with a human partner, but dogs, they get me."

Jerry lost the smile. Could it be he actually had something in common with Manning? He, too, liked to work on his own but even now found comfort in knowing that even though he was sitting in a dark corner of the parking lot with his windows down, no one was going to sneak up on him. And there was something about walking with a dog at his side that felt...right.

"You still there, McNeal?"

"Yeah, I'm here." *Just having a moment.*

"You got quiet. I thought I'd lost you."

"No, I was just listening to what you had to say."

"Yeah, I tend to ramble on if you let me."

"That's okay, Manning. Shoot me a picture when you get the new dog."

"Sure will. You take it easy, McNeal. Don't lose too much betting on those horses. And McNeal?"

"Yeah?"

"Thanks for taking my call."

"Anytime, Manning." Jerry clicked off the phone and stared at the device. It took a lot for a man to admit his own faults. "Maybe the guy's not so bad after all."

Gunter growled.

"What, I was being nice."

Gunter growled again, and Jerry realized he'd keyed on something. He looked and saw Bev standing near the front of the building, talking on the phone. While he couldn't hear what was said, he could tell by her body language that she was upset. The hand not holding the phone was dancing as if words were not enough to get her point across to the person on the other end of the line. After several moments, she ended the call, slipped the phone into her pocket, and went back inside.

"Yo, dog. You thinking what I'm thinking?"

Gunter tilted his head in response.

"What if this thing that's going to happen isn't random? What if Bev knows her assailant? You saw her on the phone. What if this is a domestic? A husband? Boyfriend? I saw more than one slash mark in my vision. That seems personal. Like the person who did it was angry. That phone call looked angry to me. What do you think? It got legs?"

Gunter yipped.

"Yeah, I think so too. Now what to do with the information?" Jerry tapped his fingers together for several moments before finally getting out and going into the hotel. There was no one at the desk, so Jerry ordered Gunter to guard the desk then went to the bathroom. When he came out, Gunter was standing in front of the counter while Bev worked behind the desk.

She looked up when he neared and he could tell she'd been crying.

Jerry approached the counter. "Everything alright?"

"Excuse me?"

"I couldn't help but overhear your phone conversation." It was a lie, but he couldn't think of any other way to get her talking. He shrugged. "My windows were down."

Tears welled in her eyes. "Oh."

Easy, Jerry, you need her to talk. "I didn't actually hear anything, just saw that you were upset."

"Oh, honey, it's nothing to trouble yourself over. It's been ages since he and I have gotten along."

"He?" This was the guy; he could feel it.

A ripe blush crept up her face. "My son. It's not his fault. It's the drugs."

Crap. Jerry was hoping it was a husband or ex. A son would be a harder sell. No matter how bad things were between her and the boy, she'd likely never believe him capable of hurting her. Not like that anyway. "He live around here?"

"I don't know where he lives. I told him I wasn't going to put up with his crap anymore and he left." Her blush deepened. "Oh, honey. I don't mean to burden you with my troubles."

"It's no burden at all. I understand how boys can be."

She sniffed and wiped at her eyes. "You got a boy?"

Jerry laughed. "Not even a wife. But I used to be one and know what I put my momma through when I was young."

"You look like you've grown up to be a fine young man. I'm sure your momma's proud of you." Tears slid down her face and she batted them away with the back of her hand. "I'm not sure I'll ever be able to say the same about my boy."

Not if he kills you. "Any chance he'll come here tonight?"

Her eyes went wide then she recovered. "No, Ray asked for money for rent, and I told him no. He's sung that song too many times – I give him money and it goes to drugs. I offered to drive him to a shelter but told him he wasn't getting any money. Actually, I think my exact words were 'over my dead body'."

A cold chill washed over Jerry. "Bev, I don't want to alarm you, but sometimes when people are seeking drugs, they do things they might not do if they were clean."

She held up a hand to stop him. "You don't have to tell me that. Why do you think I kicked him out in the first place?"

"He's tried to hurt you before?"

"Hurt me? No, I'm his mother. Ray would never hurt me. Stealing from me is another matter. He'd steal anything that isn't nailed down. He stole my dear mother's wedding rings; God rest her soul. That was the final straw – I'd finally had enough and kicked him out. He begged me to let him stay – swore he'd get his life together and promised to quit doing drugs. I told him to bring the rings back and take weekly drug tests – they have those kits at the drug store, you know – but he'd already sold the rings and couldn't remember who he'd sold them to."

"How long since you kicked him out?"

"Five months and seven days." Bev shrugged. "What can I say? I'm his mother. I might not like him right now, but I'll always love him."

Jerry felt like banging his head against the wall. Usually, he allowed things to play out. If he interfered, he might not be able to intervene when the time came. *I have to tell her.* Just as he opened his mouth to do so, Gunter clamped his teeth onto his hand, holding on so tight, Jerry felt his eyes water. He tried to pull his hand away and Gunter growled.

Jerry looked at Bev, who remained oblivious to what was going on right in front of her. He forced a smile. "I understand and wish you all the best. I think I'll take that nap now."

"Thanks for listening."

"No worries." The moment they were outside, Gunter released his hold and Jerry studied his hand, looking for puncture wounds. "What the heck, dog?"

Gunter licked his lips and headed for the Durango.

Once inside, Jerry turned to the dog. "Okay, so I take it I wasn't supposed to tell her that her son is coming here to try to kill her. I hope that means you have a plan."

Gunter yipped a playful yip.

"Listen, I'm okay with us working together. As a matter of fact, I kind of like having you around. But in the future, no teeth. That crap hurts!"

***

A cool breeze blew into the cab of the Durango and Jerry welcomed the drop in humidity. He looked at his phone to check the time: two thirty-two a.m. He'd been awake twenty-two hours and had spent most of that time behind the wheel. At least when he was driving, it was easier to stay awake. Gunter sat in the passenger seat, ears alert, his nose twitching with every sound.

A car came into the lot and Jerry pushed back into the seat. The car drove past, and Jerry got a clear look at the female driver within. She drove slowly past the building and then rounded toward the east lot. Gunter remained stoic, watching until the car was out of sight, then turning his attention back to the front of the building. Knowing the dog was on watch gave him comfort. Jerry closed his eyes.

Gunter growled. Jerry opened his eyes to find the dog wearing his police K-9 uniform he'd worn when alive. Instantly awake, Jerry looked toward the building. Seeing nothing amiss, he scanned the parking lot. Jerry touched the dog at the shoulder blades, felt him tense, and removed his hand. "What is it, boy?"

Gunter continued to stare out the front window. Jerry felt the tension as his warning bells told him it was time. He started to get out, then remembered the dome light and thumbed the wheel down to disengage it. He got out, then pushed into the door just enough to hear it click. As he did, Gunter sailed effortlessly out the passenger side window. Jerry hurried to the other side, placing his hand in front of Gunter's nose, telling him to wait.

Bev walked out the front door, heading toward her car. Jerry's heartbeat increased and he scanned the lot once more. This time, he saw a shadow of a man crouched near a car in the center of the parking lot. Jerry started toward Bev. She hesitated then must have recognized him as she began walking once again. As she did, her pursuer moved forward, stalking the woman who'd given him life. Jerry knew better than to call out to the guy, as doing so would alert Bev. He needed her to keep moving forward so he could intercept Ray before he got to his mother.

Jerry increased his pace, feeling as if everything was moving in slow motion. Gunter remained plastered to his side, matching him step for step, while whining his eagerness.

The doors to the hotel opened. The woman he'd seen drive by ran out, waving her hands and pointing toward Ray. "Bev, run, he's here!"

Instead of running, Bev turned, looking behind her. As she did, Ray made his move, running toward his mother, knife raised.

Jerry raced forward. Gunter took off like a shot, whipping around Bev just as Jerry reached her. Gunter jumped in between mother and son. Jerry pulled Bev away, watching helplessly as the blade dipped deep into the dog's side.

Ray pulled back the blade, made another attempt at the dog, and Jerry roundhouse-kicked the knife out of his hand before wrestling him to the ground. He reached for his handcuffs, surprised not to find them at his hip. *You're not a cop anymore, Jerry.* He could hear Bev crying over his left shoulder and the woman who'd alerted her asking if she was okay. He pressed his knee to Ray's back. "Call 911!"

The woman took off running toward the hotel entrance.

Jerry looked for Gunter, but he was nowhere to be found. Jerry swallowed, concentrating on his breathing as his adrenaline slowed. *Gunter's okay, Jerry. You can't kill a dead dog.* He looked over his left shoulder at the clerk. "Are you alright, Bev?"

Bev moved around to where she could see her son. She wrung her hands, her voice trembling as she spoke. "I knew you were angry, but I never dreamed you would try to hurt me."

"I asked you for help!"

"No, you asked me for more money for drugs. You want help? I'll get you help but no more money."

***

It was nearly four in the morning when the police loaded Ray into the waiting police car. Once again, Seltzer's ruse paved the way for Jerry to sail through on the pretense that he was an out-of-state trooper visiting town. As the patrol car rolled out of the parking lot, the last feeling of unease lifted. Jerry wished the same could be said for Bev, who was racked with motherly guilt. God, he hated to see women cry. "Are you okay, Bev?" He knew she wasn't, but he didn't know what else to say.

"He said he didn't mean to hurt me. He was trying to kill the dog. How could he be so strung out that he thought I was a dog?"

Because he's lying. "Maybe this is enough to get him to take steps to get clean."

"From your lips to God's ears. I'm just glad you were here to stop him. I know my son, and if he had hurt me, he wouldn't ever be able to look me in the eye again. At least now we have a chance of rebuilding our relationship after he gets clean."

All of this and she still can't admit how close she came to dying here tonight. "Happy to have helped, ma'am. If you're good, I think I'll try and get a bit of shut-eye."

Bev pulled out her cell phone. "Listen. It's a long shot but give me your phone number. I'll call you if we get a cancelation."

Jerry rattled off his cell number then walked across the lot to his Durango. As he approached, he had a feeling of being watched. He looked and saw Gunter waiting for him in the passenger side seat. Jerry's hands came together in prayer form in front of his face, trembling as he gave thanks for the dog's safe return.

Chapter Seven

The phone rang, pulling Jerry from sleep. *Savannah.* He looked at the time: six fifty a.m., less than two hours since he'd put his seat back. He swiped the phone to answer and hit the button to bring the driver's seat up to a sitting position. "Hello?"

"Shoot. Are you still in bed?"

He grabbed the back of his neck and pushed it into his hand. "No, I'm not in bed."

"Good. Are you dressed?"

"Yep."

"Awesome. I'm making breakfast. Are you hungry?"

Jerry glanced at Gunter, sitting in the passenger seat looking bright as the morning sun. "I could eat."

"Great. It will give you a chance to meet Alex."

Jerry sat up straighter. "She's not working today?"

"Not until this afternoon. Today is Thunder."

Jerry looked at the sky. "I didn't know it was supposed to rain."

"Not that kind of thunder, silly. Fireworks. You do like fireworks, don't you?"

"Not really."

"Yeah, right. Everybody likes fireworks."

"Not everyone."

"Well, I'll be there and so will Alex. You said you needed to stay close to her." Savannah's voice became serious. "Have you gotten any more information?"

"To be honest, I've been a little busy."

"Busy? What could be more important than trying to figure out what's going to happen to Alex? You promised, Jerry."

Jerry closed his eyes and placed two fingers at the bridge of his nose. "Listen, I had a rough night and..."

"A rough night? You went out drinking? Jeez, Jerry! I thought I could count on you."

Jerry clicked off the phone and offered it to Gunter. "If she calls back, you answer it."

The phone rang as he clicked his seatbelt into place. Gunter looked at him and yawned. Jerry swiped to decline the call. "And that right there is why I'm not married."

Gunter tilted his head.

"What? You don't approve?" The phone rang once more, and Jerry answered, intending to tell her he was on his way. "This could be construed as harassment, you know."

"It could? I didn't mean to harass you."

Jerry pulled the phone away from his ear and looked at the caller ID. Not Savannah. Maxine, a teenager from Michigan who also had the gift. "Max?"

"Yes, Trooper McNeal?"

He thought about correcting her but decided against it. A few moments on the phone with him and she'd know. "It's early. Are you okay?"

"I wanted to catch you before you went to work." The

line went quiet for a moment, and he knew she was reading him. He swiped to turn on the Bluetooth and Max's name showed up on the display. A second later, her voice drifted through the speakers. "You're not going to work anymore, are you?"

"Not with the police force."

"Oh."

"Don't sound so broken-hearted. I didn't get fired. Leaving was my decision."

"How are you supposed to help me if you're not a cop anymore?"

Jerry looked over his shoulder and merged onto the interstate. "Max, is something wrong? Have you gotten any more information on the lady from your dreams?"

"A little. It backed off some, but she still visits my dreams several times a week. I saw her eyes. They're green and I think her name is Virginia. She wants me to help her, Mr. McNeal. How am I supposed to do that if all I know is she has green eyes, and her name is Virginia?"

She was right; it still wasn't enough. "Max, I know it's frustrating, but it's more than you had. Are you still keeping your journal?"

"Yes."

"The key is to jot down your notes the moment you wake up. Make a note of anything you saw, smelled, or heard during the dream."

"I heard a bell."

"Good, make a note of it and anything else you can remember."

"You think the bell might be a clue?"

"It could be. That's why it's important to write everything down."

"I had a dream about you last night. That's why I

wanted to call. In my dream, you were looking for a horse with wings. It seemed important."

Jerry swallowed. "Tell me about the horse."

"It was a horse with wings. Does that mean anything?"

He didn't want to scare her, but the kid was good, and he needed all the help he could get. "Yeah, it means something. The horse is a Pegasus and I need to find it."

"I feel like they're all around you."

Wow, she's good. "They are. That's why she's so hard to find."

"The horse in my dream was black."

"That's good to know, Max. Was there anything else in your dream?"

"Gunter was there. I haven't told anyone about him, Mr. McNeal."

"That's good, Max. Hey, if we're going to be working together, I think you should call me Jerry."

"It's a good thing Gunter's dead."

Jerry looked at Gunter, who was listening to the conversation. "Why is that?"

"On account of the man last night didn't kill him."

Jerry shook his head. "Max, you sure are something."

"That's what I don't understand. I can read you and you're not even here, but this lady keeps coming to me in my dream, and I can't help her."

"I don't begin to know what half of this crap means. Sorry for the language."

Laughter floated through the speakers. "I hear worse than that at school."

"I'm sure you do. Just remember to treat everything like a clue. If you think of something, write it down, no matter how small that something is. Whether it comes to you as a vision or a dream, every detail is a message.

Sometimes you won't know the significance of it until the whole puzzle is pieced together."

"Jerry, I just had another vision."

"About the lady with green eyes?"

"No, this one was about you. You're scared. No, more than scared. Your heart is racing and it's dark. You don't have to be scared, Jerry. Gunter is there and he's big. Towering over you. He's your cloak."

"My cloak?"

"That's the way it feels. Kinda like Superman's cape – when he's wearing it, he can't get hurt. I think when Gunter is with you, it's his job to protect you."

"That's good to know, Max."

"I got to go. Mom's calling me for breakfast."

"Okay, Max, remember the journals."

"I will. Bye."

The call ended and Jerry cast a glance toward Gunter. "First I have spidey senses and now I'm Superman. Don't take this the wrong way, but this superhero status scares the crap out of me."

Gunter growled a deep growl.

Jerry sighed. "You know you're not helping, right?"

Gunter lolled his tongue out the side of his mouth and wagged his tail.

Jerry sighed. "Are you a dog or a comedian?"

***

Jerry got out of the truck, hesitating when Gunter followed. "I think you should find something else to do for a while. They're not going to like it if you upset Cat."

Gunter looked toward the house, back to Jerry, and promptly disappeared. Jerry heard the big white dog barking in the distance and hurried to the door.

When he got there, Savannah was waiting, reminding

him of a mother about to scold a child. "I can't believe you hung up on me!"

Jerry rocked back on his heels. "You sounded like my mother."

She raised an eyebrow. "You'd hang up on your mother?"

"Nope. I said you sounded like her, not that you were her."

Alex came up behind her and peeked over her shoulder. Her hair was shorter than what he's seen in the photo. Other than that, she looked the same. She looked him up and down and elbowed Savannah in the ribs. "You going to let him in, or should I arrest him for trespassing?"

Savannah blew out a sigh. "I guess he can come in."

The moment he entered, Alex smiled and extended her hand. "I'm Alex. Savannah has told me a lot about you. I'm in your debt for saving her life."

The moment their hands touched, Jerry felt a jolt. He smiled to cover it but saw Savannah bite at her bottom lip. "Just doing my job."

"Savannah told me you quit and that you might be interested in a job on Louisville PD."

Jerry let go of her hand. "Did she now?"

"I said maybe. I know you're looking at other options. I just thought since you are in town, Alex could get you a ride-along."

That's not a bad idea. It would keep me close to her. Before Jerry could say as much, Alex shook her head.

"My supervisor is not going to go for that this week. Not with everything going on."

"Come on, Alex, it's worth a try and you said it yourself – we owe Jerry for saving my life."

Alex held firm. "They're not going to give permission

for a civilian to ride along during Derby Week."

"What if I'm not a civilian?"

Alex looked at Savannah. "I thought you said he quit?"

Jerry answered for her. "Technically, I'm still on the force. My sergeant will vouch for me."

Alex reached in the drawer and handed him the same paper and pen that Savannah had offered him the day prior. "Write down your sergeant's name and number. I'll make a call and see what I can do. Don't get your hopes up; not for this week anyway."

If it's not this week, it won't matter. "Just have your supervisor call that number. My sergeant can be rather persuasive."

Alex walked out of the room to make the call, and Jerry pulled out his cell phone.

"What are you doing?"

"Texting Seltzer."

"Are you sure he'll vouch for you?"

Jerry returned the phone to his pocket. "He always does."

"You felt something earlier when you shook her hand, didn't you?"

"I did."

"Want to share?"

"There's nothing to share. Same thing as yesterday, a flying horse and a rainbow." He started to add that the feeling had intensified but decided against it. No need to worry her any more than he already had.

Cat came in, sniffed at Jerry's leg, and hissed. Jerry laughed. "Good to see you too, buddy."

Savannah called the feline over and pulled him into her lap, loving on him. "Maybe he smells the dog."

"I don't think Gunter smells. Cat probably thinks I've

come to take him back home."

Savannah turned Cat to face her. "Don't you worry, Mr. Snugglesworth. You're staying right here with me and your other mommy."

Jerry arched a brow. "What happened to Gus?"

"It didn't fit him."

"And you think Mr. Snugglesworth does?"

"Just trying it on for size."

Alex returned to the room. "Trying what on for size?"

Savannah held up Cat. "What do you think of Mr. Snugglesworth?"

Alex took the cat from her. "Sounds too much like syrup. Isn't that right, Mr. Meowgy?"

Jerry groaned. "Crap, I'm sorry, Cat. Maybe I should have kept you."

"Too late," both women said at once.

The timer went off on the stove. Savannah used an oven mitt to remove a casserole dish then hit the button on the coffee maker. "What did you find out, Alex?"

"That your friend here is a hero. He saved a hotel clerk from getting stabbed this morning."

Savannah handed Jerry a cup of coffee, then changed out the pod and hit the button once more. She took out three plates and set them on the table. "I thought you said you went out drinking."

"No, I said I had a rough night. You assumed that meant I was drinking."

Alex laughed. "Savannah assumed something? Never!"

Savannah swatted at Alex, and she ducked.

"My supervisor said you were sleeping in your car."

Savannah whipped her head around. "Why were you sleeping in your car? I told you we had extra rooms."

"What you didn't tell me was there's not a hotel room to be had for a hundred miles."

"Yeesh, I guess I forgot about that. So why didn't you call?"

"Because the second I saw the clerk, I knew there was going to be trouble. Then a man came in to get a room, and I knew he was going to die too, if I didn't stay."

Savannah's face paled and she turned away. When she returned with the casserole dish, she'd regained a bit of color. "So, what, you're picking up on everyone in the city?"

Jerry knew why she was upset. He waited for her to scoop some egg casserole onto each plate before answering, then looked at both women in turn. "I'm not a hero. I was just doing my job. I was at the hotel, and it happened that I was faced with two people who I knew were going to die if I didn't help them. What would you have me do, walk away and leave them both to die?"

Alex wrinkled her brow. "My supervisor didn't mention two incidents."

"That's because I convinced them they were connected." He pointed to his plate with his fork. "This egg casserole is good, by the way."

"Thanks, it's a bacon, egg, and cheese frittata. Why did you lie?"

"It was better than telling the police that I slashed the man's tire."

Alex laughed. "And yet you just did. I think I'd like to hear the whole story."

Jerry looked at her. "You asking as a cop or a friend?"

"I'll let you know after I hear the whole story."

Jerry told them everything that happened from the moment Bev handed him the Derby schedule.

Alex tilted her head. "But why tell the police her son slashed the tire?"

"The guy was already in trouble. He had a knife, so his slashing a tire wouldn't be a stretch. If the man had changed the tire, there was a chance he would have driven to his destination on the spare. I couldn't risk it. This way, the car had to be inspected for further damage and photographed for evidence. The guy may have been delayed longer, but according to my radar, he would live to see another day."

Alex nodded her agreement. "If I wasn't married to a psychic, I would think you a nut job."

"And now?"

"I think your reasoning makes sense. But what I don't get is why you stopped the dog from going after the guy. You said it yourself; you knew him to be the right guy. Why not stop it before things got out of hand?"

"Because it would have just delayed what I saw. If Gunter would've taken him down, he would've eventually found Bev and most likely killed her."

"And you don't think that could still happen?"

"Not according to my spidey senses." He winked. "That's what my boss called them. The woman's son told the police he saw the dog. No one else did. I think this incident was enough to get him sent to a rehab center and hopefully get his act together."

Alex looked around the room. "Is the dog here?"

Jerry nodded toward Cat, who was sunning himself near the sliding door. "If he were, that cat would be on top of that curtain rod."

Chapter Eight

Alex came into the kitchen wearing her police uniform. Jerry locked eyes with her, then turned and gave Savannah a subtle headshake. Whatever was going to happen would not be today.

Alex pressed her backside to the sink. "You can't fool me, Jerry. I saw that look."

Jerry swallowed. He hadn't intended to tell Alex she was in danger.

"You miss the uniform."

Jerry relaxed. "You got me there."

"I can't imagine not being a cop. It's all I ever wanted to be growing up."

"Looks like you're living your dream." Jerry felt a twinge of jealousy over the fact that he'd yet to find a clear path to happiness.

"Of course, I don't especially like traffic duty, but I guess someone has to do it."

Savannah grabbed a bottle of water from the fridge and handed it to Alex. "At least you'll get off before the fireworks this year."

"Yep. I'll text you when I'm done, and you can tell me where to meet you guys. And remember to park outside the city and take the bus in – traffic will be crazy downtown. I'll be able to park closer and give you a ride back to your car when the fireworks are over." Alex walked to the other side of the kitchen, removed something from a drawer, and handed it to Savannah before giving her a peck on the lips. "Here are the pins to get into Waterfront Park. Aren't they adorable? I thought they were cute, so I bought an extra one. That, or maybe that psychic crap is rubbing off on me and somehow I knew I'd be needing it."

Savannah opened her palm and closed it again. Though she smiled, Jerry could tell something was wrong. She reached her arms around Alex and gave her a ferocious hug.

"If I would've known I was going to get this kind of response, I would've given them to you last night." Alex looked at Jerry and winked, then turned her attention back to Savannah. "I've got to go. I'll text you when I'm off."

Jerry stayed at the table while Savannah followed Alex to the door. A moment later, Savannah returned and he could see her trembling.

Jerry ran his hand over the top of his head. *Please don't cry.* "Problem?"

Savannah opened her hand for him to see. "You tell me."

Jerry stared at the two rainbow pins showing the head of a horse with wings cradled in the palm of Savannah's hand. *Pegasus.*

"Don't you have anything to say?"

"They're pretty?"

"Come on, Jerry, I don't need jokes right now. I need answers."

You and me both. "I'd give them to you if I had any."

Savannah grabbed his hand and pressed the pins into his palm. "What do you feel?"

He studied the pins for several moments. "Nothing."

"What do you mean 'nothing'? You're the one who said whatever was going to happen was something to do with a rainbow horse."

"I mean this: these are just a coincidence. I'm getting nothing."

"Then why did she buy rainbow pins when she had so many other options?"

Jerry chuckled. He knew she was on the verge of tears, but he couldn't help himself. "You're kidding, right?"

"This is not funny!"

He reined in his laughter. "Close your eyes."

"Why?"

"Just do it."

She did as he said.

"Okay, picture yourself going to the store to buy the pins. They are hanging on a display on the wall."

"No, they are in a box at the counter."

"Okay, a box on the counter. Inside that box are all colors of pins. Pink, blue, red, green, gold, and rainbow. Out of all those pins, which one are you going to pick?"

She opened her eyes. "I'd pick the rainbow one."

"Why?"

"Because a rainbow symbolizes my and Alex's love?"

"Maybe. But also because it's pretty. You'd pick it out of all of the pins in the box because that is the one that made you smile." He handed her the pins. "Try to relax. Whatever is going to happen isn't going to be today."

"Are you sure?"

"I'd stake my life on it."

She smiled a weak smile. "No offense, but it's not your life I'm worried about."

"I can respect that."

***

In his six years of serving with the Pennsylvania State Police, never had Jerry experienced crowds of this magnitude – even when he'd patrolled Philadelphia, nothing compared to the horde of people currently gathered together in Louisville. While a part of him wished to be in uniform, a bigger part of him was glad he wasn't. If he had been visiting the city looking to further his career in law enforcement, this single event would convince him otherwise.

Not that there was anything wrong with the city. On the contrary, it was rather magnificent. He especially liked the way the interstate cut right through the heart of the town – so close, he could wave to people looking out the windows of some of the most prestigious hospitals around. And how fun is a city where you can get your photo taken with a 120-foot-tall baseball bat that weighs thirty-four tons or encourages you to drink bourbon along the infamous bourbon trail.

What Jerry didn't like were the crowds. One of his shrinks placed the blame on PTSD, but there were no crowds in Iraq. At least not where he patrolled. Another shrink said it was because he grew up in a small town and was never exposed to lofty groups of people. Jerry closed his eyes, picturing the man sitting in the wingback chair, one leg crossed over the other showing his sockless ankles while he meticulously chewed the eraser off the end of his pencil. He should have fired the clown the moment he used the word "lofty" to describe a crowd. It would have saved them both months of useless counseling sessions.

The truth of the matter was he'd never liked being in large groups of people simply because he could not turn off his internal radar. It had been like that since he was born. His mother told him stories of how upset he was every time he was around more than a handful of people. They attributed it to fear of strangers, but as Jerry grew old enough to be mindful of his surroundings, he knew there was more to it.

Bootcamp was particularly troublesome, as he was unable to distance himself from the things that troubled him. But as he got to know his brothers, they became family. He thought about his upcoming family reunion and pushed it aside. He would not be able to decide on that until he solved the problem at hand.

Funny how he preferred his Marine family over some of his blood kin. Most of them anyway. There were a few that got under his skin. Then again, that was true with any family.

"How is it you can look a million miles away when you're standing among so many people?"

Jerry smiled a sly smile. "Just lucky, I guess."

"You're not supposed to disappear, Jerry. You're supposed to focus your radar on Alex."

"I've already told you it won't happen tonight."

"I'm going to get some cheesecake. Want some?"

Not only had they eaten a hearty breakfast, but Savannah had hit seven food trucks since they'd arrived. *She needs an intervention. Maybe, but not by you; women are sensitive about crap like that. Don't do it, Jerry.* "Do you always eat this much?"

Savannah narrowed her eyes. "Now who's sounding

like someone's mother? No, I don't always eat this much. Unless I'm stressed and unless there's cheesecake involved."

"Why don't we take a walk instead? I think Gunter's getting restless with all these people."

"He's a ghost, Jerry. I don't think you're ever going to be able to calm him down. Besides, I'd rather have cheesecake." Savannah pushed her bottom lip out. "I'll get you one too."

"I'll make you a deal. Walk with me to the Lincoln statue and back, and if you still want cheesecake, I'll buy."

"Fine."

Jerry suppressed a laugh. If not for the lack of a foot stomp, she reminded him of a child who hadn't gotten her way. They began walking, Gunter staying close to his side.

Savannah pointed toward the sky. "Look, the air show is starting."

Jerry scanned the sky and saw four biplanes heading their way. "Do you want to stay and watch?"

"No, that's okay. The air show goes on for hours. They will fly right over. The best part is no one can stand in front of you and block your view."

The simple act of walking helped calm his nerves. "This doesn't bother you?"

"What? This?"

"The crowds."

"People? No, I like people. Why, does it bother you?"

Be a man, Jerry. "I've never liked crowds much. It messes with the radar. You're a psychic. I wonder why it doesn't bother you."

"I don't allow it to – at least not when I'm in the moment. Later, I'll be drained, but for now, I'm having fun."

Jerry heard the roar of a larger plane and looked up to see a C5 Galaxy lumbering overhead. He rolled his neck to relieve the tension.

"You good, Jerry?"

"Golden."

"What?"

"Oh, just something me and the guys say. You know, good as gold?"

"Oh."

"Maybe it's before your time."

She laughed an easy laugh. "You're not that much older than me."

They reached the Lincoln statue and Savannah pointed. "Want me to take your picture sitting in his lap?"

Jerry shook his head. "I'm good."

"You sure? It's the thing to do when you're in town."

"I'll pass."

"Okay, then you can take mine." She handed him her cell phone and got in line behind a group of people waiting to have their turn on the statue.

Jerry thought to remind her that she lived here, but a wheezing noise caught his attention. Not a wheeze, but a high-pitched whine of a jet. His mouth went dry as the aircraft neared, the whine turning into a roar. He knew that sound as well as he knew the sound of his own voice.

A-10 warthogs! Take cover, McNeal!

Jerry turned in a circle, staring out at all the people. *Why aren't they running? Can't they hear it?* He opened his mouth to warn them, but nothing came out. Not only couldn't he speak, but he couldn't run. As the jets roared overhead, Jerry closed his eyes. This was it; this was the end.

Something wet touched his hand, and he wondered for

a moment if he were bleeding. He felt it again and looked to see Gunter licking his hand. Jerry pulled his hand away. The sky was quiet. *I'm still alive.*

"Jerry!"

Jerry blinked. Focusing on the voice, he saw a woman sitting on the statue looking less than pleased.

"These people are waiting. Are you going to take my picture or what?"

Gunter whined at his side. Jerry heard Doc's voice whispering in his ear. *Get it together, McNeal. Savannah. Not Iraq, the airshow. Crap!*

***

"Are you feeling better?"

Jerry was lying on a blanket they'd stretched over the grass. Gunter lay in a low crouch at his side, keeping a close eye on those around them. Though various military aircraft continued to fly overhead, he had not had any further issues. "I'm fine. I'd be even better if you stop hovering over me."

Savannah sat beside him, wringing her hands. "I can't believe I didn't see what was happening."

"How could you? You said yourself I was just standing there."

"But why didn't I feel it?"

"I'm the last person to ask about that. I'm still trying to figure out my own curse."

"You've saved so many people, myself included. Do you really feel it's a curse?"

Sometimes. "No, I guess not."

"Liar."

Jerry raised an eyebrow. "So now you can read me?"

"We're closer. Maybe that was it. Too many people between us."

"You're probably right. My radar is all over the place, but not connecting with anyone in particular." He regretted the statement the moment he said it. "I told you before, Alex is safe today."

Savannah frowned. "It's been a while since I heard from her."

Jerry closed his eyes. "Two hours is not a long time. She's working traffic. In case you haven't noticed, there are probably a hundred thousand people in this park alone."

"You owe me cheesecake."

"What?" Jerry realized he'd fallen asleep.

"Cheesecake. You said if I still wanted some when we got back, you'd buy me one."

Jerry pulled his wallet from his pocket and handed her a twenty.

"You want one?"

Jerry returned his wallet to his pants and used his arms for a pillow. "Nope."

"Suit yourself, but don't ask me to share mine."

"I wouldn't dream of it." Jerry closed his eyes once again. He heard voices and opened his eyes, surprised to find it nearly dark.

"Welcome back." Alex sat next to Savannah with a blanket draped around the two of them. She'd changed out of her uniform, opting for jeans and a sweatshirt.

"Alex? When did you get here? How long was I asleep?"

"Hours," Savannah chimed in. "You were asleep when I came back from getting my cheesecake. I was bored, so I used the change to get ice cream. Gunter had his head resting on your chest. He opened his eyes and stared at me as if to say *Wake him and I'll bite you*. I took a picture. Do you want to see?"

Alex's eyes lit up. "I do."

So do I. "Sure."

Savannah thumbed through her phone, turned it for them to see, and sighed. "He's not in the picture."

Alex scrunched her brows together. "I'm beginning to think you two are pulling my leg."

"I wouldn't lie about this and you know it."

"He's real." Jerry looked at Gunter, lying on his side next to him. "Well, as real as a ghost dog can be."

Savanah looked in the same spot where Gunter was lying. "He's a ghost. I guess we shouldn't be surprised he doesn't show up in pictures."

"He showed up in one."

Savannah's eyes went wide. "After he was dead?"

"Yep. The first time Gunter appeared, I was following the feeling, which led me to a snowplow wreck. The whole time I was helping the driver, I knew I was missing something. And the whole time I was at the scene, this dog kept barking and howling his fool head off. It pissed me off because it was in the middle of a blizzard and this dog was obviously in distress. I was agitated that I'd helped the guy and yet the feeling was still so intense. It should have been gone as soon as I saw the man loaded into the ambulance. But it was worse. I yelled at my sergeant – telling him I was going to find that dog and have a talk with its owner. Only I didn't find the dog – I found the car that had careened into the ravine to avoid hitting the snowplow.

"Holly had been down there for hours, and yet when I found her, she was warm. Within seconds of my arrival, she was freezing. When I asked her how she'd managed to stay warm, she told me the dog had climbed in through the windshield and used his body to keep her warm until help arrived. I didn't see any dog and asked her to describe it so I could go looking for it. She got angry and told me I should know what he looks like and kept calling him my dog."

A frown flitted across Alex's face. "Why did she think it was your dog?"

"Because the ID on the dog's tag clearly identified him as a Pennsylvania State Police dog. I saw the photo myself. My boy here is the same K-9 from our station that died a couple of weeks earlier. I still don't know why she was able to capture him on film when no one else has." Gunter lifted his head and wagged his tail.

Savannah beamed. "He's happy to hear you claim him as yours."

"I guess if I have to be honest, I enjoy having him around."

"Wait? So you're saying he's here now?"

"Yes," both Savannah and Jerry answered at the same time.

Alex touched her fingertips to her head then flicked her fingers outward. "Mind blown. I sure wish I could see him."

Jerry slid a hand down Gunter's back, hoping to allow Alex to imagine Gunter's silhouette. He felt more than knew that Gunter only showed himself to people who either had the gift or had a reason to see him. From the feeling in his gut, he knew Alex would soon get her wish.

Chapter Nine

As the skies darkened, the crowd grew restless. With their heightened energy came an influx of paranormal warning signals that had Jerry on edge. He closed his eyes, remembering a particularly helpful conversation with Doc when he had been on the verge of panic after an intense battle in Iraq. Doc had looked him in the eye and said *Everyone has a built-in coping mechanism. Something they turn to when stressed – biting a lip or chewing the inside of the mouth – or maybe it's biting off fingernails. Drumming the fingers, tapping of the foot; you get the picture. Don't lose it on me now, McNeal. Find that one body movement that will help get you out of your head.* Jerry recalled asking why it had to be a body movement, and Doc said it had to be something that was always there when you needed it. Jerry had jokingly asked what if that body part got blown off. Doc had stared him down and told him: *If that happens, I'll put you back together again.* Jerry's coping mechanism turned out to be a hand placed on the back of his neck or at times ran across the top of his head.

Remembering Doc's words, Jerry placed a hand on the back of his neck to try to calm his nerves. Gunter stayed close, watching his every move. Jerry knew the dog felt his distress. *Easy, Jerry, it's just a few fireworks. You know they're coming. Everything's going to be alright. And what about what happened earlier? You knew there was going to be an airshow? Dammit, this is no time to psychoanalyze yourself. Suck it up, Marine.*

"You're awfully quiet over there, Jerry. Everything okay?"

Just arguing with myself and trying to talk myself down from crazy. Jerry peered at Savannah. "Never better."

"You knew that woman, didn't you?"

"What woman?"

"The one in the wreck. What was her name?"

"Holly. I didn't know her before the accident."

"You sure? I'm getting mixed signals. Like you knew her, yet you didn't."

Alex burst out laughing. "Better watch out, Jerry, my wife is a self-proclaimed matchmaker."

"I'd seen her around town before but hadn't ever talked to her. And I'd appreciate you staying out of my love life." *Because I don't have one.*

"You like her, though. I could tell by the way your face lit up when you said her name. Give me her number and I'll put in a good word for you."

Jerry rubbed the back of his neck. "Remember this morning when I said you sounded like my mom?"

"Yes."

"Well, you still do." A blast of small fireworks rained into the sky near the far end of the shore, and Jerry turned to the girls. "Okay, the show's over; it's time to go home."

Alex kicked his foot with hers. "If you liked that, get

ready. You've never seen a show like this before. Thunder is a bigger draw than the Derby itself."

An *umph* sounded and a single light streaked through the sky as all eyes turned toward the water. A few seconds later, a thunderous boom sounded as the sky filled with a burst of color. *Okay, that wasn't so bad. Remember to breathe, Jerry.* The thought had no sooner come into his head than the entire waterfront sounded as if the city were under attack. Jerry felt his heart rate increase. When Savannah had mentioned fireworks, he thought it would be a normal show. There was nothing ordinary about what was happening here. Explosions came from all directions, near and far, and the crowd responded in turn.

A burst of something shot into the air, reminding him of his time in the desert. Each boom and blast echoed off the bridges and buildings, and he could feel the pressure as the barrage continued without a second's pause.

The city's under attack! Jerry pushed off from the blanket, running into what was supposed to be the night. Only there was no night. With each bomb, the cityscape lit up, showing the bodies that littered the ground. Jerry picked his way around the bodies. Even in his panic, he knew to be mindful of the dead.

A man in a camo jacket stepped in front of him and yelled something Jerry couldn't hear. It didn't matter. The guy wasn't with his unit or Jerry would have recognized him. Shadows loomed before him – the sky lit up and the shadows became people. So many people. So much noise. Jerry's only thought was to get away.

Enemy fire shot up once more, and he could hear it raining down behind him. Where was his unit? *Not good, Jerry.* Each time the sky lit up, he saw people of all ages, eyes wide as if wondering how to escape. *What are all the civilians doing here? I can't help them all.*

Someone grabbed hold of his arm. He broke free – running away from the people, away from the noise, away from the vise grip that had clamped onto his heart, making it difficult to breathe. *Please let me live to see another day!*

He needed to find cover. The crowd opened up. Suddenly, he was running free on a car-littered street, heading away from the people but not escaping the noise of the bombs so loud they bounced off the buildings and set off car alarms. Something hit his back and he went down, sliding against the pavement. *I've been hit! Please, God, I'm not ready to die.*

Jerry saw an arched entrance to a building. He got up and scrambled into the archway, pressing his back against the wall. *I need to stay alive until Doc finds me.*

Jerry covered his ears with his hands and closed his eyes. Too late, he felt a presence and knew without opening his eyes that his enemy had found him. He stilled and waited for the threat to come closer, then struck out with everything he had, hitting and flailing until his enemy fell on top of him, the weight of the body comforting, as he knew it would help camouflage him from any further attacks.

Sometime later, the bombing stopped, and his panic ebbed. Jerry opened his eyes, surprised to find not the body of his enemy but Gunter lying across him. The dog lifted his head and ran his tongue along Jerry's face. Jerry ran his hands down the shepherd's side and Gunter wagged his tail. Instantly, he recalled Max's prediction and how she'd told him she'd seen Gunter covering him like a cloak. Jerry buried his head in the dog's fur. *Max was wrong – I'm not Superman.*

***

Jerry pulled out his cell phone, intending to call Savannah, his finger hovering over a different number. He started to call the number, checked the time, and opted to send a message instead, typing two words with hopeful fingers: *You busy?* He stared at the words until they blurred, then hit send, grateful when a moment later, his phone rang.

"You good, McNeal?" Doc asked before Jerry had a chance to utter a greeting.

"Not so much."

"Talk to me."

"This was a bad one, Doc. Maybe the worst one yet."

"Give me the details."

Jerry told him about the incident with the planes, about thinking he was ready for the fireworks and what had ensued.

"What finally pulled you out of it?"

Jerry thought about telling Doc about the dog then hesitated.

"Come on, McNeal, doctor-patient confidentiality, remember."

"Only you're not my real doctor."

"Still counts."

"Doc, what would you say if I told you I'm being haunted?" *There you go, Jerry, no turning back now.*

"Anyone else, I would tell them to call their shrink. You, I'd want to know if it's anyone I know."

Jerry rubbed the back of his neck, debating if he should tell Doc about the guys that had visited him since their demise. He sighed. *One ghost at a time, Jerry.* "No, it's about a ninety-pound police dog who's been hanging around for a while now. When I was running, I felt something hit my back and thought I was done for – I may have even prayed."

"There's a first for everything, McNeal."

"Yeah, well, I've been thinking, and I figure it was the dog who tackled me. I think it was his way of getting me to stop. When I came out of it, the dog had draped itself over my body. Like a – "

"Warming blanket?"

I was going to say "cape." "Yeah. And I think him doing that is what pulled me out."

"This dog, has anyone else seen it?"

Jerry chuckled. "Trying to determine if I'm sane?"

"Let's call it morbid curiosity."

"He's shown himself to a couple of people." Jerry went on to tell Doc about the first time he'd seen the dog and the incidents since. "It was a rough go at first because the dog didn't like me."

"Nonsense: you're the most likable guy I know." Doc's voice was full of sarcasm.

"Yeah, the dog didn't think so." Jerry stopped short of telling Doc what Savannah had told him about the dog being mad at him for trying to send him away. "He growled at me in the beginning, but I think he might like me now."

"I seem to remember you didn't like dogs."

"I don't." Jerry looked at Gunter and sighed. "Or at least I didn't. This one is different. He's a dog but has the attitude of a Marine."

"How so?"

"He doesn't like being told what to do, probably would just as soon fight me as hang out with me, and yet, he's had my back since the moment he appeared."

"Yep, sounds like most of the Marines I've met."

"I've never been able to figure out why he let Holly capture him on film but hasn't shown up on any other cameras or videos. She showed me the film, so I know it to be true."

"Maybe that's why."

The street was filling as people began to make their way out of the city. "I'm not following you, Doc."

"Maybe it wasn't to convince the girl. Maybe he knew getting her to see him was the only way to convince you. Let's face it, if the dog were showing himself only to you, you'd be questioning your own sanity about now."

"Doc, that train left the station a long time ago."

Doc's laughter floated through the phone. "McNeal, you may be a lot of things, but crazy isn't one of them."

"Thanks for calling me back, Doc."

"Anytime, my brother. You good, McNeal?"

"Golden, Doc."

Jerry had no sooner returned his phone to his pocket than it rang. He pulled it out and saw Savannah's name light up the screen. "Hello?"

"Jerry, where the heck are you?"

Jerry looked around for a street sign and didn't see one. "Darned if I know."

"Where'd you go? One minute we were watching fireworks, and the next, you were running off into the crowd."

"Coffee."

"You went for coffee?"

"Nope, I went in search of a bathroom because I drank too much coffee earlier. I was going to use a tree but didn't want your wife to arrest me for indecent exposure."

"Why didn't you come back?"

"I got turned around and couldn't find you." Jerry was

glad he wasn't talking to Max, who would have known he was lying as the words left his mouth. "From the looks of the traffic in the streets, we're not going anywhere for a while. I'll try looking for you again."

"Wait, I have a better idea. Meet us at the Lincoln statue."

"Works for me." Jerry slid his phone into his pocket, waited for an opening in the steady stream of people, and began making his way back to the park. As he walked toward the river, he thought about a video he'd seen on the National Geographic channel about salmon spawning and swimming upstream. Suddenly, the stream of people parted, giving Jerry a clear path – it was then he realized Gunter had moved in front of him, clearing the way.

Chapter Ten

A few short weeks ago, Jerry had never even watched a TikTok video, yet here he was sitting alone in the dark living room watching video after video. Not any video, mind you – Jerry was watching dog videos, preferring those that focused on training. He'd already saved countless videos and now found himself comparing the dogs in the videos to Gunter. A video came on that showed a German shepherd opening the front door with his paw. "Oh yeah, well, I'd like to see your dog walk through walls."

"You okay there, McNeal?" Alex didn't wait for a reply as she continued on to the kitchen.

Jerry fumbled to swipe the app closed, then shoved the phone between his legs much like a school kid caught playing with his cellphone well past his bedtime.

When Alex returned to the room, she carried two single-serving tubs of ice cream. She handed him one along with a spoon, then switched on the lamp and climbed into an oversized chair on the opposite side of the room. Wearing pajama shorts and an oversized top, she tucked her bare feet under her bottom as she pulled the lid from her container.

He lifted the lid and spooned out a bite, enjoying the rich taste of chocolate. *Be careful, Jerry. Something tells me you're about to get interrogated.*

She took a bite and pointed the spoon at him. "What's your deal, McNeal?"

Yep, she's in cop mode – handing out a treat to appear non-threatening while asking questions. He took another bite. "I'm not sure I get your drift."

"You show up at our door under the guise of dropping off a cat. And now here you're sitting alone on my couch sounding like a basketball parent who's mad their child didn't get to play in the game."

Jerry pushed the spoon into the frozen dessert. "Does my being here bother you?"

"I just want to know why you're here, and don't give me that BS about looking for work."

She was a good cop – she'd seen right past the ruse. "Why do you think I'm here?"

"We're not doing that." Cat climbed into the chair with Alex and attempted to sniff the container. Alex placed a drop of what looked to be strawberry onto the lid and set it on the table next to her. Cat sniffed it briefly before deciding to indulge in the creamy sweetness.

"Doing what?"

"This cop crap – answering a question with a question."

Jerry lifted his spoon and took a bite while contemplating his answer.

Alex surprised him by continuing. "My wife may have bought your story about going to the can, but I saw your face and watched you bolt like a scared rabbit. Savannah said you were in the Marines. I'm assuming that was a

PTSD episode."

Jerry stiffened in his seat. *Don't lie, Jerry – she'll see right through it.* "It was."

Alex placed her container on the table beside her chair. "I'm assuming you knew the risk when you went."

"I prepared myself beforehand and thought I had it under control."

"Savannah told me you had an episode when the planes flew over. Why didn't you leave then?"

Jeez, now she's trying to play therapist. "As I said, I thought I was prepared."

Alex laughed. Aside from giving him the ice cream, it was the first hint of a friendly conversation since she'd entered the room. "Nothing prepares you for Thunder over Louisville."

"That is no crap. Listen, I've been to fireworks shows since getting out of the Marines. I even worked a few events when I was with the state police. What you guys put on here is more in line with Armageddon."

"I'll take that as a compliment to our city. Now back to the original question as to why you're here. What's your angle, Mr. McNeal?"

Good work, Alex. I see detective in your future. Jerry sat back in his chair, debating his answer. He worried over telling her about the danger he saw her in, but the option was to lie and tell her he had a thing for her wife, which wouldn't help his case. Better tell her the truth and deal with the consequences. "I'm here to help you."

He expected her to laugh. She did not. "What kind of danger am I in?"

"Does that mean you believe me?"

This time, Alex laughed a hardy laugh. "I figured it was either that or my wife is pregnant, which we both know not to be the case. I hope this is over soon for Savannah's sake."

Jerry was impressed with Alex's calm exterior. "You're not worried?"

"I put my life in danger every time I put on that uniform. Besides, you did okay by my wife, so I figure I could be in worse hands. I will be in uniform when it goes down, right?"

"Good guess."

"Not really. I knew something was up when Savannah asked for me to set up the ride-along."

"And yet you said nothing."

"I wanted to be sure. So where do we go from here?"

"Normally, I would say we continue doing what we were doing but now that you know, I would like to stay on your six."

"Meaning?"

"Until whatever is going to happen takes place, we stay together. You leave the house – I go with you."

"I thought you said I would be in police uniform."

Jerry brought his fingertips together and flexed his palms in and out several times. "I don't usually broadcast my feelings to the intended target. Now that you know it might change things and I don't want to leave anything to chance."

"Target? Are you saying I might get shot?"

Maybe. "I don't know. Everything is still fuzzy."

"Is that normal?"

"It's part of the process."

"Do you always win?"

No. Don't tell her that. "I'm pretty good at my job."

"Are you still working for the Pennsylvania State Police?"

"Technically, no."

"And yet the database says you are."

Jerry sighed. "It's complicated."

"Uncomplicate it."

"Have you ever thought about becoming a detective?"

"Does it show?"

"A little." Jerry rubbed the back of his neck, trying to decide how much to tell. He wasn't worried about his own ass, but Seltzer would get in a lot of trouble if anyone learned of his part in Jerry's get-out-of-jail-free card. "Listen, I appreciate your tenacity, but I'd like to request an attorney."

"You're not under arrest."

"No, and I'd like to keep it that way."

"Will your secret help you save me?"

"It got your supervisor to agree to a police ride-along, didn't it?"

Alex yawned. "Okay, I'm heading back to bed. You should try to get some sleep. If you're planning on being my shadow, you're going to need it."

"I've done my share of traffic."

Alex pushed off the couch. She shooed Cat away and retrieved the empty ice cream cartons. "Who said anything about traffic?"

***

The second Jerry woke, he knew someone was in bed next to him. Afraid to move, he searched his mind for answers. He hadn't seen Savannah since she'd gone up to bed. Alex? Not likely, as she had gone upstairs before him. He swallowed. *Unless I climbed into the wrong bed.* He eased toward the edge of the bed, intending to sneak out of the room. The person lying next to him let out a soft moan. *Crap.*

He turned, expecting a confrontation, and Gunter rolled over onto his back, extending his feet into the air. The dog opened his eyes and wagged his tail.

Jerry pulled on his jeans, thankful he wasn't about to get shot. "I thought we agreed you were not supposed to come inside."

Gunter yawned.

"You can't be tired. You're a ghost. Ghosts don't get tired – do they?"

Another yawn.

"Fine, you can stay but only in here. You're not to scare Cat. He seems to like it here." Jerry pulled on his shirt and left the room, shutting the door behind him. He stood there for a moment staring at the door, half expecting Gunter to follow.

Jerry turned, surprised to see Alex dressed in mesh shorts and a tank top. She lifted a pair of running shoes for him to see. "Problem?"

Jerry jabbed a thumb toward his bedroom door. "I have company."

Alex's brows lifted.

Jerry shook his head. "Not that kind of company. Gunter's in the room."

Alex stepped in front of him, opened the door, and heaved a sigh. She shut the door and looked at Jerry. "A girl can hope, can't she?"

Jerry gave a nod to the shoes. "You're not going to work today."

"We," she gave a wink, "are undercover today."

"Undercover?"

"Yes, I signed up to represent the police force in today's race."

"I'm afraid I'm not following you."

"Oh, you'll be following alright. Especially if you plan on wearing jeans."

They were going to be running in a foot race. He hadn't so much as jogged since leaving Chambersburg. Jerry ran a hand over his head as the implications set in.

Alex looked him up and down. "You do run, don't you?"

"I do. Just give me a moment to change."

"Wear something you don't mind getting ruined."

Jerry arched a brow. "Just what kind of race is this?"

Alex winked. "The kind where people don't mind getting dirty."

"Sounds more like a hockey game than a race."

"Just put on something old and meet me downstairs and tell the dog he'd better not scare Mr. Meowgy."

"I told him, but I can't make him listen." Gunter lifted his head when Jerry came into the room but didn't show any signs of getting out of bed. Jerry rooted through his duffle bag and pulled out a shirt. It wasn't exactly old, nor was it one he'd miss if it met an early demise. He changed into the shirt and running shorts and traded his boots for sneakers.

Gunter lifted his head, cocking it to the side.

"Seems we'll be running in a race today. Alex said people are likely to play dirty. Maybe you should wait this one out."

Gunter lifted his lip and gave a slight growl.

Jerry held up both hands. "Okay, have it your way, but you can't say I didn't warn you."

***

Jerry walked into the kitchen, saw Alex bleeding from

what looked to be several stab wounds, and immediately sprang into action – pushing Savannah out of the way and barking orders. "Call 9-11 and grab me some bandages. Towels, blankets, anything that will stop the bleeding."

Savannah laughed. "If you do anything to mess up my handiwork, I'll brain you."

Jerry was appalled. All this time, he'd been worrying about protecting Alex and the threat was right under his nose. Then why wasn't his radar triggered? Even now, his spidey senses idled at a dull roar. He looked at Savannah, who was standing there holding a pair of scissors. "Why?"

"For the zombie run, I thought Alex told you."

Zombie run? He glanced at Alex. "This is all a joke?"

Alex gave Savannah a high five. "Not an intentional one, but it played out rather well."

Jerry was incensed. "Played out. You're both lucky I didn't see Savannah with the scissors when I saw you bleeding. This could have gone bad in so many ways."

"Geez, Jerry, lighten up. We weren't intentionally trying to get a rise out of you. We thought you'd laugh, not go berserk."

"Yeah, well, you try having the guys you serve with blown to pieces in front of your eyes. Maybe there's a limb missing, and there's nothing you can do but try to stop the bleeding until help arrives." *Easy, Jerry, they didn't know it would set you off.*

Savannah lowered the scissors. "I'm sorry."

Alex nodded her agreement. "Me too. We didn't mean any harm."

"On the bright side, your wounds look real." Savannah held up the scissors. "Your turn, Jerry."

Jerry shook his head. "I'll pass."

Alex took the scissors from Savannah and faced Jerry.

"Sorry, but no deal. The plan is to blend in."

"I'm wearing running gear."

"Yes, which makes you look like a runner, not a zombie."

Jerry smiled. "That's because I'm the real guy, and I'll be in the front of the pack. You know, the guy the zombies are chasing."

"Nice try. Since you haven't been training for a five-mile run, we will have to make you look the part." Alex took hold of Jerry's shirt and began cutting. After several slices, she motioned for Savannah, who added a few strategic wounds to Jerry's skin.

Jerry let out a sigh. All this because he didn't have the heart to abandon an abandoned cat.

Chapter Eleven

Jerry found it weird being chauffeured around, especially when the one doing the driving was a female. He had offered to drive, but Alex insisted on taking the lead, claiming she didn't want to chance changing anything. While this was sound reasoning, Jerry also figured Alex to be just as uncomfortable sitting in the passenger seat as he. She was a cop. Cops liked to be in control. He smiled inwardly, wondering how calm she'd be if she knew Gunter was in the back seat, peering over her shoulder.

They came to a red light and Alex looked at him. "You're quiet, McNeal."

She was back in cop mode, using his last name. "Just trying to figure you out."

"Ah, the tables are turned. What do you want to know?"

"You didn't tell Savannah that you know."

"Nope."

"Why not?"

"Her knowing is bad. Her knowing that I know would be even worse."

"How so?"

The light changed, and several people continued through the redlight. Alex pounded the steering wheel with her fist. "Hello? Cop sitting right here!"

Jerry cleared his throat. "You might have more credence if you were actually driving a police car."

She ignored his quip. "Because if she knew that I know, she'd want to talk about it."

"And that would be bad?"

Alex glanced in his direction. "You've met my wife, right?"

Alex was right. Savannah was worried enough for the three of them. A car stopped in front of them, and Jerry pushed on the brake he didn't have.

"Don't worry, McNeal; I'm not going to let you get hurt." She looked at him and grinned. "I need you in one piece so you can save my ass."

"Why a cop?"

"Why a cop what?"

"You said you'd always wanted to be one. Why a cop?"

She answered so quickly, it was obvious she'd given the question a lot of thought. "I've always been the square peg. When other girls were wearing dresses, I had my ball cap on backwards. My friends wanted to be cheerleaders. I wanted to take things apart to see how they work. One day, a cop came to our school. Nothing bad – just one of those career day things. He was showing pictures on a PowerPoint, and he paused the frame and said, 'This could be you someday.' I swear, McNeal, it looked like the man was staring into my soul. I took the bait. From that day forward, it was all I ever wanted to do. I guess I figured if I were a cop, I'd have some control over my life."

"How's that working out for you?"

Alex blew out a sigh. "Pretty darn good until you came into the picture."

"I could leave."

"Nah, I think it's best you hang around. I wouldn't want to be responsible for your death."

Jerry eyed Alex. "My death?"

"Sure thing. If I send you away, I get killed. If that happens, Savannah would hunt you down like a dog."

"I guess I'd better hang around for a bit and see that you stay alive."

"Reckon that'd be the best plan." Alex pulled up to a parking lot marked "reserved," flashed her badge, and waited for the attendant to pull back the barrier to allow them entrance. They'd no sooner parked when Alex pointed to the street. "Check it out. Here come some of the runners."

Jerry looked to see a group of zombies walking across the street. Arms stretched in front, they dragged mangled legs and looked much like the cast of *The Walking Dead*. "If they all move like that, the race is in the bag."

"Don't let their theatrics fool you. This is just the pre-race show of those hoping to get their pictures in the newspapers. There's a lot of bragging rights to be had – especially if the winner gets his picture on both the website and front page of the *Courier-Journal*."

Jerry glanced down at his ripped shirt and fake wounds.

"Chin up, McNeal. We're not here to win. We're here to blend in and take action if need be."

Jerry followed Alex to the back of the car, where she pulled a fanny pack out of the trunk and buckled it around her waist. "And if we need backup."

She unzipped her fanny pack to let him peek inside – ID, badge, a small service revolver, and a whistle.

"Where's my fanny pack?"

"You're not a fanny pack kind of guy." She tried to fit her cell phone in the pack, but it wouldn't work, so she powered it off and left it in the trunk.

Deciding he could do without his for a couple of hours, Jerry did the same then rolled his neck.

"Problem, McNeal?"

"No gun, no cell phone. I'm beginning to feel a bit emasculated."

Alex beamed. "I've got your back."

"I'm not used to being a kept man."

"Relax, it's just for a few hours. Besides, you said it's not happening today."

"It's not."

"Then relax and try to have a little fun."

As they began walking, Jerry felt Gunter's presence. He started to acknowledge the dog and nearly tripped over his own two feet. Gunter looked very much the part of a zombie dog. The ear that had been bitten off years earlier by a crackhead was ripped and hanging by a flap of skin. The area where he'd been shot looked fresh and exceptionally gory. There was a second bullet hole along with a knife wound. *Those happened since his return from the dead.*

Alex stopped to see what had detained him. "Are you – Jerry, it's the dog! He's real!"

What!? "You can see him?"

Alex nodded, her face ghostly white. "He looks – God, is he alright?"

Gunter lifted his lips and wagged his tail.

"He's fine."

"Wait, did he just smile?"

"Did I forget to mention he's a comedian?"

"Why is he allowing me to see him? You said he only lets people see him when they're in danger."

Or when he wants to be the star of the show. Jerry gave a chin jut, telling Alex to turn around. A man with a press badge hurried toward them, holding a camera with a high-powered lens.

"Cool makeup!" the reporter called. "Hold up. I want to get a picture of the three of you."

"I guess I'm not the only one who can see him," Alex remarked.

"Apparently not. Don't let him get too close. I don't know how Gunter will respond."

Alex dug into her fanny pack and pulled out her badge. "This is a working dog. That's close enough."

The reporter scratched his head. "That's awesome. I didn't know Louisville PD had such a great sense of humor. Can I take a photo?"

Jerry rubbed his hand over his head. "You can take one, but don't be surprised if it doesn't turn out."

The reporter looked through the camera and adjusted the lens. "Oh yeah, why's that?"

"Camera shy. Many have tried, most have failed." Alex turned away and he knew she was trying to keep from laughing.

"Challenge accepted." He held the camera to his eye once more and snapped several photos. "Man, that is some wicked good makeup. It looks so real. I need to get a close-up."

Gunter growled a warning when the man took a step closer.

The reporter halted his advance. "Okay, no close-ups, but you have to at least tell me how you got him to hold still long enough to apply the makeup."

"It's a new process." Jerry shrugged. "I'm afraid I can't give away our secret until the patent comes back."

"That's too bad. People would kill to have their dog looking like this."

"That's what I'm afraid of."

"What?"

Alex grabbed Jerry by the arm. "He said we're going to miss the race if we don't get a move on."

"Okay, one more before you go. Just the dog this time." The reporter pulled an older camera from his bag. Jerry recognized the camera, as it looked just like the one Holly used. The reporter aimed the camera at Gunter. "Fantastic. Oh, just one more question. I know you can't tell me what makeup you used, but how easy is it to apply?"

Jerry touched the top of Gunter's head. "That's the thing with this stuff – it disappears in a flash."

"So it dissolves?"

"Into thin air."

Alex elbowed him the moment the guy turned away. "You enjoyed that as much as the dog did."

"I'd enjoy it more if I could be there when he discovers the dog isn't in any of the pictures."

"Are you sure he won't be?"

Jerry ran both hands over his head and continued along the back of his neck. "When it comes to this dog, I'm not sure of anything."

***

The race began promptly at nine a.m., all zombie limping and limb-dragging forgotten as the runners tore off like someone had lit a match under them. When the crowd in front of them cleared, Alex started a steady jog. Jerry found himself both pleased and disappointed. While he didn't have any aspirations of winning, he at least thought he'd finish in a respectable place.

"You look disappointed, McNeal."

"Not at all. I love finishing last."

"Remember, we're on the job. The goal is to hang back and blend in with the crowd."

"What about the crowd ahead of us?"

"There are people in place for that."

Why couldn't I be partnered with them?

"I heard that."

No way. "You did?"

"No, but I had you for a moment."

Since he was running slow enough to talk without gulping for air, he decided to take advantage of it. "How did you and Savannah meet?"

Alex's lips curved upward. "I went to a psychic show. Saw her across the room and waited my turn to sit at her table."

Sounds familiar. "Let me guess, love at first sight."

"On my part."

"But not on hers?"

"She was in denial."

A runner with his clothes torn to shreds pushed between them, sending Alex stumbling to keep her balance.

Jerry shaped his hand into a gun, pretended to shoot the man, and blew on the end of his finger.

Alex moved beside him again. "Feel better?"

"A little." Jerry frowned at Gunter. "Don't let that happen again."

"She seems happy, so you must have changed her

mind."

"Are you digging for details?"

"Nope."

"Good, because you're not getting them." She grinned. "What's so funny?"

"I was remembering one of our early dates. I was running in a 10K, and Savannah decided to join me."

"Don't take this the wrong way, but I can't see Savannah running in a race."

"She didn't run. She decided to find a place along the route and give me water."

"That works."

"In theory. You see, she's not a runner, so she didn't know how things work. I'm running – really running – and I wanted to impress her, so I was actually trying to set a decent pace. And I see her in the distance sitting at a table at an outdoor café off to my right. She has the water in front of her and I was like, cool, I'm parched. I thought she'd come to the sidelines so I could get a drink. Only she just sat at the table in the courtyard and watched opened-mouthed as I kept going."

"She expected you to stop and get it?"

"She did. Was a bit pissy about it, in fact, asking why I didn't stop to get a drink when she'd made it a point to be there waiting for me."

"What did you tell her?"

"That I was running a race."

"Did she get over it?"

"She said she did, but she never watched me race again."

Another runner pushed between them, elbowing Jerry as he passed. Jerry looked to see Gunter, who was nowhere in sight. An instant later, the dog ran in front of the same runner who tried to stop but ended up toppling over the dog.

Alex started to stop. Jerry grabbed her arm, pulling her forward. "Leave him. He finds out the dog's with us and he'll threaten to sue the city."

"You good, McNeal?"

"Aside from the fact I just got passed by a zombie?"

"You didn't expect to win the race, did you?"

Jerry wiped the sweat from his face. "I'd settle for not coming in dead last."

"I think I can agree with that. What say we pick up the pace a bit?"

"You lead and I'll follow."

Chapter Twelve

Savannah was waiting by the door when they returned. It was clear from the crease between her eyebrows she was upset. Jerry followed Alex inside and kicked off his shoes without untying them. *Don't make eye contact, Jerry. Whatever is going on is none of your business. Just go upstairs and leave them to hash things out in private.*

Savannah stepped in front of him, blocking his way. "Not so fast, Jerry."

Crap! What did I do? Jerry searched his mind but couldn't think of anything.

Alex stooped to untie her sneakers, and Jerry guessed she was having the same internal conversation. She removed her shoes and placed them in the tray by the door before turning her attention to Savannah. "Babe, you seem upset. What's the problem?"

"What's the problem? The problem is I tried to call you a hundred times. Why didn't you answer your cell?"

"Because it's in the trunk of the car."

Savannah narrowed her eyes. "What the heck is it doing in there?"

Alex chuckled. "It wouldn't fit in my fanny pack."

"This is not a laughing matter!" Savannah turned and pointed her index finger at Jerry. "What's your excuse?"

Savannah crossed her arms, and Jerry resisted the urge to tell her she was giving off the mom vibe again. He didn't know why she was so mad – nor was he picking up on any clues on his internal radar – but it was obvious something had lit a fire under the girl. "My excuse for what?"

"For not answering my calls."

Alex answered before he had a chance – staying calm and choosing her words so as not to exacerbate the situation. "Listen, babe. I know you've been under a lot of stress lately. I'm sorry I missed your calls, but you need to chill. I don't know what you think is going on between me and Jerry, but the answer is nothing. We were at the race. I had to decide what was more important: my cell phone or my gun. I chose my gun. As for Jerry, he didn't have any pockets, and it was easier to leave the phone in the trunk than to carry it in his hand while running five miles. Could we have checked them when we were done? Yes. That's on us. To be honest, when the race was over, our only thoughts were to get out of there before traffic got any worse. That's the whole of it. If you don't believe me, go check the trunk and see for yourself."

Savannah stood with her mouth agape.

Jerry was at a loss for words. *Could that really be the root of Savannah's anger, that she thought they'd spent the day fooling around?* Savannah took in several deep breaths, and for a moment, he thought she was going to cry.

Instead, she surprised him by squaring her shoulders. "First, I'm insulted that you think I don't trust you. Second, I was not trying to check up on you. I was worried about you."

The lines in Alex's face softened. "You knew I was with Jerry. If anything was going to happen, he would be the first to know, right?"

Savannah slid a quick glance to Jerry then returned her attention to Alex. "That is exactly why I was upset."

Alex closed her eyes, then opened them once again. "It's been a long day. We both ran five miles, need to take a shower, and I don't know about Jerry, but I'm hungry. You're going to have to be clearer than that."

Savannah pulled her cell phone from her pocket and swiped the front of it several times before turning it around. "Is this clear enough for you?"

Jerry looked at the phone, then snatched it from Savannah's hand, zooming in on the photo that showed Gunter in all his mangled glory along with the bold headline, **Zombie Dog Wins Big at Derby City Zombie Race!**

"I saw this and knew it was Gunter. My first reaction was being pissed off that he allowed someone else take a photo, and yet the one I took showed nothing. Then I remembered what you'd said about him only showing himself when there was trouble – I tried calling Alex, and when she didn't answer, tried to call you. When you didn't answer, my mind thought of all the reasons neither of you answered. The more I tried to calm myself, the more I thought of different reasons. I'm not a psycho. I have good reason to worry." The tears had begun. Savannah looked at each of them before finally settling on Jerry. "I can't keep this in anymore. We have to tell her."

Alex stepped forward and wrapped her arms around Savannah. "I already know. Jerry told me. Don't blame him. I knew something was up by the way you were acting.

Nothing happened today. I should have texted you before I turned off my phone. I'm so sorry to have worried you."

They stayed embraced for a moment before Savannah pulled away. She sniffed, wiped the tears from her eyes, then looked at Jerry. "You said it could change things if you told her."

Jerry nodded. "That's why I insisted on going with Alex today. My radar told me she would be fine, but I wanted to make sure."

"What about the photo. You said Gunter only shows himself to people who need to see him." Savannah whipped her head around, looking at Alex. "Wait, does this mean you got to see him?"

Alex nodded. "I did, although I must admit I didn't expect him to look like that."

Savannah shook her head. "He doesn't. Not when I've seen him anyway. Was it makeup or real blood?" Savannah tilted her head as if considering. "It would have to be real blood unless there are makeup artists in the other realm. But why would he appear like that? Was he in pain? I mean, he's dead, so it probably didn't hurt. Tell me he wasn't in pain."

Jeez, he almost preferred Alex's interrogation. Jerry ran a hand over his head. "It was real alright. Near as I can tell, he appeared showing every wound he's received both while living and dead. The ear that had been chewed off by the crackhead, the bullet that killed him. Even the bullet he took when protecting you and the knife wound he got from Bev's son. He was dead when he got the last two and yet somehow was able to manifest those wounds on his body today."

"But why?"

Jerry hesitated. The only answer he had sounded crazy

even to him. "I think he did it as a joke. He saw everyone walking around looking like zombies and wanted to fit in. I swear, at one point, he even smiled."

Alex bobbed her head in agreement. "It's true. I saw it."

"But why even show himself in the first place? You said he only shows himself when the person is in danger."

"That's been the case, until now."

Alex spoke up. "Maybe he likes the attention."

Savannah laughed. "You know this all sounds absurd, right?"

Jerry forwarded himself the photo and handed Savannah her phone. "Not any more absurd than him coming back from the dead in the first place."

"Where is he now? Is he okay?" Savannah realized what she'd said and laughed for the first time since they'd entered. "I mean, as okay as a dead dog can be."

Jerry motioned toward Alex. "Your wife hurt his feelings."

Alex puffed her chest. "I didn't mean to."

"The moment she used her cop voice, he tucked his tail and disappeared."

Alex looked at Savannah as if begging her to take her side. "The dog was a mangled mess, but it wasn't like he was in danger of dying, so I told him he was not getting in my car covered in blood."

"Poor, poor doggy." Jerry looked at Alex and winked.

Savannah wrinkled her nose. "You stink."

Alex jutted her chin. "Okay, I suck. But I wasn't going to let that dog in my car with all that blood over him."

Savannah waved her hand in front of her face. "I didn't say you suck. I said you stink –you both do."

"Far be it for me to offend." Jerry headed toward the

stairs. As his foot touched the bottom step, he pondered the photo once more. "The photographer used an older camera."

Both Savannah and Alex answered him at once. "What?"

Jerry walked back to where they stood. "You said you were angry that Gunter didn't show up in the picture you took with your phone. That's the reason. The reporter took multiple photos of the two of us with Gunter. But he only took two of him by himself, and both were taken with an older camera. When he pulled it out, I remember thinking the camera looked like the one Holly used. Maybe it has to be a special kind of camera."

Savannah nodded her head. "I guess that could be the case. It still sucks, as my cell phone is supposed to take the best pictures."

Alex grinned. "I guess they didn't think to test it on ghosts before they made that claim."

"I don't know if I'm right. It could just be a fluke." Jerry caught a whiff of himself and headed up to his room without another word. The moment he entered the bedroom, he felt Gunter's presence. "I know you're here – I can feel you."

Gunter appeared in front of him in full form.

"I'm glad to see you. However, I don't know how I feel about your showing everyone your battle wounds. I sure hope that doesn't come back to haunt me."

Gunter moved to a lounging position, cocked his hip to the side, and placed his head between his front paws, staring up at Jerry with disapproving eyes.

"You're right. That was in poor taste. I have to admit – you make a darn good zombie. And cutting in front of the jerk like you did was pretty cool too. I guess what I'm trying to say is, for a dog, you're pretty alright."

Gunter lifted his head and wagged his tail.

***

Jerry was just about to head downstairs when he received a text from Max.

I drew this for you. Jerry clicked on the attachment, surprised to find an impressive illustration of a German shepherd materializing from within the clouds and running toward a man. Jerry sat on the bed, staring at the photo. Max had not only visualized his panic attack before it happened, but she'd also seen Gunter protecting him when he was too weak-minded to protect himself. Jerry looked at the picture once more. The dog was a giant compared to the man, who stood watching as the dog ran toward him. Though Jerry could only see the man's back, his body language showed him to be unafraid. *What are you trying to tell me, Max? That I shouldn't be afraid of the dog or that there's no need to be frightened when the dog is near?*

Jerry canceled out of the photo and thumbed a message to Max. *Thanks for the amazing picture. You are very talented.*

<Max> *Glad you like it. It came to me in a dream. I think it is the dog's way of telling you that you don't have to be afraid when he's with you.*

<Jerry> *I think you're right.*

<Max> *Tell Gunter I said hi.*

Jerry looked at the dog. "Max said to say hello."

Gunter wagged his tail.

<Jerry> *I just did. He said to tell you hello too.*

<Max> *Did he really talk?*

Jerry read her text and smiled. > *No, but he did wag his tail.*

<Max> Cool. But it would've been even cooler if he

actually talked.

<Jerry> *I agree. I've got to go for now.*

<Max> *Okay. Glad you liked my picture. See ya.*

Gunter jumped onto the bed beside him. Jerry pulled out his phone, attempting a selfie with Gunter. When he looked at the phone, he was the only one in the frame.

Jerry bumped against the dog, who felt as real as any other dog would. "Just checking."

Gunter gave Jerry a quick lick along his jawline as if to say *I'm as real as you want me to be.*

Chapter Thirteen

A mother should never have to mourn the death of a son. Nor should a wife bear the loss of a husband taken from her much too soon. Angel Parkes had done both. She'd also gazed in the face of their killer who – in her mind – had gotten away with murder. Of course, the authorities didn't think so – calling it an unfortunate incident – offering their sympathies on one hand and telling Angel her husband and son were victims of a tragic accident. While the police officer that T-boned them had lived, both Angel's husband and son died. Over what? Expired plates! Instead of calling it in and having other officers be on the lookout for the car, the officer had pursued the vehicle, reaching excessive speeds through residential streets before finally blowing through a traffic light and ramming into Trenton's Prius at nearly a hundred miles per hour. Officer Pardy Ramirez returned to duty after six months, only to be killed in the line of duty several months after that.

While Angel should have felt remorse over the woman's death, in truth, she'd felt cheated that she didn't play a part in the woman's demise – especially after Angel had gone to great lengths in planning Officer Ramirez's death. Since the policewoman had been so intent on stopping the car with expired tags, Angel was going to see that she got her wish. Only, when the woman approached her vehicle, Angel planned to be waiting with a surprise of her own. One shot fired point-blank from her husband's sawed-off shotgun. Sure, she might end up spending the rest of her life in prison, but it would be worth it to look into the eyes of the woman who destroyed her life as she pulled the trigger. It was the perfect retaliation, and Angel saw herself as the Avenging Angel – only she hadn't gotten her chance to avenge anything, and that was the catalyst that had set her on her current course.

Angel gripped the bottom of the storage shed, lifting the door up into the ceiling – her heart aching as the jet-black Mustang came into view. She stood looking at the car for several moments picturing her son, Andrew, staring out at her from behind the wheel. Angel shook off that vision as another appeared. She smiled, remembering her son's face when she'd gifted the car to him the day he received his driver's license.

Her husband, Trenton, was a sergeant in the Army, and they'd been stationed in Hawaii at the time. She'd pulled money out of savings and purchased the car without her husband's knowledge. Trenton was furious, but Angel had been able to soothe him over – at least until Andrew got his first speeding ticket on that same night. Trenton had threatened to take away his keys, but Andrew had insisted he hadn't meant to speed, claiming he was still getting used to the 'Stang's power. As usual, Angel had taken Andrew's side, and she and Trenton had gotten into yet another argument over their son. Angel sighed. There'd been too many arguments over Andrew, but there wouldn't be anymore.

Angel pulled the keys from her pocket and got inside the car. She closed her eyes, drinking in the smell. She hadn't dared to even pass a damp cloth over the dashboard for fear of removing even the tiniest of memories. The Mustang started on the first attempt, the sound of the engine bringing tears to her eyes. Andrew would have loved the way the rumble bounced off the inside of the steel cage. She pressed on the pedal and moved the horse out of its corral and into the light of day.

The horsey car – that was what Andrew called the muscle car when he was a little boy. They'd been stationed at Fort Leonard Wood, Missouri at the time, and the corporal living next door had a boss Mustang he liked to tinker on late at night, revving the engine, which would sometimes backfire. Not conducive for a sleeping child. After one such night when Andrew had been woken from sleep by the rumble of the engine, she'd gone into his room and told him it was just a car – assuring him there was nothing to cry about. The next day, she'd taken him next door and insisted the neighbor start the engine so her boy could associate the sound with the fear. Just as the engine rumbled to life, Andrew had keyed upon the emblem of the horse, pointing his tiny finger and proclaiming it to be a horsey car. The outing worked. Angel was thrilled when the next time he was woken by the sound – Andrew merely said, "The horsey car's awake" and went back to sleep without shedding a single tear.

She turned off the Mustang and went to her own car, backing it into the vacant space. She reached into her purse and removed the note she'd prepared, giving it a final read.

If you are reading this, my mission is done. I offer no

apology, as I feel no regret for my actions – only the pride of a mother avenging the death of her son. And a wife exacting revenge for her husband's murder. I don't expect anyone to understand my reasoning, as I do not fully understand it myself. I've spent too many sleepless nights trying to find another solution; however, in my mind, this is the only way. I've spoken with my husband at length since his death, and he assures me I must execute the mission in its entirety if we are to be happy together in our afterlife. He visits me often, telling me this is the reason I was not with them that day, so that I would be alive to see justice served. I can't help but think I will not find peace until I myself am dead. I pray if you are reading this, that is the case. I should have been with them that day. It is only due to a minor argument with my husband that I refused to get in the car – a decision I've regretted for much too long. I will avenge their death so that they will welcome me when they see me again. There will be no arguing in the afterlife.

A bit rambling, but it'll have to do. Angel folded the note, then reached into the back seat and grabbed the duffle bag. Closing and locking the storage unit, she put both the bag and the note in the passenger seat of the Mustang, then pulled a cloth from the console and walked to the rear of the car. She stood staring at the license plate, wishing they'd never left the safety of the island. But they had when her husband received orders to the Fort Knox Army base in Kentucky. She knew the transfer to be a real possibility, but she'd hoped they would be able to stay in paradise a while longer. Everything changed after that transfer. She had no friends and Andrew hadn't weathered the adjustment very well. He'd become sullen and refused to do the simplest tasks. He hadn't even gotten around to changing out the plates when the accident occurred.

Accident – their deaths were no accident. They were murdered and someone needs to pay. Angel sucked in her breath and screamed into the air, not caring when her anguish bounced off the steel buildings that surrounded her. She gathered herself and wished for a moment she'd brought her meds. No, she needed a clear head – something she hadn't had in the last year.

Angel bent, spat onto the cloth, and ran it over the long-expired tags. Bait. A minor traffic infraction. Only this time, the officer would get more than they bargained for. Payback. Perfect. At least it would be if it were Ramirez.

Angel returned to the Mustang, slid behind the wheel, and closed the door. She unzipped the bag, pushed the guns aside, and removed a folder. She opened it and pulled out the Derby schedule, tracing a finger around the Balloon Glow slated to take place later this evening at the Kentucky fairgrounds. It was an evening demonstration of fiery light put on by the hot air balloons that were participating in the balloon race the following morning.

Andrew had always loved watching hot air balloons, which was the reason she'd chosen this particular day to begin avenging his death. She slipped the Derby schedule back into the folder and pulled out the map, unfolding it to see the marks she'd made. If she was able to exact her revenge and escape the city without being killed, she would move on to Cincinnati, Pittsburgh, and other major cities she'd circled. The only reasoning behind her choice of cities was that they needed to be large enough to have a high crime rate. If that were the case, police should be focusing on serious crimes, not minor infractions – if the cop was worrying about the small stuff, she felt they deserved to be punished. "I AM THE PUNISHER!"

Angel unfolded the note once more and signed the

bottom before placing it and the map back inside the folder. She reached in the bag and brought out a framed photo of Trenton and Andrew standing next to the Mustang the day she'd given it to him. Good ole Trenton, smiling for the picture even though he was angry with her. He did that a lot – got angry with her and accused her of coddling their son. Maybe she did, but isn't that a mother's right? Trenton didn't have to worry about that anymore – she no longer had a son to coddle. At least not while she was alive.

Angel ran a finger across each of their images. "I'll be seeing you both soon. But not before I make things right."

***

The traffic heading into Louisville was beyond anything she'd imagined. Traffic on Dixie Highway was terrible, but from the time she entered the I-264, it was at a crawl. Unless an officer came up behind her, there was no way she would get lucky enough to be pulled over. Nor was she likely to get away after the stop.

Angel gripped the wheel when a pale green Prius moved up beside her. She looked again and realized it wasn't a Prius but a Chevy. *Hold it together, Angel. You've waited much too long for this.* Easing her grip, she went over her plan – take out as many female officers as she could before getting caught. She'd thought about taking out anyone with a badge but couldn't wrap her head around killing an innocent man. No, her victims must be women; that way, it would be easier to visualize Officer Ramirez when she pulled the trigger.

Chapter Fourteen

After nearly two weeks of shadowing Alex without picking up any new vibes, Jerry was beginning to think he'd gotten this one wrong. That, or it was still too early, as there were still plenty of events leading up to Derby Day. *Easy, Jerry, you know these things sometimes take time.*

Jerry placed his wallet in his right rear pocket. As he reached for his keys, his pinky brushed the bracelet Savannah insisted he carry, and a jolt surged through him. He picked up the bracelet and the feeling of dread intensified. *Today. Whatever is going to happen will be today.* He sat on the edge of the bed, closed his eyes, and intertwined the bracelet in his fingers. Immediately, an image of Alex flashed before his eyes then faded into a black horse. Jerry pushed his palms together in prayer form, watching behind closed eyelids as the horse turned into a rainbow of colors with wings. Jerry blew out a frustrated sigh. *What does it all mean?*

His cell rang, playing Seltzer's ringtone. Jerry opened his eyes and switched on the phone. "Seltzer?"

"McNeal, what the heck are you doing?"

"At the moment or in general?"

"I got an e-mail from the captain of the Louisville Police Department with a photo attached. Care to guess what that photo was of?"

"Crap!"

"Crap is right. The man's ready to adopt you."

"He'll change his mind when he meets me."

"You better make sure that doesn't happen. The e-mail said he wanted to thank me for sending one of my troopers down and wants to give the dog the key to the city. Said the dog is the talk of the town. Said everyone thinks he's one of theirs. What's that about anyhow?"

Jerry recognized the tone and knew what Seltzer was most upset about was that he himself had never got to see Gunter. Jerry looked at Gunter, who was currently lying on his back with his feet in the air. "Apparently, the dog thought his costume was funny."

"Funny, my ass; it's a darn public relations nightmare. Do you know what'll happen if Manning sees the picture? You'd better make sure there aren't any more photos. And darn sure not any with the two of you together. *Capiche*?"

"I understand."

"Yeah, you better make sure that dog understands. It's hard for me to cover your ass when you're on the front page of every newspaper."

"Roger that, sir."

"So, how's it going?" Seltzer's voice was calmer now. Jerry knew he'd just slipped into dad mode.

"It's going."

"Anything I can help with?"

"Not unless you're any good with puzzles."

"I take it you're not talking about jigsaw puzzles."

"No, sir."

"Ah, what the heck. Run it past me, and I'll give it a try."

"I know the who – she's a cop. And the when is today. I just don't know the what, other than I see horses."

"You're in Kentucky. You're supposed to see horses."

"That's the problem – they're everywhere, and I don't know what they mean."

"I thought you were there visiting your psychic friend. Can't you ask her?"

"I tried. The cop in question is her wife, and Savannah's not picking up anything."

"Is that normal?"

Jerry laughed. "Is anything in my life normal?"

"Maybe you need to find another friend."

Max. "You know, that's not a bad idea."

"Alright, I'll let you get to it. Remember to tell that dog to stay under the radar."

"Will do." Jerry clicked off the phone and dialed Max's number.

"Hey, this is Max. If I'm not answering, I'm either at school or grounded from my phone. Leave a message and I'll call you back when the warden lets me out of lockdown."

Please don't let her be grounded. "Max, this is Jerry. I'm working on something here. I need you to concentrate on me and let me know if you get anything. I'm seeing a black horse along with the rainbow Pegasus. If you can, call me back today. It's pretty important."

Gunter opened his eyes and wagged his tail when Jerry pocketed the phone. "Yo, dog, the sergeant isn't happy with you."

The tail stilled and Gunter lowered his legs.

"He said you need to behave yourself, or your antics are going to get us both in trouble."

Gunter disappeared.

"Chicken!"

***

Savannah and Alex were in the kitchen when he went downstairs. Savannah turned when he came into the room, read his face, and dropped the glass she was holding. Recovering, she bent and started picking up the pieces.

Alex bent to help and Savannah waved her off. "I've got this."

Alex sat at the table and motioned for Jerry to do the same. "You've got a pretty good poker face."

"So I've been told." *Too bad Savannah doesn't.* "You okay?"

"You mean aside from knowing I might get killed today?"

Savannah looked up, her eyes blazing. "This is not a joking matter!"

"Sorry, babe. You know I'm not the crying type."

Savannah opened her mouth and Jerry raised his hand. She narrowed her eyes. "What? Are you going to lie to me and tell me everything's going to be okay?"

"No. I was going to tell you not to say something you might regret."

Savannah finished cleaning up the glass and left the room without another word.

Alex watched her go. "She's going to have a rough day."

"Not any worse than yours."

"That sounds encouraging."

"What I meant was – "

354

Alex laughed. "I know what you meant. I'm not going to dwell on things I have no control over. I have a twelve-hour shift starting at eleven. How do you want to play it?"

"Business as usual. With the exception of the bathroom, I go where you go. If I tell you to do something, don't stop to let it sink in, you do it. If I say duck, you duck. If I say drop – drop to the ground without questioning the reason."

"You still think I might get shot?"

"You got a vest?"

"Yes."

"Wear it."

***

Thousands of spectators milled about the fairgrounds, watching as balloon owners inflated balloons of all colors and shapes. Among the balloons were cats, an octopus, a pirate, a cactus, an owl, and even Humpy Dumpty had made an appearance. The balloon closest to them sent a roaring flame into the belly of the balloon and Jerry stiffened. *Easy, Jerry, it's just a balloon.*

Jerry felt something press against his leg and looked to see Gunter standing next to him. The weight of the dog's body pulled Jerry back from the brink. Jerry reached a hand to Gunter's head. *Thank you.*

"What are you thinking?"

She knows you're close to panicking. Jerry forced a smile. "I'm thinking I hate people."

Alex surveyed those standing near. "You hate crowds. There's a difference."

Alex was right – it was the crowd and the fact that so many people messed with his internal radar. He had to resist following someone who set it off at every turn. Jerry pulled out his phone and looked at the screen. *Come on, Max, look at your phone.*

"It could be worse."

Jerry slipped the phone into his pocket. "How's that?"

"We could be on traffic duty."

"At least we'd be alone in the car."

Alex looked him in the eye. "Say we leave."

Okay. "You want to go?"

"No, hear me out. Say I were to call my supervisor right now and make up some story about being sick. Say he buys in to it and allows me to leave. Would that change things?"

Jerry closed his eyes and concentrated on her question. When he opened them, Alex was still staring at him. "It would change it for you."

"Meaning?"

"This person wants to kill cops."

Her eyes widened, then she recovered. "And we have a chance to stop it?"

Say no, Jerry, and you can both walk away. "Yes."

"Then we stay. Relax, McNeal – no, don't. Do whatever it is you do. Just don't have a panic attack and leave me out here on my own."

Crap. "Wouldn't think of it."

"Good to hear. How's your radar?"

"Going off like a pinball machine. Not just you." Jerry waved his arms. "This. All of it."

"Want to take a walk?"

"I'm not leaving."

"With me."

"Lead the way." Jerry followed, eyes searching the crowd as Alex weaved in and around the spectators. The threat was here. He could feel it – it and hundreds of others that pleaded for his help. *Stay focused, Jerry.*

Alex turned and headed toward the main building. Once inside, she made her way toward the ladies' room, pausing just outside the door. "I've got this."

"Yell if there's trouble."

Alex's lip curled. "You'll be the first to know."

Actually, the second. Jerry gave Gunter a nod, relaxing slightly when the dog followed Alex into the room.

Jerry leaned against the wall and pulled out his cell phone. *Where are you, Max?* He started to put the phone away, but then searched through his phone book, found Max's mother's number, and breathed a sigh of relief when the woman answered.

"Hello? Mr. McNeal?"

"Mrs. Buchanan, I left Max a voice message and need her to check her phone."

"It will have to wait until tomorrow. Max is grounded for the rest of the day."

"Mrs. Buchanan, I respect that. Trust me. I wouldn't ask if it weren't urgent."

"Urgent? Did Max do something wrong?"

"This has nothing to do with Max. But I think she can help me with a case I'm working on."

"A case? Max said you were finished with police work."

Jerry ran a hand over the back of his neck. "Please, Mrs. Buchanan, I'll explain everything later. Could you please just have Max check her messages?"

"Fine. Max! Mr. McNeal wants to talk to you."

"No, there's no time to explain everything. Just let Max listen to my message. She'll know what to do." Jerry switched off the phone to avoid further discussion. *What's taking Alex so long?* Jerry thought about opening the door to ask if she was alright, then remembered he'd sent Gunter in with her. *Relax, Jerry, don't draw unwanted attention. Just act normal.* Jerry pulled his phone from his pocket and pretended to look at the screen while scanning everyone in the lobby. He keyed on a man in a black t-shirt standing on the opposite side of the room. Thin with narrow-set eyes, Jerry knew he'd seen the man before. *Easy, Jerry, probably just a coincidence.*

Alex came out of the restroom, her hand under the arm of a woman. At that moment, every warning bell in Jerry's body went off. Instantly alert, Jerry looked for the man. The guy saw Jerry and turned, pretending to look at a poster on the wall. Jerry had been so focused on searching for a suspect, he hadn't noticed the print with two horses – one black and the other with wings – standing on their hindlegs rearing toward one another. *It's him. Easy, Jerry, don't scare him away.*

"Jerry, Angel here is not feeling well. I'm going to walk her to her car." Angel looked to be close to him in age and from her red-brimmed eyes, it was apparent she'd been crying.

Jerry felt like he was spinning out of control. He'd promised to stay with Alex, but if he followed her, the guy might see him as a threat and bolt. This was the guy. It had to be. His radar had nearly exploded when Alex came back into the room. "Go ahead. I'll be right behind you."

Alex's brows knitted together and Jerry forced a smile. Alex pulled up her chin and started for the door chatting to the woman as they walked. To Jerry's relief, Gunter stayed at Alex's side.

Jerry remained planted in place, pretended to make a call, then held the phone to his ear, all the while watching the man who had refocused his attention on Alex. Sure enough, the suspect tailed Alex and Angel as they made their way to the parking lot.

Jerry followed at a close distance. He felt the phone vibrate, glanced to see a message from Max, and pocketed it without reading it. *Too late, kiddo.*

Alex and the woman stopped at a black Mustang. The guy stayed back as Alex opened the door for the woman, helped her inside, and closed the door. As soon as Alex cleared the car, the man ducked out of view. Jerry was on him in an instant, pressing him against the hood of an SUV. Alex hurried to where they stood. "Is this the guy?"

"That or my radar needs a tune-up." The thing was, his radar should have stood down the second he grabbed the guy, but it was still soaring through his body, prickling as if every nerve ending was waking up.

"I just wanted to talk to you, Alex."

"Jeff?"

Jerry searched the man and pulled him from the hood. "You know this guy."

"Yes. We went to high school together. Jeff's a pacifist. I don't see him as being a killer."

Jeff's thin face paled. "A killer? Me? No, I just wanted to say hi and see how you're doing."

Jerry rolled his neck. The threat was here; he could feel it. He released Jeff. "Don't go anywhere."

The Mustang rumbled to life and Alex looked toward the car. "Shoot. I forgot to tell Angel her tags are expired. Hopefully, she can get them renewed before a cop pulls her over."

Jerry pulled his cell phone from his pocket. "I thought you were a cop."

Alex laughed a carefree laugh. "What can I say? I'm a sucker for damsels in distress."

Jerry swiped the phone to bring up Max's message. "It's not a horse. It's a car. A car that looks like a horse."

A black horse. Hawaii. Rainbow. Pegasus. Wings – the woman's name is Angel. The images slammed together at once as Alex approached the driver's window of the Mustang, which had Hawaii plates with a rainbow stretched across the length of it. Jerry pulled his Glock from his waist. "ALEX, DROP!"

Gunter gripped Alex's arm, pulling her forward as the sound of a shotgun blast filled the air, the pellets peppering the Charger parked next to the Mustang.

As the Charger's windows shattered, Jerry watched Alex key her shoulder mike as she scrambled to the front of the car.

"You still there, Jeff?"

"I'm here."

"Good. Get behind that car and stay out of sight."

Jerry moved forward, keeping his Glock trained on Angel. As Alex made her way to the back of the Charger, Gunter appeared in the seat beside Angel. The woman screamed, opened the door, and fell out – backing away from Gunter. The dog had appeared wearing his K-9 uniform and followed Angel from the car, growling a menacing growl.

Alex took the lead, patting the woman down for weapons and clamping restraints around her wrists. Alex glared at Angel as she told the dispatcher the suspect was in custody.

***

Jerry leaned against the hood of a police car, happy to be observing at a distance. Gunter sat at his side, both watching as Alex and another officer searched the Mustang. Alex handed a third officer a duffle bag then approached Jerry.

"There was a suicide note, which appeared to be death by cop. She was distraught at having lost both her husband and son." Alex wiped the sweat from her brow. "You were right: this was the beginning. Angel had a map showing all the cities she planned to hit after this one. There were a few newspaper articles about the deaths and another note telling of her plan to avenge their deaths. She even signed the suicide note Avenging Angel. Do you know why she tried to shoot me? Because I went back to tell her that her tags were expired."

"I guess some damsels don't like to be helped."

Alex bit at her bottom lip. "Thanks for being here."

"I almost blew it."

"Don't start that."

"Start what?"

"Playing the victim."

"Is that what I'm doing?"

"You and Savannah are good about beating yourselves up if things don't go the way you think they should. You have a gift. That doesn't make you infallible. Gee, even Superman had no power when kryptonite was involved."

"I'm no superhero."

"No, but you're my hero." Alex lifted her chin. "I'd kiss you on the cheek, but the reporters would take it out of context, and I'd have a heck of a time salvaging my rugged reputation."

"Crap."

"Problem?"

"I promised Seltzer I'd avoid the limelight."

"You go. I've got this."

"You sure?"

Alex winked. "They won't even know you were here. Hey, do me a favor."

"Name it."

"After you call for an Uber, can you give Savannah a call?"

"Chicken."

"Nope. Just don't want the boys here to see me cry." She turned without waiting for a reply.

Jerry pulled out his cell and typed a message to Max. > *You did good, kiddo. Your information saved the day. Tell your mom I said you're a hero.*

Jerry called for a ride then called Savannah.

"Jerry!? I was listening on the scanner. Is Alex okay?"

Jerry could tell from her voice that she'd been crying. "Alex is fine. She said to tell you she will be home as soon as she can."

"Is it really over, Jerry?"

"Yes. Alex is safe."

"Aren't you going to tell me what happened?"

"Nope, this is Alex's story to tell." Jerry ended the call and looked at Gunter. "Well, we saved the girl again. You know, this hero thing is a pretty tough gig. At least in the movies, the hero always ends up with the girl."

Gunter placed his head under Jerry's hand as if to say *That's okay, you've got me.* Jerry knelt and scratched the K9's head. "You know, you're right. As consolation prizes go, you're not too bad."

About the Author

Sherry A. Burton writes in multiple genres and has won numerous awards for her books. Sherry's awards include the coveted Charles Loring Brace Award, for historical accuracy within her historical fiction series, The Orphan Train Saga. Sherry is a member of the National Orphan Train Society, presents lectures on the history of the orphan trains, and is listed on the NOTC Speaker's Bureau as an approved speaker.

Originally from Kentucky, Sherry and her Retired Navy Husband now call Michigan home. Sherry enjoys traveling and spending time with her husband of more than forty years.

Be sure to read all of the Jerry McNeal series, now in a clean and cozy collection of three books each!